ON T

HE UP

McCLELLAND & STEWART

Library and Archives Canada Cataloguing in Publication

Jones, Shilo, author
On the up / Shilo Jones.

Issued in print and electronic formats.
ISBN 978-0-7710-4910-1 (softcover).—ISBN 978-0-7710-4911-8
(EPUB)

I. Title.

PS8619.O5339O5 2018   C813'.6   C2017-904800-7
                                               C2017-904801-5

Book design by Terri Nimmo
Cover art: © Sybille Sterk/Arcangel, silhouettes © Shutterstock
Inset art: © Shutterstock

Typeset in Adobe Caslon Pro by M&S, Toronto
Printed and bound in Canada

McClelland & Stewart,
a division of Penguin Random House Canada Limited,
a Penguin Random House Company
www.penguinrandomhouse.ca

1 2 3 4 5   22 21 20 19 18

For the ruck

I don't fit the big picture.
—Subhumans

I imagine Ryan phoning me. Odd hours, random days. Four years later. He sounds older than he is. Talks slow, like a guy who lives quiet. Makes an effort to ask about me. *How are you, Jasminder?* Never calls me Jaz. It's not small talk. Not a casual question between acquaintances. I can tell he means it, really wants to know. There's authenticity in Ryan's voice, and a resolve that makes it clear he's finished being afraid. If there wasn't I'm not sure I'd answer his calls. I don't owe him anything. I think Ryan believes how I am has some relationship to how he is, like if I'm doing okay then he should be doing okay too.

Is this really you? Ryan asks. *You're not lying?*

That was only then, I tell him. I only lied when I was lost in it. But usually I say: Of course it's me. Who else would it be? Don't I sound like me?

I imagine Ryan asking: *Did Mark have a good heart?* That's the expression he uses: a good heart. It reminds me of the cartoon heart painting at Hawksworth. It's impossible to know what will stick with you. A cartoon heart with dead butterflies.

Ryan must be around eighteen now. Living in North B.C. Won't tell me exactly where, and I can't say I blame him. Sometimes I laugh when he says that. A good heart? C'mon. Other days I hang up. Sometimes I ask if such a thing is possible, is it ever that straightforward?

Mark would say it is, Ryan tells me. *He'd say for sure it is.*

Ryan dreams of violence. *I don't want to*, he says. *It's not what I want.*

I know, I tell him. Me either.

Do you think you did the right thing? Ryan asks.

MAKING
MOVES

Jasminder Bansal

Everything hinges on being believed. I've spent months angling to get inside the corruption story and finally . . . a meeting with the man who employs my brother's killer. Vincent Peele, real estate attorney and the youngest board member of Marigold Group, one of the largest development firms in the country. You don't rise that far and fast without—

"—this is maybe not the best idea? Friday evening, life-changing interview with the boss, what kind of guy am I, to spring that on you with zero notice?"

Vincent uses his teeth to remove his soaked riding gloves while I tell him no problem, it's an honour, I appreciate the opportunity. I wipe moisture from a plastic patio chair and settle into the persona I've created to handle him, keeping my voice quiet and my body language subdued. The trick to getting sources to speak freely is to appear non-threatening. Mentally rehearse my pitch, how I've improved my proactive sales-oriented attitude, the steps I've taken to craft strong relationships with—

Vincent leaps out of his chair, admires the mud splattered across his fluorescent yellow rain jacket. Like a child, it seems he's having a difficult time staying still. "Just went for a killer mountain bike ride. Look at me! Covered in mud, maybe even blood. It's awesome! There are bears in the woods. Predators. March, they're hungry. Seen a bear, Jasminder? Not many bears where you're . . . anyway, cool. Tigers, though?" Vincent curls his hands into claws, pretends to snarl and scratch. "Do tigers still exist? Do I have mud in my teeth?"

Give him a you-must-be-joking hand wave, sip my tea, and decide he's the kind of okay-looking that, depending on lighting or mood, could easily become obnoxious. His face narrows from the square foundation of his beard to a sharp widow's peak. Precisely trimmed eyebrows. A mouth that hangs slightly open. He has the shitty habit of not looking directly at me, like I'm an interruption in an otherwise outstanding view. Vincent catches me sizing him up, gets the wrong idea, buries his fingers in his beard, says "uh-huh, yeah" under his breath, takes a selfie with the North Shore Mountains in the background.

I was hired as an entry-level sales associate at Marigold Group five weeks ago. Making cold calls. Harassing mortgage admin. Guiding clients to local sights. The probationary period is over. My hope is that Vincent called this meeting to hire me permanently. To get this story written I need access to his office, his files. "It's wonderful to finally meet you, Mr.—"

"Wonderful, always, sure." Vincent crosses right leg in front of left, bends at the waist, grabs his grimy cycling shoe, stretches, flexes his shoulders. "*Mmm* . . . brutally tight hamstring . . . *jeez!* Getting structurally integrated tomorrow, soma deep tissue, re-educate the body, heard of it? Nah, didn't think so. Invented locally? Pretty sure, yes. Isn't this great? Exercise and espresso! Simple needs. I live a very minimalist lifestyle, despite doing so well for myself." Vincent looks up without breaking his stretch, nods toward a group sitting at a table on the other side of the outdoor café, lowers his voice. "Those people? Giving me stink eye for stretching in a coffee shop? Uptight, not real Vancouverites, not true West Coasters, stiffs from

back east who don't understand what makes this place so special.
But anyway. I'm glad you came. Because I'm a very relaxed person,
you know, not business-uptight at all, maybe *too* casual—I thought,
well, how 'bout I call our promising new sales associate Jasminder
Ba . . . uh, Bay . . . Bi . . ."

"Bansal—"

"—right now, and see what she's doing? Give the girl some good
news heading into the weekend. Brighten her day! Of course, you
don't mind?"

"Mr. Peele? Are you offering me a full-time sales associate
position?"

Vincent waves toward the clouds ringing the mountains. "Look
at this city. Nowhere like it! We are so. Lucky."

We're at Lonsdale Quay, seated under a steel and glass atrium
on a paving stone patio a few steps from the Pacific. The corners of
the structure have gone green with algae or moss or something that
thrives in near-constant moisture, and the wind coming off Burrard
Inlet inspires me to wrap my scarf more tightly around my neck.
A blunt, red-hulled tanker inches beneath the Lions Gate Bridge,
looks close to clipping the underside of the span. Seagulls shriek
and dive into the ship's frothing wake. "So lucky, Mr. Peele. And
no problem about the short notice. I was close by. With family. In
Stanley Park."

Watch him, see if he clues into the lie.

"Family? I have some of those. Vancouver, *ooh!*"

"Lovely."

It might even be. Everyone says it is. But I'm not sure anymore.
Horizontal lines of slate-coloured water and depthless cloud interrupted by a skyline that appears blocky and indistinct, flattened, as
if carved from a single mass. And a new tower rising in the middle
of the downtown core. Needle-thin and twice as tall as the rest,
made of platinum or chrome or a material not yet discovered . . .
and an invasive organic growth erupting two thousand feet overhead,

a plague or virus spreading toward the city. No. I take a second look. Of course the malformed skyscraper doesn't exist. Visions. Hauntings? The anniversary of my brother's death is less than a week away.

"Perfect view. What it's all about? My city right there. Super world-class."

Vincent's on script, expects me to know my lines. Instead I say nothing, which seems to irritate him. He has a cyclist's physique, taut and slim beneath his riding gear: black plastic pads on his shins and elbows that make him look like an armoured insect. His mud-caked mountain bike is leaning against the flimsy patio table, threatening to collapse onto me. I'm trying not to feel put out, wary of the bike and the man, reminding myself of my investigative persona, pretty simple really, a conceptual membrane I wrap around myself when working a source, a filter between the real me and—

"Check out this bike! Brand new. As in not on the market yet? I'm on Cove's crazy elite demo team. Like it?"

"It's—"

"Huge. I know. Eight inches of travel front and back. All carbon. Nine grand for this beast. I said I spent nine thousand dollars on this bicycle?"

"But if you're on the demo team don't you get bikes for free?"

Peele leans into the handlebars, compresses his bike's front suspension. "Totally worth it. The North Shore? We invented the freeride revolution. Also did some trail maintenance, giving back to my community, accruing killer karma points. Rode Jerry Rig clean. No dab! Heard of that trail? Course not. Blind twenty-foot gaps, mad skinnies that side-loft to bermed transitions. Pros only, although I'm not quite pro. As in: too busy to formally compete. Wait! Feel it coming . . . holeshot! Post-ride endorphin high! Skin all a-tingle . . . feeling super loose! You?"

"Loose? I'm—"

Vincent frowns. "Not looking so loose. More like anxious? Fidgety? Game face, Jasminder. Big meeting with the boss."

Smile. "It's been amazing, these last few weeks at Marigold. A wonderful learning opportunity. There was a time when, to be honest, I didn't think I was much of a people person. But Marigold's in-house mentoring program, that really helped. And . . . learning how to maximize client satisfaction . . . and . . ."

Vincent looks delighted. "Hey, rain's almost stopped. Only sprinkling! Sounds pretty stock, that answer, by the way? Client satisfaction? Whatevs. Need more from you. What's this Jasminder person all about?"

What does he want to hear? "I guess what I'm saying is—"

"So about this gimongous condo development we have coming up, mega-ginormous Solstice Homes in beautiful-incredible North Vancouver, largest development Marigold's ever taken on, woot!" Vincent raises his voice to make sure everyone on the patio can hear him. "I'm in charge, of course, head honcho, big responsibility, feeling slightly stressed, truth be told, which is normal when there's like billions on the line, opening up here for you, sharing, because we're in the middle of securing the property, a very delicate and crucial time. Yes, I said billions, plural . . . sorry, did I interrupt? You were saying something boring about selling being a passion of yours?"

An espresso machine erupts inside the coffee stand. "A passion? Maybe a learned skill? A multi-billion-dollar development? That is so . . . wow."

"And me running point." Peele squeezes his front tire, frowns, digs through his tiny backpack, grabs a bicycle pump. "Truth bomb! I'm not big into selling either. I'm more of a connector." Waves the pump in the air. "Us connecting? See how I make it seem easy? Marigold, we're searching for diverse ability. The role of modern management is to match talent to task." Peele points the bicycle pump at my chest. "First impression: this Jasminder person makes people feel at ease.

You're very agreeable. And . . . *charming* isn't the right word. Pleasant? I'm not sure how to describe it. I find it quite easy to like you."

A gull flaps onto the splintered dock, snaps a yellow-black eye in my direction, scurries too close. "You're saying I'm likable?"

Vincent crouches beside his bike, clamps the pump onto his tire. "Not exactly? It's almost like . . . you're such a relief. Jasminder? What a great name. Pretty like *jasmine*, but with an *inder* tacked on? So cool. And unique! I love this country. You?"

Another gull screeches in, pecks at the first, tears out a beakful of feathers, and flies off, keening and diving through cloud. A rhythmic hissing sound as Vincent forces air into his tire. "Canada? Well, I think it's—"

"Perfect? Of course. Everyone does. People like you are why I love this country. Partly. A shining light guiding the world."

Vincent's arm ratchets back and forth. I decide the best course of action is to play along. At Langara College I learned to resist the urge to speak into silence. Sources often return to what's really on their minds if you give them space. "You mean . . . Canada's a beacon for the world?"

"On the same page! A shining beacon of rad. That's what Canada is." He stands, taps the table with the bike pump. "You're proof. We both are! Look at us, sitting together, total equals, with me maybe deciding to hire you. How great is that?" Peele puts the pump away, runs his fingers through his beard, picks out a piece of mud, flicks it in my direction.

The bastard's trying to put me in my place. This condo developer with a murdering gangster named Clint Ward on his payroll? What Peele doesn't understand is that I'm not the woman sitting in front of him, slump-shouldered, smiling at the right times and sounding unsure, deferent to his hold on my future, looking how he expects me to look, eager and expectant and hoping he chooses to be beneficent in his dealings with me. That woman? That's the me I want him to see. The real me is way over here, thinking *fuck you, Mr. Sir*, watching from a distance, taking what I need, witnessing. Things are easier when I imagine myself as someone else. "Mr. Peele, I'm truly grateful—"

Vincent tears open a PowerBar, stuffs half into his mouth, mumbles: "Okay, grateful, who isn't? Acing the interview! But I'm soaked, chilly, time is . . . almost five thirty? Already? Want to ride the bridge before dark." Peele glares at the PowerBar, tosses it on the ground. Seagulls skitter and hop. "Gross, chocolate oat? Least favourite! Anyway—"

"You're going to waste that?"

"Waste what?"

"It's nothing. Only . . . I was raised not to waste food?"

Peele mulls this over, brightens. "The seagulls will eat it. Organic. All natural."

I tell him sure, of course, angle away, watch waves circle barnacle-studded pier posts, pretend to check my phone. Vincent makes a show of scaring the gulls away. Picks up the wrapper and deposits it in the garbage. He's slightly bowlegged, walks with his weight too far forward. Tells me he's had his team looking for promising sales associates for a long time, sounds irritated until I refocus my full attention on him. Says I did mostly okay during the new-hire probation period. Areas of improvement, sure, always improving, but that I did better than expected. Grabs his water bottle, shoots a stream of pink fluid into his mouth, wipes his lips with a backhand. "Electrolytes! *Bzzzt!* Anyway, what was I talking—"

"My future?" A month more, maybe less, inside Marigold Group. Digging into the connection between Vincent Peele and Clint Ward. Is Peele washing cash through his developments? Snooping through emails both personal and corporate, bank statements, client lists, light it up online and use the story to kick-start my journalism career. "We were talking about . . . am I hired?"

"Ha, right! Almost. Because I know you understand Vancouver. Diversity, outdoorsy, all that excellent. Marigold isn't looking for licensed real estate agents, Jasminder. No. Stuck in their ways. Expectations about commission rates, always criticizing, comparing. Legal issues . . . no. We have, uh . . ." Peele smacks his lips, hesitates. "A very successful proven model? Yes! We're looking for . . . talented up-and-comers? To follow our model precisely. This is an incredible time. The opportunity . . ." Peele looks at the atrium roof and shakes his head, like he can't fully comprehend the enormity. "For a motivated self-starter like you, I like to say we create our own limitations."

"We do?"

"I'm sure of it. Welcome to the Marigold Family."

"Family of . . ."

"Of us!" Peele glares at a kid admiring his bike. "Marigold treats all our employees like family."

"I guess that could go either way?"

"Oh, ha! Like a nurturing, supportive, well-off family. We're drafting a community-oriented core philosophy to reflect how we totally dominate. Second place is for losers! And civil servants." Peele taps his phone, sticks it in my face. "See that document? Stage-two expansion, with the Solstice development being the king or lynch-whatever-pin? We're redefining work in the twenty-first century. To make it seem like more fun?"

I kick at a nasty seagull milling too close to my feet. "That's interesting. So . . . in the Marigold Family . . . you're like my boss and brother?"

"Father. On top. In a non-hierarchic or patriarchal way, of course."

I give him an excited expression. Is it feigned? I want to say absolutely. But I'm already thinking: What if I don't pursue the story? What if I take my sales associate position at Marigold seriously? It pays better than any job I've had. What about the bills my mother and I are behind on, my grinding car brakes? I fight down a shudder because what if wanting to expose Vincent Peele and Clint Ward is simply a lie I tell myself so I can live with working for a twit like

Vincent? "Okay . . . thank you? I mean, for sure, I'm excited, this is excellent—"

"Of course, we won't hire any derelict off the street. Very discerning. Gruelling process. Now, speaking of family. Tell me about your brother. The dead one."

Takes me several seconds to catch up to the question, and when I do my hands drop into my lap.

Your brother. The dead one.

Vincent puts on his helmet and fumbles with the chinstrap. "My bad. So sorry. Should we discuss your promotion some other time? Call my assistant. She might answer you." Throws a leg over his mountain bike, rocks the bike back and forth, checks his phone, seems about to ride away as I consider how much he knows.

"Amar was a gang member," I whisper, no longer certain Peele can't see the real me. Did Clint recognize me that night three years ago? Has he already told Peele who I am? And why have I insinuated myself into this circle when good sense says I should go home, grieve in silence, be afraid and stay away—

"Excuse me, Jasminder? Your brother was—"

"A gang member." My voice is loud enough to draw a few glances from surrounding tables. "That's what everyone said. He didn't live with us. I didn't know him during—"

"You didn't know your own brother?"

A gull flies overhead with something gristly dangling from its beak. "Yes, but . . . not then? I didn't know him."

"Cuz, wow. That is so insane! I remember it on the news. Drug war? Big-time violent gang—"

"Yes."

A business mantra from my research about transforming myself into a successful sales leader: *A positive mind engenders a positive reality*. Never thought I'd come to depend on nonsense, but at this point I'm willing to give anything a shot. Pessimism, negativity, have always been my weaknesses. A truth is trying to take shape, will do so if I pursue it, the dream of a journalism career still driving me, what I've held on to through years of family and friends politely and not so politely telling me to let it go, no reasonable Plan B for this girl, too stubborn or foolish to grow up and get real and if the corruption story doesn't pan out at least I'll know I tried. Gave it my best? People say that too. Cold fucking comfort, although the thought has a certain attraction, relief in failure—

Vincent squeezes his mountain bike brakes, admires his forearms. "That's incredible, Jasminder. What a sad, super-sad unhappy burden. Must be very hard. To carry that? But good for you. For carrying it."

Tell him thank you, try and steady my voice while wondering what he means.

"Because it's my understanding—correct me if I'm wrong—that you *did* carry it? As in: not a word. To anyone? The police? Even though . . ."

"I was there, yes. When it happened."

"And not a word spoken against whoever . . ."

Scoot my chair away from the table and prepare to leave. "No. I didn't see anything."

Vincent's demeanour changes too fast, from distant to deeply sympathetic. "Totally inappropriate question. I'm sorry. I wanted to hear your side. And now I can tell the Marigold Family: the older brother was a black sheep. She barely knew him. These things happen. So you weren't involved in—"

"No."

"Of course not. Not getting that gangbanger vibe! Not at all. But I see you."

"I'm sitting right here?"

Vincent inches his bike's aggressive front tire closer to my leg. "Sitting right here? Peekaboo! I got it! Thrilled to be connecting. You're like a mango smoothie, Jasminder. Very easy to swallow. I guess we're about done? Except . . . here's the thing. Acquaintance, business partner actually, runs the Aqua nightclub. Heard of it?"

"Sure. In the Shangri-La."

"Been? No. Very high end. Anyway, tight investment, robust return, but . . . a problematic industry. Great for making money, but otherwise, mega sexist. Just the way it is, though? The manager, Claire, she has to, from time to time, say some like totally objectionable things. Things that I know—because she's of course a caring feminist-type businessperson like you and me—bother her very much. Have you ever been in that position? Of having to say things you find personally objectionable to keep your job?"

"Me? Yes. I mean . . . not often? I guess I try to avoid putting myself in situations where—"

"Yay for you! For fighting the good fight. But let me say, it gets more difficult as your career advances. And you become important? So for Claire, she has to say things—because of the not-okay sexism in the music and entertainment industry—that she would never normally say. Like, 'Sweetheart, you'd look way better if you lost a few pounds.' Claire must feel horrible! Imagine me saying, 'Jasminder, you could stand to lose a few pounds.' Claire has to say stuff like that all the time! I totally feel for her. It'd be like me saying, 'Jasminder, the bohemian-college-chic look isn't doing you any favours. And maybe you should try wearing makeup if you want to succeed in this industry?' So gross, even hearing those words from my mouth as I'm telling you what Claire has to say! Thankfully for us, the real estate profession, especially on the West Coast, is way more progressive. Thankfully I don't have to say things like, "Jasminder, you look a little yesterday to be presenting penthouse condominiums.'"

Play it cool, look vaguely upset at the unfairness of it all generally but not at Peele specifically, try not to let him under my skin, but realize he is by the way I'm self-consciously picking at my skirt. "What if Claire stopped saying those things?"

"The nightclub would underperform, she'd be fired, and someone else would. Obviously."

"Sure, obviously. Vincent? Can I ask . . . I'm sorry but . . . your teeth?"

The man freezes. Touches a gloved hand to his lower lip, looks puzzled, recovers, puts on the falsely accommodating smirk I'm already becoming inured to. "My teeth? Perfect."

"Yeah, of course, except . . . obvious ortho?"

Vincent looks like he stepped on roadkill. "Yuck, no way, ortho. Me? For sure not."

"Hated that headgear! Everyone does. You must've too?" Smiling, looking happy to have connected in a personal meaningful way—

Vincent grazes the muddy mountain bike tire against my calf, pins me between his bike-straddling bulk and the table, prompts a choice. Either I ignore him or call him on invading my space. I go for option three, keep my leg steady while spilling my tea across—

"Careful! Demo model! Very pricey—"

"Oh my gosh I am so—"

Vincent jerks the bike away, freeing me. Snatches a few napkins to dab at the tea running down the bike's front fork. "My teeth are perfectly fine. By the way? Straight, white, clean, uncrowded. Perfect."

My professional persona helps me stifle a snicker. "Oh, wow. My bad. Very nice teeth. I'm sorry—"

Vincent says it's no biggie, he's got thick skin, takes more than me being wrong to shake him, hands me a soggy business card, tells me the address of an open house he needs me to attend tomorrow morning. To the south, behind the city, the evening sky transforms into an unnatural chemical green–orange punctuated by odd vertical cloud columns. Firestorm. Flashover. My brother Amar, I barely knew him, I barely knew.

Mark Ward

When I think about killing my brother, it's always in some chickenshit way. Creep on him while he's sleeping. Stab him in the neck. Poison him. Run him over. Been thinking on it since we were kids. A death with no hitting back.

"Best place on earth," Clint says, accelerating away from YVR. "Town's off the charts. Money sloshing around, fucking river, sink or swim."

A quick drag off his Colt, ash out the cracked window, me looking at him sidelong, unsteady, catching up to the fact I've landed, not soaring at nine hundred kilometres an hour, real life knocking, earthbound, sluggish, already missing Thailand's beaches, dreamland strangeness glimpsed through smudged mirror shades, my infant daughter—

"Hey! Hear me, fucker? Good flight?"

"Body scanners. Belt and shoes off. Walk into an airport, like going to prison."

"Except nobody sends you."

"Yeah. You send yourself."

"Quit moaning. Vancity!" Clint sticks a fist in my face, flashes his gold. "See that? A fucking river! Missed the early days, but it's not too late to get on board. Hey—you psyched?"

No answer. I'm lousy at lying to my brother face to face. Always have been. The bastard can scent it. An instinct. I never had it like he does. For me, it's safer to assume everyone's lying.

Clint seems about to ask again, punches my shoulder, laughs, toothy, says he's real glad I'm back in town, family reunion, his batshit soldier little bro, mad-dawg killa, yo! Ain' that right! And something in how he's eyeing me, his voice pitched too sharp, *mania*, makes me shiver, wonder if I'd survive hurling myself out of the truck commando-style, flee into the night, vanish into legend, myth. Instead I manage: "Must be cool, making bank?"

"More than cool. Get your head around what's happening. You hungry?"

"Nah. Ate on the plane."

"Smart ass. I said. You fucking hungry?"

"For what?"

Clint scowls. "For what? For more. What else?"

"I guess so? More of what?"

"You *guess* so? Fuck sakes. Kind of answer—"

"Just asking. More of what?"

"More of—fuck sakes, Marky. More of more! It's here in Vancity, more and more for the taking, but you gotta want it. You gotta be hungry. Shit."

A weird mix of emotion, feeling smarmy-superior at riling my brother up while feeling ashamed at his disappointment—

Clint hits the on-ramp leading to the bridge over the Fraser River, merges onto the highway, floors his Dodge Cummins into the red. I brace against the seat, glance at Clint to make sure he doesn't notice, but his shoulders hunch and that means he does and that's bad news because like the lying Clint can sense this shit, loves to hear a man yell I GIVE, PLEASE, I GIVE. Like when he was running dope lines, if a street-level dealer fucked up, got ripped or otherwise mishandled product, my brother would set up a grudge match, is what he called them, basically a group shit-kicking that ended with the offender begging through a mouthful of blood and broken teeth. I remember those puffed-out eyes, shattered noses, fractured jaws—how when you beat a man long enough his face takes on a cartoonish appearance, funny in an ugly way, identity erased by trauma, violence thriving on abstraction—

"Want me to slow down?" Clint, hands loose on the wheel, watching me flinch as we slide over the white line, daring me to admit I'm afraid.

"Nah. If you want?"

It's night. The Fraser River's a smooth obsidian plane. Begins deep in the mountains, born of once-blue glaciers now dirtied with ash and soot, rivulets running into one another, blind and unknowing, gradually gathering strength, compelled downhill by physical law, toward the ocean, home, I dunno, carving a path through stone towers, this vast country, all that beautiful squeaky-clean wilderness we always hear about, and I try to take something from that, a life lesson, a hidden truth to carry me through, but there's only reflecting fast-flowing water and my brother's forearms flexing as he cuts through traffic and Colt cigar smoke swirling in the truck. Time stutters, I blink, and we're two blocks ahead of where we were.

Jet-lagged. Shell-shocked. Most likely it'll pass.

"Relax, Marky. You're home now. Anyway. How's Thailand?" Clint's tone makes it clear he could give a rat's ass, is playing at being big brother concerned.

"Earnest."

"Huh? Yeah. You look shit, Marky. Thought you'd look good. Beaches. Pissing around, doing fuck all, banging slants—"

"I'm almost married."

"—but you're pale, skinny. You look shit. You training?"

"Nope?"

Clint smacks my shoulder. "Not training? Working out?"

"For what?"

"Strength matters."

I look at his cigar.

"Oh, piss off. This is nothing. I do my cardio. Besides. I'm jacked."

"You're super cut. Haven't seen you like that since—"

"Right? Seriously ripped. And check out this Dodge. Lit as fuck."

"Truck's sick."

Clint caresses the dashboard. "Paid cash. Know what? We should hit the gym. You could use it. And you should see me bench. Plus, no one knows how to spot anymore. Can't trust 'em. On their phones, whatever."

"Gym sounds rad."

"I can trust you. Family. That's rad."

Silence except for the diesel engine growling and Clint's hands grinding on the steering wheel. Real quick he asks, "You miss them?"

I tell him sure, of course.

"You just left them, fucking, hours ago."

"So? That's when you miss people most."

Clint paws through the glovebox. Always been fascinated by how my brother moves. Muscles rippling down his arms. There's an exaggerated quality to Clint's motions, like he's struggling to contain a power or potency. He pivots instead of turning. Thrusts instead of reaching out. Even the simplest gesture portends an assault. Now the hand in the glovebox darts back, smacks my chest with a dull-sounding thud that I don't feel. Clint laughs, does it again, shakes his head at my lack of response, says I still have shit reflexes, army did fuck all for me, no wonder I got blown to shit, resumes searching in the glove, left hand hanging off the wheel, truck veering across the lines—

Clint's company logo is stitched into the dash in crimson thread. *Redline Contracting*. He cusses at not finding what he's looking for, tells me to hold the wheel. "Shit's different now. Town's gone global. You feel it? Electric. Hooked into something big, jacked into the mainline—"

"Mainframe?"

"Watch the road. Wreck my truck, I kill you. Where the hell is that goddamn—"

The steering wheel vibrates beneath my hand. A single hard swerve would put the truck through the guardrail and the Ward brothers into the river. "Clint? I'm not staying."

"Currents running international. New York . . . London, uh . . . Beijing? L.A. Tokyo. Boss town! Like you seen those satellite pictures? The world at night? Cities lit up, a web of money, all connected, everywhere else dark as hell? That's where Vancity's at. Rest of the world can fuck off. Animals living in darkness."

Clint snatches a silver wolf tooth from the glove box, hollers, balances his smouldering Colt on the centre console. Uncorks the snuff container, taps a pile of blow onto the back of his hand, lays into it with me still holding the wheel. Corks the wolf tooth, tosses it in my lap without a word. I give him the wheel, mutter about the scrubbed sterile air in Vancouver and how it's too thin to get a full breath, smack the dash when I'm done with the blow because it seems like the right thing to do.

Clint glances in the rear-view, cusses, slams the brakes. A horn blares. The Colt tips onto the floor. Clint mutters about teaching the bastard riding his ass a lesson while I pick the Colt up from between my brother's feet, hand it to him. "Thing is—these people are idiots. They're owned. Morons spending the bank's money. The more I charge the more work I get." Clint laughs, cynical, throaty, makes me turn away, wish I was holding something heavy, a lead pipe, I dunno, maybe an assault rifle, something cool like the Tavor—

"Say what you want about the old man. But he knew a scam. Hated the banks. Cash is king. Old school, remember?"

Our father is the last thing I want to think about, but I say, "I remember he never got home insurance because he thought the insurance company would see what he owned, send a crew to rob him, deny his claim."

"Had that shit on lockdown." Clint flicks his half-smoked Colt out the window. "Here's the thing. You think I'm showing off? Truck cost eighty grand. Say I'm an asshole for buying it."

I tell him it's his money.

"Best remember that," Clint sneers. "Me and Vancity left you behind. We're looking in the rear-view, laughing. Remember that beater Ford Lariat the old man used to drive? Piece of shit. But that was the game back then. Decade ago, roll up in an eighty-grand truck, customer wouldn't have nothing to do with you. Smart enough to know they were paying for it. Wanted their contractors driving beater rigs and grovelling for a meal. Under the thumb. Now? Customer doesn't trust you if you're driving a shitbox. Doesn't want your ugly shitbox parked in front of his three-million-dollar rebuild. Afraid the neighbours will think he can't afford decent help." Clint laughs. "Image, right? This truck is straight-up marketing."

Clint spits out the window. I inhale a blast of ocean-stink air. Why does this city feel like someone has a boot to my neck, screaming ENJOY ENJOY ENJOY? Deeply treaded tires whir over wet pavement. Mist obscures low spots along the river. Remind myself this isn't home anymore. Clint's still talking, a wall of sound—money, work, money, respect, money, bitches, money, property—while I sink into the leather seat, unhappy with the blow making my nose run, try and remember my maybe fiancée, Daree, and my daughter, Sarah. Eighteen months old. How afraid I was to hold her. How she is of me but also entirely her own. How I violated my daughter's trust by coming here, how I always knew I would, writing on the wall, destiny, game over.

Important not to forget them. But there's something bigger than the Pacific Ocean between me and my family. This town. My brother. The wildness in how he talks about Vancouver. Raving. Drawing me in. *Make something of yourself.* I can't put the family out front. I tried. Couldn't do it. There's another need running the show. The *target*.

Which is why they're better off—

Clint tells me to hand him the wolf tooth. I do as he says. Then he yells "Worst head for business. Worst head for money. Looked down on me when you went to school for no-money bullshit. Dropped out, joined the army, fuck sakes, loser move, nearly got killed. Sense did that make? Got you nowhere, like I said. Now look at you. Ran away, knocked up a slant, ran away again. Not even thirty and busted, no work, in debt, fuck. You only get so many chances."

"I'm here to work. Pay you back."

"Yeah, cool. Funny, though. How it turned out. Me in this new truck and you—"

"Yeah."

"Looking down on me now?"

I stay quiet.

"Didn't think so. You lost. That's the take-home. You lost."

"I think you're right. I lost."

"Yeah. In the long run. They were wrong about us. The old man. School. Cops. You're the one that isn't shit."

Beneath cigar reek I smell work sweat, soaked Carhartts, chemical hair gel. I think about lighting another smoke, let the urge fade. Think about hitting the blow, maybe my first Oxy in Vancity, let that fade too. For a long time, I thought I understood my brother. Who he is. Who I am. What we are together. Then 2005 happened and everything changed.

Clint knifes into the fast lane and accelerates up Granville Street. Blasts through a very red yellow and chuckles at me reaching for the bitch bar—

"I'd . . . prefer not to die like her," I say, meaning our mother.

"If it's your time." Clint's voice drops to an ugly growl. "My work is waiting for assholes to make the wrong move. We're all just making moves, a'course, then we die. I see how afraid you are. But not me. A warrior doesn't fear death."

I almost tell my brother his half-assed martial arts warrior junk is all bullshit. I was a for-real warrior once. Several lifetimes ago, but

I remember how a C8 assault rifle feels. Bucking and popping. Feels like purpose, and for a lot of us that was enough. Holding that weapon . . . I was tapping into something legit for the first time in my life. But we rarely saw them. The OPFOR? The enemy? That's what was weird. Thought I'd be shooting point-blank. Cutting them down, first-person-shooter style, blood misting my face, was afraid I wouldn't have the stomach for it. Mostly we only heard them. Gunshots across a valley or on the other side of a village. *Pock-pock-pock.* Then hours and days of nothing. Hardly any calls or signals. We were shooting over barren fields. At concrete walls. Dirt huts. Ditches. Berms. Low and high spots. *Positions.* I never really saw who I was shooting at. Ghost stories? Bad guys? In the dust with the rest of my squad, shooting into hardscrabble orchards cut into a mountain. Shooting at boulders on the far side of a valley. Calling in coordinates for an air strike and cheering at the LIGHTROAR, GODFIRE. Laughing at a farm smote skyward by an invisible hand. Feeling we were doing good by winning, no, more than that, feeling we deserved to win, an inevitability to our triumph, our victory confirming an essential rightness in the world, killing as an act of faith in what we created, anticipating the songs sung for us heroes, all that.

But we were shit scared every time we stepped off base. Maybe never seeing them made it worse, because they sure as fuck saw us, out in the open, patrolling Kandahar, squinting through metal bars welded across a LAV window . . .

"Every warrior fears death," I say, too quietly for my brother to hear, but as soon as I say it I wonder if it's true. Maybe not. Fuck do I know? A guy can go to war and not learn a thing.

There. Secret's out.

Shaughnessy properties blur past, thirty-foot cedar hedges and ornate iron fences hiding century-old Tudor and Georgian mansions. Blue-blooded money. Several are wrapped in orange construction fencing. Sales signs out front announce the opportunity to build your dream home—

"See? Knock it down and bang it up," Clint says. "People whine. Like they wouldn't do the exact same thing. And before we paint the final coat sell it knock it down and start over. That's good-paying jobs, the economy, food on the table . . ."

We hit the crest of the hill that descends toward downtown Vancouver. High-rise condominiums and office towers mantled in low cloud, reflective floor-to-ceiling windows tinting the mist into polarized shades of teal and lavender, the city floating unreal and immaterial, making me want to stammer a prayer, give myself over, repent, pledge allegiance, swear an oath to something ancient that harkens the end of days. The rain starts up full on, coming down sideways. The truck's windshield wipers knock back and forth. Clint points to a half-finished condo tower cloaked in green safety netting. The exterior's unfinished concrete. In the dark it looks a lot like the bombed-out low-rises in Afghanistan: windowless and shattered.

Knock it down and build it up.

"—hooked up tight," Clint's saying. "Development company named Marigold Group. Guy's name is Vincent Peele. Solid guy. Thief real estate lawyer. But we're business partners. So it's all good."

"Fucking lawyer?"

"Property development. Next level."

"I just want to run crews. Clint? Can I? At night, I want to sleep—"

"—we get Peele that property—"

"—work hard during the day, honest work—"

"—Peele's a lying cheat fuck but as long as we out-lie and out-cheat him—"

"So you get this lawyer the property. How?"

Soften the target.

"Dude's a twerp, but he's tapped into real money. Like movie stars, yachts, all that. You won't believe the shit I'm going to show you."

Without meaning to, my hand slides over the puckered scar above my left knee.

"Still hurting?"

"Feels weird is all. Like I'm living in someone else's skin?"

Clint gives me a look like he's questioning something while pain radiates from my healed-over wound, up my thigh, settles into my groin. For a while I thought I'd never have kids. Then Daree got pregnant. Shocker. The floor of the LAV ripped loose by the explosion. Pressure cooker shrapnel, red-hot metal moving fast through flesh. Not even an enemy to aim at. *Where are they? You see them?* No. Ghosts, demons, fear or the carefully crafted idea of fear. Or not even that. *Signals.* Someone a few blocks away dialled a number on a cellphone, triggered—

I make an effort to swallow, breathe, tell my brother I'm not going to see our old man.

Clint grunts. "Focus on the now. Past means nothing to a warrior. Been working on my mindset. Takes discipline. Thought being the army dude you'd get it."

"No discipline can stop an IED. It only is."

Clint scoffs. "If you walk, just walk. If you sit, just sit. But whatever you do—don't wobble." He tosses the wolf tooth on the seat. "Hear me? Enough wobbling, Marky. You need to say you're ready to work for Vincent Peele."

Daree. Sarah. A red-hot bit of metal moving fast. 2005 and everything changed. We never saw the enemy. The current target lives in Point Grey. Kids piled against the factory door burning. What I owe, what I am, and then I say it, *I'm ready*, and Clint seems psyched, almost happy, and for a moment I feel like I did the right thing for once, got my brother's back, and that has to be the right thing—

Carl "Blitzo" Reed

Friday night dinner Naam restaurant: shirataki Dragon Bowl, macrobiotic special with miso gravy. Microbes. Peristalsis. Happy what I ingest makes me better than most. Happy to be here, mostly. Spider plants climbing trellises to honey-stained oak rafters. My old pal Michael Zenski's talking vencap acquisitions. I think about Holdout snorting around in my Tesla, sniffing out my stash. Suddenly envious of that potbellied pig, also feeling itchy, too hot, concerned my macrobiotic gravy exists more consciously than me, lives more in the moment. Michael says something about a tech start-up out of Williams Lake. I ask him where the hell that is, to see if he knows.

"Up north. Past Whistler."

"Are the roads paved? Does a litre of milk cost ten dollars?"

Two or three kids, Michael says, returning to the point. Damn smart kids who have no idea how smart they are, which makes our job easy. Michael says he wants an eighty-five per cent stake for throwing a few grand their way. I ask about the social sphere—are we staying true to community—fret about Michael mentioning stakes. Is he a latent vampire? Cutting-edge tech something or other, Michael answers, talking over me. Could be an app, maybe a socially responsible video game, cloud this or that. Michael can't seem to remember precisely what the Williams Lake tech geeks are pimping.

"Early stages anyway," he says. "At this point it's more about synergy, correct? Embodied potential? Are we still searching for the big idea?"

I slurp a healing noodle, admire a cheery server girl named Star, start to say something about beautifully embodied potential, but before I can make a sound Michael asks me again about the big idea—

I tell him if you talk about it long enough, something will materialize.

"Sure. But is that something saleable?"

"That's your expertise."

"I'm going to use a word, Carl. To describe these kids."

"Don't use it."

"I'd like to."

"Don't."

Michael pauses, tongues the threshold of the word *visionary*, apparently thinks better of it and retreats. That word has heavy history. Once, it applied to our groundbreaking venture capital firm, Green Lead.

The restaurant's background noise rises up, mercifully, to drown out Michael's pitch-man voice. I watch his lips move, nod into drawn-out silences, chopstick-stab noodles. Thoughts come in and out of focus. Williams Lake tech geeks with greasy skin and glued-on third eyes. Democratization of information, if not industry. Tetris played retroactively in mouldy basements. A pile of crushed Red Bull cans. Trick is to get in early. This is scraping the bottom of the business barrel, which is saying something. But who knows? Could pan out. Stay positive, manifest dreams—

"What's nice about this project is the low overhead," Michael says, sipping ethically sourced strawberry leaf, nettle, and licorice-root tea. "Capital costs nil. Zero risk. We set them up in a storage unit, throw a space heater in there, a couple laptops. In a few years, they might come up aces. It can happen."

"Huffing happens," I say, feeling perky. "Meth happens."

"How long to huff five thousand dollars in gasoline?"

"Ask Harper. Fume-addicted imperialist zombie."

People in Naam look happy from a distance. I've never pulled the trigger on a firearm of any make or sort. I'm curious about how that feels. I'm happy the people around me seem happy. I think we've done some good. Somewhere?

"Potential," Michael says, a shopworn personal buzzword, almost a threat. Subtext: we need in on this deal.

"Is that right? How does the Williams Lake tech . . . align with Green Lead's core values?"

Whoa! It's genius. Or at least nearly coherent. Core values? WTF? Maybe the most cutting question I've asked about a vencap acquisition in a decade. Michael startles, sets his tea down, spills some over his thumb, brings his thumb to his lips, sucks. Looks like a spoiled toddler for a half-second, or a porn girl dressed like a Japanese anime doll—

"I believe their project can be nurtured. Guided? Toward something— shit, Carl. Do you even remember what Green Lead's core values *are*?"

Got him. "There's only one. Green Lead invests ethically."

Michael waves me away, but something in my meal's micronutrients, precise ratios of this and that, the restaurant's socially elevated timbre, the itty-bitty speedball I injected while ensconced in my Tesla—all combine to make me feel prickish, and instead of taking the high road I press on, capable and quick, focused like a starship laser, needling my oldest friend into submission. "Michael? Who am I?"

"Quit messing around."

Set down my chopsticks. Give him a serious face. "I mean it this time. Who is I?"

"You're too old, is what."

Feeling honed, mercenary. "Do not patronize. Paternalize? Either/ or, do not. I asked you a question. Answer me."

Michael rubs his forehead, smudges his concealer. "Sole majority owner and CEO of Green Lead Investment. Happy?"

"Over the moon. But bear with me. If I am majority owner and CEO, that makes you—"

"Coo, coo," Michael whispers, and then it's gone, my moment of unfettered will, ascendant ego, petty one-upmanship, because it seems Michael's merrily cooing at me in an attempt to hurl me way off my game, and a guy with lime-green dreadlocks slouching at the table behind us yells *caw, caw* and Star goes *meow* from over by the bar and the entire restaurant erupts in animal sounds; the big bearded mofo waiting to be seated rumbles a bearish baritone growl amid more howls and caws, hisses and hoots from the patrons and I go rigid in my chair while the awful screeching barking zoo-shrieks wash over me, gritting my teeth, eyes closed, hands clamped on the table, riding this one out, thinking maybe the speedball wasn't so itty or bitty, dreaming of my Tesla's warm, womb-like interior, thinking safety, operational security, concrete-walled safe rooms, thinking maybe I'm about to bolt out of the goddamned Naam and then *poof! yee-haw!* the animal noises vanish and there's only silence and Michael looking upset with me or maybe unhappy with his veggie-nut patty?

"Uh . . . pardon?" I manage. "Coo?"

Go for a noodle slurp, try and regain the flow, noodle slips from my chopsticks, flicks miso in my eye. Blink it away, conscious of more than a few sideways glances—

"C-O-O. I am Green Lead's C-O-O."

"Ah! Gotcha."

"Do you? It's an acronym. Chief Operations Officer."

"No, it's an initialism. Google bet?"

"Mother of—"

"So . . . second in command? After me."

"You asshole."

Hit the peanut sauce. Beneath the table my legs are crossed and my foot rocks back and forth so fast I hear it hum. I'm about to shoot a ray of light from my eyes. It's actually a tractor beam. Mentally summoning Star within touching distance, me squinty-eyed staring straight at her, leaning in my chair, brow furrowed, concentrate . . . closer now, come to me, that a girl . . . until Michael waves his hand in my face, shatters the spell—

"Ouch! Do *not* do that! Very dangerous! Unleashed evil spirits. Opened netherworld portals—"

"Shush! Enough, Carl. Seriously."

"You shush. I miss Holdout." Blinking, searching for wickedness coalescing in a corner. "Management won't let me bring him in."

"It's a pig. It'll be fine."

"He has hair, not fur. Like a person."

"But it's not a person."

"He eats anything. A black hole of saggy pink skin, consuming all matter. I worry. What kind of creature eats himself sick? It's unnatural. I once saw him eat a barbecue, propane tank and all. I was in the pool and couldn't find my way out or I would've stopped him."

"The fact remains," Michael sniffs, "it's only a pig. Unsanitary. I wouldn't want it in here—"

"*Pfft*, stoolie. You know if he eats too much he won't be pot-bellied?"

"What happens?" Michael asks, mid-chew.

"He just fuckin' grows and grows."

Bit freaked out, thinking of big bangs, infinite expansion, hyper-market dynamics, a Godzilla-pig terrorizing Lotusland, me riding the swine's back, shoulda seen me halter-break this bastard, white-knuckling the reins, loosing long-repressed urges, horrifying the squares—

"Are you saying Holdout's only potbellied and cute because you starve him?"

"That offends me. He's on calorie restriction. It's healthy. Prehistoric. Feast or famine. How our nomadic ancestors ate when we roamed the veldt—"

"We're in Kitsilano. You see a fucking veldt? You starve the pig, so it eats. Imagine that."

"Those were the days? On the veldt? The internet makes me feel stupid. You offend me."

"You said that already."

"Worth reiterating."

"I want that Williams Lake deal."

"Holdout's going to eat me alive. While I sleep. I've dreamed about it."

"Then you better eat him first."

"Macrobiotic special?"

Michael smiles. I warm to him. He's still handsome when I close my eyes and imagine what he looks like.

"That was almost funny, Carl. Let's have more of that. You've been a dour dopehead recently." Michael raises his tea in cheers. "To our original vision. To having fun. To it being all about the people. Remember? Which reminds me. This development deal . . ."

I say nothing, stop listening, sink into Michael's business-drone voice, try to balance a chopstick upright on the table while the waitress, server, wage slave, whatever, the one named Star— bleach-blond dreadlocks, twenty-three, UBC student, double major in environmental studies and corporate finance because *we need good people in predatory industry*—sashays past our table. A waft of air perfumed with youthfully progressive fragrance, like a tiny blue-bell growing from a sidewalk and about to be trampled. Smart kid. Full of potential. Bright future, lots of upside. Unfortunately, Star seems intent on disturbing me, which is—no. Not okay. Dear? I lift a finger off the table to indicate, hun, not now. Business meeting. Important grown-up well-financed world-changing stuff. Come back later, though? Come back when I say. Star senses my dismissal, falters, retreats. Wowza. I'm hitting all the bases tonight. Exuding supreme confidence. Yelling over a hip-hop beat, in the Man's face with a motherfucking gat—

Michael waits until Star leaves, gives me another impatient not-nice look. "Completion of stage three will make the project the largest real estate development in the province, if not the country. Of course it's early days. Still in property acquisition. I like it."

I'm becoming aware we've switched topics. Williams Lake greaseball techies? I shoo them away. Good kids. Perhaps a bit raw. A bit . . . lumpen. We need a business plan, kids. Come see us when you have sales.

Michael's talking money. Rate of return, blah. I pick up a cloth napkin, nibble the corner, slowly stuff the bulk of it in my mouth.

". . . project of a scale similar to Concord's False Creek development. Marigold Group's spearheading. We know them. Vincent Peele? I told him we're interested. A fantastic opportunity to show-case . . ."

I'd forgotten chopsticks and noodles could be so challenging. Getting frustrated. I ask Michael if we've come a long way.

"Talking with your mouth full? A long way from your terrible twos?"

In answer, I gag on my napkin.

Star saves the day by swishing over, leaning low, gently pulling the napkin from my throat. I keep my gaze fixed on the ceiling, make a point of showing her I'm not ogling. Michael doesn't miss a beat of the pitch. The b-word is used, sacramentally. That's *billion*. Nice word. Inspiring ring to it. How you feeling today? I'm feeling danged billiony!

Mumble a potent incantation to silence Michael, inadvertantly make the walls bleed monarch butterflies, giggle like a hyena. Am I a microscopic organism residing inside the beating heart of a famous person . . . or no wait, more like a symbiotic parasite swimming in a famous person's blood, feeding on and being fed upon, and what famous person would it be? Star would know. Anyways . . . feeling experimental, which reminds me I need to create some performance art, something with me running through the woods naked, or me at Naam naked, or maybe just Star naked. Do I need a stronger online presence? Star seems to think so. Maybe me naked online? Make a mental note to ask her what the hot new site is, promptly forget, inhale deeply, take a moment to wade through Naam's full-bodied scents of incense, patchouli, weed, something yeasty and febrile I'm fairly certain isn't Star. I order a lemon cut in half, craving citrus and clarity.

"A billion-dollar development," Michael says, as if to settle it. "Vincent Peele's offer is garbage, of course. But we'll get it hammered out."

Loud enough so the entire restaurant can hear, "Property development? Sounds moneyed, but boring. You bourgeois imposter."

A few hoots and hollers from the crowd. Blitzo—dude's been around, still keepin' it real for the kidlings—

"It's my job to keep us grounded, Carl. Remember? Cash flow?"

Tuneful: "Bor-ing!"

"It will make us money."

"Money's bor-ing!"

Star smiles her approval, shakes something juicy in my direction.

Michael drags his teacup across the table, makes me suspicious he's signalling a spook. Night raid? Truth serum? So fucking yesterday they might be back in fashion. I'm finally outliving time.

"'Money's boring.' Says the obscenely rich guy."

"What about movies? Hollywood? Nah . . . too many assholes. Or the Dark Web? Bitcoin? Hey—cybernetic pirate ships! Pretenders walk the plank! It's a big world, is what I'm saying. We shouldn't have to settle. Remember my vision!" My voice rises to an inspiring crescendo. "Or how about parkour? Leaping from building to building . . . or that move where they run toward a wall and kick off and spin? Seems cool. Parkour clothing. With urban dystopian accessory pockets? To store a rusty switchblade, water purification tablets, a hennaed pet cockroach? Consider yoga pants. That Chip Wilson motherfucker is really pissing me off. Let's money the revolution."

Michael shakes his head. "We're signing on with Vincent Peele and Marigold. It's precisely the kind of diversification Green Lead requires. There's a slight complication . . . but forget it. Let me handle it."

"I got something you can handle. Coo, coo." Try and work up the energy to get upset at Michael making unilateral decisions, fail.

Star's wearing a burgundy hemp skirt and a tasselled flowy blouse. Nice outfit entirely. Easy on the eyes. The clothing line's called EcoDefenz. We backed them. Maybe a bit strident in name and branding? And what the fuck is up with that z? Take an unsatisfying bite of brown rice and wakame, consider talking to the EcoDefenz marketing people tomorrow . . . which is when I remember my daughter's coming home from Appleby College. When? Today? Next week? In a light year squared? I want to live life like a laser through space. An unerring line. Instantaneous, nothing but nothing around me, unhindered and undeterred *for evaaar.*

But Hannah. My child makes me feel stagnant. Brackish.

Star sets a dish of sliced lemon on the table, asks if my heart's in the right place. Or she would, if we were honest with one another. Instead she's silent. I'm uncomfortable with the relationship between server and patron. A fundamental power imbalance I try to subvert with ostentatious tips that have the unschemed side effect of getting me laid once in a while.

Michael's blabbing about the solstice.

"The celebration?" I ask, hopeful, thinking about shifting energy vortexes and how international capital flow is a lot like them and there's a ninety-nine-cent ebook in there somewhere, title: *Financial Wellness through the Ancient Energy of—*

Michael shakes his head. Disappointed in something I can't intuit. "Dammit, Carl. At least try to appear like you give a shit. The

Solstice property development?" He snaps his fingers twice, inches from my nose.

"I wish . . . you wouldn't . . . do that," I whisper, looking at the lemon seeds. Three have been cut. One escaped. A big part of my mind's still on the solstice. Vortexes. Sweaty naked people. Capital flow. Collusion.

"Someone has to."

"You're being confrontational. Almost unpleasant." Take out my phone. Acting like I'm acting normal puts me somewhere near normal, still spiritually uncertain but buoyed by lemony smell. Scroll for my calendar. Seeking big data. Algorithmic answers. Wrinkling my brow, studious, engaged, sweet techno-glitz don't let me down—

"Are you talking at your phone?"

"Quiet. Researching."

Put off by how fleshy my fingers look holding the sexy-sleek phone. How soft and pudgy and of the grave. We're born to rot, not riot. Forty-nine years old. Mid-century modern. There's toxic material lurking in my bones, harmless until disturbed. "I'm fucking disturbed," I mutter.

"Keep it together, Blitz," Michael whispers, using my alias as a term of endearment, making me feel like a cored fruit. "Let's get you out of here."

Phew. "Star? The cheque, dear? Holdout's getting cold."

Where's the goddamned calendar in this thing? An ad pops up, tries to sell me cryo-something. Dull body in a titanium tank. Suspended in aloe vera goop. Absorbing nutrients through my skin, osmotic? Wake me up when things make less sense . . . but right now still entranced by the phone. Subtly rounded corners smooth to the touch. It's true Steve Jobs was a genius. Not a single right angle in the natural world. An evil collision of lines. So why design right angles into our tech? The point is to make the tech appear organic, like it sprouted from seed, like alfalfa in my bowl, like Star in my bed. Seamlessness is perfection. Technology should predate us, or at least appear to. But where's the fucking calendar? My confidence fades, leaves me deflated, left out of something I can't name but know exists.

"Michael, I think I remember . . . what it's about?" I can't tell if my oldest friend and business partner has stopped talking. Did the spider plants just inch themselves closer? Is that a *maw*? Twenty-two years since the Berlin Wall came down and the universe gifted me the Nugget. A decade since I got out of prison and Green Lead began investing ethically. Pioneers in our field. Well, at least we started strong. I wonder about the fuzzy spot where you stop calling someone a friend, the even fuzzier spot where ethical investing becomes something else entirely.

There are lawyers involved. Roving packs of them. Maybe it's not so fuzzy.

Michael leans close, tries to snatch my phone, tells me I've lost my knack for holistic thought.

I ask him if we're having a run-of-the-mill domestic, and if so, can I leave?

"Consider how much commitment it would take to walk out on me."

He's right. I can't seem to spot the door.

Discouraged, I squint at the phone, fully aware doing so makes me look poor, old, and/or stupid. Star sighs. There's a pat answer out there somewhere. *Aha*, the calendar! Very similar to the old ones! Why did I need the calendar again? I pretend to tap something in, glare at Michael, feeling self-dissatisfied, certain the problem must be me, wanting the phone to reveal more than it does, collect private data, personal numerology, truth gleaned by an AI tarot reader, an algorithm coined by a lanky hooker in São Paulo who's secretly a crypto-freedom fighter working to liberate the Arctic or destroy the SPCA, her sassy algorithm introduced via Tumblr to another algorithm developed by the NSA to intercept creepily unrandom messages from the core of the earth, the two algorithms mated to produce something less than their sum, said the bespectacled guru on the rooftop in Varanasi. And a neophyte transhumanist with a dangerous idea. All hipster-smart mashed together to put a message in my inbox on my beautiful, smooth-edged, techno-organic phone, about which I will admit jealousy from a design perspective. The message will state: *You and Michael Zenski are no longer friends, never mind lovers.*

There. Settled.

That's what I want from my tech. Absolute certainty.

Am I asking too much or too little?

I could still get out of Green Lead, if not guilt-free then free. Michael's right. The world's nothing if not potential. Belief is a conscious choice. The word *free* makes my crotch tingle. Does that make me an American? "Look at my Tesla. Can you see Holdout? What's he doing? Shivering? Does his snout look dry? I'm fretting."

Michael's talking about scalability, various Silicon Valley legacies, and I'm confused, headed down a winding synaptic path, but I think we're talking Williams Lake tech geeks again. I tell him I want to invest in something I can hold in my hands. Something with actual mass. Michael laughs, says that's the exact opposite of what I said a few minutes ago, calls me analog, jabs about me being a dinosaur, a Luddite. I misquote John Zerzan, something about ricin and how to bleed a goat. My stock goes up. I see it in the fucker's eyes. The tablecloth depresses me. I think it's hemp made to look like plastic. That kind of thing should be illegal. Or at least carefully regulated. People need protecting from themselves. Something about a hemp clothing line allowing me to purchase a twenty-thousand-square-foot ski lodge in Whistler feels, in this particular space-time nexus, like a profoundly fascist intrusion. Suddenly I believe in animism. I feel the seat struggling beneath me, yearning for emancipation. Michael's had multiple plastic surgeries. His firstborn face sloughed off like reptile skin. Had it replaced with the visage of a Kathakali mask. His third wife eats

Cheerios bathed in Sprite for breakfast, has zero cavities, believes the world began an hour before she was born.

Or maybe it's the streetlight filtering in from Fourth Avenue, Rainbow Road, the constant traffic, suits in Beamers looking both rage-filled and serene, the gas station across the street, an exceptionally fit businesswoman leaning toward her Lexus, inserting a gasoline nozzle with practised ease. Man. Kitsilano. There it went. I rally for a centring breath, stop halfway, steamed broccoli lodged in my throat. A moment ago I exuded confidence. Now I can't taste my food, my ears are humming, the world appears colourless, strangely rounded. Vibes. Vortexes. Capital infusions. Solstices. Outside, the stars are hidden behind overcast skies, and the conversation continues.

Jasminder Bansal

S tuck in rush-hour gridlock congealed across the Lions Gate Bridge. Pent-up ugly energy lingering from my meeting with Vincent Peele. Suspended in low cloud, losing track of up and down, windshield wipers failing to clear sluices of rain, my car smelling damp and musty, everyone in a hurry to be somewhere else and that vibe seeps into me and I punch the horn because there's nothing else to do. Why lie about how close I was to Amar? Why betray my brother's memory to an asshole like Peele?

Because lying comes easy. In high school I lied about being Amar Bansal's sister. Of course everyone knew. Eventually my friends stopped returning calls and my teachers called more often. Worst of all was Amar. He assumed I was ashamed or afraid of him, like everyone else. But that wasn't it. I was furious because I couldn't stop looking up to him.

Breaking the real estate corruption story, bringing a truth to the public, or do I just want to see Clint Ward suffer? So what if my objective journalistic integrity is compromised? Neutrality is a privilege I don't have. What did Thompson say? You can't be objective about Nixon. Besides, no one believes that shit anymore. Write a three-hundred-word nut graph, blast it online, and don't expect to get paid because no one reads more than the lead, which might be *why bother?*

What if the story isn't worth the sacrifice? A twenty-six-year-old working part-time as a movie theatre usher while I attended real estate sales and marketing certificate courses. The half-truths and outright lies I've told my family. The forced enthusiasm with clients and colleagues at Marigold. And rekindling a relationship with Eric Hull, a guy I dated for a few months at Langara who works in real estate, to get a resumé reference for Marigold. Now that I'm inside I don't need Eric anymore. Should I end it tonight?

Playing a role, pretending to be someone I'm not. I think it came naturally to Amar. But for me?

My foot slips off the clutch and my Honda jerks forward, shudders as my brakes grind the car to a stop. The grating metal-on-metal sound is so bad that people in surrounding cars glance over, drawn to disaster. The bridge deck is rain-slick and narrow. I squint against oncoming traffic, hope to hell my car doesn't stall or worse. My defrost is shit, only clears a half-circle directly above the dash, forces me to drive hunched to the side, one hand on the wheel while I swipe at the windshield with a soaked scarf.

I see you, Jasminder. That's what Peele said. But I think he's wrong. I don't think he sees me at all, not yet and hopefully never.

At a standstill. Tail lights vanish as the bridge descends to Stanley Park. Braided-steel cables rise into the honeycombed steel structure overhead. Car horns and pelting rain—or a ship horn. From out in the harbour? Am I imagining it? They don't blast ship horns out there, do they? At Langara I did a story on women who work the tankers anchored in Burrard Inlet. Picked up on the docks and boated out. Returned to land the next morning. I was six months into my program when Amar died. I couldn't face sitting in class.

Fog on the Lions Gate Bridge drifting like dry ice across a dance floor. My brother was dancing when he was shot. I can't remember what song was playing. Why is the memory silent except for a single gunshot when I *know* there must've been music playing in the club? The doubt creeps into my memory of that night, makes me question what I saw.

Strobe lights flickering on the dance floor; headlights too bright on the bridge. Remembering Amar dancing when I see them up ahead. Apparitions coming in and out of focus. My hands gripped at ten and two while I tell myself I'm not really seeing this. A troupe or clan of dancers spinning and weaving through stuck vehicles. Towering creatures with hooked beaks and forked antlers, draped in cloaks and hides.

They have to be performers wearing costumes and wooden stilts. Closer now, still shifting and blurry but moving toward me. Soundless. Relentless. Why can't I remember the song? The animal dancers leap onto hoods, shatter windshields. Claws scrape against doors and a shrill shrieking reaches me. Is that the dancing creatures shrieking? Or only my wrecked brakes? Clint Ward murdered my brother and I'm putting myself near him and I don't know why, what I expect to accomplish except please tell me there's a truth taking shape.

"Must be time for a congrats?" Eric shouts over a roaring circular saw. "Full time with Marigold and Vincent Peele?"

I'm following Eric through a condo display unit being constructed inside a vacant retail space in Gastown, trying not to dwell on what I saw on the bridge. Eric doesn't sound entirely happy about the news, and neither am I. Eric hops over a pile of two-by-four offcuts while I fight back a sneeze from the sawdust haze. "Must be?"

Eric's wearing his real-estate-agent-as-construction-supervisor outfit: white hard hat, safety goggles tinted yellow, plaid shirt tucked into pressed khakis. Even in work boots he's smaller than me, has a habit of standing with his legs locked, chest out and chin up, like an image from a doctor's brochure on proper posture. Eric's about to say something when a construction worker reeking of weed and straining under a soaked sheet of plywood trips on an extension cord, staggers, nearly smashes into me. The guy cusses, says sorry, asks Eric where he wants the fucking plywood stacked. Eric frantically scans the work site. "Uh, how much plywood is there?"

The worker shakes the plywood in Eric's direction to show him it isn't light, says how should he know. Isn't Eric the boss? Eric can't seem to decide if he's the boss, and if he is, where to pile the plywood. Every inch of space is crammed with lumber, stacked drywall, tile boxes, metal scaffolding. The guy says goddamned fuck, chucks the plywood on the offcuts at Eric's feet, storms outside.

Eric tips his hard hat, tries to smile. "Twenty-four hours and we open for pre-sales. Hot neighbourhood, this part of Gastown. Finally revitalizing. Jaz? Here—" He hands me a set of blueprints, asks me to help hold them open. "Two thousand square feet to work with. So we're building—get this, it's wild—two different display units in here." Eric points at a half-finished structure looming behind us. "That's the two-bedroom. Seven hundred square feet."

The two-bedroom is elevated on a platform built a few feet off the retail floor. It's partially framed in with regularly spaced two-by-fours. The store lights are on overhead, and the unit is further lit by shop lights on industrial yellow stands. I squint against the glare, realize the shop lights are putting off a lot of heat and I'm beginning to sweat. The thought hits that maybe I wasn't dressed appropriately for my interview today. What did Vincent say? Hippie college chick. A rush of frustration and self-doubt that I stomp down, remind myself it doesn't matter, I got the job. Hammers smacking a staccato rhythm are interrupted by a frustrated shout. A carpenter and his crew are trying to finish framing in the walls, but they're being slowed by the hardwood guys already working beneath them.

"Why are they installing the hardwood so early?"

Eric uses his forearm to mop the sweat off his face. "Yeah. Why? Good question."

I glance at the blueprints. Apparently the plan is to construct two separate entry tunnels from the front door. Customers will walk down a darkened hallway a lot like the ones leading to a movie theatre and emerge into a perfectly constructed ideal made to be temporary, an illusion or magic show where at the end everyone claps and throws half a million into the magician's hat. That is if Eric Hull can get his shit together. "Look. The framers are tripping all over the hardwood guys. Hardwood shouldn't be going in until—"

"How is it everyone knows this but me?" Eric moans. "The hardwood guys said they needed to finish here and move to another—"

I try not to laugh. "You bought that bullshit? It's Friday night. You haven't even got the thing framed. Hardwood goes in last, or right before the paint. You think the hardwood guys want to be here first thing Saturday morning?"

Eric looks panicked, asks how I know so much.

"I spent high-school summers painting houses."

"Perfect!" Eric leans in for a kiss. I deflect with the blueprints, fight the memory of a beaked half-human creature shattering a car windshield. Eric says he's sorry he's gotta bail on dinner but he could really use some help—the weed-smelling guy drops another piece of plywood at our feet and a dust cloud billows around us—and could I stick around, maybe grab us some takeout sushi.

"On two conditions." I check the blueprints. "First you tell Mr. Chronic to move the insulation to that corner and stack the plywood where the insulation is now."

Eric pinches the blueprints, tugs me toward him. "He's gonna hate that. He already moved the plywood—"

"Just tell him. That's what bosses do. This isn't a sales negotiation. He's pissed because he isn't getting paid to make decisions, even about something stupid like where to put plywood. That's your job, and you're not doing it."

Eric's excuse-making is interrupted by the hardwood guy scream-ing holy fuck while he cradles his hand and hops across the plat-form—

Eric takes a step toward the display suite, hesitates, asks if I think the guy's okay.

"Probably nail-gunned his finger. Happens all the time. But you could ask him."

Eric says nothing.

"Hey!" I yell at the hardwood guy. "Get bone?"

The guy walks to the edge of the platform, shields his eyes against the shop lights. Torn jeans and a threadbare Pixies T-shirt. Early thirties. I tap the blueprints against my shoulder. Eric's irritating inability to deal is helping remind me that I'm here to break things off with him. The hardwood guy holds his hand up, makes sure I see the blood running down his palm, says, "No bone, stapled my thumb-web thing."

"We have a first aid kit. You need it?"

"Actually, Jaz, I don't think we—"

The hardwood guy laughs, says it'll stop bleeding soon enough, returns to his work.

I grab Eric's elbow. "This is where you make a crack about him not bleeding all over your expensive hardwood. Lighten the mood?"

Eric looks about to be sick, manages to stammer the updated plywood-pile instructions to Mr. Chronic, who whinges about how having to do everything twice is total bullshit, no wonder these hamster cages are so bullshit expensive, which seems reason-able enough.

Eric and I hurry to the back, where he spreads the blueprints on a piece of plywood stretched across two sawhorses. The half-finished condo suite, ringed by shop lights and broader darkness, looks like the armature of a lunar pod or a museum reconstruction of a prehistoric dwelling. Eric's blathering about high-end fixtures and costs per square foot. The guy in the Pixies shirt catches me watching him.

What would I say? To break the ice? That must'a hurt? Amar always knew what to say. Reporters, cops, groupies, rivals—always ready with a slick line.

Dealing with the construction crew on Eric's behalf leaves me feeling capable but on the outside of things. Eric knows my brother was murdered, but he has no idea about Vincent Peele's connection to Clint Ward. No way a guy like him could keep his mouth shut. Criminal activity? Please. Do that, you're no better than them. That's what Eric would say. Let the police handle it. Besides, what do you possibly hope to accomplish? Order, civility, security. The bedrock of Eric Hull. Even now, after he's ditched his journalistic aspirations and devoted himself to hawking real estate, there's still a pretentious twang in Eric's voice when he speaks to me, a South Van girl. Eric was born and raised in Lonsdale. Grew up gazing across Burrard Inlet. Feels possessive of Vancouver, the city beyond reproach, a treasured trinket he covets and secrets away. But he's involved in the story now, whether he knows it or not. I fold my arms and worry about guilt, and more specifically why I don't feel much of it—

Eric rolls up the blueprints. "What's condition two?"

"You impart a smidge of your vast realtor wisdom and tell me how to run my first open house for Marigold."

"Open house? Fantastic! When?"

"Tomorrow morning."

Eric laughs. "Yup, sounds like Peele. No concern for anyone but himself. See? If you came and worked with us, that would never happen—"

"Nothing ever gets dumped last minute on a Western Rim agent? You volunteered to be in this sweltering dust pit all Friday night—"

Eric raises his hands in surrender. "Okay, okay. But I'm not sure I understand what you need. You did amazing during the probation period. Keep doing more of the same?"

I thread my arm through Eric's. "Advice? Insight? I've never been solo on an open house."

"Don't stress. These widgets sell themselves. But that's my advice: make sure the unit sells tomorrow. That's what Peele expects."

"Other than that I'm good to go?"

Eric scrolls through a menu on his phone. "Absolutely. Except . . . it's important to be . . . animated. Is that the right word? Do you want gyoza?"

"Cartoons are animated. Or is that anime?"

This is a man who once spent an entire meal explaining the difference between anime and cartoons.

"Uh, sorry, of course you're right, *animated* is the wrong word. Important to show enthusiasm? To be communicative."

"Am I not enthusiastic?"

The guy in the Pixies shirt wraps a strip of duct tape around his injured hand.

"Oh, sure, yeah," Eric says in his most aggravating falsely conciliatory tone. "You have enthusiasm. But . . . people sense when your heart's not in it, you know? I believe that. We're more in tune with one another than we—"

"Say it. Please."

Eric falters. Takes off his hard hat, rubs the back of his neck. "You're quiet sometimes, Jaz. It throws people off. When you're talking, it's easier to warm to you." Puts the hard hat back on, tries to smile. "You have a nice voice. When you're with a client, your enthusiasm needs to be evident, your excitedness. Excitement? This is an exciting time for our clients. We should be excited too . . ."

"I am excited. How about we say 'excited' some more? Will that help?"

Eric swats me with the blueprints. "Okay . . . but still. Clients want their agents to be confident, to display a certain joie de vivre, vivaciousness—"

"I fucking know what it means."

The circular saw screams, startling Eric. He glances at the work crew to see if anyone notices. "It's the tiniest of tweaks. Because you asked for my opinion, for a place to begin, you know, improving. A tweak can make all the difference—"

"A tweak? I'm not sure exactly what—"

"A slight adjustment. Do you practise in front of the mirror?"

"Excuse me?"

Eric sighs. "Speaking. Enunciating. Are you upset?"

I sit on the plywood table, remember it's covered in sawdust, stand up, brush myself off. "Forget it. No. Upset? I'm not exactly skipping the light fandango."

"Is that something your mother says?"

"She used to. So what? What the hell are *you* saying? Practise in front of—"

"If you want. To try?"

I should be getting angry, but mostly I'm tired. "Eric, I asked for advice on how to run an open house, not how to speak the language. Are you saying people have a hard time understanding me? Because of my—"

Eric waves at a woman in the doorway carrying two massive binders stuffed with fabric samples. Hammer noise quiets as the carpenters pause to decide if she's worth paying attention to, then quickly resumes.

Eric tries to brush past me. "Anyway, it's nothing. Want to help me pick window coverings?"

"Not in the slightest. You remember I was born here? On Knight Street. I don't have an—"

"Well, maybe. But there's this perception. Among a particular group of people who happen to make up the majority of our client base. I'm not saying it's right. We have to work within it, even though—between you and me—it sucks. Speaking in front of the mirror might help. More for them than for you. But also try making eye contact more frequently. Not aggressively, but in an appropriately engaged fashion. Constructive, communicative eye contact works wonders. We're dealing with language barriers, all kinds of cultural assumptions. And stop fiddling with your hands—"

"My hands?"

"Stop fidgeting with them. Like you're doing now."

The saleswoman tiptoes into the construction site, winces at the noise. I decide I want to leave before we're introduced. A half-finished journalism diploma and a Hail Mary story. Maybe it's time to take this real estate racket, and Eric Hull, more seriously. Who's the dipshit now, Jasminder? "Enthusiasm. Speak proper English. Got it. Thanks, Eric. Anything else?"

"Takeout sushi? I'm buying."

I tell him sure, but only because I'm in no position to pass up a free meal, and after slipping outside and walking a few unnoticed blocks I find myself standing directly in front of the nightclub, now converted to a trendy brand-strategy agency, where Amar was shot point-blank in the back of the head and his name means forever, long life, luck, the everlasting.

Parked across from Andy Livingstone Field, psyching myself for sushi with Eric. Up the volume on the stereo, a playlist of early punk and current dance pop, violent rebellion and vapid conformity, alternating through the extremes. I haven't spoken to anyone about the visions. Sky ripped apart over Point Grey. Yaletown condominium with a femur still blood-wet and as large as an airplane chained to the exterior. North Shore Mountains torn from granite bedrock, flipped upside down, hovering. Half-animal, half-human dancers circling Canada Place plaza. Blue fire consuming the Nine O'Clock Gun. Misshapen skinless creatures emerging from a Saint Laurent handbag in a window display on Robson Street.

They began a few months after Amar died. *Post-bereavement hallucinatory experiences.* Ghosts of loved ones glimpsed in bathroom mirrors. Their voices singing a favourite song (Amar's secret fave was Color Me Badd's "I Wanna Sex You Up," partly because it was on the soundtrack to *New Jack City*; his public fave was Tupac's "California Love"). Usually I'm not lucky enough to see Amar. All I see is this city. Only happened once or twice a year, until now. Enough time in between to pretend they were isolated incidents. But coming more frequently as the anniversary of my brother's death approaches. Eighty-six thousand four hundred seconds in a day. And of those maybe only a half-dozen are inexplicable, horrifying, beautiful. So isn't that an acceptable ratio? Of mental normalness and day-to-day grieving and keeping on versus the other stuff? All things considered?

There's a soccer tournament at Andy Livingstone. Three different games. A city block glowing bright enough to accurately kick a checkered ball. In a local entrepreneur magazine, I read about a guy who invented a new way to light mud huts in Africa. He took a clear-plastic water bottle, stuck it through the roof. It collects and redirects sunlight into the hut. Cost-effective, efficient. I think he won some sort of award? The soccer ball spins through the air. Men in stockings chase after it while rain needles through fluorescent light, narrows to a single point, aimed, wilful. My sunroof's leaking onto the passenger seat. Damp fast-food wrappers disintegrate into the carpet. I grab a flannel blanket from the backseat, wrap it around my shoulders, hold my hands to the heat vent. Is it time to consider my next move with Vincent Peele?

Up the volume on a Subhumans song called "Oh Canaduh." Working at Marigold is partly about money. At least I admit that to myself. Partly about paying bills. It's also about imagining the story that will transform my life forever, reveal the highly regarded journalist I always knew myself to be—

My phone vibrates. Must be Eric wanting to change his sushi order. Ignore it, happy to be hate-dreaming about an unlikely future while Wimpy shrieks about the sea getting blacker and the sky turning brown. Recorded thirty years ago. What a strange feeling, wanting wealth and success but feeling cynical about it at the same time, desiring and despising, a weird mental split like that disorder everyone used to believe in, split personality, rack 'em up, never a dull moment.

It won't work. The thought is buried in my skull, undermining everything I do. *Why are you even trying?* Sometimes, when I'm well rested or feeling confident, I have the energy to choke it down. Other times, like now, when I'm tired and stressed, the thought is right in front, evident in how I pull away from people, in how hard it can be to leave my apartment, do stupid chores, never mind live a twentysomething life full of Kitsilano parties, holiday travel, Bellinis, Pinterest repurposing, community activism, caring—

Lady Gaga comes on, suggests I just dance.

Reach into my purse, find a Ziploc filled with photos, while outside the soccer players cheer a goal.

Amar standing beside his first car, a slammed pearl-black Prelude. T-shirt tucked in. Hair cropped short. All the world in his smile. Amar and my younger sister, Meeta, on a rare family outing to the blueberry fields in Delta, faces smeared with inky summer stain. Amar standing neat and nervous in front of the fake fireplace in our tiny South Van apartment with the first girl he ever brought home, a blonde named Rebecca so small-minded and idiotic I spent dinner dropping peas onto her lap, waiting for her to notice. A photo of Amar hanging with a group of friends outside Oakridge mall. Spiky gelled hair, gold chains, oversized shirts. Amar's turned away from the camera, slumping, trying to hide the cigarette in his hand. I took the photo to blackmail him, was going to threaten to give it to our mother unless Amar bought me and my friends coolers. I never made the threat. Another photo, one of the last, of a bulked-up, pissed-off Amar in a downtown nightclub, arm draped over the shoulder of an ugly tattooed white guy named Clint Ward.

Amar and Clint came up around the same time. Met in one of the gyms Amar frequented. Hung out a bit. But by then I'm sure Amar no longer had true friends. He had associates. Business partners.

Alliances. Connects. He had dealings. Territory. Corners. Dope lines. Double-crossings. Fallouts. He had muscle and payback, beef, heat, pigs, rats, weed, smack, crystal, gats, Glocks, nines, AKs, green. He had image. A rep. He was gettin' paid. Makin' bank. He had to prove points. Make examples of. Teach lessons. Motherfuckers had to bleed. By the time this last photo was taken Amar was a criminal. A vicious new breed of Indo-Canadian gangster, the media called him, which made me wonder: who were the old breed? And soon after the photo was taken Amar had a bullet in the head. An unsolved murder. A nightclub full of witnesses and not a single person who'd say a word—

Not even me.

Like Amar used to say. A little mouse.

Neighbourhood rumours about Clint being the killer never went anywhere. Newspapers moved on when the drug war ended. New weather systems blew in, new imagined terrors. Cambodians. Somali refugees, children of the snow. Afghans. First Nations gangs. Latino cartels. Muslims of every description. Always another threat from somewhere else. Fear is a lot of what Western culture is. Which means no one wants to remember. We live like rabbits ducking into holes.

Looking at my brother's picture, it feels like my life lacks present or future. Everyone endures an occasional rut. But what happens when the rut is so deep and lasts so long it alters something integral?

There's no way to link Clint to Amar's murder. All I have is memory. Lights spinning across a dance floor. My brother dancing, laughing, snapping his fingers, waving, trying to pull me onto the floor. Me shaking my head no, far too shy to leave my seat, intimidated by the glam club-girls swarming around him or maybe intimidated by the man he'd grown into. The bass rattling my chest, making my voice sound hollow. Maybe if I'd had the courage to dance with my brother he'd still be alive. Then a concussive crack I felt more than heard. And Clint Ward motionless in the middle of the dance floor, face shadowed by a hoodie and ball cap, mouth hanging open like he'd surprised himself. I ran for the door, not my brother. Let the crowd carry me into the rain.

Little mouse.

Was Amar right? Am I doomed, or a secret superstar?

Mark Ward

"—taxed to shit so you junkies can live easy—"

"Not a junkie."

"Splitting hairs? How's it feel? Ditching your woman and baby daughter?"

"Feels shit."

"Juuun-kieee . . ."

"Daree's sorted. Has her head on. Easier without me. *Farang.* Makes shit hard—"

"*Ooh*, life's haaard for a loser . . . Ox-eee . . . juuun-kieee . . ."

Smoking bowls, glaring at the GPS screen on the dash, trying to tune my dickhead brother out. A glowing red dot tells me where I'm located, halfway up the North Shore Mountains at the corner of Southborough Drive and Kenwood Road, parked across from the Capilano Golf and Country Club, deep in the British Properties, deep in enemy territory, lofty aerie of rich pricks, oh the horror that the neighbourhood's strict whites-only policy has fallen by the wayside but hey-ho times have changed and money is money and the TV news says they arrive with suitcases full of cash. There's a buzzing in my ears and I'm very grateful for the red dot on the GPS screen, like it's giving me an irrefutable proof, an affirmation I am in fact where I think I am, that I exist in this particular time and place.

Clint stabs his index finger into my arm, tells me to stop fucking chewing my fingernails. I say I'm chewing my knuckles and nail folds, not my fingernails, you ignorant idiot. Clint says piss off, just stop it, Marky, it's creeping me out, the scritching-rat-chewing sound, takes a solid hit, cough-laughs, says fuck me I thought you'd be better, dude. I set my head against the cold window, close my eyes, tell him I think I am better because I can't tell if I'm me anymore? Clint stops laughing, says what the fuck, shut up, always your problem, nattering instead of getting shit done.

We're perched over Vancouver, the downtown core nestled in the darkness of Burrard Inlet. I try to pay attention, see things straight, the people down there living their lives, day to day, normal people . . . but then I get a not-cool suffocating feeling because none of it feels real, the city, the ocean, even the leather upholstery under my ass, like there's some kind of . . . wall between the world out there and me in here, and it takes a considerable amount of effort to remind myself Clint's alive, whatever that means, and me too . . . and the effort of trying to keep it straight leaves me rundown and ragged—

"Wait a sec," Clint says, flicking a gold Zippo to flame and lighting two incense sticks. Stinking too-sweet smoke curls inside the cab, hits the roof and spreads outward, descends when it reaches the windshield, settles around our waists. I wipe my nose on my sleeve while Clint lets the incense burn down. We don't say anything for a long time. Smoke fills the cab. My eyes water. A city. A small town made good. People living their lives. Decent people? People with hopes and dreams and loves is what I'm supposed to believe. Someone might've won something? We won? They say we won, which is why those people down there are free to live their lives. Another victory for the righteous, we made it, LIGHTROAR, thank heavens that's over, it was a close call but we triumphed,

DEATHFIRE, we the magnificent-ascendant, we the blessed who
are meant to be—

Clint closes his eyes. Cups his hands, pulls incense smoke toward
his face. It's an odd gesture for my brother. Measured. Serene. He
takes a few slow breaths, drawing the smoke into his lungs. His face
slackens. A muscle that twitches constantly, at the hinge of his jaw,
relaxes. My older brother. Handsome like a LAV III. Built with
martial intent.

"Seen what you're doing," I tell him, not meaning to sound so
bitchy.

"What?"

"Seen it in Thailand. It's Buddhist. You saw it on TV. You're looking like you're meditating."

"Doesn't make it less true. So fucking what, you went to Thailand?
Hey, if you could be born at any time, what would you choose?"

"Two thirty-eight p.m."

"No, I mean age, smartass. Era. You know?"

"Now seems pretty good."

"But there's no code. No honour. I'd choose the warrior nobility
of Japan. *Buke*. Samurai? Shit was for realz."

"They weren't all samurai. Most of them were peasants."

"Not me. I'd be a—"

"You said you had somewhere for me to sleep?"

"Feeling tired?" Clint opens his eyes. Tosses the incense out the
window, drapes his arm over my shoulders. "Little bro need some
shut-eye?"

"Yeah, jet lag." Weird to have my brother's arm across my shoulders. The weight of him. The bulk. His heart pumping shared blood.
He's always been bigger than me. Used to pin me down and leak
a long drip of spit in my face, then suck it up before it dropped. "Jet
lag, I guess. And Oxy. And weed."

"And blow. Smarten up. Glad you're here. Family."

"Me too." Nothing else to say.

"Means something." Clint squeezes my shoulders. His breath smells of cigar. He's not a bad guy. That's what I was wrong about, growing up. We all were. I let him take the flak. Be the black sheep. Then that thing in 2005. He pulled me off my first target. Saved that sick fuck's life. So Clint's not the bad one. I think I am. It's me. I'm the bad guy here. All the shit I've done, it must be me. At least Clint believes in honour, family. Takes care of our old man. Paid his medical bills while I fucked off. For a long time, I told myself I did it to impress Clint. Nearly beat that sicko to death. Lied to myself. Blamed my brother.

When what he gave me was—

"You feel it?" Clint whispers. "This town? The opportunity . . ."

To be what I am.

50 Cent's on the stereo, talking shit about bitches. My brother's forehead settles against my temple. His arm's still draped over my shoulders. We're real close. Holding each other. Not saying anything. Condensation rises up the windshield. It's still raining. Thrumming. There's a forest outside. Trees. Dirt. Canada? I'm not sure. Living things? Animals? Veins pulse along Clint's forearm. He was always more veiny than me. More muscular. Breathing his sour smell. *Hold me.* The two of us alone in the truck, breath settling into a matching rhythm. The smell of my brother like childhood, like memory. The time, ten years old, he ate shit on a buddy's Yamaha and I fireman-carried him to the nearest gravel road. He was crying even though he was the one who never did. His chest shuddering as he tried to keep the tears in. The smell of him then, same as now. The weight. The animal aliveness of him. The stubborn warmth. The Dodge diesel spitting and growling beside the deserted golf course. A real sweet truck. Polished chrome rims. Big mudders. A grand per tire. Rolling around town, running crews, boss man, my brother. Me and Clint aren't talking. He made something of himself. *I love you, brother.* What a sweet fucking truck. *Please help me.* I'm getting choked up. It's nice. *I feel you're alive, brother.* Unstable. Give me some more

blow. We're still holding one another, breathing together. Saw the LAV VC with the steering wheel blown through him. Saw the factory outside Bangkok. Saw inside everything. Can't think about the war. Need another Oxy. My wife and baby daughter. OPFOR pushed a button on a cellphone. *Hold me.* I don't want to blame them. We did this to me, not them. Marky got all blowed up. BLOOD RAIN. GODFIRE. Making bank. On the up. The city lit bright. *I'm sorry.* The city on fire. *I'm sorry.* The children in the factory on fire. *Please, no.* My brother's weight heavy against me, his breathing slow, his skin too warm. *I'll kill you for this truck.* Rain hitting the windshield, hissing in flame. My brother's arm across my shoulders, embracing and pinning me down. *We're in this together.* Could'a been any dumb bastard on top of that bomb. Turned out it was Marky. I KILLED FOR YOU. *Hold me.* YOU MADE ME. Living things, a dark forest to roam through, stolen territory, the triumphant kill. *Where's the enemy?* Don't ask me to. *Help me. Please, my brother—*

"No one knows you like I do," Clint whispers.

We're still touching.

I don't want to let go but it's better if I move first or he'll call me a fag, so I do.

"No one ever will," Clint says, moving to the far side of the truck. "We've been through it. I'm talking blood. Everything flows from that. Blood loyalty. *Buke.* It still matters. You ready?"

"I'm . . . real thirsty."

The light changes, or I change how I'm seeing the light, and my older brother, the one who held me because he knew I needed it, is gone.

"Get us a drink right now. Rich prick's house." Clint rolls his head, slow, then side to side, stretching.

"Now? Just flew in . . . I can't . . . what?"

"Don't be a dogfucker, Marky. Don't be that guy."

Clint takes off his rings and chains, drops them in the centre console, pulls a balaclava over his head. His eyes bulge white in the holes cut in the mask. Night creature. Takes me a while to realize what he's doing. Gearing up. *Home invasion.* Truth is I've always liked how it sounds. Covert. Daring. A late-night insertion. OPFOR. A raid on a fortified compound. A filthy rat dragged from a hole. Better than shooting at rocks across a valley.

Clint drops something in my lap. Looks like a baseball torn apart at the seams. One end heavier than the other. Loaded with steel pellets. My hand tightens on the SAP. Cold leather yields to warm grip. Clint shrugs a black hoodie over his head. I want to say something. I shouldn't be here. Don't ask me to. This isn't who I am anymore. Have a daughter and—

Clint nods toward the city. "See? Fucking told you. Best place on earth."

* * *

I was the smart one, people said when we were growing up. Teachers said it, if not in so many words. I was the Ward brother that had potential if I stayed out of trouble. I was going to *rise above.* Took me a long while to realize they weren't talking about me in particular but more of an idea. *Equal opportunity. Work hard and you'll succeed.* I was also the talker. Loved drama class. Played Hamlet in *Hamlet.* Kept them entertained. All eyes on me. Stage lights beaming down. People will say anything if they know you come from a shit family. Makes them feel better just saying it. *You got a good head on you.* Shit like that. *You're not like your older brother.* Tried to build me into something special, something they could tolerate. Invest every waking moment in your own happiness and other people's unhappiness begins to feel like a personal affront. The truth of things poses a threat to your carefully constructed paradise of self-aggrandizing bullshit. Unhappiness is ugly, and real, and of the dirt and body, of earth and death, and completely distasteful unless it's being used to sell something, as some sort of cynical strategy. Which is fine, because fuck them. Trouble is, I believed what everyone said. But something happened along the way. Wish I could say it was Afghanistan. *The war changed me.* No. Wasn't that. Wish it was. That's something people could get behind. I could go silent. Give them a thousand-yard stare so they'd nod and say *uh-huh, yeah man, that must'a been hard.* But that's not it. Wasn't the war at all. War felt a lot like our shithole town in the Fraser Valley, only more outright. More honest about what it was, about who was getting fucked. War felt nothing but familiar.

The lines clearly marked. Us and them.

Out in the darkness, out in the rain. Following Clint as he slides down a gravel ditch and climbs over a chain-link fence securing the golf course. Ten seconds after we leave the truck we're strolling across a manicured green, footsteps squishing in soaked grass, not hurrying, not worried, nearly invisible. I'm taking it in, the rough balaclava against my throat, the SAP's reassuring weight, nerves and anticipation, allure in the wilful rending of routine. Good or bad, it can go either way, and inviting the unknown is half the joy.

It's cooler on the mountain. Rain thickens to sleet. I think about the guys strolling the golf course on a weekday morning in June, wearing cutesy pastel, thirty grand in clubs, laughing, life's good.

And now here we are. Trespassers.

The first time me and Clint broke into a house I was nine and he was eleven. Got in through a bathroom window. In Chilliwack, a suburban wreck an hour outside Vancity, up in a neighbourhood of ranchers spread out on big lots on a hill called Little Mountain, an isolated enclave for the town's better-off. Elevated above us commoners stuck in the floodplain with our laid-off fathers and apartments with mouldy walls and tobacco-yellow lamps and single-pane windows glazed thick with winter ice.

I went in first. Nine years old. Punched out the screen and

wormed into that pretty bathroom. Slipped off the toilet and nearly brained myself against the marble vanity. Inhaled the aerosol lilac stink of the wife's hairspray. Family'd left only five minutes earlier. Me and Clint, hidden in the ornamental hedges, watched them drive off, made our move.

And the silence in that first house. Welcoming. Opening its arms. So much space I almost got lost in the bathroom. Marble and fancy-assed stone tile around the claw-foot tub, shining silver fixtures, real nice for back then. For a moment that fancy bathroom was mine. The nice things in it were mine, not the empty fridge back home, no-name ketchup and peeling lino, a TV that never worked right, smashed-in fake wood panelling and the stink of my old man's failure. I stood in that fancy person's bathroom letting the expensive smells sink in, enjoying being somewhere I shouldn't, doing something I shouldn't. And dreaming of being someone I wasn't. Freedom's different things to different people. Might be casting a ballot. Getting a decent job. For me growing up, freedom was standing in a house I had no business being in, smelling lilac hairspray, waiting to hear the homeowner's car pull into the driveway, waiting to run for my fucking life. So to celebrate the occasion I grabbed the wife's hairbrush, stuffed it in my pocket.

I still have that hairbrush. Took it overseas, kept it tucked in my tacvest. Her rich-lady smell is long gone. But I remember leaving the bathroom, walking alone through that silent house, the feeling like approaching a cathedral altar, awed at all the shit that family owned, how new it was, wanting to stop and try out the Sega, play some *Sonic*, then letting Clint in the front door. Nodding as he slipped inside, conspiratorial, like we'd uncovered a secret tomb stuffed with treasure. It wasn't my brother's first house. Clint made right for the jewellery. Now I know the real treasure is feeling almost equal, if only for a few stolen seconds.

So yeah, my blood's surging as we stroll across the golf course, although the feeling's dulled some over the years. Just another mission, soldier. The SAP held loose in my hand, brushing my thigh as I walk. Every step brings a jolt of pain from my ruined leg, keeps me sharp.

"Show you something," Clint says, whirling to face me.

His phone lights up his balaclava, his shiny gloves, and I imagine the sight from a distance, fucking strange, two masked men trapped inside a ghostly sphere of light in the middle of a pitch-black golf course—

"Heat, dude. Put that shit away."

Clint laughs. "Nah. Only us out here. Look."

A few numbers flash on the screen.

"Know what that is? Old man's vitals. App reads the vitals, sends them to me in real time."

I peer at the phone, the numbers stacked along the screen, ask what the hell he's talking about?

"That's him. Dad. Heart rate right there. Blood pressure. I'm guessing he's asleep. Which is good. Doesn't happen much."

It's the closest I've been to my father in years. ". . . he's all right?"

"Asks for you."

The SAP now heavy in my hand. The intentional rending of routine. "Where was he, back when I was asking for him?"

"You going to feast on that forever? Mr. Perfect with the wife and daughter?" Clint pockets the phone, plunging us into darkness. We're facing one another in the middle of the golf course, rain pounding, armed, angry. "I'll get the app to text you."

"Fuck off. He know about that thing?"

"Course not."

"Yeah. Cuz it'd drive him up a wall."

"He's over the wall, Marky. Updates twice a day. And if anything goes wrong, a close call—blood pressure, heart rate—you get a warning beep and a suggestion about what's going on."

"He's had close calls?"

"A few." Clint starts walking.

Wiping the rain from my eyes when a not-awesome thought hits, because I've seen my brother clap a dumb motherfucker on the back at the same time he's leading him into the woods. "What's this thing tonight?"

"Worried? Maybe you should've paid up. What's the soldier in you say?"

I think on that. Only one thing Clint wants to hear. "Family."

We're halfway across the golf course. A steep hill on the other side, densely wooded, leads to a cul-de-sac of mansions. "Wait. Can't see proper. Light from your phone messed my eyes."

"Putz. Give it a sec. You get used to seeing in the dark." Clint hops another chain-link fence, lands in knee-high grass browned by winter. "Don't steal anything. Don't say anything. And for fucking hell, don't let anyone out of the house."

Scramble over the fence, catch my jeans, rip a hole in the calf. Clint makes a backhanded comment about stealth and the military. I ask about the target as we enter the woods and begin storming our way up the hill and my feet sink deep in rotten leaves and moss and I feel like I'm arriving into myself, consciousness, whatever-the-fuck but it feels okay, an animal aliveness, soaked forest scent crisp in my nose and is this feeling real, something I can count on? The tree canopy blocks the bulk of the rain, sends it down in heavy drops. I don't really care who he is. A target. A victim. Just seems like a normal-sounding thing to ask.

"Deserves it. Trust me."

We slow where the forest thins at the edge of the yard. Lower into a crouch. The house is huge, four storeys, gleaming white concrete, broad curves and bold cantilevers dug into a granite slope with a view over the golf course to the city beyond. Looks like a spaceship about to launch, something created by a secretive government program. Design like this used to stand for something. An idea, a hope. Now it stands for money and some rich prick's pseudo-sophistication. We stay crouched in the woods for a long while, silent, watching. All the lights are out. Nothing's moving.

There are a lot of things we could be. Subversive shit always comes smashing in from the dark. No one wants to acknowledge it, though. Not now, when it's all about dialogue and discussion and socially oriented business partnerships and alliances and understanding. I call bullshit. We let them sweet-talk us. But we'll see who remembers. I'm talking Narodnaya Volya. The motherfucking Mollies. Red Army. J2M. WUO. Direct Action in the eighties here at home. And dozens more around the globe. Exploiters and exploited. So it's been a couple hundred years. That's an eye blink. European monarchy lasted a thousand. We're cutting our fucking baby teeth. Clint has his so-called Asian warrior philosophy. My inspiration's more recent. There's still a war going on. That was clear to me two decades ago when I busted into that bathroom and saw what money means. Until then I thought everyone went hungry at the end of the month. Thought it was normal to have the electricity shut off. I was nine. Didn't know any better. For me and my brother that was normal.

Like us and the Afghans. Sweatin' broke-ass brown people in their huts. Never sat right, especially when I was in it, my Colt Canada raised high, screaming *Aram shoo! Aram shoo!* at the frightened kids and worn-out women when we kicked their doors down, and how the older folks in the huts nodded and ignored us, their gaze never leaving their *palaw* pots they were so used to it—

"Couple things you should know." Clint slips a set of matte-black brass knuckles over his fingers. "One, the house is alarmed. So we're quick about it. Not panicky, but quick. Two, father fucked up. But he has a teenaged son. Simon. Plays hockey. Big kid for his age. Dad's a nothin' lawyer who overstepped. But Simon . . . you know? Teenagers. Hot-headed."

Clint asks for the time.

I tell him eleven seventeen in the p.m. Way too early for nightwork. Three thirty's the sweet spot. "Should wait a while."

Clint runs the knuckles over his lips. "Nah. In this fucking wet?"

On the move, sprinting across the lawn and around the covered pool. Clint's two hundred twenty pounds of night terror smashes into the patio door at full speed, ripping it from its hinges. Glass shatters. The sound shoots fire up my legs, through my groin, into my heart and head, gets me feeling I'm exactly where I need to be, stars aligned, destiny? Here in the mountains we have ten, maybe fifteen minutes before the cops arrive. Plenty of time. Eons.

I leap inside the house while Clint brushes broken glass from his forearms. Lilac hairspray fills my nose, not from this mansion but from the one twenty years ago, makes me gag, smash the SAP through a neat-o glass sculpture. Race across a cavernous open concept main floor and up a flight of stairs three at a time despite my leg killing me, BLOODFIRE, swinging the SAP into walls, leaving head-sized holes. A landing, right turn, another flight of stairs. Someone's screaming. Panic. Horror. Screaming terror in their mud huts in Afghanistan, screaming terror in their mansions in Vancouver. Night sounds, bloodletting, trespass. THIS IS OURS AND OURS ONLY. My brother roaring behind me. We kicked down the doors of their huts and made their women scream. We threw flash bangs in their huts and blinded the enemy—

Top landing, sitting area, marble floor, fancy-ass white leather armchairs every rich prick owns overlooking double-height windows facing the city and there's still a war on, a ragged bit of metal ripping through flesh. Light spills from beneath a door at the end of the hall. I'm tearing smirky contemporary paintings off the walls, art that says nothing, risks nothing, has no conviction. Clint shoves past me. Bedroom door swings open. LOOK AWAY. Desk-jockey lawyer wearing pyjamas with baby-blue sailboats, makes me laugh-scream. Clint's roaring down the hall. A goddamned bull, head tucked low. An armoured vehicle ripping through the desert and the LIGHTROAR, *please help me, we called it down like gods—*

✳

"Still on point, Marky."

I shrug, but it's nice to hear. Tuck the SAP in my pocket, step over the kid named Simon, slip into the bathroom. Flick on the light. Look at myself in the mirror, black balaclava, featureless face, everyone and no one, YOU MADE ME AND NOW YOU WANT ME GONE, spit in the sink, realize I got more than that, hurl in the toilet, flush, lilac stink clears a bit, rinse my mouth, find a bottle of Pine-Sol in the cupboard, consider guzzling it and hanging myself with the waist-belt from the kid's bathrobe, decide Clint would bust in and fuck it up and besides I got a goal, a purpose, and then I'm out. Bathroom's full of teenager shit. Products, I dunno. Hair gel, avocado skin cream. Nothing catches my eye. Disappointed, I stagger down the stairs behind Clint, trying not to limp too bad. The wife's on the phone in the master bedroom. 911. Screaming. Hysterical. Totally standard.

Make our way to the kitchen. A gas stove so large it deserves the word *range*. Clint wraps a hand in his wife-beater, opens a fridge made to blend into exotic-wood cabinetry, pulls out two beers. Hipster microbrew. Only the bestest for these folks. Knock the cap off against the countertop, drink the motherfucker in a gulp, drop the bottle, listen to it shatter, think about *Inspector Gadget*, my favourite cartoon growing up, those telescoping robotic arms, grab another beer, tune the wife's screaming out, what can I steal from this shithole, decide I'm feeling not bad.

"Sick crib," Clint says, slipping the knuckles into his hoodie. "Cheers."

"Cheers. Gangster crib."

We clink bottles. Clint hurls his empty across the house, into a glass fireplace in the living room. *Poof!* It's a trippy fireplace, sixties-style oval-shaped, looks like it's hovering above the floor, a real conversation piece. There was a time, not long ago, when we believed we would colonize the moon. Travel to the stars. When we believed robots would labour in our stead and the future looked—

"Simon Bryant." Clint reaches for another beer. "What a dickbag name."

Living room's painted white. Hurts my eyes. Only colour is from a huge painting on the I guess it'd be the north wall, some abstract thing, geometric but with flashy Day-Glo oranges and yellows that make me think of a nineties snowboard jacket. The woman's still shrieking, the sound echoing and crashing through the room and Clint slides a ten-inch chef's knife from the oak butcher's block, Kasumi, honed piece of steel.

"Nice blade," I say, admiring. "Good hand?"

"Decent weight. Not too flimsy. Selfie, dude." Clint holds up his phone, leans against the counter. "Get in here."

I down a second beer, step beside my brother, try and ignore the wife but the sound of her sets off a warning *beepbeepbeep* and with each beep there's a red flash behind my eyes like from staring directly into the sun—

Clint brandishes the Kasumi. "Hold the SAP so we can see it."

"To the happy family," I say, laughing, trying not to throw up in front of Clint, the kitchen shaking and trembling or maybe it's me?

"Here's to family, period." Clint snaps the selfie, lifts the Kasumi so the blade's against my neck, and I try and shrug him off but the fucker tenses, keeps the blade pressed against my throat and the woman's screaming *beepbeepbeep* and Clint snaps another selfie, this one with him holding the blade to my neck, which is fuck.

Something on the countertop catches my eye as we walk out. Bobby pins in a silver bowl. I lift one up, bring it to my nose. Sure smells like a lawyer's wife. Exotic. Cloves or cardamom? Sophisticated, highbrow. It's not perfect, but it'll do. I'm about to stuff the bobby pin in my pocket when Clint reminds me not to take anything.

"I'm not leaving empty-handed."

"Stealing weakens it."

"That what your boss says?"

"I don't have bosses. I have partners."

"She won't even know it's gone."

Clint looks about to argue, storms out the shattered door. I sniff the bobby pin, set it down, wish I'd bought some Skittles at the airport. Clint asks for the time as we slip into the woods. I lean toward the light shining from the house because the one on my watch got broke. "Uh, it's—"

A twig-snapping sound and I'm ducked low, scanning the treeline. Just a branch breaking or the bolt of a high-calibre rifle being drawn back? Out in the open, exposed, easy target? Stare into the black woods. Can't see a thing. Maybe the soft glint of painted metal? The enemy out there, dug in, waiting, sighting and I swear I *feel* the crosshairs settling on my chest—

Clint follows my gaze into the woods. Barely breathing, listening, and after a minute or so my brother gets impatient, says fuck it dude there's nothin' there.

"You didn't hear anything? Like a rifle?"

"Maybe an animal?"

"No."

"Didn't hear nothing. Relax. That was slick. Plenty of time to piss in the pool."

Carl "Blitzo" Reed

Countdown to something special. Seated in my sweet-ass monochromatic Tesla Roadster a few blocks from Naam. Rain sounding rainy on the windshield. Inside, ensconced in black calfskin grown in test tubes—no animals harmed—I'm mostly invisible to passersby. It's cold enough to see my breath, but comforting to know I remain warm on the inside.

Holdout's pouting. Rubs his whiskered chin against my leg, tells me he got cold waiting for me to wake up, says he felt excluded locked in the car while I was out socializing, says I need to include him more, asks if I'm embarrassed of him. I say you're a pig, be glad I don't stuff an apple in your mouth and fire up the grill. Holdout sniffs, calls me an anthropocentric reprobate, says my species is in decline, says he's thinking of organizing, asks if I realize my advancing years have spawned a pussy-footed Canadian conservatism, says the nice thing about Yanks is at least they're genuine assholes, says the only thing worse than an asshole is the guy riding the asshole's coattails and feeling superior about himself. Then the pig pivots his rhetoric, gets personal again, asks what I'm afraid of in the near term, mentions phoning my wife, hits me in a sore spot.

"Heather? Do I have to? And hey, I left you a warm blankie. Where is it?"

"I ate it," Holdout answers, spiteful. "Should I talk about your wife some more?"

Then I'm like, "Never mind, where's my rig, or did you eat that too?"

"How was your meeting with Michael?" Smarmy, flinging two hooves on the dash, in my face like he owns the joint.

"Crystalline. Are you current with the new tech? Seriously indispensable this or that."

"Wondering how you lived without it?"

"Totally. Wondering how I lived without it in advance of owning it."

"That ache."

Scratching under the seat for my rig: "Everything improved. Always and forever."

"You're not getting any better though, *hmm*, Carl?"

Holdout grins in a way that makes me whimper, "Please don't eat me?"

"What? You need to see me for me. Your one true friend."

"I'm sorry. The fear bubbles up. A certain light. A stomach growl or ambiguous gesture. Can I buy you a protein bar?"

"You should get out," the pig says, suddenly serious.

"This is my car."

"Out of Green Lead. Trust your gut. Disband. Disavow. You guys are old news."

"You've always been jealous."

Holdout snorts. "Of Zenski? Pernicious bean counter. Leg humper. Who needs 'im?"

I'm silent, listening to the rain, and after a few breaths Holdout says he's afraid of people who have all the answers and I say me too, me too and that seems to satisfy him because he nuzzles close, rests his head on my thigh, says we'll pull through, we've been through worse, and I watch rain track down the window, glad for the company, feeling bolstered but still worried that the starving pig plans a coup, schemes to eat me alive. I ask him why he sounded so dire when he told me I should get out of Green Lead, tell him his tone gave me the jitters. Holdout shrugs, which is more of a neck than a shoulder gesture for a pig, says isn't it clear, can't I sense what's coming, and when I ask what, he closes his eyes and snuffles to sleep.

Hidden in the patent-protected insides of this vehicle is a tiny mechanical part, no bigger than my pinkie, machined to atomic tolerances, an integral piece of the whole. I've forgotten what this part is called, so I call it the Nugget. And because of the Nugget this vehicle operates without sound or blood oil, and because of the Nugget I can afford this vehicle. The shape of nature is a secret I'm sworn to keep. There is justice, but only for the initiated. Green Lead's first investment triumph is buried in my Tesla. My only and—I will not say—final triumph.

My stomach churns. Pet Holdout to calm myself, feel his leathery pink skin shudder as he snores, count piggy freckle constellations. I'm forcing a delay. A gulf of time opened between having and not having. My rig's under the seat. Sweating? Cold shakes? Pain is essential to a meaningful life. Those fortunate to live pain-free have to invent ever more unlikely sources of such. The radical decentring of suffering. How long since we've had our basic physical needs accounted for? A century, give or take, depending on what part of the world a person hails from? That's nothing. An evolutionary instant. And who knew? That attaining physical security would be such a problem? Who could predict—futurists, soothsayers—who could predict that what comes next, in absence of a desperate lifelong struggle to be fed, clothed, housed, not eaten alive, properly fucked . . . who knew that what comes next isn't necessarily happiness, fulfillment, but rather—

A computer chip stitched to your privates?

Maybe the pig is right. A so-called sentient species that can't tell if it's in rapid ascent or irreversible decline. We asked, and so what if we don't like the answer.

I decide to up the self-inflicted pain ante; phone my wife.

Eventually Heather Elizabeth Reed, age forty-four, loving wife and mother, careerist master of political mindfuckery, embattled minister of the environment for the province of British Columbia, answers. We stammer at each other, interpreting marital moods and signals, then inquire about one another's day. I believe I tell her I feel like a stoner kid scribbling lyrics to a love song and reading them in the morning, sober and crestfallen. Heather responds by asking if it's raining even though I know she can hear torrents drumming on the roof. Fact checking. Confirming a hypothesis. She always was the practical one. Competent in a mechanistic, nut-shrivelling way that leaves no room for error, spark of creation, basic human uncertainty.

In other words, back when we occasionally slept in the same bed, I woke up convinced my wife is a living manifestation of my fear of machines. A very advanced robot. Soft on the inside, somehow. But in all things I remain a skeptic, and I think my wife's murky-soft interiors held me from murder. Either that or I love her.

"Our daughter will be here soon," I say, with effort, focusing on the Tesla's gorgeous steering wheel. Sexual organs should be so pretty. "Spring break. I remembered. Did you?"

A prolonged pause that serves as an answer. I'm scrabbling for my rig. Marvellous that I can always count on domestic silence to crumple my will. Holdout wakes up, gets involved in the search, roots around the seats. "A pig's nose is very sensitive," I tell my wife.

"Heavens fuck, Carl. This could've waited. It's almost midnight—"

"Mind Night?" Holdout whispers, wide-eyed. "Heard of that program, draconian, psionic experiments done on—"

MIND KNIGHT.

"Uh, Heather? Mind Knight? Cortextual Cavalry? I feel your signal! Did you run an electric current through an iPad immersed in a jar of sourdough starter, take it out, hit *I'm Feeling Lucky*, utter the magic words? Cuz I've heard that sometimes works? Heather . . . I almost hear you . . . across vast space-time distances—"

"It's called a cellphone."

"I'm clairgustant," Holdout brags. "I can tell how someone died by scarfing the spirit residue of their last supper. Usually I just taste myself."

"Holdout, shut up! Heather, wait a sec!" Reach in the glove, find a flashlight, hold it an inch from my face, close my eyes, turn the light on and off, aiming for eight pulses a second, constructing a DIY Dream Machine, arcing Slater-sexy through rolling alpha waves. "Whoa! Heather! I'm opening my mind field to you. Minister of the environment? Ha! That's my girl! I shoulda known you're infiltrating some twenty-first-century corporate-state MKUltra, not only henpecking poor people about recycling etiquette. Okay, let's do this. I'm game for anything, but you know me, last minute willies, kinda freaking—"

"Carl? What's that clicking sound? What the fuck are you doing? And is someone with you?"

"Not . . . right now?" Finger getting tired from pressing the flashlight button, managing only two or three flashes a second, way too slow to slip into the hypnagogic sweet spot.

"You wish," Heather says, which makes me not want to screw around delaying myself gratification much longer. "I'm going to hang up, Carl. I hope you're doing okay. Really. I'm going to hang up."

Toss the flashlight at Holdout. He gobbles it whole, belches, puffs his belly to reveal the radiant light within, arcs an overweening eyebrow in my direction. "Yo. Blitz. I ingested the numen. What have you done lately?"

Splay my fingers against my piggy's illuminated insides, hoping my celebrated Hello Kitty shadow puppet will silence the lippy upstart. See Beelzebub in fly form cast against the Tesla interior. Holdout opens his mouth and the fly zips right in while I try very hard to let Heather hang up. But instead I tell my wife: "She's slipping."

"Who? Carl?"

"I mean our daughter? Hannah? I think she's slipping."

"What? And hey—pot meet kettle?"

Stern. Unforgiving. Not in the mood for game-playing.

"You know what I mean. At Appleby?"

Making rational sense now, fortified. Talking into the phone on my lap while busily arranging components on the passenger seat. Needle. Strap. Spoon. Multi-tasking. Components arranged in a tidy quadrant in a much larger grid called ad hoc. Holdout perches on the dash, beady-eyed, listening in.

"Stop staring at me like that," I hiss as the light dims in Holdout's digestive juices. "I've installed countermeasures to you."

"Carl, what?"

The pig flutters his lashes, fakes innocence. "Me? Staring like how?"

"Accusing eyes! Judging! You know I hate prolonged eye con—"

"Carl? What the actual hell—"

Direct Holdout's attention to the phone. "*Shh!* Grades? Heather? Grades . . . um . . . Hannah! Right! *Jeesh*, Heather. Appleby College? Concerns about Hannah not applying her talent. I'm . . . worried about her."

"You? Worried? Why? Is your vape clogged? Hannah's not your pet project. She's a human being. A sixteen-year-old human being."

That's what I'm worried about. "Still? We need to present a united front. That's what her . . . uh, maybe the fucking guidance counsellor said. And . . . in fact I'm disappointed by your rather distanced, um, even callous approach to pare—"

"United? Carl? Against what?"

Against the future. "Against her slipping! Heather? Family much? Hannah's coming home. Is that what I'm saying? Will you . . . be here?"

"There? With you? Ugh. From when to when?"

"Queen bee," Holdout whispers, "flying around, harshing mellows, buzzing in our ears, *bzzz*—"

"*Shh!*" Shrugging off my coat: "For a weekend? At least?"

"... *bzzz* ... *bzzz* ..."

Then, by way of brute retaliation, my wife says, "If Hannah develops an eating disorder, takes to the taste of lipstick and ice cubes, it's because of the pressure you put on her. Understand? Shit, Carl. Grades? Applying her talent? Christ in fuck. You've become a tired, officious little man. Next you'll be talking about her *progression*. Should she do a stint in Africa, charity work to beef up her resumé? Does she need another language? What about her friends? Have you vetted them? Are they all woollen vests and Point Grey vistas? Fuck you, Carl. Know what? I hope our daughter's way stoned, got three cocks in her right now. Or whatever she's into. Seize the day! Isn't that what you bastards like to shout—as long as it's only you doing the seizing—"

"Three sounds not so ba—I mean, no thank you! Obscenity laws? I don't think you can say that in our supposedly civilized country."

"Chill, Carl. Seriously. Three meaty cocks. Problem?"

"Anyways. Grades."

"Fuck her grades. You want to bring Hannah inside? Change her so she fits in? Into *this*? That's not the point, remember? The point is she lives so far outside she forces the world to change for her. And by the way, private school was your bullshit idea."

Holdout, looking inspired: "*Mmm* . . . love that rabble-rouser Heather Hellcat in da hou—"

"So who's repressed now, Carl? Pearl-clutcher! If you're a progressive, we're well and truly fucked. Hannah's fine. Let the girl live. Remember how that feels?"

"No."

"See? Told you."

"Are you a robot?"

"Excuse me?"

"Cyborg maybe? Holdout says he smells it on you. Chemical lubricants? Or have you hooked yourself up to a machine that helps you experience things that aren't there so you can live a more complete life?"

My wife stunned silent. This is fleeting victory.

Not that I'm particularly pining for a family reunion. It's about enforcing an obligation, a vow made long ago and slippery-eeled out of, day after day, year after year. It's about a marital reckoning. The strap tight on my arm. Our self-created suffering defines us. "It's . . . a goddamned, y'know . . . crucial time for her, Heather. Standardized testing?" Grasping a bit. Sounding uncertain. Drill down to specifics. "Entrance to . . . and . . . fucking scholarships? Decisions she makes now . . . have real impact? Consequences? Paths narrowing, career opportunity, all that? Very competitive education environment. Different than when we were in school, wasting time getting high and reading novels. What if Hannah ends up cutting hair for a living?"

Startled gasp. "Classist! If Hannah wants to cut hair, fine. What did you mean, about Holdout? That the pig? Thought you got rid of—"

"Hairdresser's fine? Seriously? Private school tuition? Wasted potential? I mean—"

"*Potential?* See? That's exactly it. You want her to achieve. I want her to be happy. But you know what? I can't believe you. All that Marxist wankery and it comes to this. To each according to her whatever-the-fuck? You talk a good game, little man. But being happy is special enough, Carl. And rare enough. Which you, of all people, should know. Shit. I'd trade everything for three cocks and a hair salon. Then I'd be happy, or at least less bored, which is maybe the same thing."

I think I'm smiling. "Open your own establishment? The Cocksnip Salon?"

"Ouch. You sayin' something?"

My wife's smiling too. I can hear it. My rig's right there. Holdout's snuffling against my calf. My monochromatic Tesla improves me, a silly idea I know is logically untrue but emotionally . . . what can

I say? I'm invested. What should I say? *I miss you. Please, I miss you. Come home. Stand in the rain with me. Run on the beach with me. Stupid movie things. Swim naked. Ice cream in winter.* Instead: "Are you smiling?"

"I think so? It's been a while."

"Me too."

"That's good, Carl. I think that's good. Fuck this place. *Grrr.* It brings out the . . . not so nice in me? Combative, scheming—"

"—venal?"

"Maybe some time at home would help re-centre . . ."

I miss you. Would that be enough? For sure not. "What would it take?"

"Are you offering?"

"If I could see an end point, hope of future resolution, maybe."

"That's just it. You have to put the work in without knowing how it turns out."

"Belief? Faith?"

"Yes."

I'm not smiling anymore. "It could all be—"

"For nothing? Yes. That's probably even likely. At this point."

Suddenly so exhausted I can barely keep my eyes open. *Probably even likely.* So casual, how she says it. Clinical, a diagnosis, like it's the most obvious thing, written in every authoritative textbook, and where was I, skipped that class, peaking in the corner of the school parking lot. Then the terror hits as I realize there's an entire trajectory of future possibility my wife has not only considered but already neatly come to terms with. I'm choking in her dust. "Would you? If I did try?"

"I might . . . be willing to take it on faith? For the last time."

"You'd have to come home."

"After the legislature. Sure."

Holdout shakes his head, whispers no, Heather has to take the ferry home now, stick to my guns, be a manly man, this is important, a matter of mutual commitment to our marriage, talk is cheap, proof in the pudding.

I press my palm over the phone. "Come home tonight? She'll never agree."

"Do you want her to agree? Really? Is that what you want? Think about it."

"I want to start this very expensive vehicle."

"Just driiive off."

"Yes. Drive right the fuck off. Very fast."

"Freedom. The road. Aggro old man speeding."

"All those."

"Thank fuck I'm so lucid," Holdout says. "I remain true to us. Not the opportunistic traitor Zenski. Not that gold-digging Heather chick. You owe me."

"I do. I owe you big time. One day, I'll lay down and let you eat me alive while we make love. Truth is the idea's becoming oddly attractive, the generosity of it, a nurturing impulse; there's something heroic about feeding myself to another living being, reinventing myself as the avant-garde headmaster of an ecophagic cult." Then into the phone: "Heather? You have to come home now, in time to meet—"

"Now?" Irritated, raising the drawbridge. "Carl, it's late. Why now?"

"Let me talk to her."

"Heather! Do you want to talk to Holdout? Get an unbiased opinion?"

"The *pig*? Oh Christ, Carl—"

"Turn it back around, ask if someone's with *her*," Holdout says, a cruel spark in his ungulate eyes.

I cover the phone. "With Heather?"

"Oh, c'mon. In that oak-panelled office? *Cluck cluck!* This very second, on the phone with you, she's—"

"Heather! Is someone with *you*?"

"Things are coming to a head," Holdout growls while gnawing on an army-green Bug-Out Bag he found under the passenger seat. "Cataclysm. Final conflict."

"Things are coming into my head!" I yell, mimicking Holdout's grave tone. "Cataclysm lurks in my skull and bones—"

"Ahead? Skull and Bones? Do not put words in the pig's mouth. Carl? Or however it works? Use your own words. Who am I talking to?"

Distraught, close to breaking down—

"You heard me. Wife! We're too polarized and self-interested to recognize one another as human beings, never mind hear each other out. That spells imminent mutually assured destruction."

A horrified, thoroughly satisfying gasp. "Spells of destruction? Is that a threat? Don't do anything unusually stupid. Okay? Or self-destructive? Not again. I will not have ... *that* ... hanging over my head every time we argue because you're being a ninny—"

"We don't have much time," Holdout says, nodding at my rig.

"We don't have much time," I tell Heather. "We're running out of time, like, pronto. Sand through the hourglass. Can't you feel it? The end is nigh."

"Nigh? Nothing's fucking nigh! What's it now? Lizard men? Asteroids? Mayans? Black-swan death machines? Blood moons? We have time. Do not do this. Not through the pig—"

"Hannah," Holdout advises, my peerless sage. "Bring it back around. Moral high road, sign off easy, big win, man of the house, no looking back—"

"Fine, Heather. But what's best for Hannah? Eh? I'm talking about our daughter's future. *Jeesh.* Bad moons? What are *you* talking about? You on that Wiccan kick agai—"

Holdout waves his cloven hooves. "Easy now, tone it down, high road ..."

A fierce exhale, "Just let Hannah be. Back off. Stay away from her."

"No can do. She's a child, a teenager, not an adult. I for one intend to be involved in her life." We're a hair's breadth from *I raised that girl since I got out of prison,* and my significantly better half knows it's true. Ace in hole. You chose a late-blooming political career over family, woman. "Well, uh, Heather? I know our daughter better than you. And I, for one, am sincerely worried about her recent blips. Bleeps? Anyway, we need to talk. Doesn't talking always help?"

"Not if everything you say is demonstrable bullshit."

"Hostility? All right. That's all I got. Apologies for interrupting your otherwise productive evening, honourable minister."

There. Un-fucking-stoppable.

A muffled curse followed by an agreement for a family weekend that comes like worrying a splinter from skin. I get ready to hang up, satisfied, greedy for a well-deserved blast of stimulant when my wife lowers her voice, asks if I'm compromised.

I stop cinching the dope strap to my arm, unsure what to say. Compromised? I'm tempted to feed her the line about being a high-functioning something-or-other, but I'm afraid of her metallic cackle. Instead I ask what she means.

"I mean will you remember a goddamned word of this conversation?"

"I'm getting older. Anything's possible."

"Shit."

My initial masochistic self-denial has become a burden. Nerves are pinging. I smack my lips, try and muster a response, flick my Zippo, tell my wife this conversation is taking for . . . ever, to which there's another sharp intake of breath.

Then an image of Heather in her early twenties, southeast of Pemberton, way down the In-Shuck-Ch Forest Service Road on our way to Sloquet Hot Springs, sitting in the passenger seat of my Chevy, turquoise Lillooet Lake shimmering in the background, late-summer leaves airborne behind us, my future wife smiling somewhat in my direction, bare feet smudging through dust on the dashboard, toenails unpainted, carefree, idyllic, add a daisy in her hair and the ensuing decades might seem worthwhile, the romantic sublime, but I've grown suspicious of these images, sporadic, without context, past and futureless, no longer certain of the line between memory and something far less appealing.

There was a shared ideal. That much remains certain. Life in the moment. An eternal now. Living like a newt with bulbous blue eyes. A process of consciously devolving oneself to discover an unspoiled essence, but the battle was lost, or maybe there wasn't an essence, or maybe we were successful in our pursuit and this *is* the essence—

I ask Holdout if he has my Zippo.

". . . North Van property . . . corrupt little asshat named Vincent Peele," my wife's saying. "Carl? This government has well-established plans for that property. Understand? Political shitstorm if Peele scoops it from under us." Then again, something about the solstice and a word that sounds like Bo-shee, which is obviously the hot new thing out of Riga, Hampi, maybe Addis. My wife sounds like she's in the bathroom. Sitting on the toilet. Urinating.

"I don't have your Zippo," Holdout says, showing me he has it clamped between his teeth.

"Excuse me?" I ask Heather, meaning it. "Bo-shee?"

"Yes. Bo Xi intends to run money through—"

"Riiight. Gotcha! I'll try anything once. Bo-shee! Like the new ayahuasca? Does it cause vomiting? Why should the kids have all the fun?"

"Mother of hell. You're in for how many million and you have no idea."

"Who's in who for what?"

"Listen: this government needs that North Van property. I'm campaigning on it becoming a green space. Well-heeled riding. Serious party financing on the line. Understand? It's my political future. Green Lead's going to sabotage Vincent Peele. Follow? We need you to . . ."

Blah blah blah blah. The point is, we flirted, she's coming around. Can't stay mad forever! Plans are being made. A surprise party for Blitzo? My own peeps trying to keep me in the dark? I'll play along. We're doing a group holiday, flying somewhere sticky and desperate for a bacchanalian Bo-shee intercultural solstice celebration eco-journey. Maybe it was my idea? I can at least take credit. I don't have to clarify because I'm certain I have it parsed. Vincent Peele must be the eco-lodge owner. A classic Canadian guy. Concerned about his operation's resource footprint, equitable pay, authentic experience. "Heather? How 'bout a Wreck Beach bonfire when you're home? Sounds invigorating. Bo-shee with balanced stones?"

"Fucking forget it. I'll talk to Michael again. It was important, though, in case you were wondering."

I wasn't.

Jasminder Bansal

I suffer through takeout sushi with Eric feeling overly conscious of being overly quiet. Eric's all irritating smiles and clingy hand-holding while I help him manage the construction crew. Later, standing outside the condo display units, hunched under an umbrella, shivering in a wind sweeping across the ocean, Eric grabs my arm and gives me the look he always does when he's about to ask me over. Before he can say a word I interrupt, tell him I have a mirror to practise in front of. He blusters, says something about me being stressed, and that's how I leave him, my heart quickening as I walk past my car, knowing I should go home, regroup for the open house tomorrow, begin again . . .

But there's a history I have, a past life I regress into, and this afternoon when Vincent Peele asked about Amar I knew how the day would end. So instead of saying goodnight to Eric and getting in my car, I continue east, boot heels clicking loud and oddly reas-suring on the slippery cobblestone sidewalk. I feel Eric's questioning glance against my back. Is he going to follow me, demand to know where I'm off to at this hour? Part of me wants him to. Then he heads back inside the display suite. Eric Hull is not a man to run after a date and impose himself. A true gentleman. He'll go home, pour himself a cup of orange juice, brush his teeth, go to bed, sleep perfectly for seven-point-five hours, wake up, do it again.

Cabs and replica steam trolleys rush by, hissing spray, passengers' faces blurred by rain and motion, and for some reason seeing those indeterminate souls peering through the streaked glass frightens me in a vague way that settles into my stride, makes me quicken my pace. Weaving through huddled club kids done up for a night out, teal mascara, angled bangs, and pitched chattering, heads bent to text. Feeling envious and lonesome. Where are my friends? Lost touch, let them go, or vice versa? The people I pass are my age, but I'm nothing like them, not anymore; there's something trivial about their lives, flimsy, or maybe something ruined about me? I was never a social butterfly, never realized how much I relied on my siblings for friendship until Meeta was married and Amar was gone.

Hurrying beneath faux-antique street lamps; yellow bulbs clustered in threes and suspended on ornate wrought-iron posts, crossing the street because one side of Water is cordoned off for filming, umbrella reflectors glowing pale as a fifties starlet while stainless-steel panel lights cast strictly envisioned shadows against brick facade backdrops. Catering trucks, coffee and maple-dip donuts, sequestered stars worried about catching colds. It might be a pretty night, but I'm keeping my head down. Thinking about real estate: how to sell it; the story: how to write it. *My business dreams align with my core values—*

"Hey, easy girl. Back up back up back up . . ."

A firm hand settles on my shoulder; I offer a mumbled apology for no reason besides habit.

"There's a line, yeah? Ladies get in free but you have to wait—"

"Please tell Sim," I say, surprised at how faint my voice sounds, wondering at the urge to run. "Tell Sim that Jaz is here."

"What? Speak up." The bouncer bulks into my face. "Can't hear—"

"Sim Grewal," I repeat, raising my voice. "Tell your boss it's

Jasminder Bansal." The bouncer towers over me, an Indo-Canadian man with a black leather jacket and slicked hair, good-looking in a focused, intense way. A crowd surrounds us, men mostly, whites and Asians and Indians shouldering for position, sucking cigarettes and vapes shaped like rifle cartridges, craning their necks, curious about this girl out alone and trying to barge her way into—

"Sim? Not how this works," the bouncer says. "I'm not your errand boy." His eyes light up. "Although there are certain errands . . ."

A few jeers and nasty catcalls. I imagine a piano falling from a sixth-storey window, flattening the crowd. The bouncer hesitates long enough for me to compose a confident smile. The rain's nailing down and everyone's soaked, bored, impatient, more than happy for the drama I'm providing. In fact, what they hope is that I get tossed on my ass so one of them can come over, say *hey baby what's up how about you and me—*

The bouncer shoves forward, calls my bluff, forces me to step from under the awning and into the rain and right when I'm about to retreat a woman shouts from inside the club, tells the bouncer to fuck off and let me through, she knows me, I'm with Sim. The girl's dressed as some kind of animal, a flamingo or fluffy kitten responsible for the well-being of a plastic barrel filled with ice-chilled beer. A Styrofoam Corona logo's draped from her neck. Her name escapes me. She's been here a while. Long enough to move up from busgirl to front-door beer-girl. Sarah? Cindy? It doesn't matter. I peek around the bouncer and give her a smile of thanks. She shrugs, hands a guy a Corona dripping with condensation, wipes her hands on her skirt, stares at the rain dripping off the awning. The bouncer pats my shoulder, yells at someone trying to cut in. I slip through an arched doorway beneath a cursive sign that says *Cherry's* in pink neon timed to pulse and throb with the beat.

✳

"Busy?" I ask Sim.

"Mad busy. Right product, right price. People doing well, need to blow off steam, they come here. Doing shit, need to blow off steam—"

"—they come here."

Sim's laugh still makes me smile. More than that. It makes me wish—

"But busy's better than broke." Sim's tone is all business, like I'm a booze rep he's chatting up and nothing more. "It's all good, except for the city threatening to pull my permit."

We're seated on a red velour sofa in Sim's office, in front of a panel of one-way glass that provides an unobstructed view into the club. The walls are insulated for sound, reducing the Top 40 to a predictable thump. "Thought that was done? Tourism optics? The Olympics are over."

"We're a cash cow they want to keep milking. Which is fine. Same everywhere. Look at Vegas. All in the open. Take it or leave it. Vegas is the most honest city in the world." Sim spins a gold ring on his middle finger, makes a laughing sound that isn't a laugh at all.

"A city of gamblers and thieves is the most honest? Sounds about right."

"This town wants to play it both ways. Wants to be all upstanding and self-righteous and condemn my club, but at the same time, they wanna get paid."

"Sucks," I say, wanting to move closer but holding back, unsure of how much I can be myself with him, going through the list of what's changed between us, the lies and half-truths to keep straight, what he knows and doesn't. Not wanting him to find out about me working at Marigold. It was Sim who clued me in to the connection between Vincent Peele and Clint Ward. Mentioned it offhand at my nephew's birthday six months ago. He said he's keeping an eye on Clint, even though I told him to let it go. Said he heard the wannabe was trying to move out of dope and into real estate. Said it's a real common career move among aging gangsters. A scumbag dope dealer turned bagman for a big-money developer? Got my journalistic curiosity up, to say the least. Two weeks later, I was enrolled in a real estate marketing course and reconnecting with Eric. Sim hasn't put any of it together. Like most people in my life, he has a habit of underestimating his little mouse—

"It's the lying that gets me," Sim growls. "Be upfront about it. Admit what you are."

Sim came up with my brother. He finds out I'm at Marigold because of him, he'll hit the roof. "How much is the ask?"

Sim gives me a questioning look.

"You don't have to say, but how much do you pay them to keep the club open?"

Sim takes a sip of bottled water. "Still digging dirt, huh? Keeping them honest? Glad to hear it. Anyway, it's not crippling. It's the principle. Say fifty grand a year. Cash."

"To one—"

"Gets sprinkled around. Inspection, zoning, cops."

Make a note to make a note of that, try and find a source working for the city who wants to talk.

A woman's dancing on stage, dressed like a sexy cyborg, gold-painted skin and shiny silver short-shorts with a matching silver wig, a tiny top and knee-high boots with thick metal buckles and chunky heels. *Fuck-me boots.* The music slows. The dancer pauses beside the not-very-polished brass pole, moves her arms and legs in quick, jerky motions, robotic, while the crowd hoots and guffaws and fist bumps.

"Quite the performance."

"She's top-tier. Makes it look easy."

"I meant the men watching."

"Them too. Keep to script, most of them, and the ones who don't get tossed."

"We all have our roles."

Sim shifts. "C'mon. It's a game. You never wanted to be someone else?"

"All the time. You?"

Sim goes quiet. He was never one to rush in. Always thought it through. Maybe that's why he's still alive and my brother isn't. I watch him sip his mineral water. He's slumped against the couch, relaxed, in control. Being near him . . . fuck you, Sim. That's what I want to say. Fuck you. But it's not only his fault. Neither of us has the strength to end it clean. Kissing him, being kissed back, a kiss that proves something, answers a question—would it be the real me, kissing this man behind a wall of one-way glass?

"I was someone else, remember?" Sim glances at his watch. "Wasn't all that." He stands, moves to his desk, frowns at a few papers. "About the journalism school thing? Been meaning to mention it. You want—"

"Gin and soda's all I want. Please."

Sim phones the bartender, orders my drink. "I mean my offer stands. If you decide to finish your degree. Not free money, but a loan."

I pluck at a loose thread, tell him it's only a diploma, not a full degree, but maybe someday. The dancer inverts herself on the pole, which seems to be one of her favourite moves. The men watching her also have a limited number of moves. I count six:

1. Hip-hop nodding with a gangster-serious pursed-lips look while glaring at the dancer.
2. Brooding, shoulders slumped, not impressed, bored/cool, pretending to ignore the dancer like he's waiting in a drive-thru line at Wendy's.
3. Laughing, dancing in his seat, making come-hither gestures at the dancer. The too-jovial guy everyone hates.
4. Holding a wad of cash, occasionally catching the dancer's eye but mostly staring at the cash.

5. Intellectually studying the dancer like she's a conceptual painting or a split-open frog on a dissection tray.
6. Sitting with a blank expression, flicking bills at the dancer as if discarding used tissue.

"Jaz?"

I startle. "Yeah?"

"I said . . . you good?"

A waitress wearing a fluffy pink tail skitters into the office, hands me my drink, leaves. I rattle my gin and soda and ignore the worried look in Sim's eyes. It's partly why I see him so rarely. That worry never leaves his face when I'm around. He used to be the big man with the even bigger smile.

"It's a trick question. You never come here when you're good."

Sim asks about my mother and Meeta, the neutral topic of family. I offer brief, noncommittal answers. He settles beside me, leans into the sofa, crosses his arms. His head's shaved close. He's wearing a custom suit in a beautiful grey-blue that brings out the depth in his eyes, makes me think of Bentleys parked in London sub-basements. Before he bought this club it was a notorious dive. Carting girls out on stretchers nearly every week. Sim put an end to the prostitution ring that ran out of the second floor. But I have no illusions about who he is. I tell him I'm sorry me being here upsets him, ask if he wants me to leave.

"I think so, Jaz," he says, quiet. "I know that's what should happen."

I can't remember if I've ever heard Sim raise his voice. We used to hop the fence at Mountain View Cemetery, me and Sim and Amar and sometimes Meeta, and scare the shit out of each other playing hide-and-seek among the gravestones and crystal-specked granite mausoleums. But that kind of yelling—childish, fun, a way of confirming ourselves in the big wide world—no longer counts.

"I think about him a lot this time of year," I say. "Three years next Saturday. I think I want to stop thinking about him. Shouldn't I have stopped by now?" And I almost tell Sim the truth about the things I've been seeing since Amar's death, but instead I take a sip of my drink, pretend to check my phone.

Sim's quiet for a long time. I watch the men watch the women in the club. A stainless-steel ladder descends from a second-storey dressing room onto the stage. Men cluster at the bottom of the ladder, cheering as the girls teeter down. I wonder what it's like to stand at the top of that ladder, above an oval trapdoor cut into the floor, and look down at those hungry faces, how you'd have to fight to stay whole, take a deep breath as you step onto the top rung—

My prosperity thoughts create my prosperous world.

—submerging yourself into that hunger, knowing it's wrecking you but doing it anyway, or maybe doing it partly because you know it's wrecking you, no coming through it, no other side, and how being wrecked confirms an unspoken suspicion about the world. Taking satisfaction in the fact that although it's wrecking you at least you were right about what it is and does, at least you have that and always will.

Some girls, maybe they're strong enough. But me?

From my seat on Sim's couch I have a view into the upstairs dressing room. It's a dizzying perspective into a foreshortened space. A side table spray-painted gold. A woman's bare calf. Part of a sparkling mirror ringed in Hollywood vanity lights. *I attract my ideal clients and customers with my energy.* I could handle the dancing, if I had to. Being on stage with the music and lights, alone and apart. But the talking? Socializing on the floor, drawing clients backstage for a private dance? No. And the ones who want to talk would be the worst. Who want to prove they're different. They'd ask questions about where I'm from. My *cultural heritage*, if they were university students. I'd have to wear a belly dancing outfit. Wink and talk about the *Kama Sutra*. Tell the sensitive ones I'm going to school part-time, tell them it's not a bad job, it's liberating, pays well. Tell them we're vilified, that society can't stand a woman in charge of her own money, her own body. The guy'd nod and say wow there's more to it than I thought, then I'd hit him with the pitch. Come upstairs, hun. Fifty bucks a song—

"I think about him too," Sim says. "Can't believe it's been three years."

I set my empty glass on a chrome table, already wishing I hadn't mentioned Amar. Shake my head at Sim's offer to order me another drink, fold my hands in my lap, try and think of something cheery to say. Something positive, small talk, a harmless bit of nothing to round out the visit, then excuse myself, glad to see you're doing well, Sim, and that's goodbye. *Whatever I can dream, I can achieve.* No wonder Sim bowed out. My brother was Sim's best friend. It was hard enough, hiding our relationship from Amar. The conversations about when we'd tell everyone. When Amar was gone Sim and I had no reason to hide, and nothing made sense. And now? The man in front of me is my last link to that world.

"Saw him again," Sim says, and from his tone I don't have to ask who.

"No," I say, mentally rehearsing the lies I need, so easy now, the lying truth, and maybe that's what living is, the point where you can't tell the difference or the difference no longer matters. "I was wrong. It wasn't Clint. The light . . . it was noisy . . . maybe he was there, in the club, but it wasn't him who—"

"You saw who you saw. Now you're afraid."

Afraid? Or not ready? I need enough time at Marigold to break the story. Then Sim can do whatever needs to be done. "I was in shock. I wasn't thinking."

"Don't protect that motherfucker. You came to me that night and you told me, Jaz. You trust me. Trusted me? I don't know. But you looked me in the eye and you said a name, and we both know it was the *right* name. Clint-fucking-Ward. Three years now, we've been carrying him. Look what it's done to us, while he's free and easy. But it'll come around."

Look what it's done to us.

"You saw him when?"

"Other day. Condo job off Clark. Backed by his real estate buddy, I bet. Trash, both of them, money or not. Clint was standing outside, surrounded by his crew, all tatted up, playing the big shot. Dude thinks he's out. Sucker motherfucker."

"Sim? Leave it alone for a while."

Sim glares at his hands. Hopefully thinking I'm still grieving, too broken to deal. The bass goes quiet. The dance is over. I'm not the person I was before Amar's death, but Sim believes I am. The audience turns toward a boxing match on the massive flat screens suspended from the ceiling. The dancer crawls across the stage on her hands and knees, gathering ten- and twenty-dollar bills in a threadbare baby's blanket. A few men approach, slip cash between her fingers and beneath her costume. She smiles, cups their cheeks, kisses them on the forehead as if in blessing, nods toward the stairs. She makes most of her income from her regulars.

Mark Ward

S traight jacked. I'll make bank and get the thing I gotta do done
and then adios to this greed-pit town. Clint can have his yup-
pie boss trip, whatever. Maybe I'll head back to Bangkok, try and
make a go with Daree and Sarah. Open a campground for back-
packers in Northern Thailand. Bob Marley on repeat. Slacklines.
Hammocks. Shitty Thai weed.

Could be worse. A lot worse.

We hop in the truck and Clint fires her up and tears off without
the headlights. Cuts away from the golf course. Feels sweet, speeding
across a mountainside in pitch black, and if we're lucky we're already
dead. I light a cigarette, groove on the smoke stinging my lungs,
cancer, bad choices I'm free to make, piss off, no one asked for your
permission. Lean my head against the window, try and think of
more happy future shit about my daughter, fail, mood skips, pinch a
chunk of arm skin, try and tear it off, see what's underneath. Clint
says fuck sakes stop it Marky, so I do. Clint turns the headlights on
when we hit Millstream, the last road before the rainforest stretching from here to fuck knows. The British Properties are a maze of
looped boulevards and cul-de-sacs. Only a couple roads lead to the
highway, and if a cop rolls up and doesn't like what he sees—

Clint asks what the fuck's the matter. Maybe sounds worried. I try and laugh, tell him I'm living the dream, but by the time I think of something to say it seems like too long since he asked, so instead I say nothing because what's flashing through my head is *Am I alive* repeating over and over like those scrolling TSX tickers with symbols like RBC and ENB and IMO and ABX up down gains losses profits *tick-ticktick* and I'd short that motherfucker Marky Patrick Ward (MPW) for sure and *Am I alive* fifty-two-week low market capitalization can I be monetized it's a for-serious question and I'm tempted to sink my cigarette into my wrist, try and feel a hundred per cent here but end of the day, does it matter?

Blood's smeared beneath Clint's right eye. I tell him. He licks his index finger, wipes it off, and I wish I had a bag of gummy-candy raspberries.

"Man, that bitch can scream," I say, which is when I figure out what's really bugging me. Truth is I can't get the sound out of my head. Reach in my backpack, pull out a shaving kit stuffed with pill bottles, pop two Oxys while Clint shakes his head.

"You need to watch that shit." All paternal.

"Bad things. Can happen."

"Keep a lid on. I need your badass warrior self, not some doped-up junkie that needs babysitting." Clint cranks the truck around a switchback while headlights come up quick behind us. "Okay, so here comes a motherfucker."

Take a look, the vehicle approaching like it's aiming to ram us off the road and—

Am I alive.

Clint shouts something, slams on the brakes, forces the vehicle following us to swerve into the oncoming lane to avoid rear-ending him, but before the guy can pass Clint veers hard left and cuts him off so now the guy floors it and speeds by on my side. A two-seater Datsun with rusted-out wheel wells. I get a look at the driver, scrappy-looking old dude, and the weird thing is he's giving me a solid not-friendly stare-down like he knows me somehow, and I dunno from the look of him I'm thinking soldier, I'm thinking boots on the ground and after Clint's done screaming out the window he glances over, says, "Sweet. Not a cop. Hey Marky you look total shit don't throw up."

". . . following me?" Struggling for breath, lingering afterimage, sniper's nest, crosshairs seeking my heart, a haunting or hunting.

"Following *you*? Nah. You're nothing."

Acrid taste in my mouth, gunpowder, burning blood and I tell my brother yeah, I guess he's right.

Clint slows the Dodge in front of a Spanish-style mansion with a clay tile roof. Makes a call, says *Breezy in Vancity* and a steel gate glides open.

"Dope grow?" I ask, wincing at being such a gluehead.

"Nice work tonight, Marky. Stay on it."

A stamped-concrete driveway slopes steeply downhill. Clint kills the engine, puts it in neutral and coasts, slightly unnerving, like we're floating, about to slip off the mountain and wreck into the city below. Another awful time-stuttering deal hits and the ragged feeling makes my gut curl around the beer and Oxys and it takes a lot of swallowing to keep from throwing up again. The house is dark. Motion-sensing floodlights click on as we approach, blinding, making me shield my eyes. Clint inches the truck against the side of the house where it won't be seen from the street while muted sirens sound across the mountain.

"Day late dollar short," Clint says, laughing at the cops. He shows me the selfie of us in the kitchen, him holding the Kasumi to my throat.

"Custom cabinets," I say. "Pretty woodgrain. You're holding the blade wrong."

Clint gives me a weird look. Blink and we're marching up the front steps, dripping water inside a giant foyer, leaving muddy puddles on hideous pink-and-gold-veined granite. A gold-foil balustrade winds up a spiral stairway. Ornate moulding—looks like it got squished through a pasta maker—frames the walls. Floral wallpaper. Not a single piece of furniture in sight. Clint stomps toward the TV noise coming from down the hall, some action flick, yells and blasts and machine-gun fire. The house reeks of lemony disinfectant and Pop-Tarts nuked too long, splattered the fruit stuffing.

Clint vanishes into a room before we reach the main living area. I follow behind, forget where I am, launch into space, shout Daree's name in a placeless panic. Clint yells at me to shut up and get in there. Lights are out when I enter. A smallish guy, I'm guessing Asian, wearing only jeans, his back turned to me, is sitting cross-legged in front of a massive flat screen mounted to the wall, playing *Call of Duty* like he means it. Dude's back is all ink, a blur of swirls and lines I can't make out in the flickering TV light. The room's huge. No furniture in here either. Clint sneaks up, puts his cocked index finger to the guy's head, says *boom!*

"Whatever, Cee, asshole," the kid says, not taking his eyes off the video game but using my brother's ultra-secret gangland AKA so I know we're all good, not here to totally fuck him up. "I knew it was you. Honkey. Get lost. I'm playing—"

"Just like that. And you're done, and this grow—"

"I'm on it." The kid's still staring at the screen, but he sounds upset. Like, wounded pride? "I said I knew it was you. I opened the gate to let you in. Duh."

"Look at you," my brother says, pinching his nostrils so his voice sounds funny. "Dogfucker. And also, it stinks of ass in here."

"Whatever. No one's stealthin', Cee. 'Specially not some fat whitey dickbag"—the kid glances over his shoulder at me—"and his scabby tweaker boyfriend."

Clint shoves the game console with his toe. "Turn the sound down. You're killing me."

An armoured transport carrier explodes on screen, makes me think of Hot Lips, my favourite penny candy.

The kid winces. "Shit! See that? You're *wrecking* it—"

"Turn it down."

"Fine. Get your boyfriend to the hospital, hick. They have medicine for that shit."

I'm standing by the door, listening real close. It all sounds friendly enough, but there's a serious edge. When the kid turns I get a look at him. Yup, Chinese. A Benelli M4 Super 90 semi-automatic shotgun is lying on the floor beside a few empty Monster energy drink cans, some Nerds boxes, a half-eaten bag of caramel popcorn. The Benelli's a sweet weapon. Eight rounds without a reload. I imagine the kid getting tossed halfway across the room when he fires the thing. Maybe he gets lucky on the first shot, but after that the kick lifts the barrel to the roof and it's over. I'm about to comment on the lousy weapon selection or maybe ask for some Nerds when Clint turns the TV off, plunging us into darkness.

"*Aargh*," the kid yells, smacking for the pause button.

"Just like that, you lazy slant," Clint repeats, laughing now, buddy-buddy, and the empty room amplifies the laughter in not a nice way but the kid laughs too, high-pitched, calls my brother a racist white-trash hick, stands and flicks a light on. He's lean and super ripped. Close-cropped, unwashed hair. A thin gold chain with twin golden scrolls stamped with two characters in fuck knows what language swings from his neck. Fist bumps all around, then Clint introduces the guy as Bo Leung and Bo corrects him by saying call me Doyle.

"Any Nerds left, Doyle?"

Doyle shakes a Nerds box, tosses it. I fumble the catch, pick it up, pop a few in my mouth, crunch 'em, say they taste like strawberry battery acid, ask Doyle if he has any better candy, like something more chewy?

"Clint? Fuck is this guy? Candy?"

"Mark, stop picking your arms like a gir—"

"Craving sweet." Stuff my hands in my hoodie, feel something warm and wet beneath my fingernails. "Scratchy air in this shithole. Can't you feel it? I like that Benelli though. Doyle? Give it to me."

"Fuck's up with the tweaker? Clint? Should he be here?"

"That's my brother," Clint says, like it's more than enough answer. "He goes where I say. He's good. Right, Mark?"

"Benelli's sweet is all. Eight rounds. Built Yank-proof. Doyle? I said give it to me."

Doyle goes quiet. Takes a step back.

Seeing the shotgun lying on the floor makes my fingertips tingle, makes my nuts cinch tight, and I wonder what the kick feels like, could I handle it in the prone shooter's position? "Fuck you guys worried about? No harm in me taking a look. Least I'm trained."

"No," Clint says, "the shotgun's for Doyle. Don't touch it."

"How's the barrel choke affect the shot pattern?"

Doyle shrugs, glances at Clint.

Try and wipe the grin from my face, fail. "He hasn't fired it."

"No."

"So let me have a look. Fuck's the big deal?"

"No."

Doyle's doing some not-cool shit, sliding beside Clint, putting himself between me and the Benelli, which is fuck. So now it's silent. We're eyeing one another, three assholes in an empty room in a dope-grow mansion in the British Properties. Maybe the next-door neighbour's an executive. Other one's a surgeon. They're so much better than us, 'cept they're not, cuz here we are. Doyle's tapping his hands on his thighs, *tappity-tap*, nervous about something or maybe still upset about his video game getting fucked up.

"Leave it alone, brother," Clint says again, slow. "Shotgun's Doyle's."

"If you say so. It's Doyle's."

"It's mine." Doyle says, trying to sound hard.

"Good," Clint says. "Come on in, Marky. Come in and be cool."

I walk farther into the room, hand Doyle a smoke as a peace offering. He asks if I'm the real-life soldier. I tell him that's bullshit, I own a patisserie in south France, and he asks what's a patisserie and I have a quick laugh while I light a smoke. Doyle asks if I ever killed anyone and I ask have you and this time we both have a laugh, but really I'm looking at him and thinking: no.

Not yet.

Clint's looking at me in that sideways way I've been seeing a bunch, like he's rethinking something important, my place or role in like the grand fucking scheme of things and right when I'm about to say fuck's your problem Doyle howls and sweep-kicks my brother, surprise attack! Clint blocks, grabs Doyle's leg, returns some kind of TV martial-arts war cry, flips Doyle on his back beside the Benelli. Doyle knocks Clint's feet out from under him. Clint yells, falls to the carpet, and now the two of them are at my feet, grunting, smacking, struggling for advantage. The Benelli's right there. I guess I could fire three or four rounds, blow the both of them apart, and it's a dope grow so end of story, but instead I toe the shotgun out of the way so they don't roll over it, turn the TV on and stare at the paused video game screen, first-person shooter, OPFOR's face exploding in pink mist, nice shot Doyle.

Clint manoeuvres Doyle into a variation of a scissor lock, cranks his legs around Doyle's neck. Doyle chokes, goes bright red. Spit leaks from his mouth. His hands paw at Clint's legs, trying to break the lock—

"You're fucked, Doyle. Been in that lock many a time. It's over."

Takes Doyle maybe five seconds to tap out, which is pretty good, bet it felt like forever.

Gasping, Doyle rolls away, rubs his neck, gets his breath, calls Clint a honkey, a skid. Clint laughs, says shut the fuck up chink. Curious, I ask Doyle how he feels about being called a chink. Doyle scoots to the wall, sits. Still not breathing right. Tells me it ain't no thing, Clint's an adopted brother they're so tight; then he laughs, picks his smoldering cigarette out of the carpet, puts the tiny carpet fire out by spitting on it and rubbing the spit with his fingers, fights for a drag. Plasticky burning stink displaces the smell of Doyle's ass. I don't know Doyle well enough to tell if he means what he says, but I know for sure he's not Clint's brother.

The walls are painted a washed-out Pepto-Bismol pink. A few posters are tacked up. Tupac leaning against a polished black Ferrari, shades on, shirt off, in full gangland pose down. Snoop strolling in vintage pimp suit, way stoned, with a huge marijuana leaf in rasta colours framing his image. Bruce Lee scowling and screaming like a boss. An orange-robed Shaolin monk wielding a wicked curved sword. Another poster of a bright yellow Lamborghini hovering in an empty white space like a fucking art gallery. On the bare carpet beneath the posters is a low wooden bench covered in half-burned candles, bright blue fake flowers, incense, a ceramic Buddha and a few plastic statues from the dollar store, of which I recognize an elephant and maybe a monkey or dragon?

I crouch down and pick up one of the fake jade statues. The elephant. Weighs nothing. "This fucked-up altar yours, Doyle?" Messing with him, testing.

"Tweaker says he wants my dick?"

"It's a shrine, you idiots," Clint says. "Confucius. Sacred shit."

Me and Doyle share a look. Apparently we decide to keep quiet.

Clint mumbles something vaguely Asian-sounding, bows his head. Doyle laughs, calls Clint a gook, says his people are taking over, says Clint's on his fat gook tip, to which Clint responds by roaring, running at Doyle, lifting him up, dropping him on the carpet, then resetting the video game and fake-bowing across the room.

Doyle gets up, sputtering and cussing.

I watch the two of them and wonder if this is the kind of multi-cultural harmony my university profs had in mind. If not, too bad. Meet the global citizenry, motherfuckers. The Oxys in my gut are

making themselves comfy, helping me believe this is real, not a vir-
tual reality or video game where I can press reset or a dream or
hallucination where I can will myself to wake up. I return the plastic
elephant to the shrine, feeling some kind of connection with the
meat-thing that calls itself Doyle . . . I dunno, empathy or kinship or
only shared circumstance, the recognition we're both fucked?
Cigarette smoke swirls around my face, forms into a fire-breathing
serpent, and at first I'm psyched but then things go shitty because
the serpent's face morphs, looks like the blown up LAV VC whose
name I can never remember so I smack at the air to dissipate the
smoke and make the blown-up face go away. Doyle laughs . . . at
what? Maybe me? Clint says he's starving, asks if Doyle has any
food besides bullshit candy. Doyle says maybe Star Wars frozen
nuggets, turns on the TV, restarts the game, our cue to leave.

"Fridge is empty."

Clint says no wonder the kid's skin and bones, leads me downstairs, uses a couple keys on a reinforced steel door. The basement's
dug deep into the mountain. Undercroft, vault, flesh-eating stone.
Ten-foot ceilings but no windows. Air smells of no-bullshit bud,
chemical fertilizer, nitrates and so on, same shit the OPFOR uses to
make IEDs, blow a bastard like me to the moon, meet my god if I had
one and what would I say to Him or Her if I did? Press reset?

The grow's chilly and damp from an industrial-sized AC system.
Cold slows spider mites. Mature plants are growing in tidy rows on
metal shelves, one at knee and another at chest height, stretching the
full length of the room. A solid amount of quality bud. A blower fan
feeds stale air into flexible aluminum tubing that snakes through a
hole cut in the ceiling and out the fireplace chimney. Fertilizer's
stacked neatly along the far wall. There's a workbench with pruning
shears, a vacuum sealer, other day-to-day standard operating type shit.
Nothing's out of place. There's not a speck of dust.

"Looks legit," I say, nodding, doing a quick financial calc in my head,
feeling wealthy, sacred, holy, imbued with otherworldly knowledge,

feeling hydroponic light sink into my skin, absorbing energy, changing, regenerating, money, moulting, I dunno, aliens, exoskeletons,
ancient temples, feeling beyond, a creature of light, angel.

"Pro install," Clint brags. "I got a crew—electricians, HVAC
guys—that set up grows for a flat fee, real tight, and I lease the
equipment to independents. Not my weed, though. I'm done sling-
ing dope."

I pinch a moist bud between thumb and forefinger, mostly to
steady myself, suddenly worried over this thing called mental health,
military shrink, retrain my brain, good fucking luck. "Done with
dope? You mean off the street?"

"No. I mean out of weed. Rips happening all the time. Looked
into the government medical market, couldn't be fucked with all
that lying. More money in real estate, less hassle."

I tell him that saddens me. We wander deeper into the grow,
stepping over extension cords. Plastic sheeting flaps beside a fan.
Thousands of bright green seedlings are growing in inch-deep plastic trays. Fed from tubes dripping concentrated solution. I take a
long breath as goosebumps rise on my arms. "So peaceful. I love it
in here."

"Me too," Clint says, turning to face me. "I miss it. Remember
our first grow? Spot-planted outside, that shitty shake—"

"We could be anywhere," I say. "Bottom of the ocean. Centre of
the earth. Outer space—"

"—had to smoke like a fucking ounce to feel—"

"—a room wrapped in plastic. Drip tubes leaking nutrients.
Electric sunlight. Hermetic. All we need to survive—"

"—but we sold that shake, made enough to move into coke—"

"—and the efficiency of it. Stark. Pure. *Prisca theologica.* Everything
inessential stripped out, every lie—"

"—never thought we'd make it this far—"

"—could we live forever?"

Clint laughs. "Live forever? Not if you bust through that door."

Points to a shotgun mounted on a jury-rigged camera tripod. "Pressure plate. Blow a thief bastard in half. Come on. I'm freezing. We crash here tonight. Tomorrow you get your own pad, Coal Harbour, awesome for hookers, all stainless."

✳

Sitting on a sopping wet balcony overlooking the city, slurping Mr. Noodles from microwaveable plastic bowls. Red and white light flashes through the window behind us as Doyle works his way through *Call of Duty* for the bazillionth time. Clint's quiet, which only happens when he's eating. I watch my brother inhale his third bowl of noodles, amazed at how quick we become accustomed to things, thinking how far I'd go for him, a blurriness that doesn't let me see clearly enough to uncover an answer. Far enough, I guess.

Doyle comes out, sets a plastic shopping bag in my lap, vanishes.

"Three phones," Clint explains, telling me one's for him exclusively. "The second's for anyone in the business. Third's for personal. You can keep the SAP." Clint hands me an envelope. I'm guessing three grand cash, widen my eyes all beggar-grateful, make a show of sniffing the money like a fiend.

"That a fucking thank-you?"

"Nope."

"Use it to get a haircut. Thought the army taught self-respect." Clint finishes his noodles, tosses the bowl over the railing. "Sold off most of my dope lines, too," he says, almost wistfully. "Worked exclusive agreements for the crews that took over my old neighbourhoods. Only active in two territories. West Side and West Van."

"Yuppies won't stab you for a dime bag."

I count twenty-seven cranes rising over the city. A thought forms in the back of my mind. Brutal and inspired, even in its unpolished state. West Side and West Van. Poshest neighbourhoods in the city filled with upper-class drug addicts. A mountain of Afghan heroin.

A direct line on that poison from an old military connect, lace it with an assload of fentanyl and the motherfuckers start dropping—

"What you thinking about?"

"What am I here for?"

"You start work tomorrow."

"It's already tomorrow."

"Then you start today. Truck in the garage. Tools in the lockbox. See how I take care of your worthless ass? You're gonna pick up a kid named Ryan at the Cash Corner. Six o'clock. He's a mouthy fucker but shows up, works not bad, does as he's told. Grab another warm body or two while you're there. Lotsa digging. Grunts get nine an hour, no more." Clint stands up, pats my shoulder, leaves.

Gulp a couple pills, sit alone, glaring at the city while my skin ripples into stone like a cathedral grotesque, soaked and shivering but not feeling cold, wrapped in silken opiate warmth, trying to stay focused, work though the angles on the thought that hit me. Truth is I'm excited. After a while I force myself to flap my wings, fly to Doyle's room. He's curled on his side in the TV glow, a pillow clutched to his chest, a few feet from the Benelli. Looks twelve years old. I shake him awake, ask if he has a computer. He nods, tells me the password, *takingnames*, rolls over and falls back asleep.

Guzzle water from the kitchen faucet, get settled in the dining room, back to the wall, stare at the blank screen. I heard about a fire in a clothing factory outside Bangkok when I was deployed in Afghanistan. News stream, shit stream, child slaves locked behind steel doors when the warehouse caught fire, boo hoo for them. Radio man, eleven-second story while we blasted through Kandahar, rolling coal in the LAV, righteous pricks waving our boom sticks. Tuned out the radio man's message, didn't think much about it. No. Thought *nothing* about it. Happens every day. Round the world. Eight-year-old gets his arm ripped off in a shrimp boat on the Burmese coast while the catch goes to make cat food. Here kitty kitty! Six-year-olds forced to bob tourist nob in Lao. Whatevs! Kids burned alive while sewing our wicking outerwear? Oops, glitch in the supply chain? We'll get that sorted? Naw. Fucking liars. Collateral damage. Cost overruns. Threat level critical. But here's the thing: a few seconds after hearing about those kids, Marky got blowed up. BIG TIME BOOM! Marky got blowed up, kids got burned up. And when I came to it was nothing but fire, piled against the door burning and I felt them—I still do—not their ghosts or spirits but like they're more real and whole than me or my brother or that city down there, and we're the ghouls cursed to haunt them.

Lost half a year to a hospital bed, Oxy up and next thing I know I'm in a sweltering manufacturing district in Bang Phli, across the street from where it happened, sitting in muck and dog piss against a scorching corrugated steel wall, drinking warm Singha and chain-smoking, and the fucked up thing is I couldn't tell if it happened like the radio said. The company rebuilt the warehouse after it burned, brand spanking new, no memorial shrine with cutesy plastic flowers or photos or letters, nothing, like those kids never happened.

But they did happen.

Still happening. Right this second.

I get online. Go to the website of a high-end outdoor clothing company called Karakoram. Click to the employee page, pull up the image of Mr. Craig Williams, Vancouver boy, suntanned, trim, self-satisfied in that particularly nauseating West Coast manner, speckled grey-blond hair and a shitty-shit smile. Mr. Williams, his biography says, is a U of T finance alum, committed biathlete, and dedicated family man. So good for him. Mr. Williams got a promotion after the Bang Phli fire for how well he handled the PR fallout. Here's an upstanding family man who knows how to make lemonade.

Then I'm on YouTube, clicking links the algorithm recommends, watching the first few seconds of whatever video pops up with the sound turned off: a man leaping into a swimming pool under stormy skies; GoPro footage of a motorcyclist careening off an overpass; a toddler dancing in front of a television; a woman illustrating the proper way to carve a pineapple; a sunglass-wearing Labradoodle on a stand-up paddleboard; a flood somewhere tropical carrying mud huts into a massive sinkhole; a girl hanging upside down by her ankles and covered head to toe in whip cream; a jihadi waving a sword; something huge and unnamed skimming beneath a fishing boat in the Atlantic; a calico kitten about to leap from a fridge; a survivalist giving a firing-range tutorial on the AR-15, a morbidly obese man lifting a lemon meringue pie to his mouth; a time-lapse of flooded coastlines; a skinny kid dressed in black, eyes ringed in purple eyeliner, trying to consume an old woman alive on a brightly lit subway and the woman fighting back, clawing at him, and as the images scour my mind I hear a woman in a mansion screaming *you are a soldier and yet you are afraid* and the idea springs forward, how remarkable that a life can pivot on a single flash of coherence, and then it's back to the image of Mr. Craig Williams, hale and grinning, so super alive—

Jasminder Bansal

The smell of cigarette smoke and powdered carpet cleaner lingers in my apartment building. Up the steps, a chipped plastic handrail painted bronze, scratched and beat-up walls, a lapdog's half-crazed barking, an old man's throaty cough. I imagine tenants moving in and out over the sixty years the building's been around. Was it once considered respectable, a decent place to live? Before the boiler went in the middle of winter and it took the landlord three frigid weeks to fix? Before the infestations? Mice. Mites. Fleas. Bedbugs. Before the dope pads arrived with tenants running extension cords to hall outlets because their power had been disconnected? Before landlords started charging monthly fees for access to the laundry room, storage lockers, parking stalls?

My mother and I live together in a one-bedroom apartment, but I rarely see her. I try to spend as little time here as possible. Simply entering the building leaves me feeling exhausted and ashamed. Should we be going grocery shopping together, getting on each other's nerves but sticking together like families are supposed to, being stronger at the end of the struggle?

My failures have made me a better entrepreneur.

Tonight my mother, Pardeep Bansal, is working in the hall closet she's converted into her office. Lit by two screens on a desk inside the recessed darkness. My mother came out swinging in her early work. Stark, uncompromising photographs and videos that felt like a smack in the face and an embrace all at once. Now she spends eighteen hours a day fiddling with code-generated colour gradients and pre-made filters in her editing software, snipping a half-second from one clip and adding it to another, reversing them, splicing isolated moments of newsreel footage of Amar's death to weather reports from around the world, drawn to the catastrophic and unpredictable, lost in minutiae and a sense of futility but still trying to discover or create a space for her grief that doesn't come prepackaged.

She doesn't move as I enter, doesn't acknowledge me.

The lights are out. She's seated on the same office chair Meeta caught her fingers in a decade ago, crushed to bleeding. The television in the closet is tuned to the weather channel, the volume off. A satellite image of swirling clouds massing over the Pacific. Another weather system rolling in. A blond woman gestures with a laser pointer, makes ominous expressions at the cloud graphics. The second screen is frozen on an image of Amar stepping out of his Escalade, but my mother has shifted the focus beyond Amar's shoulder to the crowd of gangsters and wannabes surrounding him. She's motionless except for her fingers tracing the touchpad, the occasional key click on a computer on long-term loan from a friend at an artist-run centre. I'm preoccupied with worrying about the open house for Marigold tomorrow and am about to walk behind her and into the kitchen, see if there's any food, try and get my beauty sleep when she says, "Something happen today?"

Still staring at her project.

"No. Why?"

"Something about how you came in. See this? Clouds from this storm in Manila appear to magnify the reflection here? In the window behind the police officer? Behind Amar? This might turn out to be an all right day, if I can just . . ."

I have a memory of my mother as a beautiful, independent woman in a spectacular crimson sari, even though I never saw her wearing one. An artist and performer. A woman of conviction and passion who chose to leave her country and move to Canada on her own to pursue her art. She once asked her kids to be her accomplices in the kidnapping of an unhappy-looking capybara at the Langley petting zoo. She let us wear our school clothes inside out and backwards and laughed when other kids tried to correct us. Her favourite purse was from Japan, shaped like a pink octopus. She painted tiny fairy doors on alley walls and told us they were real and we left snacks for our fairy neighbours like we did for Santa Claus. Her favourite expression—to all three of us kids, each stressed out and uptight in our own way—was *take it down a notch*. After my mother left India her parents never spoke to her again, and despite her worldliness she wasn't prepared for the ease with which my local-boy photographer father would cut his losses once he started feeling weighed down by the *oppressive bourgeois institution* of family.

I'm standing directly behind her, staring at my brother's image. "Mom, I can't do this now. I have an open house in less than six hours. I need—"

"So now the realty makes you work on Satur—"

"They don't *make*—"

"But if you don't do it you—"

"I won't get the job. No."

"Well, great for them. For hiring someone as aspiring and diligent as you."

I try and let it slide. Take it down a notch? But instead I retaliate, snark that the electric bill came in, that we're already late—

A few quick finger swipes and she hits play on the project timeline. Scattered images roll across the screen, but as I watch there's this feeling like something's being revealed. When did I stop believing in my mother and her work? I remember her grant application, a project summary about moving beyond linear narrative time, the thought domain of Eurocentric empiricist culture, and the countless arguments we had about my decision to study journalism, my mother telling me there's no such thing as truth, just stuff you believe in and stuff you don't and isn't that liberating, shouldn't I embrace that anarchic sensibility instead of wasting my life being used as a fresh face to prop up the old authorities?

My mother's shoulders tighten at my mention of money. "It's always worked out for us, hasn't it? Despite your fretting it's always—"

"Always? The summer we lived in a gravel pit in Squamish?"

"I wish we could live in a big expensive house, so you'd see how much better and happier life would be. Or not. You have an incredible throwing arm because you spent that summer throwing rocks at pop cans with your brother. And besides, it was a Debordian experiment, an extended *dérive*. You learned a lot in that camp, even if you aren't aware of or refuse to admit it."

My mother turns to face me. She's fifty-one but looks a decade older. Her skin is loose around her chin and jaw but tight across her brow. When she thinks I'm not looking she blinks rapidly, like she's having trouble focusing. Her faded house robe hangs half open. I try not to think about what Amar's death has done to her. She was always the impulsive free spirit. Not telling her bad news comes naturally; I've been doing it since forever. I try and remember the last time she saw her doctor. Two months ago? Six? How often do they recommend? Is she taking her medications? I remind myself to check her pillbox. A year ago I found half her meds in the garbage. The doctor said you can't force her to take them. She makes her own choices. I said yeah but should she?

The weather girl waves her laser pointer at a storm massing west of Vancouver Island. I used to blame my mother for not letting go of her grief. As if she were holding it in her hand like I'm holding hers now. Not understanding it was grief holding her, not understanding that I wanted her to let Amar go so she could show me how.

"I'll get the bill paid," she says.

I didn't tell her what I saw in the nightclub. How could I? "It's not a big deal. I'll do it. Didn't mean to bring it up."

She pulls her hand away, digs through a few sketches on her desk. "Shit! Almost forgot. Someone called for you."

"For me? Here?"

"I took a message. She was nice enough, if a bit snooty. Didn't leave a name. She asked me to write it down. Word for word. Said she's happy to have you on board? Must be someone from your realty? She said start with Bo Xi?"

"What?"

"Start with Bo Xi."

I snatch the notepad. "Bo Xi? Who's that? It couldn't have been for me."

"She used your full name. But she didn't elaborate."

I notice how worried she is, feign forgetfulness, tell her thanks while she turns to her screens. I ask if I can put on some music. No answer serves as an okay. I squeeze past her desk. The living room is my bedroom: a single bed with sheets tacked to the ceiling to provide at least the appearance of privacy. My mother, on one of her better days, said the bed looks like a Tracey Emin sculpture. Said private shame can be wielded intentionally, can become strength. Said ugliness can be reclaimed, used as a weapon to undermine a power you disagree with or are hateful of.

The boom box is an old Sony Xplod. Dig through a shoebox looking for a CD, watch my hands shake, drop the box and scatter the CDs across the carpet. Finally manage to put D.O.A. on, once my mother's favourite band, although she doesn't listen to music much anymore. I wait for her to tell me to turn it off. She doesn't, but I keep the volume depressingly low. Who the hell is this Bo Xi? Hear my stomach growl, realize I'm craving a decent meal, fruits and veggies, check the fridge, nothing, wonder if I have enough change for a slice of pizza, find a package of edamame in the back of the freezer, decide that'll do.

The apartment is hot and stuffy, inspires an awful thought about germs or viruses thriving. I turn down a baseboard heater, crack a window. Our building is on Knight Street, a busy four-lane arterial linking the American border and several Lower Mainland suburbs to Vancouver. We face south toward the bridge. Semis, most headed to the shipyards on the north side of the city, shudder and groan up the hill leading from the river delta onto the rocky higher-elevation land this part of the city is built on. Black exhaust spits from chrome stacks. Particulate settles over everything; in spring I have to wipe the balcony down; the rags look like I used them to clean a barbecue.

Amar and Sim once found an abandoned truck tire in a vacant lot nearby and rolled it down the middle of the street at three in the morning, whooping and cheering as it picked up speed toward the Fraser. I press my forehead to the window, feel the glass tremble. Anonymous phone calls. Sources. Clues. Contacts. *You have your whole life ahead of you*, one of my Langara professors said after Amar died, when I told him I was dropping out. Was that supposed to make me feel better?

The microwave beeps over Joey Shithead shrieking over a semi-truck gearing down out on Knight Street.

✳

Approximately twenty-four square feet. That's what's mine. The square footage of my bed. Double if I include the space beneath, which is where I store my stuff. And that twenty-four square feet depends on the rent being paid, which depends on my sister, Meeta, which depends on her husband, Will Blevins. Which means my mother and I have nothing. Even in *my* so-called personal space I know I could easily be sleeping in my car or a shelter, one bit of bad luck or shitty decision away, or maybe it'll be something completely out of my control (because what's truly in my control?), a reneviction, property owner flips the building, makes good financial sense, who knows? So in my twenty-four square feet there's no true rest, just tension and an undercurrent of uncertainty and fear. Worse, there's also gratitude, the feeling of being lucky to have this . . . but it's gratitude complicated by the sense of being held under something or someone and knowing that showing gratitude for my twenty-four square feet is what's expected of me. Much like how during my meeting with Vincent Peele I constructed a persona to show him I know how lucky I am. Sitting in my bed with my knees curled up, warm, dry, a half-eaten bowl of edamame beside me, feeling the self-hatred that comes from being complicit in my own suppression, and then I'm online and there he is, a man named Bo Xi.

In twenty minutes I learn about several corporations Mr. Xi is involved with: gold mining in South America; infrastructure contracting in Central Africa; luxury property development around the globe. Way down on page fourteen I stumble across a blog post from 2004 written by a disgruntled former employee, a British geotechnical engineer hired to do soil samples for a diamond mine in Angola. The post is a nearly incoherent screed in which the man accuses the company, owned by one of Bo Xi's subsidiary investment firms, of hiring military contractors to incite rebel violence and using the near civil war as a diversion to bypass regulatory hurdles.

And that's it. A grudge-fuelled rant. Rumours and unsubstantiated allegations. But I wonder how many Vincent Peeles and Clint Wards this mystery named Bo Xi employs around the globe.

Awake at sunrise after an anxious sleep with the dream residue of an awful cawing noise in my head. My first thought is a worry about money, which leads straight to the open house later this morning, then to Vincent Peele, Clint Ward, Amar. Look out the window at the bridge over the Fraser River and for a moment the landscape appears in a single scale, cigarette butts as big as warehouses and apartment buildings as small as cigarette butts, equivalent, perspective pressed into a depthless plane, the greasy morning sun the same size as a pebble, or is it the other way around?

SURVIVE

TO

THRIVE

Mark Ward

Saturday, six-o-fucking-clock in the a.m., twelve hours after landing in Vancity. Driving one of Clint's work trucks toward the Cash Corner, early 2000s Ford, not as sick as the Cummins but still dandy, feels good being behind the wheel, eating an overripe apple I bought at 7-Eleven, dark outside, windshield wipers on, work boots on, missing Thailand's sunshine but not the humidity, should I call Daree? Otherwise feeling flat, wondering what next-level dope comes after the Oxys, which at this point are mostly maintenance. Lots of crap careening through my head, jumbled, mostly excited to get to work, smell fresh-dug dirt, cut lumber, diesel exhaust from the Bobcat.

Left off 2nd onto Ontario, drive down 3rd and the unemployed guys are slouched around the Cash Corner, wearing torn jeans and filthy hoodies or soaked flannel, heads tucked against the cold, stooped, some lucky enough to be sipping coffee, more leaning in doorways and under a stunted fir, seeking shelter, murky figures, ghostly, which is what being poor does: turns you immaterial, a spectre, neither here nor there, able to see the world, the things you want, but not touch them.

I crank the heat in the cab and pull to the curb. In five seconds I got a dozen guys around the truck, a tight semicircle, eyeing me as

I eye them, most not saying a word. I spend a minute fucking with the stereo, switching stations, ignoring the men out in the rain to make sure they know what's up. Ash and burned metal clog my mouth and nose—the scent of fear and anger and hope and hate from labouring men who need money when there's not enough work to go around. The unholy trinity. There's some shoving, a flare-up, a few guys fuck off, not wanting to bother. I roll down the window and tell them I got a drainage job over on Alma, maybe a sewer line, lots of digging, hauling gravel, maybe some paving-stone work, and a white kid with a wispy beard and bloodshot eyes under a floppy fake rasta hat says how much and I say nothing for you, hippy, because he's soft, slumming, down on the corner by choice and not forced circumstance and there are guys here who need the work way more.

"You," I say, pointing to a kid, big shaved head, big ears, small black eyes, who's built pretty solid. Kid doesn't bother asking how much, tosses his backpack in the truck box, hovers around the passenger door, waiting, not wanting to sit bitch.

A ripple in the crowd. A tweaker pushes through, scabbed and strung out, sees me, zeros in, pounds on the truck, shouts *please Mr. Bossman please* until I tell him to get lost. So I guess I'm the bossman now? Point to another guy, older, brown, maybe Latino, and he walks real slow around the front of the truck, taking time to finish his smoke.

"Hey dude I'm right here. Hey! Mark? I'm here like Clint said."

Hearing my name gets my attention. Kid's pressed against my door. Short. Was looking right over him. Wavy brown hair, bright-looking, smiling all enthusiastic even in the shit weather at this shit hour. "You Ryan? Fuck you so happy about?"

Ryan lifts a dollar-store toolbox caked in mud. The lid's been torn off and duct-taped back on, and the thing's layered with tattered stickers from Mustang and Viper and Malibu Boats and other pricey shit I'm guessing the kid has zero chance of owning. "Working! Fucking right. Hey . . . Clint calls me Twll."

"So?" I'm about to tell the kid it's a stupid nickname, but whatever, his voice pitches all teenaged-excited when he says it, buddy-buddy with the boss. "Twll. Know what it means?"

"Course. Means like dude or bro in . . . Irish?"

"Sure."

"Ireland looks rad. Like *Trainspotting*." The kid laughs, not some fakey bullshit laugh but genuine-sounding, makes me sad in a way I'm not gonna sit around analyzing. "That scene where the dope-head . . . remember?"

"Yeah."

"And he shits himself!"

Realize I'm chewing my cuticle bloody, stuff my hands in my hoodie, feel the bottle of knock-off Oxys I scored on my way to the Cash Corner. "Yeah. That guy shitting himself was all-time funny. And remember the baby dying?"

Ryan glances over his shoulder. "That wasn't funny though."

"Nope?"

"Okay. Hey? You can call me Twll. If you want? You're Clint's brother, right? He told me about you a bit. You got a nickname? Clint says it's cool when everyone on a crew has nicknames, says we gotta stick together in this business, you know—"

The ugly big-headed kid leans on the hood, says, "Like ragheads do with trucking?" then gives Ryan a shitty sneer, like, *hey, see the brown on your nose?*

I'm guessing they're only a few years apart in age. Ryan sees the sneery look too, puffs up his chest, proud to know the boss person-ally, and now the two teenagers are gonna be locked in bullshit competition for the rest of the day, trying to see who can one-up the other and impress the boss, and I guess that's something I could use to my or Clint's advantage, business-wise, but like Clint says I'm lousy at business, and instead the earlier feeling of sadness when I heard Ryan laugh bleeds into nausea and I'm real close to tearing off, hitting the Oxys and the Sea-to-Sky, driving North until the tank's empty, fleeing into the woods and not coming back.

What I do instead is light a smoke, ask the ugly kid his name. He says Tony, sullen, like he's doing me a favour by telling me, shuffles closer. Ryan gives him space, adjusts his ball cap to better shield his face from the rain.

I ash my smoke at Tony. He notices, pretends not to. "Ragheads, eh Tony? What about Jews?"

Tony scowls. "Fuckin' Jews too, yeah."

"Hey Tony? What's a Jew?"

Tony squints up at me. "It's like . . . uh?"

"Tony? Go away. Before I change my mind about you working."

Ryan hides a snicker behind his hand.

Tony calls me something I don't hear, shoves Ryan in a pretend-accident way, stalks behind the truck.

Flick my butt out the window, watch it sputter. "Breaker Boy."

Ryan brightens. "Breaker Boy? Rad. Your nickname? Sounds badass. What's it mean?"

"I'm shitting you. Forget it. Twll? Get that dickbag Tony and get in."

Big smile at me using his nickname, but saying it leaves a nasty taste in my mouth. Clint was always quick to believe the old man's claim we got some Welsh in us, but truth is we're from nowhere.

"So where's Clint?" Ryan asks.

"Fuck business of yours? You know I just told you to do something?"

"Clint promised to top up my phone."

"My brother says lotsa shit. How long you worked for him?"

"Four months."

"Then you should know that."

I do up the window, surprised to see Ryan's wearing a quality pair of steel-toes. The rest of the guys on the corner scowl and swear and wander off.

My crew for the day crams inside the Ford, bringing smells of stale sweat, dope and cigarette smoke, cheap booze, the stink of soaked work clothes left in backpacks overnight, and the four of us stuffed in the truck, pressed together, touching, it strikes me as wacked out, intimate, like we're in this together even though of course we're not, sooner run each other over than help each other out, and there's this undercurrent, too, of being sardined in the LAV, warrior brotherhood, all that *rah-rah* military solidarity or business teamwork bullshit. But the thing is Ryan ends up squished beside me, riding bitch, and I smell him, you know, his like unique fucking boyish scent, and I get this mentally-not-cool feeling like where me and Ryan are touching shoulders there's a warmth, something being I dunno transmitted, closeness, and for a few seconds I feel this warmth and closeness and it's something I want to keep feeling, something to cherish and protect. Which is a shitbag big-hero fantasy trip because all I am is nothing or worse, garbage, pollution, disease, death. And in the silence as I'm sitting with my shoulder pressed to the smiley-faced kid named Ryan feeling for sure he's really truly alive I start to worry maybe these strangers in the truck know I'm feeling this and they're secretly thinking what a loser, what a pathetic wacked-out weakling.

So to shake all this not-okay nonsense I elbow Ryan in the ribs, tell him to scoot the hell over. Punch the gas, roar from the curb, come close to clipping a junkie, drive a few blocks in moody silence, not bothering with more introductions, trying to get the baby-shampoo scent of my daughter out of my nose. We pass a hipster coffee shop done in reclaimed wood and an art gallery beneath a shiny new condominium not a block away from the Cash Corner, five hundred square feet for a half-million, neighbourhood's changed, Olympics and so on, gentrifying like all East Van, which let's cut the shit should now be called Kits East.

Ryan puts his hands in front of the heat vents to warm up. He's got the smallest hands I've ever seen, chubby fingers, but his nails are caked in dirt and I'm betting the kid knows how to work. "Cold morning," I say. "Damp."

"Oh man that's not cold I know cold dude this is B.C. it never gets cold here, not like where I'm from," Ryan answers, one stream of chirpy-chipper sound, making me hope I don't regret letting him in the truck. The Latino guy stares out the window, doesn't say a word, so he's up one in my books.

"Okay, it's six thirty in the morning," I say, "and usually I'm not super chatty this early, yeah? But where you from?"

Ryan rubs his hands together, eager, flashes me a grin, and I gotta say, it's the realest thing I've seen since I said goodbye to my family in Bangkok. And why the big smile? Because the kid's happy someone asked about him, that's why. Ryan says he's from Northern Ontario, strikes me as a bit evasive, and I sing a few lines from the Neil Young song, decide not to ask anything more.

Ryan laughs when I'm done singing, says he's heard that song sung better. He's bouncing in his seat but trying not to, trying to play it cool, not be too excited or needy, and of course that makes it worse. Real happy to be in a warm truck, driving to a job, to work and get paid, and I try and think back to when that was all I needed, a day filled up with that straightforward satisfaction. How old was I? Seventeen. Just out of high school. Working a few years for my brother before I went to UBC.

I ask the Latino guy his name and he looks at me and nods. Okay. Put a shovel in his hand and he'll understand real quick.

Ryan watches me light a smoke and of course he wants one but he has the pride and self-restraint not to bum this soon after meeting the boss, so for that I give him one. Tony sees us smoking and asks for one and I say no, because I can, and Ryan gives Tony a drag of his when he thinks I'm not looking.

We hit Oak Street and drive south to 12th, then west down 12th, beneath hundred-year-old oak trees still winter-bare, and pretty mauve and mustard-yellow character homes. Seems every third house is being gutted or torn down. Not much traffic. We're about to hit Alma when the car in front of us, a polished Mercedes, slams its brakes for no reason, forcing me to do the same. The Ford screeches to a stop. Tools in the truck box slam and smash. I wince, thinking about the fifteen-hundred-dollar concrete saw. The Mercedes rolls forward a few feet and turns left with no signal.

"Bet that's a chink," Tony says.

"What, man?" Ryan says, still friendly.

"I said. Bet that's a fucking chink."

We get a glimpse of the driver as the Mercedes turns and Tony pumps his fist, which is when I pull the Ford to the curb and tell the nasty fuckhead to get out.

"What?" Tony squeals, acting over-the-top victimized. Seems getting fired ten minutes into a job wasn't included on Tony's list of potential outcomes for the morning.

I don't look at him.

Maybe Tony takes me ignoring him as a sign of weakness or maybe he's as dumb as he looks because he starts arguing, saying, "Fuck no, I'm not getting out. What, and *walk*? We're in the middle of nowhere. Rules, man. You at least have to give me bus fare—"

"Hey, dude," Ryan says, "maybe you should . . ."

Tony clues in to something very important. Senses it. The old Latino, no fool, is already out of the truck, waiting for Tony to get lost. Tony scowls, makes a sneering sound, maybe the one thing he's good at, snatches his backpack, flips me off as he walks by, his stride all fakey swinging-crotch macho. Ryan shuffles over so he's more in the middle of the bench seat, ashes his smoke, pretends not to watch me. The Latino dude crawls in and I see his back's real stiff, hurting him bad. I give Tony a celebratory honk as we leave him behind. No one says a word until Ryan pipes up, says, "I hate that shit too, man."

Jasminder Bansal

Marigold Group's newest full-time sales associate presiding over her first open house, start to finish, all me. High-spirited and hopeful even though I'm inhabiting my real estate sales persona and not the authentic me . . . but the truth is I've already mentally spent the commission from selling this unit ten times over, in increasingly wasteful and decadent ways, "treating myself," as my sister likes to say before purchasing something lavish and ridiculous.

It's almost noon. I've been in the unit for four hours; have shown it to over a dozen potential buyers without generating much interest. But I think I'm doing okay.

The current clients—the Chens, a lovely young couple in their late twenties, and their pinched, Prada-wearing agent, Ms. Lee—have a certain idea of how a condominium viewing should progress. My goals are more divergent: I need to sell this thing, but I'd also like to get an idea of what it's like for international buyers in Vancouver. I gesture toward a stainless-steel sink, try and remember the name of the manufacturer while Ms. Lee flashes a not-kind smirk.

"Mr. Chen? Hi. Isn't this a lovely unit? How are you feeling about your real estate experience in Vancouver?"

Mr. Chen, no surprise, doesn't answer. Pretends not to hear. The question was too direct. Mr. Chen removes his glasses, crushes his index finger and thumb into his eyes hard enough to force a nasally sigh. I feel for Mr. Chen. He's likely had a long flight, if not more than one, after an even longer workweek. Maybe Mr. Chen is wondering: *What the fuck is going on? Who is this sloppy-looking head case of no easily discernible heritage? Is this how they do real estate in this backwater? How many more shitboxes do I have to see today? Then the flight home tomorrow. Not worth the hassle, but man this place sure feels like a palace—*

Mr. Chen could be thinking those things.

Now he steadies himself against the kitchen counter, taps a cigarette half out of the pack, taps it back in, and for some reason the gesture makes me think the man is a gambler, reminds me of the roulette table. Ms. Chen makes her way through the kitchen, anxiously opening and closing cupboards like she's searching for a half-empty cylinder of ketchup Pringles.

"I think they're all empty, Ms. Chen. It's a new condo." Realize I'm fidgeting with my hands like Eric said and, even worse, that I'm having trouble connecting. I blurt: "This is an incredible unit. Wouldn't you agree?"

An awkward silence. I decide to give the Chens some space, grab my phone, watch an eleven-second video of a man walking down the street get smoked by a runaway bratwurst cart. I think he lived.

Well-mannered Mr. Chen excuses himself, steps onto the balcony, lights his cigarette, leaves me and Ms. Chen squaring off around the sink while the realtor checks her phone. Ms. Chen looks like a nereid that hasn't quite broken the surface, but I get the feeling she's a talker, bottled up, could be an opportunity for me, a new angle, the international real estate investor's wife comes clean about loopholes and double-dealing. "Are you enjoying Vancouver?"

"She enjoys it very much," the agent answers without looking up.

"Thanks. Ms. Chen? Are you excited about mov—"

"I am very sure she is."

"Ms. Chen? Vancouver?"

Ms. Chen shakes her head, could be a no or a yes or a third option, less binary.

"I'm new at this job. Can I get that out in the open? Is there anything you'd like to know?"

Ms. Lee pockets the phone, asks if the dishwasher is a Miele.

"A melee? Hit points?"

"No. Miele? European?"

"Oh, European? No."

"Not European?"

"Not a Miele. Pretty sure."

Now all three of us, the domestic womanly sisterhood, crowd around the sink while Mr. Chen the inveterate backroom gambler smokes cigarettes on the balcony and wonders if he's up high enough to guarantee a quick death and what kind of cruel widow-crushing taxes and tariffs and fees would kick in if he died in a foreign land and fuck it with his luck he'd probably make the leap and get stuck in those clouds, more solid than Xi Jinping—

This must be the right moment? To play my hand?

Last gasp, open my file folder to a note that reads:

> *Seller will take 680k not joking that's 60k less*
> *than asking time-sensitive offer hurry!*

What I find amazing is how two outwardly rational people will react in completely different ways to the same piece of information. Ms. Chen reads the note, wraps her dove-like hands around her midsection, glides into the middle of the kitchen, whirls a three-sixty, bolts for the bathroom. I have no idea why she did that.

Ms. Lee, on the other hand, laughs like a stone-cold crook.

I crumple the note. "Did you see her run out of here, Ms. Lee? That was so not the reaction I intended. Is something the matter?"

Ms. Lee snuffle-laughs, dabs her eyes, points at me.

"Me? What about me? Is what just happened against the rules? The note appeared for three seconds. I didn't even write it. I found it in the cupboard under the sink."

The passion I have for my work enables me to create value.

Ms. Lee hurries to the washroom, taps on the door, says something soft and soothing to Ms. Chen. I shuffle onto the balcony, bummed, failing, wondering how to link Bo Xi to Vincent Peele and Vincent Peele to Clint Ward, expose the truth, be granted recognition for my talent. Apparently I had unrealistic hopes that the note would get these folks a condo and me a commission. Mr. Chen interrupts his staring-into-the-clouds to give me an absolutely neutral shrug-smile combo.

I'm in the advantageous position of blocking the sliding glass door. Mr. Chen could brush me out of the way if he wanted to, but I must outweigh him by forty pounds. The situation could devolve into some kind of slapstick physical struggle. One that I would likely win. That's the look I hope I'm giving him. It says: You are trapped. It says: I am in charge now, so please answer my questions. For Mr. Chen the easiest course of action is no action at all. Like a criminal or canine, he just needs to stay down.

"Hi there, Mr. Chen? Hi. Vancouver? Welcome!" The sliding glass door thunks closed behind me. We're alone. Mr. Chen seems uncomfortable. Car horns blare below, seagulls screech and circle above. "Ahhh . . . love that Canadian fresh air! Great . . . location. Amenity room."

Mr. Chen has really got the whole soaking-wet-leaning-against-the-balcony-railing-smoking-cancer-sticks thing down. His slacks are bunched around a thin leather belt; his white dress shirt carries weeks of layered wrinkles; his cuffs are unbuttoned and rolled above his elbows. Mr. Chen looks like a man who is not yet old but has already worked very hard for a very long time and is now wondering: Why?

Mr. Chen's honesty of presence is quite sexually compelling. I'm drawn to his elbows, their saggy-tired skin like turkey wattle. His smoke-yellow fingers. His jaw, still tidy, the last feature to fade. I appreciate his obvious and unaffected weariness, his refusal to pretend otherwise. My current persona might have a secret smoking habit, might like to smoke a cigarette with this Mr. Chen.

So I ask him for one.

Mr. Chen hands me a cigarette, tentative at first, then decisive, like a child stuffing french fries into a hyena cage. The filter is dry and papery between my lips. I like looking beyond the smoking cigarette ember and seeing Mr. Chen leaning against the railing, his face lifted in profile. What kind of man lifts his face to the rain while smoking on a balcony in a foreign country? The rain turns his cheap dress shirt translucent, exposing his shoulders and ribs, the bones of him, his structure like the cages of construction cranes rising behind. His hair is matted around his eyes in a way that reminds me of an unwell child, a boy languishing on a hospital bed. The rain helps me see Mr. Chen, or the small part of him I'm permitted to see.

"So. China. What city?" It'd be nice to smoke in silence. Watch clouds flirt with condos. I'm certain Mr. Chen would prefer silence. But there's a reason I'm on the balcony.

He exhales. In no hurry. "Wuxi. You know?"

—aaand he couldn't be bothered to do me any favours, say the biggest city closest to his so I can pretend to know where he's talking about and not come off like a provincial dolt.

"Wuxi? Never heard of it. Sorry. I haven't travelled much. Actually, never. Is it a big city?"

Mr. Chen says okay size, asks where I live.

"Mostly at my mom's. Sometimes sister's. Until I can get my own—"

"But from—"

"Oh, here. Canada. It's actually not that uncommon for people my age to live at home? Especially in Vancouver. I'm trying to save to move out—"

"Really?"

"I guess living with my mother could be permanent if I continue to suck at saving, but hopefully—"

"I mean Canada. Really?"

In what sense of *really*? "My mother was born in Patiala, Punjab. Know it?"

"India . . . yes." He seems displeased. "But your mother only?"

Change of subject. "Are you a gambler?"

"Sorry?"

"Do you gamble? Roulette? Poker? My brother tried to teach me. I never got into it, couldn't take it seriously."

"Gamble? Not so much." Mr. Chen leans until he can see into the condo, glances at his cigarette, then at me. He touches his hair, seems surprised by how soaked he is, whispers, "Some time."

That's all he says: some time. Out of nowhere, and mostly to himself. Could be a language thing? But it doesn't feel that way. I have no idea what he means, am about to clarify when he laughs nervously. "We are in Unit 301 in where?"

I find myself smiling a real-me smile. "Unit 304. At the Maquette."

"I see. So many."

There are several things my authentic self would like to say. I'd like to ask Mr. Chen more about his town. His work. His home. What he does in his spare time. What's an average day like? What does he usually eat for breakfast? What does he think about his colleagues, his government, his country? I'd like to ask Ms. Chen the same things. Talk to them. I'd like to . . . I think I'd like to tell them what it's like here, for me? And be honest about it? How at twenty-six my journalism dream is starting to feel like smoking a cigarette down to the filter? But I'm working. What should my sales persona say in this situation? "That's fantastic. Great unit . . . uh, in-floor heating? Vancouver real estate is always a sound investment?"

Mr. Chen scratches his eyebrow. "Very nice. But my wife and I are looking for a home."

And *whump* just like that no life-changing commission, no treating myself or even fixing my brakes.

Mr. Chen flicks his cigarette over the railing, really not appropriate in terms of community spirit? I open the sliding glass door, feeling the fight drain out. Mr. Chen slips into the condo. All that and I didn't even get a decently controversial quote out of him. Wuxi? Some time? Who cares? Sales and investigative personas. Corrupt developers. Killers. There's a lot of cloud out there, not much light. I head inside, trying not to think what happens if Vincent Peele discovers who I am.

Ms. Lee opens a pricey-looking leather file folder, writes something with an emerald-green pen made to look antique. Her penmanship is like swordplay, all slash and thrust. Ms. Chen gives me a perfunctory half-wave, wanders into the hall without a backward glance. Her husband, startled by his wife's unannounced departure, hurries after her.

Ms. Lee and I exchange a not-very-friendly look. I stay the course, remain optimistic, hand the woman a Marigold Group business card. She slips my card into her file folder, and when she raises the folder to her chest my card flutters to the ground. She glances at it lying on the floor. Makes no effort to retrieve it.

I treasure the freedom my business affords.

"Thank you for your time, Ms. Lee."

The slightest of nods. "We were under the impression your realty is Asian owned."

"It is?"

"But you're not."

"Asian owned?"

Pursed lips become a not-quite-apologetic smile. "Asia is a large place. Thank you for your time, Miss Bansal."

Carl "Blitzo" Reed

Brand strategy meeting at an as-yet-unnamed organic hop farm/craft brewery in a valley sideways from Pemberton. Huddled inside voluminous orange robes, carrying a carved cedar staff adorned with tinsel, sitting at the head of a table made of rough-hewn planks, under a threatening sky, whispering incantations, brooding on the politics of the street. Thinking about liberation in the form of a brick. Smashed windows, simpler times. Black bloc. Infiltration. Worried my robes make me look like a sunburned scrotum. Worried about toxins, off-gassing, fluoride. Worrying I should be worrying about formaldehyde. Brain in a jar? Worried that *flouride* and *formaldehyde* rhyme, is someone trying to tell me something? Worrying about what to worry about next: asbestos, lead, radon, modified genes. STP, TPD, JIDA, IND. Terrified of acronyms, gnomic language, being left in the dark, being left behind. Nostalgia for nuclear, ducking under desks, sirens blaring, musty bomb shelters, those were the days, back when averting catastrophe meant lowering your centre of gravity.

Shit's gotten complicated.

"Carl? What do you think?"

That's Michael. Dang it. "Uh . . . penetrating?"

"About the microbrewery? Where we are? Right now?"

"You saying this was this my idea?"

Surrounded by densely forested mountains, clouds, vales, not to mention nearly a dozen squirrelly youth, entrepreneurial up-and-comers, untested, totally untrustworthy. Lacking secrets or skeletons. I'm feeling exposed. Pinpointed. The whole thing's staged. Movie studio lights. A painted canvas backdrop. I'm trying to spot the surveillance cameras, listening for the insectile buzz of an Agency drone. Somewhere in Alaska, secluded in a mountain bunker, scarfing Twizzlers, a snot-nosed kid is happily joysticking his way into my mind. It's all a game to him. None of these people are unreal. I'm feeling painfully certain. If I don't move, the drone's camera won't see me. I last ten, maybe fifteen seconds of absolute stillness, then do an impressive bump of meth off a carrot still sticky with dark, wet dirt.

Fresh plucked.

"Tasty," I say, relishing the crunch of carrot, realizing I'm being photo-manipulated, wondering if there's a cargo container full of alternate futures buried in the potato fields.

"We have a wicked-cool greenhouse," the pumpkin-haired girl on my right says, eyeing my carrot, then my meth. "Hydroponics. Early harvest."

"Early Harvest? I met that chick back in oh-six," I tell her, trying not to reveal too much. "She's a Burner. That is not a compliment."

"An empowering solution," Holdout says, clueless, trying to stay upright on the bucking table. "Free-range creativity."

Someone mentions the do-ocracy, the gift economy, then reaches for my stash. I smash the offender's hand, express my discontent for default culture. Explain that, alas, more often than not, violence *is* necessary. Ask where the brewery's firing range is. Ask to inspect ordnance. Ask what their battle-tested methodology is for disabling the government's light armoured vehicles during a real-world shit-hits-the-fan situation. Am met with blank looks, fiddling fingers. An uncomfortably cleared throat or two.

"What? No RPGs? No AKs?" Holdout says. He is a pig, after all.

I glare at Pumpkin Girl. "Drone evasion strategy?"

Nothing.

Holdout, gravely: "Surveillance never sleeps."

"Indeed. You have to survive to thrive."

"This is where we part ways," Pumpkin Girl says, blowing me a kiss. "Violence is never justified."

"This is where I leave you all behind," I correct, wishing I'd brought more cash, afraid it might not be clear to her, afraid she might be getting her own ideas.

Ahem, someone says. Then a voice, disembodied, cruel, floats across the gathering. I flinch, stricken. Something about *connecting with the consumer*. I hiss, waggle my fingers, utter a spell of renewal, call upon the tree of life. Someone boos. The voice continues: . . . *organics are our brand's unique selling feature . . .*

Pumpkin Girl says wait a minute, organics aren't unique any-more, we need to go a step further. *Micro-niche*. Yes, someone else says, but broad enough to appeal. The table erupts in youthful patter: What are our customers feeling when they enjoy our craft brew? The goal is to create emotional resonance, a link between our brew and an imagined ideal happiness, something psychosexual maybe? No, no, we're targeting Millennials. The goal is emotional *rescue*. We have to save them from themselves. They're adrift in anomie. That's an electronica band? No, a surf break in Tofino? No, an overpass in Langley? Our customers are feeling happy with our product, is the consensus. This is about inclusivity! This is about helping people feel happy. Simple as that. I like it! Me too! Selling craft beer is about generosity, egalitarianism, offering a helping hand, community. Like Gandhi, but responsibly drunk—

Holdout, crunched in lotus: "I want to be reborn a babirusa. Serious horn envy."

—uh, anyway, so our customers are drinking our craft brew made with locally sourced organic hops, and that's really radical. I mean, fully revolutionary, but not in the sense of, ick, personal sacrifices, or ick, tough choices, or ick, taking a stand. Wait! Are we endorsing a regressive rhetoric? Is the word *revolution* a bit patriarchal? Twentieth-century? Combative? Angry white male? Or perhaps—just blue-skying here—perhaps there's an energy that could prove useful? A vitality. Virility? Sipping our consciously created craft beer. That's a radical incursion. A thrust, yes, to use an outmoded diction. Because it's a political statement, today, to say: I am happy. I am one hundred per cent committed to my own happiness. Above all else. It's the new free love, but with less swass. Right, great. Me too!

Voices blur into a maddening natter. I elect to remain unfazed, hover above the fray. Magnanimous. Let the kids battle this one out. I did my time in the trenches. The torch will be passed. But they seem so young, guileless, unprepared. Virginal. Finally a decent train of thought. I do a bump to keep it rolling. The voices continue: an old dichotomy destroyed, steering clear of the aggressive-destructive tendency in conventional ideology, seeking a less-directly-confrontational path, nurturing the mindful consumer-citizen—

"People fucking died so you can have weekends!" I shout at the doe-eyed nymphs, getting straight to brass tacks.

Pumpkin Girl lifts her index finger. "Excuse me, is that even true? I'd like to see citations."

"What? You think they gave us that shit of their own volition? From the goodness of their hearts? Here, they said, have two full days to yourselves! La-de-da! Next up, a living wage! You think they stopped using six-year-olds to sweep chimneys because they had an irreversible crisis of conscience? You think we can't regress"—I snap my fingers—"like right fucking quick? They will pounce, you hear me? *Pounce.* You are either predator or prey. You wanna talk universal suffrage? Yeah, because no one got bloodied fighting for *that.* Time to pick a side, you sanctimonious, thin-skinned little wisps."

"Wisps?" Holdout says. "Or WASPS?"

"Yes, like those guys, but considerably less substantial. Everywhere and nowhere. Which makes them even more dangerous. I'm getting freaked."

Holdout looks around, anxious. "Feeling surrounded? Hard to put a bullet through a cloud of mist."

"Excuse me, no," Pumpkin Girl says, "it's actually very easy."

I resist the urge to smack her with my staff, afraid it'll whoosh right through her.

Holdout rubs his nose in a pile of meth, snorts, says it is odd, how the only clearly defined feature on these kids is their lips.

"Weird purplish and bright red or blue lips," I say, noticing. "Like berry stains . . . no, like stains from those lollipops you wear on your finger like a huge ring. Like they've been sucking saccharine all day long."

Pumpkin Girl harrumphs. "That was then. Things are so much better now."

"And who do you have to thank for that, missy?"

Silence again, perfect and absolute except for Holdout's snuffling. A dozen sets of elven eyes glare at me. Making me feel guilty about making them feel. Is everything worth doing best done alone, forget the ethos of radical acceptance—

Clapping. From the other end of the table. It's Michael, AKA Troutman, my long-lost comrade, making me shiver. Still got my back, old friend, right where I like you.

"The give-us-your-weekends speech," Michael says. "Been a while, Blitz. Thought you'd forgotten."

A kid with a purple faux-hawk who introduced himself as crazydays18 lifts a marketing plan handwritten on hemp paper, sniffs: "To return to point, if we might? *Organic* remains a powerful buzzword. What we're doing effects real-world change."

"Did you just say *buzzword*?" Holdout says, eyes beading.

"This guy's been planted to misdirect," I tell the others. "Tread careful."

crazydays18 giggles, pours some drugs into a hand-carved wooden goblet.

I shake my staff at the sky, feeling over the weather, while the disembodied cyber-nymphs prattle about *differentiation, mark-ups, contemporary lifestyle choices.*

"A powerful collusion is occurring," I observe, thankfully shielded from drone strikes by my flowing robes, which are secretly made of metalized Mylar, "between technology and corporate interests. You all are proof of that. Consider, if you will, the internet. The world's largest shopping mall."

"We have a more nuanced view of capital," says crazydays18. "Its aleatory, potentially transgressive flow."

"Shop the Revolution," Pumpkin Girl says cheerfully, pointing to the slogan emblazoned on her T-shirt, prompting me to hitch myself to another sizable bump. "Which is why this hop farm is such a radical project, Mr. Reed. Blitzo? We're modelling alternatives outside the—"

"Robot!" I shriek. Across the valley, Mount Currie the Mountain Spirit grumbles that he's looking forward to Singularity, says at least robots can be programmed to pack out their toilet paper.

"But isn't this why you invest ethically?" crazydays18 asks. "Isn't this what Green Lead is all about? I mean, forging mindful investment partnerships? Cultivating the next big thing?"

The assembled wait for a response while I consider the viability of biological weapons–dealing. Must be more interesting people in that line of work. Full-bodied Eastern European men and women who remain uncowed by body hair, still believe in sin, and fuck like it's wartime, bombs away. Not these guileless, moonbeam-walking selfies who fuck like spoiled kittens lapping at a saucer of milk. Seems high-stakes vencap has lost its charm. Been co-opted. I point at Holdout, leave him to explain what we're about in thirty seconds or less, knowing the kids'll tune out the last twenty seconds anyway.

All eyes turn to the pig.

"Fuck if I know where this is going," Holdout says, "except I'm real hungry."

"Besides, what about the state?" crazydays18 says, buoyed by my silence. "The true source of repression? Taxes? The military industrial—"

"Owned. Outmoded. Overridden. You need to stay current. All is almost lost, and that's when shit gets good. Subvert! Disrupt!"

"Who has the time?"

"True. I'm like, totally swamped."

"Waaay too much on my plate—"

I loom, stab my staff through a MacBook screen, watch the sucklings flinch.

"Fraktur," Pumpkin Girl says, awed as she traces a rune through Holdout's drool, a gesture I find strangely soothing.

"You have an attractive nose," I tell her, feeling chivalrous, imagining a bestriding, handing her both carrot and—

The story of our brew begins in a verdant garden . . .

"Where the hell is that disembodied voice coming from?" Holdout interrupts.

"Change *verdant* to *bountiful*," the kid beside me says, making me blink. *Bountiful, British Columbia?* Vas deferens. Illegitimate spawn. Seer stones? Christ in a teepee? Got me a couple'a all those!

The kid at my elbow continues, "The label should read: The story of our beer—"

"*Brew*," Pumpkin Girl corrects, indignant. "Beer is for Bridgers."

Self-righteousness and an inability to recognize what's at stake. That's what irks me most about these nymphs.

The story of our brew begins in a bountiful garden . . .

I ask the kid his name.

"Frisk," he answers.

Many enthusiastic nods of assent for the word *bountiful*. It appears another consensus has been reached. As to what, I can't quite say, never mind remember how I voted, but it's nice to be on the winning side. I wave my staff, bless the gathering, exclaim, "We should all have sex, or whatever the next thing is, to seal the deal."

"I have plenty of sex," Pumpkin Girl says, "but not with you."

Holdout, suddenly irrepressible, frolics across the table, scatters MacBooks, overturns crystal decanters of GHB, gobbles a platter of lightly poached river-caught salmon and still-warm bannock while eyeing my crushed ketamine and flirting with a golden-haired princess named Zen who introduced herself as the hop farm's earth electress.

Michael's at the far end of the table, returned to being boring, reading the farm's hastily scrawled financials, squinty-eyed, ignoring the parade. I zap outward, link to Holdout's mental field, issue a command, make my piggy-muffin charge Michael, scatter the paper-work. Ponder the link between druidism and international currency trading. Something about castration anxiety, no doubt. Michael yelps, tips off his chair, prompts me to stand, smash my staff on the table, and shout, "Roar!"

"Pooh-pooh," Holdout sniffs, jealous of being upstaged. "Populist."

I sit down, satisfied, and in the prolonged pause I remember my sixteen-year-old daughter, Hannah-fannah-bo-banna, her life at Appleby, so far away. I wonder what she's eating, if anything. My hands begin to shake. There must be an emotion for this.

Michael picks himself out of the mud, vanishes, reappears directly in my face, filling my field of vision, eyes bulging, screaming, "This was your idea! A fucking organic brewery, Carl? We're Green Lead. *Lead?* This isn't leading! This isn't even *advancing.* We were going to change the world. Clean energy. Perpetual motion. Space colonies! Mythopoeics! Now another brewery . . . no, not even that, a potato field full of needy grubsters for eight point three million—" Michael presses his hands to his face, mutters something, looks around wildly. "I shouldn't be here. Wasting my life with you. Peele's waiting for us to sign on the Solstice property and I'm out here freezing—"

"Fresh Plucked," I say, imperial, stroking my goatee, on target, anticipating an imminent counter-counter-insurgency in the form of a speedball—

"Fresh what?"

"The name of the brewery, you lump. I christen this exciting new venture: Fresh Plucked."

The kids cheer my name: Blitzo! Blitzo! Michael spittles. My skin superheats, fuelled by past regressions, melts my business partner and former best friend on the spot.

"It's settled then, Michael? How are the numbers?" Michael-the-Defeated-Puddle gets petty, refuses to answer. "Fine then, be shitty. I for one like this project, Mr. Zenski. We need to think smaller. Micro-politics. Locally sourced. This carrot has a unique story to tell. I want to know who sowed this carrot, in what garden plot—GPS-coordinate accuracy, please. I want to know how long this carrot was in the ground, what nutrients it was fed, who tended it, was it stroked, how often the skies rained and sunned, was there a non-denominational or maybe politely neo-pagan celebration of gratitude when this carrot was harvested. Nothing wrong with having the wealth and privilege to cultivate intimate relationships with my food while the rest of the world goes hungry. Can't fault it. Not without sounding like a dick. *Jeesh*, Michael Zenski, you're a cynical old dinosaur. Be happy like me! Where's the ketamine? Whoa! Sure, I'll share. Here, do a bump off my staff. Man, you all look so sparkly and light-soaked. How do you get that glow? Is it a powder you shake on your skin? Aerosol? CGI? I'm terrified of scalpels. Men in masks. Can one of you cuties tell me the creation story of this meth? We'll talk defensive perimeters later. Let Team Blitzo show you the ropes—"

"Me too!" someone shouts.

"I like it!"

"I'm a huge fan!"

A kid dressed in a burlap sack stands, spreads his arms, asks if he can prick my brain.

"Say what?"

The kid laughs, pretending he didn't slip up, making light of a tense situation. Weather booms and thunders. My staff vibrates, dowsing the treasonous source. Mount Currie's going nuts, dropping f-bombs, threatening to avalanche the valley if we don't get rid of the narc. Then the kid in burlap explains he heard fireside rumours about a so-so commune in the early eighties, an idea well past its due date, way up Bute Inlet, direct action against a logging camp, spiked trees and sand-filled fuel tanks, and oh-shit-looky-here my current wife now in politics, the Establishment, hobnobbing with the power elite, how times change, and my vencap company hooked up to Tesla, well-known haterz and fascists, and all that has to *mean* something, right?

Elect to deliver a cutting rebuttal. "Well, maybe not really?"

"So you deny it?"

"You calling me a sellout?"

Burlap Sack takes a nibble of heritage parsnip, chews. "I'm calling you out."

"*Ooh*, you are so not our tribe," Holdout says into a gust of chill wind while I wave my staff at the sky and thunderclouds gather above the assembled and a killer tornado forms wrathful in my mind.

Michael-the-Puddle, now re-formed into a creature resembling a human being, apparently realizes we might've been set up, threatens to call the brewery deal off unless Burlap Sack can recite the St. Paul Principles.

Burlap Sack stares at his nose, looks as smart as three dumb people, doesn't answer Michael's question about the StPP. We were almost duped! I reach inside my robes, grab a satchel of garlic powder and a backup supply of something cooked crystalline—

"Frauds," Holdout growls, which is cool, I didn't know pigs could do that. "Spy fuckers! Querulous lollygaggers!"

Michael tells Holdout to settle down while steering me to my seat. The wrathful tornado clouds thin, disperse, too bad, could'a been cool.

"So. You kids want to hear it from the horse's mouth?" Michael dips his pinkie in a mountain of powder, runs it over his gums. Not quite like the old days, but it's a start. "Was April of eighty-three, first of all, you lying McParland—"

"Not them," I say, slumping inward. "Not now. They don't deserve it. Please?"

"They can't touch us," Troutman says, a worrisome line, an echo. "And besides. Love and light? We're role models. The story'll serve as a warning."

Lay my head on the table, close my eyes, let my mind unspool while Troutman says the kids have no idea who they're dealing with. Tells them the story of the Bute Eight. How we made it a full three years up that godforsaken inlet, eating peanut butter from five-gallon drums, killing mosquitos with fly swatters. A man on grizzly watch every night. But bears weren't the only things hunting us.

"What happened?" Pumpkin Girl asks, a question still seeking an answer.

"There was me," Troutman says, "and Blitzo here, and his girl-friend the Vulcan, and two more I won't name. We were in from the beginning. The rest drifted in, Tincan Bill and Larry, Marjorie and Coral. Drawn to the idea, see? The potential. Like flies to shit, it turned out, but we didn't know that then. This was when believing took commitment. Sacrifice. We were decades late, living in the shadow of those who came before, conscious of the big shoes. Most of the early crew, the Yippies and so on, subversive if ineffectual pop artists of our tribe, were already working in Vancouver, hawking junk bonds on Howe, or nestled in the Slocan, experimenting with advanced hybrid strains. The fervour had passed. The *fashion*. In a way it was a good thing. Culled poseurs from true believers. But we went up that inlet anyway. Blitzo here had us all primed to begin again. Said there's nothing more intriguing than a dead idea. Said the evolution of human consciousness is a circle—"

"Oval," Holdout corrects.

"What?"

"Elliptic," I mumble into my arm. "Circles are unlikely. That degree of precision—"

"Aren't ellipses precise too?" Pumpkin Girl wants to know.

"Some kind of mostly spherical shape? Anyway, we're talking a clean slate, kids."

I lift my head. "Nothing's clean. Nothing and nobody. That's what's so beautiful."

Pumpkin Girl, captious eyebrow cocked: "That right? Because—"

"Everyone's some kind of horrid. It's what makes us worth loving."

In unison: "Ick! Ew! Ick!"

"Ever try loving someone better than you? I mean light years better? Damn near impossible. Think of the Almighty. No one really loves that fucker—they just want to please him. Striving, falling short, striving, feeling unworthy, guilty, resentful—nah. Way easier to love someone who's worse. Christ had it easiest of all, loving us fallen, being all smug and beneficent, all like wow look at how much I love these losers. A world full of perfect people—know what that is?"

Michael kisses my neck. "A world without love."

"Can I go pee?" Frisk asks, shy.

I say yes, ask him how long he's known Burlap Sack, who vouched for him, then make a hurry-up motion at Michael, tell him to get on with the Bute Eight if he must—

"Where were we?" Michael asks.

"Clean slate," Pumpkin Girl says, diligent schoolgirl.

"Right. The ancient urge," Michael continues, running his fingers through my hair, "to start over. Be reborn. That's why we headed into the Canadian wilds."

"*Ooooo* . . . the Canadian wilds . . . ," moans the whole table. "*Aaaaah* . . . the great outdoors . . ."

crazydays18 preens his faux-hawk. "By a clean slate you mean, totally empty?"

"You scared?" Holdout says.

crazydays18 nods, nuzzles Pumpkin Girl. I say come on over here you two, check out these robes, secret pockets, tucked-in illicits.

Michael shoos them away. "Impossible, right? Idealism is always about death, either fear of or lust for. Attempting to begin again— you're taking aim at immortality. To become godlike. Of course the enterprise is doomed. Death is the only achievable human perfection. We learned that the hard way, out there in the cedars and sphagnum."

"Life must've been so ick back then," Pumpkin Girl says. "Everything's perfect now."

"Attainment," I say. "On demand."

Frisk returns, says he had the best pee ever.

Holdout tells him happiness is appreciating the little things.

"Blitz spent—how long in Auroville?"

"Two lifetimes," I mumble, waiting for an opportune moment to snort something. "It didn't stick."

Troutman laughs. "You feel that, kids? Two lifetimes sweating his bodyweight every day, a guru's finger lodged deep. Thing is, Blitzo here had—has—the one thing we lacked. Vision. We had the desire, but we were scattered. Was easy . . ." Troutman's voice falters, gets scratchy, ". . . to follow this man. Believe what you will."

A tableful of doe eyes focus on me, trying to reconcile fantastic rumour with let-down reality.

Pumpkin Girl counts with her fingers, frowns. "But that's nine."

Troutman sighs. "What?"

"Nine people in the commune," she says. And then she carefully recites our names one by one.

"My Gia, child!" I yell. "Forest for trees? We did that to fuck with the Tool!" I shake my staff, shower myself in tinsel, try and lift my head off the table, fail, feel a eulogy in the breeze, not quite ready to call it a life.

"Was a time of cross-pollination," Troutman continues, his voice billowing over the fields. "No right or wrong path. We'd read Abbie and Abbey. But we were years late and way up Bute. Nearest road was three hundred kilometres south. North was empty until Bella Coola. Ends of the earth. Still is. But not empty, heck no. Not a blank slate, not by a long shot, and never was. In the footsteps of that murderer, Al Waddington, and his failed colonial project to put a road through them thar hills. Haunted by Klatsassin's war cry and gavel strike of the Hanging Judge. The valley felt impenetrable. It wasn't. Thought we'd chosen a spot well out of the way of the logging companies. We hadn't. Crown land got sold, a backroom deal putting our camp smack in the middle of a timber lot."

"It wasn't that long ago," I tell him. "You don't have to do that gothic-horror tall-tale voice?"

The kids are quiet, enraptured by Michael's ghost story. I lean into him, feel his warmth, try not to hope for more.

"We started small. Slashed tires. Stole chainsaws. But those loggers . . . it was their livelihood. They responded the only way they knew how. Winter of eighty-five was setting in. We were bushed. Cabin fever. Plagued by violent dream-visions. Unlikely heroes rose, shifting alliances among the clans. Usually the logging crews were laid off in October. But the mucky-mucks on the board of directors were afraid if they left the Homathko camp unguarded we'd burn it to the ground. And they were right. Both sides were dug in. So the high-ups voted to keep a crew in all winter. Turns out the men they selected were . . . reactionary. Let's say . . . hardened. Violent strikebreakers, entrenched neo-Nazis, right-winger paranoids. Not average working men at all. Full of hate, every one of them. Thugs were given a very specific task, understand? *Defend our property,* the suits said. The Vulcan, Larry, and Coral were smart, sensed the inevitable electrics, caught a boat in mid-December.

That was a long winter. Socked in so thick you couldn't see five feet. Felt like living in a deprivation chamber, and in the absence of coherent stimuli our minds started playing tricks. Time spring came around, Marjorie and Tincan Bill were dead. Plus three of the goon squad."

Someone's cellphone rings. A techno beat with a raven cawing.

"Fought the wrong war," Troutman says. "Those guys weren't our natural enemies. Another place, different social circumstances, they'd a been our brothers. Suits set us against one another. So Blitzo here walked into the courthouse, copped to two deaths. Other one went as an accidental drowning. But this man you see before you spent from eighty-six until—"

"February twentieth, zero-one."

"—in federal prison. Not easy, staying quiet for fifteen years. The best part of a man's life? Conceived his daughter behind bars?" Michael glares at the crew. "Well. Let's just say . . . I hope you've been listening."

Troutman presses his head to mine, whispers a promise I can't hear. I respond, kiss his neck, tell him language is an impediment to communication, tell him I want to get preverbal, that I miss him, that he's still fucking hot. Michael's smile is so like yesterday, so like memory, it makes me forget the decades between us, how we fucked on the banks of the glacier-grey Homathko, beside spawning incarnadine salmon, feathers in our hair, mudsmeared, tender-bodied, lit by sunlight reflecting off the ice field, and now Michael kisses me, says he's sorry, all these years, he never thought it would—and one of the moonbeam brewery kids tugs on my sleeve, interrupts, asks how come he never heard the whole story.

Michael pulls away, laughs, says because he made the whole thing up, careful who you let shit in your ear, son. A collective sigh. Drugs are passed around. Holdout wiggles his head into my robes, nuzzles his wet snout to my nipple, says it's time to move on.

"So how'd you get all your money, Blitzo?" the kid wearing the burlap sack asks.

Holdout manoeuvres into battle position. "There's a bomb surgically implanted in my belly," he tells the kid. "One wrong word and I detonate."

"That's, uh, kind of a lot of pressure?"

Bomb. I think about my old accomplice Caltrop, how long it's been, perhaps time to pay the devil a visit. Last of the real radicals. Fifteen years older than me. Escaped a second tour in 'Nam, snuck up north. An image of the former soldier moving through the mist, face painted green and black, crouched low, silent, hunting. Dude needs to get in on this action.

I decide Burlap Sack's not a narc. He's a strikebreaker and corporate spook. Deep undercover. Suspicions confirmed by a look he gives me, I dip my fingers in the garlic powder. The genealogical link between vampirism and union-smashing is strong indeed.

"That was a real cool story," Burlap Sack says. "About trees and whatever? But can we talk marketing narrative, Mr. Blitzo?" The kid reaches down, slow so he doesn't startle me, picks up a sketchbook, flashes a drawing. "We've done a few sketches for our brewery logo. Would you mind—"

"Show me!" I thunder, snatching the sketchbook and flipping through it. The spectrum changes. Burlap Sack has no idea what he's stumbled upon. Tool of techno-corporate hegemony. But man, the kid can draw. "You're an autodidact?"

The kid looks sheepish. Too young to be properly afraid.

"Channelling secrets," Holdout says, agreeable, his hoof blurring a charcoal print. I shove him off the drawing.

"Inadvertently, of course," Michael says, looking over my shoulder, maybe sensing something. "Which is the only way secrets should be channelled."

I'm flipping through the sketchbook, engrossed. Plans, blueprints, schematics. It's all right here. I must contact Caltrop. Time is narrowing. A window, some kind of opportunity? My staff vibrates. The air's suddenly turbocharged. I ask Michael to remind me who wants the North Vancouver property?

"I told you. Bo Xi."

"Bo Xi?" Frisk says. "Heard of that guy. Super-rich businessman. Big into—"

"Me too!"

"—corruption charges, African blood diamonds, all sorts of nasty."

Michael, quiet, so close his lips brush my earlobe: "You see it now, Blitz? You see it?"

"All these years. Is it really him?"

"Yes. All this time. And now he's close."

"You know this dude?" Pumpkin Girl asks, snoopy-snoopster. "He sounds like total bad vibes."

Michael grabs Burlap Sack's banjo, feeds it to Holdout. "Lotsa people have heard of him, but no one really knows who he is."

I flip through the sketchbook. Pencil drawings. Secrets. Schemes. Caltrop will know what to do. A soldier should always have answers, otherwise he's just an asshole. The dream materializes. I've always trusted dreams; they're the only things worth waking up for.

"Kid," I mumble at Burlap Sack while studying a so-so drawing of a horse in a field, realizing it's an emu but the perspective's off ten degrees and that makes all the difference. "You're going to take us through time."

"So Mr. Blitzo," crazydays18 says, plucking a pierced eyebrow, grubby financial mercenary, sticking it to me despite the olive branch on offer, "you buying the farm?"

Mark Ward

The Alma job ends up being a shitshow. Clint halted work a few weeks back because the customer wasn't paying, and between then and now the partially excavated trench running along the foundation caved in and filled with freezing mud-water. I send Ryan into the trench with an electric water pump to try and expose the foundation footing where our drainage pipe needs to run. Kid ends up soaked to the waist, shivering, but he works hard down there in the muck without a single word of bitch so I let him sit in the Ford for a while to warm up. The old guy, turns out he's a Guatemalan named Ramon, heads toward the corner store at coffee break and never makes it back.

Lunchtime, me and Ryan sit in the Ford with the engine idling and the heat blasting. I eat a tuna sandwich, another pulpy apple, drink coffee from a Thermos, and am about to eat another sandwich when I realize all Ryan has is a chunk of soggy Subway that looks pulled from a bin. Give him half my second sandwich, a bag of chips, another smoke, some coffee, telling him he better not be a mooch motherfucker cuz I hate those. He waves me off, asks if he can get on the saw.

"What saw?"

"Concrete saw. It's in the truck." Ryan takes a bite of tuna sand-wich, looks at the torn-up front yard like it's the most fascinating thing ever. "Paving-stone patio around back. Half finished. Whoever was here had no clue. You should let me rip the stones up. All slumped in anyway. Rebuild the patio. Cut the edge in. Bet I could finish that patio this afternoon, you stay out of my way."

I tap the steering wheel, crank the defrost to defog the wind-shield, try and find a way to be pissed off at the kid. "You're here to dig."

"Okay, you're the boss, but just sayin' that's a waste of money. Clint's not paying me fifteen bucks cash to dig."

"Saw weighs more than you."

Ryan gives me a look like now he's certain he should be running crew, not me. "Been doing this since back home. Longer than you I bet."

"Clint let you run the saw?"

"No."

So for telling the truth I say, "All right, go work on the patio. I hate that ditch too. But I see you run the saw dry or sink the blade into the dirt, it's over. Diamond blades cost fifty bucks a pop."

"They cost fifty-eight." Ryan looks at the clouds. "Ditch is going to keep filling with water. You need a new pump."

"Not my company. Not my problem."

"Your site though. When's Clint coming?"

"Look, I don't know what my brother told you, but Clint doesn't work on site anymore. Your phone's not getting topped up. You stay hired, it's me making the call."

Ryan stuffs a handful of potato chips in his mouth. "He'll top up my phone. Clint and me hang out. Even went to Whistler."

"Meaning what? That you and my brother are besties and I can't fire you?"

"How long you gonna be around? Because you look . . . what happened to your leg?"

"I worked with Clint for seven years, off and on. After high school. Then in university. So I might be around longer than you think."

Damn. Didn't mean to mention school.

"University?" Ryan asks, curious but cautious. "Doing what?"

"Lotsa shit."

"Then why you here? In the rain?"

I take a long drag. It's obvious Ryan loves this work. Was made for it. It's not cool to slag someone's work because it doesn't suit you, especially when that work might be the best and only thing the guy has. "It's all right," I say, only half lying. "Working outside, no bullshit, can say what I want, piss in the yard. There's a lot to be said for it."

Ryan looks satisfied. "I like it too. Fresh air. Smoke when I want. Sometimes girls walk by."

I clench my hands on my lap to keep from cradling my ruined leg. "How old are you, Ryan?"

"Eighteen."

"For real. Lie and you'll never see that concrete saw."

"Fifteen."

"Just turned?"

Ryan doesn't answer.

What sends a fifteen-year-old kid out of school and across the country? Nothing I want to think on for too long.

A few minutes later we're in the yard. We spend two hours levelling sand and laying the paving-stone patio. It's circular, about fifteen feet across. The entire outside edge has to be cut on a symmetrical curve, stone by stone so each cut line matches with the next, or else the whole thing looks like dogshit. This is not easy to accomplish with a concrete saw. The thing weighs thirty pounds and takes two hands to hold, so you have to cut bent over awkwardly, with the toe of your boot holding the stone in place as you cut. The saw's attached to a hose that sprays water at the blade to keep the dust down, which means you're soaked and constantly tripping over the hose while holding the saw. The blade's twelve inches diameter. Teeth lined with diamonds. One slip and you're getting cut, even with steel-toes. But worst of all's the fucking noise. A diamond blade ripping through concrete is louder than any chainsaw, a piercing high-pitched scream audible ten blocks away.

Ryan uses a pallet and a piece of plywood to set up a cutting station clear of tripping hazards. Checks the saw blade, the dust filter, and fuel. Turns on the water and is about to yank the pull cord up when I stop him, ask about ear protection. He shrugs. I call him an idiot. He laughs. I tell him he's wearing ear protection and hand him a set of earmuffs from the toolbox. He puts them on and fires up the saw.

"You want me to measure and mark your cuts?" I yell.

Ryan gives me a look like what the fuck?

"Measure the cuts?"

Ryan shakes his head no, grabs a stone from the stack, sets it on the cutting station, eyes the patio, settles the spinning diamond blade gently onto the stone while I move away from the spraying water. The kid makes the first cut, then another, then another, and one by one the stones slip together and line up perfectly and fifteen minutes later there's a graceful arc of cut stones curving along the edge of the patio. Ryan isn't even marking his cuts with a soapstone pencil, just eyeballing each one, visualizing where the blade needs to set down and hitting the curve exactly right every time, something I've only seen one other guy—a fifty-five-year-old German stonemason named Jurgen—be able to do.

An hour later I've smoked five cigarettes, munched a bag of sours, popped an Oxy or two, and the patio's finished, a perfect circle, each stone cut crisp with the ones beside it. I figure Ryan just made Clint around five grand, tell him the patio looks sweet. Tell him he's a mean bastard on the concrete saw. Ryan, soaked and covered in muddy grey dust up to his waist, flashes me a real open smile, says okay but what about another smoke since you know I'm good for it?

I spend an unaccounted-for while sitting in the Ford, watching Ryan bail muck-water out of the trench, running my fingers over the weird hole in my thigh where a chunk of me got burned and blasted off. Scar-heat carries through my Carhartts. Breathing not very regular. Chest too tight. Set an Oxy between my molars and crunch down, adding a bit of tooth pressure to the pill every time the clock on my phone rolls over to a fresh minute, ignoring the bitter chemical taste, and in this way it takes me eighteen minutes to get the whole pill in my gut, which I figure is okay in terms of self-enforced time release and limiting the risk of overdose, stopped breathing, skin turning a pretty robin's-egg blue.

At one point I try to adjust how I'm sitting and my leg smacks the steering wheel and my shriek makes Ryan climb out of the trench and stare at the truck until I roll down the window, yell hey, dogfucker, back to work with you. Slump against the seat, use my index finger to clear a four-inch-square viewing window in the condensation, watch Ryan struggle in the ditch beside that huge house, partially obscured by rhododendron, dogwood, see him wrestling with a piece-of-shit water pump that keeps getting clogged and overheating so he has to use buckets to get the water out of the trench, scrambling up the slick, muddy sides, a losing battle, dug in, wartime, OPFOR. Feeling lousy for deserting the kid but knowing I couldn't make it across the yard, what a fucking waste, a living embarrassment, *Canadian Armed Forces QOL (Quality of Life) Level Determination Private Basic Mark Patrick Ward Level One: Mild interference with the ability to carry out the usual and accustomed activities of independent living, recreational and community activities, and/ or personal relationships due to the entitled condition or bracketed entitled conditions* and so fucking on, made my own bed, no one's fault but mine, tough shit. I put the cellphones Clint gave me on the seat, moving slow and careful, thinking I might need to call someone, who can I call, reach out to, say I'M HERE HELP ME I'M STILL HERE—

Mind stuttering, detonators and dusty roads, Daree, Sarah, my brother making bank, zero risk, it always goes up and the heat from my leg creeps into my chest, makes my heart go *zippity-pop* and now I'm too hot but shivering, wiping sweat from my face when my phone beeps, a text, and when I open it I see a list of numbers 85-142/86-36.7 and for a few seconds I stare at the screen, moaning, not knowing what the fuck while—*whoosh-ffft*—my breathing full-on fucking stops, chest seizes, like getting kicked in the solar plexus but worse, game over for Marky, thrashing around, forgetting where or what I am, lungs not inhaling, smacking for the door handle, suffocating, dying, locked inside a smouldering metal cage, piled against the door burning, leaving Ryan alone in the trench fighting an invisible enemy and after a while of this free-floating breathless terror I realize the numbers on the cellphone aren't an IED detonation code. I'm looking at my father's vitals.

Dave Ward. The old man.

Air rushes into my lungs. Gasping. Clutching at the wheel. Bio-data sent from Clint's fucking app. Stabilize, get a few breaths, trash the text and call Daree for the first time since I got to Vancity. Daree answers quick thank holy fuck and the first thing she says is my name, pronounced wrong, *Maak* instead of Mark which makes me sad for no specific reason and I ask is Sarah there, can I talk to my baby daughter and Daree says it's late, she's sleeping.

I say well fuck sakes wake her up, it's important. I need to hear Sarah breathe and Daree says it's late here, asks if I'm okay and I say sure, fuck yeah. Missing my daughter is all, why won't you wake her up she's a baby she'll fall back asleep quick even if she's crying I need to hear her *breathe*, please, it's important, my voice rising now, shouting why are you keeping her from me. Forcing myself to calm down, realizing this was a shit idea, wanting to hang up but feeling shit about that too, saying I miss you guys over and over, Daree saying my name over and over, both of us drowning in this shitty frantic energy and me asking her to come to Vancouver, bring Sarah, it'll be okay we'll make it work and Daree finally going quiet so I say, "Please change your mind. Come to Canada. It doesn't have to be forever."

"No. My mind won't change—"

"You don't want—"

"We do want—"

"Then why the fuck—"

"Because do you want? Really us there?"

Which is when I say no, fuck it, you're right, you know what I want more than anything and Daree asks what tell me please even though she's crying, like she needs to hear me say it, tell her and the baby to fuck right off, that I'll never see them again, but instead of giving her the satisfaction I say, "I want my name in lights. Like in front of a stadium. Big bright lights for everyone to see."

And then I hang up. Drag my hood over my head and limp into the rain, help Ryan in the trench, lay and level thirty feet of drainage pipe. At the end of the day I offer the kid a ride home. Ryan says he lives in Burnaby and I say well fuck that I'm not sitting in traffic for two hours. I end up dropping him off at the Commercial SkyTrain station. It's crowded, packed with commuters, black and grey umbrellas brushing against one another, people looking sullen, trapped beneath something bigger than the weather, rain hammering down, spraying off the pavement, pretty only because I'm warm and dry inside the truck.

Ryan shoves through the crowd, goes to the ticket machine, presses a few buttons but doesn't put any money in, glances over his shoulder. On a hunch I drive away, circle, park down an alley. Ryan slinks out of the station a few minutes later, looking super cagey, sidestepping around commuters who refuse to acknowledge his right to be on a sidewalk. He heads south down Commercial, hops a fence, vanishes into a blackberry thicket covering a steep hill leading down to the SkyTrain tracks. There's an overpass down there. It'll be dry. Ryan's going home.

Jasminder Bansal

Driving the Stanley Park loop, stressed about not selling Unit 304. Feeling put off by the mountains and ocean, wishing for a Mumbai slum even though I've never been, hope springing eternal in smog and snarled traffic. Anything instead of all this too-perfect natural blech beauty. Thinking about people from high school and Langara; knowing I'll never call them or go to class reunions. Thinking about networking, how to become a more productive person, sell more units. Thinking extroverts have it easier, that I need to pay more attention when meeting people, cultivate connections. Questioning my relationship with Eric, why I chickened out from calling it off last night. Deliberately not thinking about Sim or Vincent Peele or my brother. Marvelling that consciously not thinking about something is more draining than simply thinking about it.

The clouds have lifted over the city but are still hanging stubbornly against the North Shore Mountains, threading through green-grey trees, fuck off pretty Vancouver sky, fuck off happy Vancouver people jogging on the seawall. The road is damp and slick, coated in algae in the shady spots beneath hemlock and cedar. Worried I'm going to fail at selling condos. What can I do differently?

The Honda's back end slides out, a rear tire bumps the curb, a quick grinding sound that'll cost a few hundred bucks to fix, and I ease off the gas and straighten the car, glance in the rear-view, feeling looked down on. Worried I've forgotten the real reason I'm at Marigold. Maybe I've already failed and the inevitable personal realization and self-reckoning is lagging behind the current available evidence, and everyone knows it but me—

It's started and I have no idea where to begin.

My phone rings. I pull over and answer. Vincent says he's sorry, wow, terrible idea to ask me to host an open house on such short notice, huge imposition but success never sleeps and neither does he now that he's doing a soft-launch trial for a new wearable nutrition patch called Verve, have I heard of it? Staying super loose dermally absorbing white willow bark, garcinia, green coffee bean plus sixteen hundred per cent of his daily recommended B12 which he can totally feel so he was up all night killing it trading mega-volatile junior oils and anyway how am I?

Struggle to compose myself, find a vantage point, high ground. "Honestly? I've been better. I think I let the stress of the open house get to me? Terrible sleep."

"Yeah? Gotta try these food patches, no time for being tired, but the reason I'm calling is that unit should've been a lock—"

Dig through my purse, pop a preventative Advil, watch a toddler in a blue rain slicker throw a handful of sand at a Canada goose, decide to borrow an idea from Eric Hull, get in front of this mess and tell Vincent I know, I was having trouble connecting and I'm working on using eye contact more effectively?

"Eye contact? Excellent! But to expand on what we talked about during your interview? In terms of presentation? Someone had this conversation with me early in my career and it was quite helpful. Our clients, local and international, all of them very well . . . ah . . . heeled? Wealthy clients. Lots of them! So there's an expectation of—"

I switch the phone to my other ear. "You're saying I need to dress—"

"Better. Attire? Okay? Casual is good? Chillaxed, always. But business casual . . . or even better . . . West Coast casual. Techies, designers? Find your own personal but appropriate style. With flair, like: wow! How about this? For inspiration? Think . . . a chrome Mies table with like tiny pink cherry blossoms in an antique Japanese vase? Or maybe something, you know, culturally appropriate to your uniqueness? And, uh, heritage?"

"Oh, sure, heritage. I get it. As in how? Exactly?"

Vincent grinds his teeth. "Um, you're the one who's . . . wait! Let you speak! How about you tell me? What I mean?"

"Oh, okay. You mean like a lotus flower resting on the dash of a tinted Ford Mustang parked in front of Caprice Nightclub?"

"Totally on the same page. Personally expressive, but within strictly predetermined parameters. Just a sec . . . ugh . . . this trading platform is stuuupid slooow. My traaade is taking fooooreverrr. Come on you stuuupid thiiing . . . there! It went through! Two hundred grand to an Albertan with an eye patch and a pickaxe! Gotta play to win. That's my balanced, long-term investment strategy. Anyway, okay? No biggie. We don't need to spend any more of my time on your problem, Jasminder. I'm looking forward to seeing you . . . do better?"

Dude's not getting off that easy. "Vincent? Wait a sec? I'm sorry, but could you give me a few more examples? Of what you expect?"

"Now? On my way out the door. Sorry. Did I mention my gruelling training ride? What don't you get?"

My mood's improving. Is the Advil kicking in? Or maybe it's the opportunity to manoeuvre Vincent into saying something he really doesn't want to say—

"I guess I need clarification on how you interpret business casual? Because for me—"

"Something a bit more tailored? And pressed? And also . . . neutral?"

"Neutral? Help me with that?"

"It's just . . . I'm out the door in ninety seconds. Sustained endurance phase. Very serious about having fun mountain biking. Grinding it out! You like donuts?"

"Yes but, trying to eat, y'know—"

·"Eat clean? You should definitely do that. Can't out-train a poor diet. I'm a honey cruller guy myself. After a ride, I can eat a dozen of the things. I don't, because I'm disciplined and way better than that. Burn four thousand calories this morning. *Poof!* Gonna have to wear some more nutrition—"

"Do they make those patches in honey cruller?"

"Honey . . . ha! Jasminder? Easy to like! Anyway, take home: busy week ahead of you, dress more appropriately, mega-wealthy clients, do better, awesome."

"Vincent? You keep saying *appropriate*. You clearly have an idea of appropriate in mind. Could you communicate that to me, clearly?"

A long pause. "I mean . . . greys and blacks?"

"Oh. Got it. So no striped knee socks and plaid skirts or corduroy pants or red cardigans? No more of those?"

"Not no more, just . . . less? Not a company rule. Ugh! No way. A friendly suggestion? This isn't some crony old-boys' business club. This is Marigold! In Vancouver! In 2011! Of course I'd never tell you, directly, how to dress. That would suck! You being gifted the power to guess how to please me is way better than me telling you how to do it, don't you think? But many of your colleagues, the females like you, I think they like black? Because it's slimming? And easy?"

It's not easy if I need to buy a whole new wardrobe. I force a smile so the bastard hears it in my voice. "Business casual in grey and black. I'll work on that. Vincent? I'm really grateful—"

"Sure. Of course. Listen. I affirm lifelong learning. I went through the same thing, and now look at me. Dominating! Exciting times! There's a whole city out there . . ."

He's gone, leaves me wanting to throw my phone into traffic, hating the fact he can call whenever he wants.

I spend the rest of a lousy Saturday searching second-hand stores for business outfits I can afford, then drive to my sister's house in Shaughnessy at seven. Meeta's late. No one's home. The house is a restored Southern colonial perched on a half-acre of rolling lawn and obsessively sheared topiary. I settle on the porch swing, listen to water percolate through a stacked slate fountain, check my phone. No messages. Check my email. Nothing. Spend a few minutes watching YouTube music compilations, liking how the Dead Kennedys singing *let's lynch the landlord* contrasts with the sea-breeze twill linens on Meeta's porch swing. The music makes me think of my mother in a vague, semi-conscious way, as if she's the one who's gone, not Amar. A half-hour slips by and I'm freezing, irritated. Grab a shawl from my Honda, wrap it over my shoulders, and when the car door slams closed I wonder what it would be like if I didn't have Meeta and instead of sleeping at her place when I don't have the strength to go home I had to—

This is the persona of a twenty-six-year-old Canadian woman with six months of post-secondary education who sleeps in the backseat of her Prelude. The rubber seal around her sunroof is cracked and separating. Water's been dripping on her legs all night. She's piled clothes over her head in the hope that someone peering through the window won't see her. It's still early, pre-dawn. The light is diffuse, cloud-softened, and cold. Her car is wedged between two dumpsters behind a Chinese restaurant. Seagulls peck and tear at overstuffed garbage bags, scratch and skitter across the car roof, leave the windshield smeared in rotten eggshells, coffee grounds, regurgitated cigarette butts.

It's not a good sleeping spot. She's parked illegally on private property. Soon the restaurant employees will arrive, if they haven't already. She doesn't want to put dishwashers and prep cooks in the position of having to bang on the car and ask her to leave, or call the cops. A good spot is both private and public, in a neighbourhood not too posh but not completely down and out. For this reason she avoids parking anywhere west of Cambie and north of Venables. Younger guys living in camper vans with their dogs might feel okay parked outside the warehouses around Powell, but she doesn't. A good spot is somewhere the parking meter guys don't check often and there are no NIMBY homeowners out for morning walks who will hassle or rat on her.

Last night she slept with her head rammed into the armrest and her knees pushed against the door and she can feel the knot in her shoulder that will move through her neck to become a brutal headache by midafternoon. Her sleeping bag is bunched and twisted around her waist. Everything is damp, sticky, frigid. The overwhelming sensation is of discomfort, followed by an anxiety she's too proud to call fear. The young Canadian woman is wearing the same clothes she wore yesterday, plus an extra pair of wool socks, a fleece jacket, and a toque. But the damp gets in.

Something thunks on the roof, startling her. Only a gull. She grimaces against the gross taste in her mouth, tries to remember what woke her up. Was it the awful seagulls? Or did she hear someone working a sharp piece of metal into the locked door? She waits and listens, breathing silently, trying to hear beyond the noise of feeding seagulls. Is someone standing outside her car? Sometimes, often, every single night, she lies awake thinking about what she'd do if someone tried to smash into her Honda and harm her. She imagines scenarios that end with her successfully driving away her attacker with the minimal amount of harm to either party. She wonders:

What are suitable weapons of self-defence in this situation? A kitchen knife? How big? Paring-knife size? Or bigger? She knows nothing about knives in particular or violence in general. She's frustrated at herself for not knowing what weapon she should have, for seeming to know so little about anything. She reminds herself she never expected to be in this situation, that she needs to think more positively about herself, and the fact that she uses the phrase *think positively about myself* without irony, without the smirky humour she was known for at Langara, makes her very worried about what she's losing or has already lost.

What she wants is to be alone in her bed—a real bed—and watch shitty TV all morning. She wants the luxury of time, of not being forced to get up to turn on the car heater, pee, brush her teeth. She wants to walk naked and safe from her bedroom to her bathroom. She realizes she has to pee very badly. She wants to blow-dry her hair. She wants her makeup in a single drawer instead of a travel bag with a busted zipper. She wants her notebooks and files out of the damp.

Completely awake now, and freezing. She blows on her cupped hands. No one knows she sleeps in her car. That's how she thinks of it: *I sleep in my car.* It's like camping. She doesn't live on the street. Only real homeless people live on the street. Even now the social stratification is clearly defined. Other, much less fortunate people live on the street. They go to shelters. They use food banks. She's just sleeping in her car until things turn around. Things *will* turn around. True, she didn't expect to be sleeping in her car through the winter. It was one thing in summer, when it was warm and mostly dry and she could relax at the beach until late evening, reading and people-watching. Winter is different.

She decides to get up, tosses the tangled mess of blankets and clothes off her head, peers outside. The parking lot's empty. The damp is in everything. The day hasn't begun and she's already exhausted. She feels another cold coming on. She's been sick almost constantly this winter. A gull hops past the window and the motion conjures the image of a man peering in. But there's no one. She's irritated with herself for forgetting to fill her water bottle. Even a small sip would be better than nothing. The nasty taste in her mouth won't leave until she's brushed her teeth, which won't happen until she drives to a community rec centre. She knows the locations and hours of every rec centre in the city. Sometimes she sees people she knows, regulars, and they're largely silent with one another, no small talk in the change room, because morning is a private time, before the day, before there should be other people at all.

The thought of driving reminds the woman about her ruined brakes. How much is a brake job? And the thought of not having any money reminds her she feels disgusting: disgusting unbrushed teeth, disgusting clammy sweaty skin, disgusting unwashed hair. How can she see anyone like this? How can she go to work? This feeling will remain even after she showers. It will be in her voice, in how she walks, in her smile. The feeling will remain until she learns to forgive herself or cultivate the hatred that masquerades as strength. She wonders if people can sense or intuit her living situation? Do they *know*? Her brakes might cost as much as five hundred dollars. Maybe more. She doesn't have a mechanic she trusts, is afraid of getting ripped off.

She resolves not to think about money for the time being. It's too early. But the thought is always with her. Money. It's not a thing anymore, on the outside; it's another fear, hardwired, internal. There is no respite. Her breath rises inside the Honda while more gulls, attracted by the buffet of rotting food scraps in the bins outside, arrive to feed. The birds tear and thrash against one another. She wants to be generous, understand they're animals living instinctively, but right now she can see only ugliness in their grey-black bodies and flicking beaks.

She's woken to the sound of insane screaming very close by. She's woken to the sound of a woman being thrown against her Honda and stayed silent, motionless, dying of shame but not moving to help, choosing cowardly self-preservation over her humanity. She's confronted the fact that the idea and reality of herself are two different things and vary depending on circumstance. She's woken to the sound of a cop's flashlight banging on her windshield. She's seen a cop in uniform and felt only fear.

At Langara College she sat in elegant lecture halls with raised seating arranged in a semicircle around a polished-oak podium. The lecture halls had excellent acoustics. The woman was attentive, hard-working, earned excellent grades. She's been honked at while peeing beside her car. She's been screamed at by a woman in an apartment while peeing against a cedar hedge. At Langara she heard lectures and had heated discussions on topics such as truth to power, authenticity, credibility, advocacy, objective truth, harm limitation, neutrality or the impossibility thereof. She learned words that revealed intellectually invigorating ideas and the ideas revealed a system of value she didn't know she believed in until she was at school: faith in the tenacity and fuck-you stubbornness of truth. Some of her classmates agonized over its existence. She was too pragmatic or dull or clear-headed or literal-minded to involve herself in that conversation. Truth exists.

She tells herself this now, as she shivers with cold, and the statement is so cherished it has yet to become caustic. She tucks her hands in her armpits. Mornings are the only time she has to think. In the evening she'll be too tired. Now—and particularly on mornings like this—she feels the vitality of the conversations she had in college, their impact on and proximity to her lived reality, waning. They're becoming an abstraction, a luxury. Soon she'll disappear from the conversation altogether.

She uses a baby wipe to clean her face. Another to scrub her hands. The Honda stinks of fast-food wrappers, dirty laundry, coconut hand sanitizer. Some of her former classmates are doing all right in their careers and she wonders why she isn't, what is it about her specifically, what fault of personality or attitude or genetics is holding her back, and what does she need to do to change? Her legs are cramping. She can't feel her right shoulder. She doesn't believe in luck, bad or good, or in fate, in being born unlucky, in having a bad go, in being beaten before she began, but she's beginning to understand the allure of such beliefs, their despairing comfort. She's not yet angry, although sometimes she wishes she were. She remains stubborn in the belief that her life will turn around.

The dream of radical self-transformation is always with her, as is the desire to run. *Who can I be somewhere else?* Her full bladder is nearly unbearable. She estimates how long it'll take to wriggle out of her sodden cocoon, crawl into the front seat, start the car, warm it up, drive to the YMCA, dig her towel and bathroom handbag out of the mess, hurry inside the YMCA? At least thirty-five minutes. She decides she's going to pee outside, soon, behind the restaurant. She notes how little that bothers her this morning. She'll pee behind the dumpsters with the seagulls and whoever the fuck else eyeing her. She doesn't care. She knows it's a mistake to conflate career and material success with self-worth but look at her, she thinks: *Look at me.* It's impossible not to conflate them.

She wonders—

My sister's SUV rolls up the driveway. Afraid I might startle her, I stand and wave so she recognizes me while she's still safely inside her vehicle. Meeta honks a greeting. The sound feels abrasive but I smile anyway, hope I don't look so tired she gets worried.

Mark Ward

Sunday morning recon mission, three a.m., nice and early. Wake up, eat a boiled egg, take the elevator down to the parking garage beneath the Coal Harbour condo Clint hooked me up with yesterday after work, climb in the Ford, drive to Jericho Beach, park outside a house overlooking the Pacific, get comfy, smoke, study the Williams house, real keen. Looks like the offspring of a wwii bunker and a Fabergé egg, like a prison for rich people. A palace, one of many owned by Mr. Craig Williams. A palace here, a palace there, sprinkled around the globe. Why not? The man's worked hard, deserves his money.

Sitting alone in the Ford, breath visible, rain beating down, feeling purposeful, reconning Williams's money-can't-buy-taste mansion, fixing his location in my mind, picturing him sleeping safe and sound, warm and tucked in, thinking about the homeless in the city, sleeping rough and cold, men, women, children, and that gets me thinking about the kids in Mr. Williams's outerwear factory, flames rising up, factory walls superheating, DEATHFIRE, cinders sticking to flesh, lungs inflating tiny chests, hair igniting, a writhing horror piled against the locked doors, GODFIRE, toxic smoke, we made their women scream, how long did it take to die like that, fifteen minutes, an hour? And then it hits me, like it sometimes does, raw emotion, unfettered, so powerful it smacks my head against the seat, makes every muscle in my body tense, makes me shake, spit, snarl, a savagery of raging heart and righteousness.

And after that li'l episode? Mellow, easy. Emptied out.

Roll down the window, let the rain in, think about how brutal we are to ourselves, to one another, to life on earth. How vicious the culture is to what's best in us. Was it always this way? And how there's only a single story now, a total lack of viable alternative visions. Not that long ago there was still talk of alternatives—most of them puerile or idiotic or straight-up absurd, sure, shunned and lunatic rants, but still necessary, as difference is necessary to any fully functioning ecosystem—and how the conversation of alternatives has largely vanished except among an impotent coterie.

These questions, like rain on the roof, beating incessantly, thrumming through my head while I study a mansion with darkened windows and dream of an old-fashioned bloodletting, conscious of not making the best rational sense, or maybe of being too rational, aware of the flaws in my thinking, or at least some of them. Market dynamics. Negative externality. Aware that all killers, to one extent or another, rationalize their actions. Put differently: If the world were a better place, would the thought of kicking in Mr. Williams's door . . . feel so commanding?

. . . and wondering, at what point, precisely, I went fully batshit insane?

Was it back in April of 2005 when I found Mr. Alfred Combs, kiddie-porn-king extraordinaire, reclining on his Corbusier? When I beat the man with a tire iron until my brother stepped in to stop me from killing him?

Was that when I went insane?

Or was it when I fled the crime scene and went to work as per usual? Did I go insane the day after the near-murder, when I waited for the guilt, grief, regret, and—unlike poor Raskolnikov—it never arrived, and in fact the opposite, I found myself smiling, not overjoyed but content, feeling like I'd done something nice for a stranger, a kind gesture, like holding the door open for an elderly lady? Was I insane for feeling I had made a definitive, concrete, and specific contribution to making the world a better place by almost murdering Mr. Alfred Combs? Was I insane not so much for the act, because murder is common, but for my response to it, which was basically: I need to go back and finish the job, proper?

Everything unknown, everything uncertain.

Maybe that's as it should be.

At five a.m. the lights in Craig Williams's waterfront home turn on, interrupting me, probably a good thing. At five fifteen the target emerges. The entryway light reveals Williams's face clearly, a bold-looking man, strong nose and chin, a take-charge kind of guy wearing minimalist running shoes designed to strengthen the ankles, a stylish cobalt-blue track suit and a light blue running jacket with the hood up to shed rain. Our biathlete out for a morning training run. Staying fit, eating well, courting longevity.

Mr. Williams pauses at the edge of his property, taps his watch, no doubt synching to his online fitness tracker, then begins jogging west toward the university endowment lands. I watch him go, and satisfied with the morning's work, fire up the Ford.

Drive to Pacific Centre mall, hunker down and try to sleep until the Apple Store opens, slink inside, buy a laptop from some sneering, golf-shirt-wearing techie, think about Doyle's shotgun, laying into the joint, *chk-boom chk-boom*, scattering bystanders and those creepo-cult Apple salespeople, let's see the tech wizards trouble-shoot a buckshot cone, I disown you, usurper, pretender, no one opened a laptop and started speaking in tongues, no one ever flayed their flesh for a fucking cellphone, I disavow you, liar, naked emperor, walking out of the store sweating, feeling like a bug in the program, feeling outdated and obsolete, stunned by fluorescent light, self-conscious, stupid, bloodshot eyes and picked scabs, secretly hoping there's an updated version of me out there, beta copy, ready to be downloaded, made compatible.

Carl "Blitzo" Reed

Private jet from Whistler to Calgary. Window seat. In the rain shadow east of the Coast Mountains, rocketing over rolling blue-green pine forests bisected by crisp, clear-cut geometry. In gentle terrain like this loggers use a machine called a feller buncher. Like a go-fast boat, there's nothing quite as imaginative as naming an object after what it does. I press my face against the Plexiglas, try and discern a pattern hidden in the clear-cuts, pipe and power lines, these needy scrawls like contemporary Nazca lines, wonder and awe and flawed understanding, only instead of ancient astro-astronomy this is astro-investment. Astro-industry.

Perhaps the feeling is the same. Everything refers to something else, but it's no longer possible to grasp the whole. Fragments will have to do. The risk is in focusing on the wrong fragment, a diversionary red herring. The enemy knows we have finite resources: energy, time, even money. They've become very sophisticated in their disinformation strategies. Psychological manipulation. The tactic now is to reveal everything, betray all secrets, overwhelm the processor, a flash grenade aimed at the collective mind. If everything's true, nothing is.

"Michael? Why am I dressed like a matador?"

"You don't remember? After the brewery meeting? You challenged Holdout to a—"

"Nah, I'd never. But I am so loving these sparkly pink sequins."

The patterns are there for those willing to look. This I accept as a matter of faith. "Like in these drawings," I say, holding up the sketchbook appropriated from the brewery kid in the burlap sack. "Tell me I'm off my rocker?"

Michael sets his tablet down, picks up the sketchbook, studies it. The man is an umbilical cord connecting me to earth. It's a love-hate thing.

Holdout's excited to be on the plane. Curlicue tail acquiver, snuffling, hopping on seats, trying to see out. I tell him he's way too cute, sucking up. The pig answers by choking down a mouthful of aisle carpet. The brewery kids weren't wrong about the subversive power of happiness. Their timing's off, is all. Mistaking reification for actualization. Mistaking a multitude of niche products for meaningful choice—

"Yup. You're way off your rocker. Nothing here but shitty drawings."

"Try flipping it upside down?"

Michael takes a look, says no, just upside-down shitty drawings, his tone not unkind, tears a page from the sketchbook and feeds it to Holdout. I watch the pig's lips saw back and forth across the page and think about the images being rearranged in his gut. Blurred by stomach acid. Organic alchemy.

"Why'd you tell the poseurs about Bute?"

"I didn't," he says. "I told you."

I reach out to hold my friend's hand, happy to discover he's still warm, fears of vampirism lingering. Truth is I didn't kill anybody out there in the sullied wilds. But I gave the command to Caltrop, if not in so many words, and for fifteen years Heather and I made love in a six-by-eight cinderblock room while oily-faced guards peered through the observation window. Wasn't as sexy as it sounds. Michael's the reason I wasn't murdered in jail. He was outside, staying connected, making sure we still had *juice*, and not of the fresh-pressed variety. It would've been very easy for Michael to cut me loose. Justifiable, even. And if the situation were reversed—

"Green Lead is winding down," Michael says. "Everything does. You feel it. It's okay."

"I'm still seeking inspiration."

"You're too old to be inspired. Bow out with dignity."

"You think it's really Bo Xi?"

"You forgot about him."

"Uh . . ."

"If it is Bo Xi, Caltrop's on it. Our job is to not fuck the operation up."

"Operation? What?"

"Just . . . let me deal with Vincent Peele, Carl. He's an errand boy, but he's not an idiot."

"And that'll be that. We could . . . let it go? Move on? Couldn't we?"

Michael glares out the window. "Bo Xi was chair of the board. He pushed to send the goon squad into Bute—"

"So long ago, almost like it never happened."

"Marjorie? Tincan Bill? You'd let them become a never-happened?"

"The North Vancouver property development is a lure."

"We draw the enemy into the open." Michael smiles. "Vincent calls his boss Tectonic. So big he makes the earth move. I shouldn't need to tell you to be careful, but I will anyway. Be careful."

"I'd like to get kind of insanely high." The oddity is, those years of incarceration were the best of my marriage. Conjugal visits. Nothing like fifteen scheduled minutes a week to add urgency. We should all be so lucky. "What's in Calgary that could possibly be worth going to Calgary?"

Michael says good question, picks up his tablet. "A meeting at the Delta with an aide from the prime minister's office."

"Prime-ministerial projects?" I'm fighting it down. Panic. Need. Michael knows me better than that, so I grab my rig, ask what their ask is, start prepping something uplifting.

"The prime minister's aide intends to sell us on a scheme to seed the atmosphere with experimental chemicals. A covert global warming reduction strategy. Of course the prime minister himself is completely hands-off. Admission of guilt, tar sands politics—"

"Carbon-based fuels are the next tobacco. The next drunk driving," Holdout says.

I pat my piggy on the ass, say yeah, we'll be biking around, wagging our fingers at the blue-collar reprobates who have to drive between work and home because they can't afford to live downtown.

Holdout gobbles a plastic seat cover. "Social shaming. There'll be bylaws. Zoning. No vehicles within twenty metres of a building entrance. Prohibitive licensing fees to own a vehicle that consumes more than x litres per kilometre. Only the rich will have the money to drive, and only the poor will need to."

"Perfection demands sacrifice," I say.

Michael smiles, sad. "The more certain we are, the less tolerant we become."

Holdout wriggles between me and Michael, leaks snot on my lap. *I love you in all your unglory.* "Nobody says, 'I might be wrong, let's go to war!'"

"I'm imperfect, those motherfuckers deserve to die!"

The three of us laugh, nudge one another, chillin' with my crew.

"Hold me again," I say to Michael. "It was nice."

"No."

"Touch—"

"No, Blitz."

"Then leap out of the airplane with me. At least? You were wrong about death being the only achievable human perfection. There's another. Even more terrifying."

"So?"

"So let's make the leap. I'd trade five seconds of perfection with you for whatever else this life has in store."

Michael sets his hand in mine. "Spending too much time with the brewery kids? You're being—"

"Emotional? Fuck you."

Holdout curls in my lap, pretends not to listen.

"Hysterical."

"Okay then, fuck you twice. The most destructive phrase ever uttered: *You're being too emotional.* How much war? How much killing could've been prevented if we only allowed ourselves to be—"

"Rage. Jealousy. Hate. They all motivate murder. They're called crimes of passion."

"True. But all the big killing's done for a reason. Logic. Intellect. Tyranny."

"I think you're wrong. I think emotion comes first, hatred, *then* the rationalization, then the killing."

"Then why's it so much easier to convince yourself murder is justified—on a rational level—than it is to actually *feel* okay about it? Because the intellect's a liar, that's why. A lying, petty tyrant. I can hate someone, or a group of people, sure, hate them so much I dream about killing them. But without an attempt at rational justification it would stop there. It's the mind that convinces me I can live with myself. The mind makes big killing possible."

"If you don't have the desire, there's nothing to rationalize."

"It seems a safe bet to say every one of us has the desire. At some point."

"What I'm hearing is . . . you don't want to go through with Bo Xi?"

Holdout lifts his head, growls.

"Michael? Was my potbellied pig growling at me? It's so unsettling I need to do a speedball. You in?"

"What?"

"Huh? Drawbacks to the prime-ministerial global warming thingamajig?"

"The program might be a dry run for disseminating a swarm of hostile nanobots. Think locusts, only with more bite. And one more thing, before you hit that. Bo Xi and Vincent Peele's development project? Remember why Green Lead is investing? Our cover story?"

I rattle my brain, say no.

"Still in prototype. A cutting-edge self-contained communal waste recycling and regeneration system."

"A condominium that eats its own shit?"

"Zero-waste lifestyle. Zero-style. Anyway, it's a selling feature. You don't remember the play? Dammit, Carl. I've been telling you for weeks."

I lie, tell him bells are ringing.

"Your wife wants the North Van property to build a green space."

"A what?"

"A park."

"Oh, yeah. Heather might've mentioned. So you're feeding her intel about Peele and Marigold."

"You're certainly not. Anyway, plan is we pull out at the eleventh hour, Peele fails to secure the property, Bo Xi surfaces to push the deal through, we close the book on him, end of story is your wife gets the one-of-a-kind property and there's a new park in North Vancouver. Happy ending. Except. Listen up, Carl. This is important. Peele's recruited . . . two unique assets. Wannabe players. Mid-level Valley Boys."

"Ruffians?"

"For sure. Brothers."

"Sounds hot."

"These two are total throwaways. But possessing a certain skill set. One of ours, a real estate lawyer we planted inside Marigold, got roughed up—"

"Roughed up?"

"Beat half to death. In front of his wife and son. Couple nights ago. Who knows what he told the gangsters. We're vulnerable. Okay? So I was wondering—"

"Funny. Mind-meld. I was thinking about contacting him."

"Who?"

"Caltrop. Our redoubtable man-at-arms?"

Michael slips his hand from mine, puts it on my shoulder. "You still able to make contact? He still . . . answers your call?"

At a certain level of influence the causal chain disintegrates. The logic of *A* following *B* no longer holds. That's what the brewery kids don't understand. They demand instant turnaround between action and result. Impatient. Foolish. I've learned to play the long game, but I envy their lack of substance, gumming their way through fire-lit dances in Playa dust. It's exhausting, trying to keep track of the systems, seeking a through line, a thread to follow. Complexity's emergent, leaves me feeling glitchy. I rub my temples, acutely aware of my limitations. The plane's nose dips into a pocket of unsettled air, sends my insides lofting. "Michael? Are we still doing good?"

"On the whole?"

"Yes. And including Caltrop?"

"You're still kicking your own ass. It's destroying you. Your family."

"I wanted to know everything. Ran myself ragged trying to stay current. Now I get exhausted trying to keep everything out."

"Crotchety."

"If you won't love me, there's only one thing that will make me a better person."

"I need you to stop talking like that."

Atonement. Guilt is a powerful motivator. To do a little more good than bad in the world. Caltrop didn't just murder those stooges. He strung them up. Gutted them. Fed their insides to ravens. Might've been a wolverine, too, elusive bastards. And how much good needs to be done, to make up for—

Michael turns to the window. Cloudless western light streams in, chiselling his face. I make to kiss his cheek but he nudges me aside, tugs the shade down. "Cut yourself some slack, Carl. You think the Homathko goons are still paying for it?"

"Brock Hollings shot himself in the face in eighty-nine. Andy 'Crank' McCoy drove his Harley into a telephone pole in ninety-four. The last died in 2002, crushed by a big piece of steel on a rig outside Fort Mac. So do I think they're still paying? Yes and no."

Michael squeezes my hand. "Those were natural deaths, Carl. Natural all the way. Am I wrong?"

I tell him I wouldn't be the one to ask. I was in prison. But Caltrop wasn't.

"What's done is done. You'd do better to focus on the living. Your daughter."

The living? I almost spit. Michael's in the mood for giving credit where it isn't due. The girl's a paragon, but sometimes I have to make sure she's not plugged into an outlet. Like her mother, but with more ambition, which is . . . whoa. These kids. At nine they can recite the elements of the periodic table, play a Bach concerto, hack into Goldman Sachs, write a love poem in iambic pentameter. But ask how they feel and they draw a blank, or they natter until they create a blank. The next revolution will be an unpredictable affair, defined by completely inappropriate affect. A comrade will get blown up and the kids will burst into laughter. They'll sob while making love. Wires crossed. Perhaps it's better that way? The problem with war is its reductive appeal. If war makes sense, maybe it's better if the kids don't.

Mark Ward

Vincent Peele has an office, a suit, and a mouth. The office, like Peele, is contemporary in the West Coast style, pseudo-scruff designed for effect from start to finish. Rough-cut cedar planks provide texture against polished steel and granite. A view north over the city. Posh without being stuffy. Relaxed while conveying the essential message: we're rich, but we're cool, so we're even better. All Clint told me is the guy's a real estate lawyer for the development branch of Marigold Group, the company spearheading Solstice Homes, and our inside contact for securing the North Van property.

Peele's behind his desk, talking, muddy blue eyes not focused on much of anything. Me and Clint are facing the lawyer, Clint sitting hunched forward, me flung back in my chair like Peele's carrying something virulent. I'm watching the lawyer's hands. Peele likes fluttering them around, wiggling his fingers like a fucking necromancer. Creepy pale hands. Never seen a day of real work. It hits me that Peele's practising this set of oratory gestures on us. Rehearsing. He's a little older than me and Clint. Early thirties. Impeccably crafted beard. Hair parted neat to the side. Dark-framed glasses. Looks ridiculous, like a news reporter from the eighties.

"People complain," Peele says above the electric whine of a bus out on Broadway. "In such an incredibly vibrant market that's bound to happen, sourpusses . . ."

Peele wasn't born rich. I can see that. But not poor either. The middle, now close to making it big. Maybe the worst.

"But—gentlemen? I don't say this to anyone, but you two . . . I have the feeling we're on the same page? You know what gets me a little down?" Peele taps his desk, pauses, like he's struggling to articulate a transcendent truth. "I'm an upfront guy. Used to play lacrosse. Can't play lacrosse without being an upfront guy. Agreed?"

Me and Clint say fuck all. My brother's wearing a cheap-ass suit I've never seen before. The black fabric's saggy and stretched; makes him look like a flooring salesman. Clint doesn't know a thing about lacrosse, and neither do I, and that's why Peele's talking about it. Who knows lacrosse? Not many people. I have half a mind to ask Peele what position he played, but the sneaky prick probably has enough brains to google whatever he's bullshitting about. Instead I look at the art: one First Nations painting, two generic abstract things, Asian calligraphy on scrolls manufactured to look old, a landscape of a farm in the Prairies. A collection chosen to say absolutely nothing except to point to the owner's diverse and accommodating taste.

Peele pauses mid-thought, scratches his beard, studies his immaculate fingernails.

"Seven hundred times a day," I tell him.

"Pardon me?"

"That's how often a man touches his beard."

Peele frowns. "I did not know that. Factoid! Where was I?"

"You were feeling a little down? Beards also collect fecal matter."

A photocopier beeps and whirs in the reception room behind Peele's office door. Marigold occupies the top two floors of an unremarkable six-storey office building. Smaller operation than I thought. Residential one floor beneath us, commercial and development here on the sixth floor. Maybe five people on staff.

"Fecal—"

"Particles in the air. Like a walking shit sponge."

Clint sighs, presses his fists together, glares at the floor.

"Oh, sure. Ha!" Peele waves a stack of papers at Clint. "Good thing I'm meticulous about personal hygiene. Almost OCD?" The lawyer gives me a pointed look, rubs hand sanitizer into his palms, fills the room with raspberry-ginger smell. Then he stands abruptly, snatches a Kleenex from a desk drawer, hands it to me, points at my arm. "Unlike you, uh . . . Mark?" Peele gives me a disgusted look, retreats behind his desk. So I'm bleeding a bit from something. Press the Kleenex to my elbow. Then a thought from nowhere, not totally welcome, maybe connected to the traffic noises outside, car horns, commuters, and I wonder what Ryan's sleeping spot looks like. What kind of blankets? Is he invisible until you step on him?

"Can I confide in you gentlemen?" Peele says, grimacing while I sop blood from my arm. I can tell he's not quite sure what to think of me, so I'm feeling not bad. I consider asking Peele if the beard's new, but before I can get a word in the lawyer takes a breath and launches. "Of course. Best part of my job is the people I meet. Different backgrounds, different ideas. Like you two? Very different than me! Nothing in common at all. If you're not meeting new people all the time, it's easy to slip into a rut of thought. People challenge you. To reconsider how you feel? Take that first-edition painting I see you admiring, Mark."

Hearing my name from the guy's mouth, I dunno, it makes me grit my teeth, pine for an Oxy. Peele sees I hate him saying my name, picks his lower lip, repeats my name, very slow, tonguing it. The man has eyes like the lead singer of a boy band and the mouth of a piranha.

"Do you like that painting? Does it resonate with you?"

"Which one?"

"The one with the . . . you know? On the left? Bright colours and the . . . uh, swirly things?"

"The Northwest Coast First Nations painting? Those are ovoids."

Peele leaps to his feet. "That's the one, Mark! Ovoids? First Nations? No probs! I appreciate you didn't say 'Indian.' Cultural sensitivity is important to the Marigold Family. I'm all about tolerance and having fun. We do lungi Fridays! To show how in tune we are? But some people . . . aren't quite as in tune as us? An issue of education? Are you educated?"

"High school, yeah."

Peele runs his fingers through his hair, or tries to, but can't get through the sticky product. "But not university?"

"Nah. Fucked it."

Peele checks his phone, fires off a text. Clint does the same.

My brother's been sitting quietly through all this. Almost attentively. But under the cheap suit, Clint's shoulders are bunched. Man has the finest blue-collar bullshit detector around. Peele must be killing him. Which proves how bad he needs this deal—

"Studying where?"

"UBC. For a bit."

Peele tosses his phone on the desk and settles into his seat, legs crossed at the knees, creepo hands folded on his lap. I slump lower in my chair, yawn, stretch my feet out, fold my hands behind my head, push my crotch up at Peele so my nuts are centred in his field of view.

The lawyer gives me a solid look of contempt, feels real familiar, been seeing it my whole life. I ball up the bloody Kleenex, drop it on the floor.

"Mark, great school. The University of British Columbia. Right here in stunning Vancouver! Ovoids, Indians, awesome. My alma mater. We're fortunate to have world-class schools. In fact, we're fortunate in so many ways." Peele jerks his chin at the mountain view framing his desk. "I'm like, wow, gratitude. Of course everyone wants to move here!" A percussive laugh, completely self-satisfied. "I mean, look what we have!"

Peele raises his hand, begins ticking the list with his fingers. "Oceans! Mountains! Rivers! Lakes! Incredible opportunities for outdoor recreation. I won't bore you with how good of a mountain biker I am. Do you guys ride? I could show you some incredible trails—"

"No," Clint says, stretching, making sure Peele sees the tats on his hands and neck. "Used to dirt bike. Not much anymore. Work. Fucked-up back."

Peele's tongue flicks across his lips. "Dirt bike? Ugh, but okay. Shared use. Plenty of room. You can go ride up-valley, in ... wherever? Abbotsford? That's what makes this place so amazing. Mountain bike, ski or snowboard, surf, trail run, rock climb—the list goes on and on!"

"Sled?" I ask.

"Pardon me? As in, Ski-Doo?"

"Yeah. Backcountry sledneck?"

"Motorized?"

"Full fuckin' throttle. *Waaa! Waaa!*"

"Um, no? Not here? Maybe Prince George?"

I got both hands clenched on the chair, trying not to drown in the aggro-competitive energy flowing from the lawyer. Peele glances at his phone, scratches his beard, lifts a second finger. "And then we have Vancouver's cutting-edge food. Ethnic, everything inclusive. Sushi. Dim sum. Tacos. Big fan of fusion dim sum tacos. I eat out like every night I'm not in a cooking class. And don't forget food trucks! An integral part of what makes Vancouver so desirable—"

"They have food trucks everywhere. In every city. All over the world."

"Sure. But not like here."

A third finger comes up, wiggles at me. I picture the room on fire with the lawyer tied to his desk while he says, "Then we have our incredible weather. For Canada? Warm, lovely weather. At least you don't have to shovel it!" Peele mimes shovelling snow, chuckles.

"And, I mean, weather's free, right? Free is good . . . if you're poor! Look at it out there. Gorgeous. March and it's already—what? Ten degrees? Friend came in from Winterpeg yesterday. Minus thirty-five. Ha! And that's not counting wind chill! I was like, no way. Uh-uh. No thanks. You poor souls. You losers suffering out there in Winterpeg and wherever, basically everywhere east and north of here, which is everywhere. I mean, life's too short! Why would anyone ever live there? I said that to them. I'm a casual, upfront kind of guy, so I said: 'Why do you live in that freezing hellhole?' They said: 'Work.' I said: '*Pffft*. I'm staying right here, thank you very much, where I belong.'"

Clint fires up a round of *Angry Birds*. Peele has a side table covered in trophies and framed photos of him mountain biking and snowboarding. He sees me looking at the pictures, says he's no longer so competitive, it's all about having fun, raises a fourth finger. "Then we have . . . I mean, look at that downtown core. A lovely, livable city. Masterpiece of urban planning. Did you know, planners visit from all over the world to study how amazing we are? Had you heard that? Walkability means something to families today, especially when we tell them it should. Who wants a car? Not me. Not smart, in-tune urbanites my age and younger. We've done polls. Cars are expensive, ugly, polluting, very twentieth century. Wrapped up with Arab oil, acid rain, manufacturing, dying industry. Even strip malls. Can you imagine? *Strip malls?* Ugh . . . obesity? Thigh chafing? Who wants that? Biiig branding problem. Ha! Get it? Biiig!" Peele pauses to see if I laugh. I don't. "Anyway, Mark, live where you work. That's the future for people who can afford it. We're not even putting parking garages in our developments, which is super sustainable, allows us to get like ten more units in each building. So we win twice! That's how committed we are to green cities. A statement, really, about what's important in life. It's about creating a city where everyone, all kinds of people, productive, well educated, high-earning, money from all over the world, can come and walk to work and raise a family and go mountain biking. Helping manifest that super-inclusive vision."

There's basically only one thing you can do, I realize, and that's hold your breath. So I do. Kind of a game, to see if my breath gives out before Peele stops talking. Clint giggles, shows me his phone, a picture of a stacked naked chick pressure-washing a mud-caked ATV.

Peele asks if he can take a peek.

My brother says what?

"Your phone? What you were showing Mark? Being distracted, rude, not fully present for me talking?"

Clint lifts the phone so Peele can see the naked chick. Peele stuffs a bit of beard in his mouth, chews, seems about to say something, stops himself. His hands do their fluttering thing, then he tells my brother to maybe put the phone on his desk? So Clint can pay proper attention?

What's gonna happen is we shit-kick this two-faced lawyer, maybe light him on fire if I'm lucky. Because no way is Clint gonna take that from—

My brother stands, rolls his head side to side, sets his phone on the edge of Peele's desk, sits down. Peele looks like a coyote scenting a half-eaten doe and I feel him sucking the air from the room, suffocating me—

Peele lifts a fifth finger, actually a thumb. "And as I was saying, Vancouver! This is what it's all about. We're a global city now. Part of a vast network of global citizens." Peele does a circular hand motion to indicate the expansiveness of the globe. "Multicultural. Conscientious. Accepting. Of course I go to Pride. It's funny! I mean . . . fun? Those people are so . . . alive! This city, it's changing. And that's good. I mean, Mark, don't move to one of the world's most vibrant and dynamic cities and complain about how expensive it is! Don't do that. That's not West Coast at all. Get lost, we're too inclusive for you! Sourpuss, downer, you missed the boat! Because this city . . . it's more like a village, really. Or a family? A big happy interracial family with like three doting parents, two of which are same sex—"

Clint looks up. "Need three working people in a house to afford—"

"Shit," I say. "Need six. Average income—"

"See?" Peele says, nodding vigorously. "How living in such a desirable city is changing us in ways we have yet to fathom? Like, restructuring the . . . *hmm* . . . stodgy conventional oldness of our lives into something more progressive, seeping edge? Single-family homes? Wasteful, antiquated. Who wants to live like their grand-parents? Money's tight because you're a loser? We get like ten Vancouverites to a house, multiple mortgages, easy-peasy! Resource efficient. Very quiet inoffensive sex. Can't upset the neighbours in the next room! Like in the old country, or Bangladesh, or wherever. Either that or the houses sit empty, accumulating wealth simply by existing. Wow! Anyway, gentlemen, I affirm our global city. Allow me to toot my own horn? *Toot toot*, ha! I've been in this business a long time. Like, four years. Two more, maybe eighteen months depending on what the market does, and I retire. Truth! I've sold property to all kinds of people. They come to Vancouver for a visit, to see family, or on holiday, and they come to me and they say: 'We're staying. We love it. It's absolutely one hundred per cent the mega-best place on earth!' And what do I tell them? I say: 'I already know that! I was here way before you, but welcome anyway!'" Peele spreads his arms, as if embracing the entire population of Metro Vancouver. "I say: 'What's your price range? What neighbourhood are you inter-ested in? They're all incredible, just different. Let's get you set up!'"

I exhale, mentally shovel the horseshit away from my neck.

Peele's beaming. Ten years, maybe less, he'll be in public office, and he knows it.

I give him three slow claps. "Fuck yeah, Peele. All that sounds good. You're way more chill than I thought. Mind if I smoke?"

Peele shudders, checks his watch, mumbles the time with a hint of irritation and right when he finishes there's a knock on the door.

I crack my knuckles, shift in my seat, impatient to get the fuck out of this airless office. Another guy rushes in, breathless, sweaty, looks like the kind who's always pissed off. Wearing Eddie Bauer khakis with a coffee-stained crotch. Tucked-in dress shirt, probably the same brand. Clean-shaven. About five ten, midforties, thick-shouldered, balding, head and neck sunburned even though it's the end of winter. Just holidayed in Vallarta, Cancun, maybe Maui since he's doing well for himself and doesn't have to worry about the exchange rate. Just flew home. Start of the construction season. About to roll up the sleeves.

"Perfect, great, wonderful," Peele says while me and Clint shake hands with the new guy. Peele introduces Russ Fuller, project manager for the Solstice Homes development. Clint and I share a look. Finally getting to business.

"So. Coffee? Tea? Guava juice? Call Harvey? My assistant?"

Fuller settles into an armchair facing Peele's desk. I slide a look in his direction, tell Peele: "Whiskey. Booze. Whatever."

Fuller almost smiles. "What he said. I'm in."

"Whi—? Whiskey? Ha! It's ten o'clock on Sunday morning . . . but different strokes." Peele presses a button on his phone. I lift three fingers to indicate me, Clint, and Fuller are all in for whiskey. Peele looks at Clint, double-checking. Clint nods. Peele tells whoever's unfortunate enough to work directly under him to bring Scotch, three glasses, and a kale-goji-mango juice with bone marrow extract. Fuller and me share another look. All right. Solidarity. The horseshit smell's clearing a bit.

Peele natters about the impressive big-time projects Fuller's managed until the drinks arrive. Best thing to happen all day. Fuller grunts, takes a solid late-morning swig, and we get to it. Fuller says Clint did damn fine work on those projects down in Steveston, and—was it—Coquitlam?

"PoCo," Clint corrects.

"Bur-quitlam?" Peele, giggling around his straw. "Sur-lang? Slangley?"

Fuller takes a swig, rattles his ice, studies Clint's cheap suit and tats. "Vincent filled me in. On why you're here so early."

Peele's pretending to pick his fingernails, watching Fuller and Clint real close. Says let's do a rundown of the Solstice development, Russ.

"Not sure what you boys know about big goddamn development projects," Fuller says in a voice like he's unhitching a belt buckle, "but what they are is giant assembly lines. Only instead of the product getting made by rolling through the assembly line, it's made by rolling work crews through the site. One after the other. No tolerance for error. One subtrade's late or fucks up, throws the entire project out of whack, snowballs, eating shit."

"Dominos," Peele quips. "One goes down . . ."

Fuller avoids looking at the lawyer directly. "Say you got your concrete formers all set to go, skilled carpentry trade, expensive, and they do their job fine, but there's a fuck-up with the cocksucking rebar, supply's gone, bought from under your nose, have to wait, only you can't wait, because the concrete's being poured in two fucking days. Follow? Concrete trucks, pump trucks, all that shit's booked ten, twelve months in advance in this town. Two-fifty an hour for a pump truck, big job like ours we might have five of 'em running at once. Schedule's real tight. So now there's no shit-eating rebar. And if there's no asshole rebar there's no concrete being poured, cuz this isn't Meh-hico and we have codes, all Robertson's hippy-trippy bullshit to tiptoe around. Hey—fill that up, son! Grassy-ass. Little more . . . *ahh*, fuck me dead. Now that's a drink! Long hair can't hide that red neck, boy! Shit, was just in Varadero, shithole all-inclusive, do yourself a favour, never go there, locals got no sense of jump to it. Anyway . . . open bar, old lady got sunburned like she does every year, blistered t' holy hell, had to hear about it all day, rub fucking aloe vera, my hands still stink, sonsabitch pinkos didn't factor Fuller's mojito pitchers into their bottom line! Drank 'em outta house 'n home, told 'em bring me the goddamn bottle, can't you see

I'm married to a lobster! Christ in commie hell. Nice cars, though. This is all right whiskey, Peele, not bad—"

"Actually, it's Scotch."

Fuller raises his glass. "That right?"

"Scotch whisky."

"Huh. You say potato I say—"

"No," Peele says, "they're entirely different alcohols. Scotch whisky is made exclusively in Scotland from malted barley. You're thinking bourbon whiskey, American, made from—"

"Gives a shit? Better than the rotgut rum the Cubans—"

"All tastes like Crown to me," I say, clinking glasses with Fuller.

"Um, sorry, that's blended rye," Peele says, which makes Fuller take a swig to hide his grin. I pour myself another drink from Peele's fancy-ass crystal decanter. Clint finishes his booze, shows me another titty pic. So I'm feeling like I'm here? Fuller takes a look at the titty pic, laughs good and loud and now I'm laughing too, feeling A-okay, asking Vincent Peele if he wants to tell us what's in fuckin' Irish whiskey?

Fuller cackles, snorts booze up his nose, sneezes across Peele's desk. Peele gasps, retreats to the window, calls his assistant to bring disinfectant while Fuller says man he needed bastards like us in Varadero. I say to rub aloe vera on your wife? Fuller smacks my shoulder, says he'd pay me to, wingman, take one for the team, look out for those pinchers! I say no thanks but ask Vincent, he knows all about beauty products. Fuller says yeah look at that goddamn beard, for Chrissakes, Peele, what the hell is that thing? I say forty-dollar bottle of beard oil? Fuller says what in heavenly fuck's beard oil?

Clint's laughing too, me and Clint laughing together while Fuller laugh-chokes his way to a chesty wheeze, belches, catches his breath, rattles his ice, lifts his glass to his face, squints an eye half closed and stares inside like he's trying to discover a hidden wellspring of liquor down there. Peele says nothing, does an admirable job of being cool, not getting baited; this is one dangerous prick. Peele sucks on his mud smoothie, wipes his beard with a backhand, looks out the window, waits until his dogs quiet. "Just like that. You guys? Ten minutes in a room and you're all ... well, gentlemen? Russ? Solstice Homes? North Shore single track is calling."

"Peele, goddamn. 'K boys, so ... where were we?"

"Up a creek?" Clint says.

"No concrete," I add, crunching an ice cube. "Cuz of no bastard rebar?"

"Ah, yep. Up a crick, bet yer ass. So we got no concrete? So what? But after concrete you got iron workers, tough sonsabitches as you know, they're pissed off, also tight schedule for them, expensive sitting around jerking it, not to mention the goddamn crane operators, whiners, thousand bucks a day, then the rest of the trades stacked up and costing money every second that slips by. One missed deadline throws the whole shitshow out of whack—"

"Tell them more about the money," Peele interrupts, then corrects himself. "The *capital*."

Fuller glares at the wall behind the lawyer. "Time we break ground, Mr. Peele and his team o' beans have pushed enough paper to secure financing from the motherfucker bank. We're running the whole shebang on borrowed cash. Debt! Lots and lots of debt, boys! Bank sets specific completion benchmarks. Follow? We don't get, say, all the wiring done by a certain date, thief banker starts making noise. Maybe ups the interest rate, maybe refuses to bankroll the next stage of the project, hamstrings the job 'til we renegotiate the loan, basically legal extortion ..."

Fuller settles into his chair, eyes his empty glass, runs a hand across his sunburned forehead.

Peele grabs Fuller's glass, deposits it on a side table. Fuller scowls at the lawyer's back.

"You worked with Peele long?" I ask Fuller.

"Couple years," Fuller says, wiping his hands on his thighs. "Tight ship."

"Thank you, Russ. Tell the Ward brothers about our timeline," Peele says. "If you would be so kind?"

Fuller shrugs. "It's shit."

"Ha, yes, shit," Peele says, settling against his desk. "Solstice Homes has an accelerated timeline for completion. Usually a project like this would run . . . how long, Mr. Fuller?"

Fuller waves a hand like he could give a fuck. "Couple years?"

"Right. At Marigold, we're more ambitious. We want our customers to be enjoying appreciation on their investments six months after we receive operating capital from the bank."

"Never gonna happen . . . ," Fuller mutters, looking at Clint. "You know how it is, son. Even in residential. Shit happens. Material's late, weather's lousy, crews are useless, half of 'em hungover and the other half stoned, someone gets killed. Happens."

Peele raises his hand. "Which is why we're taking steps to ensure any potential . . . friction . . . in the long chain of events that must occur for this project to be completed on time are removed. Which is, in part, your job, Mr. Ward," referring to the older brother, Clint."

"We're de-frictioning?" I say, unable to help myself.

"Lubricating?" Fuller says, shaking his head like he can't believe the shit he has to put up with.

"Lubricating," Peele repeats, testing the word. "Ensuring a smoooth ride."

"Well, someone's getting fucked," Fuller says, face grim like he's remembering something he'd rather forget. "Long as it ain't me this time."

Fuller stands abruptly, says good luck to me and Clint, storms out without a word to Peele. An assistant scurries through the open door, wipes Peele's desk clean. When the assistant's gone Peele wags a file at us, says there's some paperwork that must be completed before we continue.

"I'm not signing a thing," I tell the yup lawyer, mostly to piss my brother off. Clint tells me to shut it, looks a bit like the old man, makes me snicker, squirm in my chair, desperate to get out of Peele's office and oxy up.

Peele slides some papers to Clint. My brother signs without reading. They stare at me. Normal-life people in the reception room are chatting, laughing, bullshitting about sports scores, the weather, sounding happy to be at work even though it's Sunday. What would Daree and Sarah and me be doing in Vancouver on a Sunday? Peele hands me a fancy silver pen. I resist ramming it in his eye.

"Your brother is my client now, Mark. I'm delighted to represent him. We share protected privilege. It's a prerequisite for further discussion."

I finish my drink, tell Clint to quit looking at me like that, sign.

Peele stuffs the papers in his desk. "I like you two. The Ward Brothers. Nice ring. Bit of an odd couple, though? I would've thought you, Mark, would be wearing the suit—and by the way, Clint, you need a new suit. I'll hook you up with my tailor. Mark, considering you went to university? That might sound terribly classist. I apologize. What did you study?"

"Labour studies. Critical theory. Art."

"Wow!" Peele says, pretending to flinch. "Art? Labour? No wonder you're dressed like a skid. What do you make of that, Clint?"

"Nothin'. Like I said. Me and Marky get shit done."

"I'm counting on it. No degree, though, Mark? You dropped out of UBC to . . . join the Canadian Forces? Fight the war on terror in Afghanistan?"

A few seconds tick by. "I never said that."

"Isn't that what *you* said, Clint? When we discussed your brother's past? At length?"

Clint scratches his neck, says it's the truth.

A stinging too-hot feeling spreads over my skin because Clint's giving me his gangster-boss stare-down. I cup my hands over my wrecked leg, realize I'm wincing, and worse, Peele's leaning over his desk, biting his lip, barely breathing, feeding on me hurting. Which is fuck. Me sitting here drinking the lawyer's booze and laughing with Russ Fuller, and Peele didn't care because he's the one really laughing, and maybe my brother and Fuller were in-secret laughing at me too because I'm the nothing asshole caught thinking he's all high and mighty. "You got it, Peele. Fought a war for you. Thank me anytime." I turn to face my brother. "Clint? This guy? You told him—"

"When did it happen?" Peele asks, looking at my leg real keen. "Your . . ."

"Big boom? June 18, 2007."

Peele's hands fold and unfold, and when they settle his expression is sympathetic and sad. "Incredible. I commend you, Mark. Risking your life to defend my freedoms. It must've been horrible. Almost four years ago. How do you cope?"

"Stay on the move, you forget you're someone else." I almost say *but this city's bringing me back*, manage to clamp my mouth shut.

"And what about your horrific crime? Was that you, Mark? Clint says it was. What you did to Mr. Combs back in . . . Clint?"

Clint clenches his fist, watches his forearm tats ripple. "I said oh-five."

"Clint, why the fu—"

"Thank you, Clint. Two thousand and five. Bludgeoned an innocent man on his sofa, classy—"

"You stay seated in the fucking chair, Mark," Clint yells, pointing me down like a mutt. "This is big. You had it easy. Cuz of me. Now you buck up."

I dunno. I guess I could say piss off, walk out. Maybe I could do that. If Peele lets me . . . but then it's too late because Peele's lips pull back thin and blue until his teeth and gums are visible and as I watch pinned to my chair his lips stretch and fold down his chin and over his face until all of him is this vicious black-gummed razor-toothed mouth perched on a scrawny pencil-pusher neck and I moan *help me please* because a forked black tongue slips between Peele's teeth, rises into the air and shakes and trembles and I hear a rattling sound like bones knocking together and what Peele's doing is calling them to him and beside me Clint reveals this horror in him too and without looking out the window I know the whole city is nothing but these walking sharp-toothed wide-open mouths with black tongues reaching to the sky and they're all tuned to the rattling hunger coming from Peele—

"With us now, Mark?" Peele hisses. "Stay seated. Because Clint owes *me*."

Choking, covering my face, trying to breathe, trying not to hear rattling bone-dry clacking and a woman screaming and feeling my lips stretch, pull back—

Peele laughs, says something I can't hear. My brother slaps me so hard my teeth knock together and when I find the courage to look at Peele it's only a dickbag lawyer spewing bullshit.

"Ah ... the Ward Brothers! Clint? You didn't tell him how much you owe? And that's fine. Everything's above board. In case you were getting the wrong idea, Mark? Are you some sort of negative-minded cynic? Syndicated mortgage. Pooled investment capital. Clint's money is hard at work. Using extreme leverage to—"

"You fucked us," I whisper.

"Not us," Clint says, meeting my glare. "Never us."

"We're only talking, Mark. Shooting the breeze? No harm. Do syndicated mortgages upset you? Why is that? Confused? Lacking financial skills? Disoriented? What are you hiding?"

"Peele, get off him. I told you what his kick is."

"Clint?" Room's going all fucked, leaning in, wiping sand from my eyes, Doyle's Benelli, *hold me*, Kandahar road dust, a cellphone ring—

"A killing rage, Mark?" Peele leans so close he's almost touching me and I want to stay strong so bad but what I do, chickenshit nobody, is flinch and shy away. "You a killer, Mark?"

"I'm okay now. That's . . . all done?" But someone whispers *burning, piled against the door, screaming*.

"What's he saying, Clint?" Peele asks. "Burning? You said he was primed."

"He's talking about the war, Peele, fuck—"

"Is he? Maybe. Maybe not. Mark, you unstable?" Peele lifts an index finger to silence my brother, never looks away from me, "Syndicated mortgages, words on paper, no one to blame. *Kill*. Only a word. *Kill*. See? Words don't mean anything. Only us gents shooting the breeze."

"I told you," Clint says to Peele, like I'm not even here. "Marky's game. Let me walk him through it."

Jasminder Bansal

"The trouble is the news agencies expect us to work for free, or close to it," I tell Meeta, who, since marrying her high-school sweetheart, Will Blevins, at eighteen, prefers to be called Maddy. We're at the Granville Island Market, on a Sunday morning grocery excursion for my sister's cooked-from-scratch nightly meals. "And there aren't many jobs in this city. Even if I re-enrol at Langara and graduate there's no guarantee I'll find work, and definitely nothing that pays like real estate. But let's say I do get an internship. I'm there a couple years, working for nearly nothing? Eventually they let me write for some blog, and then I'm twenty-eight, thirty—"

Meeta drags her six-year-old son Andrew from under a craft table, tells him not to dirty his cricket whites before practice. "You're going to be thirty anyway."

"I suppose I am."

"And Will says there are no guarantees in life."

"I suppose there aren't."

My sister leans over a display of imported radicchio. Folds a white-veined leaf, furrows her brow, says she can't tell if it's fresh. She has a colour-coded meal planner on her phone, organized by ingredient and nutrient lists. Errands and chores for home and community fill Meeta's days. Library fundraisers. Park cleanups. PTA meetings. Takes a long time to hand-pluck pomegranate seeds for a salad dressing. I used to feel superior about the real-world seriousness of my ambition. Now I worry I'm envious.

"How's Mom?" Meeta asks without looking up from the radicchio.

"Working on her project."

"Still? That has to end—"

"—when she decides to end it."

"I wish you'd move out," Meeta says, nudging her stroller when my niece, Chloe, babbles for attention. "Find roommates. It's not healthy, you being there. For either of you." My sister catches my questioning look. "It's not that we don't like having you stay over. Occasionally. It's just . . . Will says people our age never want to grow up."

"I won't leave her," I say, barely audible over the throng of enthusiastic shoppers, earning a reproachful glance that makes it clear Meeta's as shocked as everyone that I'm the one floundering, high-school star student, the daughter who was sure she had it figured out and was foolish enough to let everyone know.

"Who's it helping, Jaz? No one." Meeta's tone reveals that she mistakes her good fortune for earned reward.

"It's helping me. You've never looked for a decent rental in this market. And I bet if you asked Mom she'd say—"

"People must do it, though," Meeta interrupts, embarrassed by me broadcasting the family financial situation in public. "I mean . . . there *are* people who do it. Have journalism careers? And lives. Families."

"I think I have a life?"

"You know what I—"

"Of course. Yes."

"Then why can't you?"

Meeta's wearing head-to-toe Dolce & Gabbana: ankle-length pants in wool for fifteen hundred, T-strap brocade pumps with flower embroidery for another thousand, knit cardigan with encrusted lace for a cool two k. Topped with a personal accent Vincent Peele would approve of, a thirty-dollar silk *dupatta* draped loosely around her neck, so people are clear about where she's from.

"Jaz? I mean, real estate? For now, I get it. But you're so much better than that."

"Maybe I'm not. There are things I like about it."

"Of course you're better. Creative but more grounded than . . ."

"Mom?"

Meeta doesn't answer. She grew up hating our mother's art practice, believes it was a selfish choice, that she should've focused on a more pragmatic, financially viable career. Sacrifice for the family? I get it. But now here she is saying I'm better than needing to pay the bills and should focus on my creative side? The truth is Meeta has no idea what it means to hold a job. My sister does what she wants, period, yet manages to talk about her life like she works sixty-hour weeks.

A man in his early forties, handsome, well dressed, selects oranges one at a time, carefully inspecting each one, a slight squeeze, a discerning once-over. I wonder if he's thinking about his family when he does this, will his son or daughter enjoy this orange? Will he set the orange down in front of his partner and watch him eat, vaguely satisfied? What should I say to my sister? Tell her yes, maybe I could've returned to Langara after Amar's death. Or maybe I should tell her I *did* get an internship while I was still in school, a spot with local radio, not exactly the *Globe* and just writing ad copy, but a start, and it took the station manager less than a week to discover I was sister to Amar Bansal, drug lord, gangster, a man who was accused—it was revealed after he died, at the trial of an associate—of ordering a hit on a rival, propping the body in the backseat of a gold-trimmed Cadillac Escalade and spending an evening driving the corpse through his drug territories, showing it off, a warning and a boast.

"Anything's possible if you work hard enough," Maddy sniffs, squeezing Andrew's shoulder. "Like raising a family. It's a ton of work, trust me."

I bite my tongue, resist telling her most people have to work *and* raise a family. I don't want to start another argument. I'm gauging to see if it's a good time to hit her up for a loan. Not a lot, a few hundred, enough to fix my brakes until I sell a condo and a commission comes through.

Image is everything. Amar's words when I teased him about how long he took getting ready for a night at the clubs. Amar opening the Escalade's rear door and the dead man's head slumped against the headrest and his associates peering inside, saying baller dude you fuckin' gangsta, you boss, no one steppin' to Bansal—

"Do you think about him?" I ask Meeta before I can stop myself.

My sister falters. Lifts an avocado, asks what's in season.

"Nothing. It's March in the Northern Hemisphere."

Sighs in disappointment, plunks three avocados in her shopping basket.

"Meeta? I said: Do you think about him at all?" Too loud to ignore because I'm ashamed about asking even once, especially in front of the kids, and that shame blurs to anger—at Meeta, Amar, myself. And at Clint Ward. *He'll get his,* Sim said. It's awful how I've learned to cope by being angry.

"Jaz? Let me go."

I'm clutching Meeta's arm. Hard enough to stretch her blouse. I release her, step back, feeling short of breath. "You're still embarrassed of him."

"He destroyed this family."

"Amar is this family. All of him. What he did—all of it is us, too."

"He was, you mean."

"*Is.* A person doesn't stop being family because they're gone—"

"Only because you let him stay. You and Mom both. But for me, he's gone. I have another family."

Meeta makes a show of rearranging Chloe's blankets, asks when Mom and I plan to visit her house for dinner. I mutter something noncommittal. Family looms large in my sister's conception of the world. Like a domestic black hole, everything in a life must inevitably bend toward it.

Granville Island is pretty much the last place I want to be this morning, but it's one of Meeta's favourites; I suspect she's soothed by vegetables better travelled than most of the world's population. She spears her stroller through knotted shoppers and asks if I gave up on journalism too soon, another way of saying she thinks I did.

Instead of answering I pull out my phone, read a message from Eric asking about the open house. Drop the phone in my purse, wonder how long I'll need to dodge him before he clues in we're finished, and then another pang of guilt at being so self-centred but isn't that common to people in crisis, all my emotional energy spent putting out fires.

Meeta pins Andrew between her hip and a vegetable stand while she inspects heritage tomatoes with ugly yellow stripes. Andrew squirms, plucks a four-dollar tomato from the bottom of a pyramid, sends the stack tumbling, squeals joyfully. I smile to myself, relieved, feeling I made at least one right decision in my life. Distracted, I begin picking up tomatoes while Meeta chastises her son in a manner that's for the benefit of anyone listening.

"Is this all you wanted to talk about?" I ask. "My lousy career choices?"

"Wanted to see you. Too tired last night. Andrew misses his aunty. I miss my sister. Who texted? Eric? How's it going with him?"

I swallow, resist walking out.

Meeta balances her shopping basket on the stroller's handlebar, sips her decaf latte, fusses over the baby's spittle while I watch, vaguely horrified. Then she says she doesn't know why I went to school, wasted my money, if I was going to quit halfway through.

"Because I wanted it more than anything." What if I tell her I'm working for a development company linked to Amar's killer? That I am pursuing my career? Would she support me?

Meeta, whose husband is heir to a family fortune made in several lucrative varieties of nastiness—internet gaming sites, e-cigarettes—lifts her nose, tells me Will thinks people our age are entitled, don't really want to work, want everything handed to them.

Money and wealth come easily to me.

"I don't feel great about all my choices," I tell her, too strident. "But at least they're mine to make."

There. One step away from calling her a kept woman. Yet another person I'm pushing away, bit by bit, every time we see one another. Meeta lifts an eyebrow, has the class or compassion or good sense to keep quiet.

"Okay, you know what?" I say, forcing a smile. "I'm sorry I brought it up. Not the best couple days. This week will be better. Can we talk about something else?"

"I would've loved to see my sister on TV." Meeta lays a sympathetic hand on my forearm. She looks centred and youthful, like she sleeps twelve hours a night and enjoys hour-long massages every other day, which she does, and that's wonderful, but what frustrates me is she still has the gall to complain when other people are overworked, run ragged, and otherwise too busy to accommodate her and her family's considerable needs.

"Maybe next year I'll be in the annual commercial with Marigold. Then you can see me on TV. Singing the jingle? *It's al-ways a good time for pro-perty—*"

"Will says you should've studied a trade. There's lots of work for tradespeople these days."

"Except I can barely make scrambled eggs, never mind build a house. There's this impediment called aptitude."

You fall short of perceived potential, people feel justified in providing unasked-for advice. Constantly. Like: we're only trying to help.

Meeta asks a craft-cheese vendor if Gouda is gluten-free. Andrew, seeing his mother isn't watching, pulls a stolen tomato from his pocket, drops it on the floor, smashes it with his heel. Tomato slime splashes across my only decent pair of boots. Andrew picks up the gooey tomato, slips it in Chloe's blanket. I ignore him, pretend to rub my eyes, too tired to do much else, try and take comfort in the fact that at least I'm inside Marigold, and maybe nothing gets written and nothing happens, but right now I need this feeling of mattering.

Mark Ward

B ack to the wall, sitting in the alley behind Peele's office. Not feeling shit hot. Made it outside before I threw up. Thinking about Peele, what comes next, my first bit of work for my new boss. Clint lights a blunt, hands it to me, asks how I'm doing. I'm quiet, looking down the alley, watching lunchtime crowds hurry along Broadway, a poodle in a lavender sweater, a bike courier balanced in a track stand. "Sorry bro. Didn't mean it."

Clint's kicking rocks against the cinderblock wall. "Pologizing for?"

"Lawyer got to me. Slimiest scumbag ever. And I've seen Afghan narco-kings sitting pretty in their personal fiefdoms."

Clint takes a hit off the blunt, checks his phone. "Don't sweat it. Peele's a pro. Getting under skin is what he does. But he's got no meat. No code. Besides. Best to have a guy like that in our corner."

"You think?" Tap the blunt against a garbage can, start to say something, change my mind while a tinted Audi rips through the alley, almost runs my brother down. Clint cusses, picks up a baseball-sized rock, whips it at the Audi. I wait to hear if it hits, then ask what I looked like in there.

"Looked like?"

"Yeah. I always wonder how people know? When I'm ... not feeling so great? Did I look different?"

Clint's face scrunches like it's the stupidest question ever. "You fucking looked like you. Peele had a one-up. He was testing."

I run my fingers over the piss-stained asphalt. "Not . . . shaking and spitting? Like I'm crazy? Cuz the military shrink said . . ." I should stand, walk, focus on my breathing, but the truth is I'm so tired I could pass out in the alley and not give a hoot.

Clint kicks another piece of gravel. It ricochets off the wall and thuds into my good leg. "Marky. Relax. I told Peele about you beating that pervert. Had to. Peele offered me an in. These syndicated mortgages Marigold runs, they're special elite. Not offered to any asshole." Clint flicks me a glance like he's wondering if he should say more, and if it wasn't for the blunt loosening his tongue he probably wouldn't, but he blurts, "Speaking of coming up, you should see who Peele has working for him and he doesn't even know." Clint laughs, takes off his suit jacket, tosses it on the ground. "Bitch is selling real estate for him. Course she's a glorified tour guide, showing Peele's clients properties to run money through. Anyway, Jasminder Bansal. Remember?"

"Uh, nope?" I want to grab Clint's jacket, use it as a pillow, curl up.

"C'mon. Bansal? Amar Bansal? Indo-fucking-Canadian? Brutal bastard. Much respect. Rolled with him. Not side by side, but business. Shot three years ago. While you were in . . . fuck knows?"

"Bansal? Yeah. The pretty boy? This chick Peele's got working for him is Bansal's sister?"

Clint flicks the smouldering blunt into a puddle, clamps a shaky hand on my shoulder. "Never told you this. Amar was all me. Point blank. On the dance floor. Real proud. After him, I moved on North Surrey." I try and speak. Clint digs his fingernails into the soft spot where bicep meets bone. "You shoulda seen it, bro. Biggie thumping. Lights spinning. Bitches dancing. Like a music video." Clint's face is wrapping around, warping, blocking my view of the alley, the city, and when he speaks I think no I'm not the crazy one but of course that's wrong, of course I am.

"The sister's at Marigold cuz of me," Clint says. "Not a fucking coincidence."

Takes me a while to clue in. "You're going to—"

Clint wipes his hands on his pants like he didn't like touching me. "Not sure what yet. Dunno what she thinks she knows. But it's a problem. Threatens the thing we got with Peele, he finds out I didn't tell him about Amar. Man, the world's shit, Marky. That's why family means so much."

I'm thinking if the Bansal sister put herself in this kind of risk to get at Clint, she probably feels the same. And the weird thing is I'm trying to feel something about my brother's admission, outrage or anger, but there's only a hissing radio noise in my head and if I listen real hard maybe I'll know what to do. "Clint? I need out. Please?"

"Yeah, fuck off. You're barely in." Clint digs in his pants pocket, pulls out his phone, scrolls to a photo. A girl, mid-teens, dressed in a navy blazer and a pleated tartan skirt, walking down the marble steps outside a brick building that's either a private school or a castle. "Forget the Bansal thing. This is your work. Slutty daughter goes viral." Clint holds the phone so I can see. "Look at that cutie. Easy."

"Clint? I really think I need—"

"Doin' you a favour with this one. Total cutie. Think?"

"Yeah. Cutie." But looking at the girl's picture and feeling nothing. Not interested . . . and not *not* interested . . . but nothing at all. Course this one's just a kid. But when was the last time I noticed or thought about being with someone? About getting laid? A long time now. Touching, being touched. A real long while.

"Daughter of the competing bid." Clint pockets the phone. "Mother's some uppity politician. So y'know, a public figure exposed.

Father's a rich-boy addict. Name's . . . uh, Carl Reed? Runs an investment company, things get thorny around there . . ." Clint frowns,
spits against the wall. "Reed's got a side deal with Peele. Peele went
through it with me, it's nothing, but out of courtesy, right, you
approach the old man first. Daddy gets to decide: lean on wifey so
she pulls the government bid, or—"

I light a smoke, tell my brother it felt good working on site.

Clint pockets his phone. "Twll show up?"

"He works not bad. Said you guys hang out?"

A few skaters roll by, teenagers in black skinny jeans, vintage
T-shirts, Vans. One of them ollies over a manhole and as he lands
he looks over, catches my eye, and I see something about me bugs
him but he puts his head down, boardslides onto Broadway.

"Me?" Clint says, watching the skaters disappear. "Hang with
that puke? Course he's bullshitting. Up my ass to let him run a crew."

Something feels off in Clint's voice. Like doth fucking protest?
"Kid seems all right."

Clint pauses. Pretend-uppercuts the cinderblock wall. "You know
he uses?"

Ash my smoke. "Huh?"

"Yeah. Can't believe a word. Don't tell him I told you. See the shit
I gotta put up with?" Clint roundhouses the wall. "Job got held up so
no work tomorrow. I'll phone Twll, have him meet you Tuesday
morning. Maybe I'll come by. Help out. Feels like all I do is drive
around." Clint sighs. "Good thing that Cummins is sick as hell. And
hey, the Reed daughter's for you alone. I'll give a shout. Otherwise,
don't bug me."

I'm about to say no problem when my phone beeps. Clint raises
an eyebrow at a photo of a fancy gilded ballroom packed with fancy
smiling people wearing fancy evening gowns and tuxes, a sparkling
chandelier hanging from the ceiling—

Clint snatches my smoke, takes a drag, laughs in admiration.
"Peele, that motherfucker. See? Big shot. In our corner."

A banner draped across the back wall says *Vancouver Police Gala*. Peele's on stage in a slick black tux, handing an oversized cheque to the chief of police. I'm about to delete the image when another arrives. Peele wearing a downhill helmet and body armour airing a gap on a full-suspension mountain bike. I groan, show Clint. He hands me my smoke, looks at the photo, tosses a couple punches through the air. Then a third message arrives.

"Fuck you, Peele." I drop the phone on the pavement. Burning pressure builds behind my eyes. Clint tells me to look at the text, so I do, and this time it's blood violence murder, a dude in a suit slumped against the steering wheel of a silver Mercedes with all the windows shot out. Clint says yeah, that's Vincent saying yo what's up from his big-fish boss Tectonic, some super-secret Chinese guy, all I know is that's who we're securing the North Van property for, don't sweat it, Marky, don't let that chickenshit Vincent Peele in your head, sending pissy messages, bullshit mind games—

Jasminder Bansal

Monday sales meeting at Marigold. I've been awake since five. Met a client at seven. Toured a development site in Richmond, close to the Cambie Line. Determined not to let my failure at the open house set me back.

My ideas come to life through my business.

Seated on a lumpy beanbag chair around a neon-green table shaped in a series of asymmetrical curves. The table has a plastic play crate on it, like in a daycare. The crate is overflowing with puzzles and brainteaser games. A foosball table and an original Pac-Man arcade game square off in opposite corners of the room. A miniature basketball net. A fish tank full of gold-green fish.

Vincent calls this the Flowroom, but I've heard employees refer to it, not affectionately, as the Playroom. It's the secret room Marigold's clients never see, Vincent told me, a space reserved for synergistic creative interplay. The real estate game is changing, Jasminder. New money. Young money. International money. That's partly why we brought you on board—

I shift in the beanbag chair, let the thought go. Only two of my colleagues are present this morning; the third is away on business. A man about my age, wearing grey slacks and a tweed jacket with patches on the sleeves, like a dotty professor, smiles in my direction and asks if I've tried the shower.

"Excuse me?"

"The shower," he says, nodding toward a bamboo wall curving around an enclosed private space. Several unlit tiki torches guard the entrance, along with a potted palm tree draped with pink and blue leis.

"Vincent says he does some of his best next-level thinking in the shower. So he had one installed in the Play—the Flowroom. It's pretty cool. Completely glassed in. Quadruple showerheads. About a month ago I decided to try it. In the middle of a sales meeting. To see, you know, if the man walked the talk. Vincent was midsentence. I hopped in the shower for fifteen minutes. Came out towelling my hair. Vincent grinned, gave me a fist-bump, asked if I was feeling the flow."

"Were you?"

The guy taps his temple. "Like you wouldn't believe! Freestyle flow. Went in that shower, let my mind wander. Free association. Like a well-paid poet? Came up with a new tactic for a client I was having trouble resonating with. Deal went through that week."

"That's wonderful. Congratulations." I smile. "It's neat? This room. But our clients—"

"Peele's a visionary," the man says as he extends his hand. "Beckett Pearl. Beckett. With two *t*s." Beckett grabs the tips of my fingers, gently, and I introduce myself as Jaz Bansal, the new girl. He points to the foosball table. "Why should tech start-ups monopolize all the fun? This industry is changing. Our workspaces should reflect that."

"That's exactly what Vincent said."

"Terrific leadership."

I'm about to ask Beckett how long he's been with Marigold when Vincent bursts into the room, nods in our direction, yells *Strava!*, jogs on the spot, pushes a few buttons on his watch. Wearing eighties-style high-cut running shorts and a shiny synthetic shirt. Earbuds in. Drenched in sweat. Shoes and legs caked in mud.

"A minute and a half more, people," Vincent says, his voice too loud because his music's still playing. Tinny electronica fills the room. Beckett knocks a Slinky off the table, picks it up, slinks it between his hands. I try to remain open-minded. Many powerful wealth-generating ideas come from eccentricity and idiosyncrasy and plain wackiness. A Flowroom? After the last little while I'm up for anything. I notice an old Game Boy on the table, say sweet I remember these, start up a game of *Mario*. Beckett says he has high score; he's never been bested.

Mario boops a coin.

Vincent's timer beeps. He does deep-knee lunges around the table, drops, does twenty push-ups while Beckett pumps his head to the electronica coming from Vincent's earbuds, yells what was your time?

"Thirty-nine minutes. Off my personal best at thirty-six. Still a ways to go to match Rick Rypien. Man, that boy can dance."

Beckett sees my raised eyebrows, says, "Grouse Grind. Crazy-intense workout. Vincent does it twice a week."

"Three times now, Becks," Vincent lowers into a squat, lifts his arms, rises. "Used to do it only on rest days but the phase ramped up." Does a couple more squats, hops up, flashes me a hang loose, pauses in front of the Pac-Man, smacks a few buttons, lunges, almost trips over a beanbag chair. "Training for the Test of Metal. You should race with me, Becks. It's sold out, but I can get you a bib like no probs. You could keep up for a few minutes. It'd be fun to drop you. Team! I'm gonna ask Mabes—her full name is Mabel, Jasminder, but only I call her Mabes, not you, we've known each other since forever—to get me a smoothie. Any suggestions? Office has a tab over at Grassroots, big perk, take advantage."

Mario rides a warp pipe. I'm smiling, thinking about what kind of smoothie I should try. There are so many options.

"Soy almond," Beckett says.

"Oh, way too heavy," a girl I've yet to meet, seated across the curving green table, says. She has close-cropped red hair and is dressed like she's about to leave for a dinner date: elegant bordering on severe. "I suggest coconut ginger."

"Coconut ginger?" Vincent says. "Wow, Elodie. Totally avant-garde. Reminds me . . . met a sculptor the other day? Commissioned him, said yeah, do me one of those whatevers. And make it bigger!" Vincent jogs behind me, showers me with sweat, calls his assistant about the smoothie. "How's Jasminder this morning? Trail run? Yoga? Happy to meet the family team?"

"Jaz," I say. "No exercise yet?" I lift my coffee mug sheepishly. "Only caffeine."

"Yes, of course. But hey, Jasminder's better than Jaz. A nice, inclusive name. I encourage you not to shorten it."

"Jasminder is a lovely name," Elodie says while she fights to maintain her posture in the slumping beanbag chair.

"Thank you," I say, hoping we switch topics.

Beckett looks up from his tea. "Hey, Vincent, about the race, the Test of—"

"*Shh!* Time's up. Check my stats! Average heart? A little high. Working a bit hard on the finish. Sprinted from the SeaBus. Could be fighting something off. Maybe a cold, nothing major. Won't have to skip any workouts." He vanishes behind the curving bamboo wall, emerges with a towel, wipes his face, dries his hair, tosses the towel on the table. He must catch my look because he asks, "Something the matter, Jasminder?"

Shit. "Uh, well? I guess I'm not used to—"

"Of course not." Vincent smiles at a motherly-looking lady who hands him a metal cup dripping condensation. He slurps at the smoothie, wipes his beard with the towel. "Takes some people a while to get used to our offices being so chillaxed. See, already you're being challenged. Personal growth is our number-one asset.

Working at Marigold is like . . . perpetual personal revolution."

Beckett sticks an empty cob pipe between his teeth. "A constant process of . . ." He falters, swings the Slinky in a pendulum.

"Reinvention?" Elodie offers.

"Bang on!" Vincent throws himself into a beanbag chair. "You'll be fine, Jasminder. The revolution has been serialized! Deputized! Media eyes!" Vincent rubs a patch on his upper arm, giggles. "Wow. This wearable nutrition thingy's really kicking in. Liftoff! So . . . team? Last week's deals? Who's first on the recap?"

Beckett and Elodie share a fake-friendly glance.

"I'll go first," Elodie says.

Vincent claps. "Perfect. A volunteer! Go on. My heart rate is . . . oh. Still too high. Focused breathing. Where were we—wait! Elodie. Have something for you."

Vincent hands Elodie an odd-looking stuffed animal. I almost drop the Game Boy, have to rein in a laugh. A line of tension runs from Elodie's jaw down the side of her neck and through her arm to the hand holding the stuffed animal. Her voice loses its severe edge, sounds deflated. "Is this . . . Quatchi?"

"Sumi," Beckett corrects.

"Sumi, yes," Vincent says. "My favourite! Sue me! Lovely. Very cleverly done, Olympic marketing people. Brilliant. Sell me! Sue me! Quite nail-on-head, am I right, Jasminder?"

This morning I walked by Elodie's office and caught a glimpse of the woman's war wall, decorated with her framed degrees and awards. Elodie has an MBA from Columbia. Now she's holding a child's toy that resembles a stuffed rat wearing a cartoon superhero's cape.

"Nail-on-head?" I ask. "I'm not sure what you mean?"

Vincent frowns, but only for a fraction. "Beckett? Would you be so kind as to fill Jasminde—"

"Already on it," Beckett interrupts, waving his tablet in my direction. "Liberated information, Jasminder. Ahem! *Sumi. An animal guardian spirit with the wings of the Thunderbird and legs of an*

American black bear who wears a killer-whale-like hat in an artistic style of Haida people. She lives in the mountains of British Columbia and is a passionate environmentalist. Her name comes from the Salish word sumesh, *meaning 'guardian spirit.' Her favourite sport is alpine skiing in monoski.*" Beckett snaps his laptop closed. "The internet hath provided. Gosh. Where would we be without it?"

"At the library," Elodie says, her voice hollow. I'm still up in the air about her.

"Is that a typo?" Vincent asks. "Shouldn't it be: 'Her favourite sport is alpine skiing *with* a monoski?'"

Elodie twists the stuffed animal's cape around her index finger.

"Certainly you must be right," Beckett says enthusiastically. "How about we make our contribution, Vincent, get that egregious typo corrected?"

I'm only half listening, back to playing *Mario*, thinking about the showings I'm scheduled for this week, tallying hypothetical commissions, feeling optimistic for the first time in years and maybe Beckett's right, this Flowroom place *is* kinda cool.

"Sounds like a plan, Becks. I love contributing. To friends, work, community. And Wikipedia. If you're not contributing you're—"

"Depleting," Elodie says, dragging a fingernail across Sumi's eye.

"See Sumesh, sacred guardian," Beckett rumbles in a voice that might be trying to imitate a Salish man.

Vincent jolts to his feet, smacks at the nutrition patch on his arm. "Flowroom! This thought has legs! What if we pay the Olympic people to let us use Sumi in our marketing material—"

"Love it!" Beckett gasps.

"Right on! New development, mix Sumi into the strategy, Millennials, big into their comics—"

Elodie bristles. "Graphic novels."

"—yes, as if, Elodie. But picture it: Sumi on her penthouse patio, kickin' it in a Carine Gilson satin-silk robe, English Bay sunset in the background. Then another image of Sumi on a . . . not a fucking monoski! Beckett? Make a note: we change that to a snowboard." Vincent rocks from side to side, jumps, pretend-grabs his snowboard. "Boned stalefish! Swish-swoosh! Two feet of fresh! Carving sick powder turns, taking freshie facials in defence of our old-growth forests. Who's feeling the flow here, people? Me! Our West Coast superheroine Sumi fully living the West Coast gnar—"

"YOLO!" Beckett shouts.

"And that's just in the morning! Afternoon, Sumi's chillin' on Robson, eating the best sustainable sashimi in the world. Who's peckish? Should I call Mabes, takeout sashimi—"

"So delicious," Elodie says, brightening. "Vancouver sushi."

Peele nods. "World-class. Al pastor tacos."

"Exceptional," Beckett says. "Japadog."

"I am deeply suspicious of people who do not consume ethnic food," Elodie says, looking directly at me.

"Right," Beckett says. "It's borderline ra—"

"Absolutely," Elodie says. "It's like: I love dim sum. How can I be ra—"

"I like chicken fingers," I say. "Plum sauce?"

Elodie glances at Beckett who glances at Vincent who smacks his lips, says, "I had those. Upscaled, lovely, forty dollars a plate at—"

I laugh, say nope, not those, I can't get enough of the fast-food ones with the watery see-through plum sauce.

Beckett grabs his stomach. "Yuck, contaminated with—"

"Let's move on," Vincent says, grimacing. "Another Flowroom idea! Whenever something is beyond awesome, totally next-level, we say . . . that is so Sumi! You guys in? Is that so Sumi or what?"

All three of us agree it's so Sumi. I take a sip of coffee, think about calling Meeta, setting a date for that family dinner she's always harping on about.

Vincent holds up his phone. "Elodie? Do you mind? Can I . . . just . . . a photo with Sumi? For our feed? A year after the Olympics and we're still celebrating. That's how Vancouver parties. The fun city! Our enthusiasm is like . . . endless."

Elodie lifts the stuffed animal to her face. Tries to smile. Red lipstick's smeared across her front tooth. Beckett tells her. She uses Sumi's cape to wipe it off. Vincent takes the photo. Takes another sip of his half-finished smoothie, spends a few seconds posting, then shouts, "So Sumi!"

"So Sumi!" everyone shouts back.

"Go family team!" Vincent says, beaming, looking completely impressed with everything. Checks his watch, mutters about a lunch meeting, says we'll have to hurry, asks Elodie for the dollar amount, gross, of the properties she closed last week. Elodie smiles for the first time all morning, and after the meeting Vincent congratulates Beckett on dropping out of film school, shouts *So Sumi!* while doing an awful white-boy hip-hop dance. Beckett leaps up to join him. I'm leaving when Vincent grabs my arm, not hard but not gentle, asks if I want to go skimboarding when the weather gets warm and I tell him yes, absolutely, and I don't mean it at all, but I do, a little, because it sounds fun?

Vincent tells me I look happy, asks if I'm happy and I think for a second and say yes again, absolutely, but what I'm thinking is whoever said money can't buy happiness wasn't born broke. Vincent says what a score you are, Jasminder, a total keeper.

Carl "Blitzo" Reed

Hot tub party at a house that looks suspiciously like my own. Coral's going on about how little five million will get you in this town, in houses or drugs I can't tell. Larry's nodding, sleepy, threading his sasquatch-like shoulder hair into Coral's dreadlocks. I'm surreptitiously sticking the hot tub jet against my bare arse. Mist blocks the view over the ocean. Someone mentions fecal counts. I do a mental check of my bowels, realize they're talking English Bay.

"She's slipped under," Coral says in a voice like she's speaking through a wall of glass.

"Haven't we all," Larry says, ever the prankster.

"Sweet way to murder a Monday, Blitz. You got some life."

Half life? Second life? I try to say something quippy, give up, try to determine if it's day or night, give up, blame it on my kaleidoscopic Oakleys, ask when the surprise solstice eco-party is?

Right now, someone whispers in my ear, inspiring a collusive smile. From behind, someone else asks has Blitzo ever been to the Orgasmatron. I'm momentarily taken aback by the realization there are several hundred strangers in my architecturally award-winning home.

"This house . . . recycles itself," I manage. "Negative carbon footprint, net positive energy. Where's my cellphone? House is on the

Internet of Things, gives impromptu lectures about how the government subsidizes me to own it. Has a promising career as a techno-futurist huckster. Says we are forever in its debt."

"Huckster?" I take a look, drawn by the stoner drawl. It's the Whistler liftee I picked up hitchhiking on the Upper Levels. Cute blond highlights, vaguely Australian by association, hasn't been around long, needs to see the world, expand horizons. "Like hucking a fat five-four? And also, do you have any Yop? Red-berry flavour?"

"Supposedly. You want to rock this jet with me?"

"These walls can talk," Larry warns.

I wriggle against the jet, find a comfy spot, ask if anyone else cherishes a time when the world was mute and dumb. Realize I'm clutching a tiny object, smaller than a pencil eraser. Lift it an inch from my face. Fuck is this? Some sort of ball bearing? Can I snort it? Coral asks if I found her hash.

At the mention of a controlled substance the sinister ball bearing sprouts iridescent wings and a tiny camera-eye. Nano-bot, death from above, Jesus wood sprites! I toss the spy-bot in the air. It fires up, *whirrr*, emits a self-replicating exhaust cloud and whoa now there's a few dozen swirling overhead—

Holdout, sensing my distress, snaps at the nano death cloud like a pitbull chomping papillons. Crunches down, says he told me not to trust that backstabber Zenski. "And it's called the Integratron," Holdout corrects, firing a jealous glare at my strapping young snow-boarder. "Not Orgasmatron."

"Whatevs, brah. You been?"

"Architect revealed the inner workings of the structure," I say, too strident, reopening the conversation about my house, afraid I'm being ignored, losing touch. "Note the fanciful duct-work exposed on the exterior walls? It's like . . . wearing your intestines draped on your dinner jacket."

"I landed that cab seven-two bolts, digs me?" Blond Highlights brags to Holdout, who shrugs, says he's tired of the bipedal bias in contemporary athletics, says it doesn't count cuz it was only on the trampoline, which makes Blond Highlights drop his half-smoked blunt in the hot tub and wander off. Holdout dives in, emerges chewing the blunt, says he doesn't hate Mondays, he hates capitalism.

A familiar reedy-needly voice: "Are you going to properly attribute that?"

"Pumpkin Girl?" I lift my Oakleys. "You followed me home?"

Pumpkin Girl waves, naked and side-ponytailed astride a plastic merry-go-round lion I vaguely remember commanding Holdout to thieve from the PNE. Holdout acts out, head-butts the lion, sends Pumpkin Girl scattering, makes me doubt the whole free-range parenting thing.

"My light in you, recognizes, the light in you, and gives gratitude, for you," Coral mumbles, nibbling on Larry's ear.

Pumpkin Girl dusts herself off, steals an orange emergency blanket from a Scientologist passed out on my lawn, wraps it around her waist, says she's bailing, asks who wants to see Chip Wilson's house, it's way more steeze.

Gets my neighbourly ire up. "Chip's house? Steeze? How so?"

"I heard he lines his formal-wear closet with stretched baby-seal bladders. Says he likes the smell of them desiccating into his Armani. Says it reminds him of his first Bikram lesson."

Larry says that does sound sleaze.

Holdout scratches his chin. "Uh, Pumpkin Girl? Can I tag along? Sounds like a guy I should eat."

"Not a chance, porky," Pumpkin Girl yells over her shoulder.

"She was nice enough," Larry says, "but I never saw her smile."

Something submerged in the frothing hot tub tickles my big toe. "They do that to kids nowadays. Lop the laughter foreskin off at birth. Supposed to keep things cleaner. A real shame." Watching my house with a wary eye, feeling it outsmart me, wishing it were yesterday so this would all be over.

"Is that in Joshua Tree? The Integratron?" Coral wants to know. She's an okay kid, curious, needs to put the time in. Larry explains about sound baths, polygonal structures, astral travel. Takes all of a minute.

Coral slips Larry's finger in her mouth.

"I miss Kalalau," Holdout says after devouring Pumpkin Girl's plastic lion and washing it down with a puddle of spilled vodka-yerba mate. "Incredible foraging."

A radical reversal! Pain in my sinuses! Sycophants! Cascadia apologists! The ritual of resistance? Things have taken a corporatist turn. Remember: they tried to kill Castro with an exploding cigar. I avoid synthetics, men with sharpened teeth, hothouse my own hovercraft. Extraordinary measures. Seems to work thus far. Bet your ass my safe room is fully stocked. The best parts of me are embalmed beneath the Hotel Nacional. At night my medulla oblongata strolls the Malecón, searching for viable investment property and wooing sea bass with smuggled greenbacks—

"Integratron! I helped fund such an enterprise," I shout, marshalling forces for a conversational *flèche*, slumping into the water to be nearer whatever softness is interested in my thigh. "Coral's right. It was Joshua Tree, by the way, Southern California, where it landed." Firm, declarative, not wanting to be upstaged, feeling a bit dickish, lording over my peons. "We built it on Cortez. Not a single nail. All wooden pegs. Nails rust, fuck up auras, magnetic fields, think of a spiked tree. Used a stolen csis prototype space-slingshot attached to twin arbutus trees to send it into orbit. Slingshot made of tanned moose guts and braided Red Ensigns. Swapped the ensigns for black flags, cranked the fucker back with an early Unimog. This was decades before the A-bomb, or something. Calcs were rudimentary. Pioneering work, really. We were aiming for Tikal."

"Electromagnetic plasma?" Coral asks.

"Resonant frequencies," I tell her, thinking about my Tesla, the strange story of the Nugget, Caltrop stringing those goons up, my many years in prison, Michael calling me an idealist, slave to perfection, how what goes around, recharged cellular structure, maybe this isn't my first time casing the block, forever stylized, make me something less—

"Immutable law of attraction," Larry says, passing me a golden dinner plate heaped with offerings. "I had breakfast with Ted Kaczynski. Told me he saw your neat-o polygonal sphere zipping overhead. Heard it sing in ultra wideband. Told me it made him dream of heartwood."

I nod, sagely I gather. "That makes sense, in terms of trajectory and so forth. Thermodynamics. Gravity waves. Heavy shit. Not to be toyed with. What'd Ted eat?"

"Bratwurst and eggs smothered in maple syrup."

"Niiice . . ."

Two men materialize, young bodies painted in red ochre, feathers and turquoise draped around their necks. One settles beside me, runs his toes through the foam, asks about the connection between Aztecs and aliens.

"Mayans," I correct, wishing the sky would stop falling. "They're still alive, you know. Is that war paint?"

"I'm against war," the painted boy says.

I look around, try and spot the blood-slick sacrificial altar, or at the very least, an overgrown pyramid to the sky. Quetzalcoatl is my muse, I almost say, but a previous vow keeps me silent. I want to pray for rain. Dance around a spark-spitting fire and sing the rain from the sky. I want to know less, but still believe I'm in the middle of things.

"Are you a cop?" Coral asks one of the boys, triggering a run for the hills and an attempt to consume scattered pills before confiscation and inevitable resale. Holdout, as usual, gets more than his fair share.

The painted boy rubs his nipples, repeats he's against war.

Coral begins to cry.

Larry strides verbally forth, says the painted boy needs to cultivate a more positive attitude, decide what he's *for*. I object, say it's unfair to tell the boy what kind of attitude to cultivate. It exposes a domineering impulse.

"I feel you," Larry says, retiring. He's an old friend, knows when to say when. With us in Bute. A trucker-saint. He should get more screen time.

"Who's the pretty mermaid?" someone says, impostering in my voice.

Larry pats Holdout's head. "I guess what I asked Ted was, nothing goes up forever, and have we peaked? And if we've peaked, we wouldn't know it, uh, until it's too late?"

"What'd Ted say?"

"Thought I was talking ballistic apogee. Got a little worked up. Had syrup in his beard."

I giggle, swat at the water. "Stop tickling. It almost hurts. Overdeveloped erogenous zones."

The painted boys are apparently comfortable enough to slip into the hot tub. One of them reaches into the froth, grabs something that looks like a waterlogged muskrat. Star's face emerges from the foam, water goddess. A painted boy hauls her onto the patio, presses his lips to hers, repeats, crunches on her chest, repeats. She's motionless so long I think about her serving me eggs Florentine at Naam; then she spits an arc of water, a mermaid fountain, and begins gasping, calling my name.

My phone rings. *Wife!* I yelp, drop the phone in the tub, scalded by the possibility of Heather's voice, hungry for closure or tofurky.

"Gangster," one of the painted boys mumbles, pretend-shooting me with a Tommy gun.

"Things can only get better from here," I tell Larry, who looks doubtful. "Can't you feel it? Second by second. Just being alive makes us better. We don't even have to try."

"What do you believe in?" Coral asks the painted boys.

"Everything!"

Impeccable reasoning, says no one at all.

"But I wasn't even alive in the sixties," Coral says as a painted boy's lips meet mine. A nice kid, that Coral, if a mote wearisome, heavily invested in her alienation. Practise forgiveness. Awaken. Rise up? The ochre-painted boy whispers he's an old spirit speaking in the voice of all that is lost. Larry mutters about a continuum, contactees, a space convention beneath the scalding desert sun, a man who dynamited himself to death in a cave carved inside a sacred stone. Painted Boy slides onto my lap and I feel young indeed.

Mark Ward

Standing on a suburban street in North Van, in a newish development called Raven Woods. The rain's been demoted to an irritating mist that drifts down from the mountains and up from the ocean. We're above the Dollarton Highway, only a stone's throw from the water, but since we're hemmed in by McMansions there's no view. A few development signs, a rezoning application with an architectural rendering of the affected area, unerring black lines and empty white space, wiping the territory clean, remapping it, something about selling or being sold.

Clint tromps off the sidewalk and into an overgrown lot bordering a chunk of forest. I follow, pushing through rain-soaked brush while cedar branches dump frigid water down the back of my neck, imagining all the unseemly shit that must've gone down in these woods over the years, and how creeping through a forest behind my brother reminds me of playing war games on Vedder Mountain when we were kids, shooting BBs at each other, heads wrapped in black T-shirts, pretending to be ninjas, clueless, and of course not much has changed.

Difference is now the enemy has a face. *Craig Williams.* The target. A strike package assembled. Sometimes you do things, make a decision, knowing it's right but without knowing why. Like me returning to Vancouver. Pay off my brother, sure. But now I got a handle on what's driving me. It lives right here, in this deserted lot, its accumulated nighttime terrors, bad first dates and broken noses, tarp shelters, overdoses—

Clint breaks out of the forest onto a rocky knoll. Looks like a cross between a black bear and a gold-rush pioneer, snorting, licking rain from his lips, madman gleam in his eye, an explorer smashing through the unknown by sheer force of will, greedy and cutthroat. Easy to put a man like my brother down. Ignore him. Undercut him. Crass, crude, ignorant. A relic. A shame. Truth is in another day and age he'd be leading a crew into the wilds and the soft-skinned aristocrats would be paying him to do it, secretly plotting to have him killed when he returns. Same as now. Easy to fear a man like Clint, a guy who doesn't ask all polite to be let inside but smashes down the door. I push through a stand of huckleberry, thinking there's got to be a way to save him.

Clint stomps on the ground. "Right here everything changes, Marky," he shouts, using his heel to dig a trough in the mud. "This dirt is freedom."

Squint in his direction, fumble a smoke from a soaked pack, didn't know we were going fucking trekking, wish I'd popped another Oxy. Clint's upped his rhetorical game in the past few years, hanging out with worse company. It's dangerous to underestimate my brother; there's a difference between stupid and uneducated. Rain drips off my nose and ruins the first smoke, then my lighter gets wet. Clint hands me his lighter, butane with a linear blue flame. We move under a good-sized cedar that does nothing to shelter us from the mist.

"Welcome to Solstice Homes," my brother says.

"Go big or go home. Or both?"

Spent last night naked, cold, high, lying on a strip of sand on the backside of Stanley Park, the biggest rock I could lift on my chest, crushing my lungs, waves coming in, tide rising, trying to see the stars but not the Reed daughter. So, a normal Sunday night?

Clint's eyes narrow. "This is something to take serious."

"That North Van job when I flew in? That was Peele's doing?"

Clint doesn't answer.

After a while I say, "I like it. What'd the old man say?"

"You don't got land, you don't got shit."

Bow my head to shield my smoke while I take a drag. I do like it. But not for the reasons Clint does. I'm thinking mental Molotov, psychological insurrection. I like it because this hillside's going to be bulldozed, old-growth forest chopped down, wildlife scattered and starved, roads and homes put in, shiny condo towers with luxury penthouses, daycares for kiddies whose moms and pops work sixty-hour weeks plus commute, designed-injury-free playgrounds, a woodsy community centre, an outdoor pavilion for summer performances, folk singers twanging about togetherness, the environment, ridiculous horseshit about how if we try really hard we can make it all work out, everyone feeling good about themselves, aren't we great, aren't we all that, and in the centre of it all, in the very guts of these people's lives there's gonna be a sickness, a corruption, the blood of that real estate lawyer, the sound of his wife's screams, all the dirt this kind of operation attracts, blood money pouring in from all corners of the globe, sex slavery, international dope and gun running, human trafficking, investment fraud, labour and resource exploitation, proxy dictatorships, and maybe it'll be felt, in the quiet moments of the day, a passing doubt marring a self-righteous surface shine, a tickle in the throat or base of the neck, a sudden fear over muesli and yogurt on another wet Wednesday morning.

"Well?" Clint says.

"Fuck sakes. Trying to sell me a lot? I said I like it."

And even if there is no subconscious fear, no passing doubt, the long-term strategic goal of PSYWAR is to infiltrate and spread the infection.

That's where we've been going wrong. Can't attack this thing head on. Protests, singalongs, prayers. Too late for that. Asymmetrical warfare is the only viable tactic. You have to force-feed the beast its own tail, offer it your children, your spirit, feed it everything you are, remake yourself in its poisonous image. You sacrifice yourself to it. That's how you survive.

YOU MADE ME.

Clint smiles. "Glad you're coming around. Fucking commie. The old man was half right—"

"That's more than usual."

"—without land, you're shit. But without money, you're sweet fuck all."

Self-transformation. Every guerrilla op requires a fluid identity, even if it's only a fake ID and a pasted-on accent. My brother standing in his boxers on a Persian carpet in the middle of a windowless oak-panelled room on the top floor of a brick three-storey walk-up in Gastown, arms spread horizontal while a white-haired tailor takes his measurements with a focus bordering on meditative. I'm seated on an antique high-backed chair, its dark hardwood lacquered to a gloss that matches the shine in Clint's gold money clip. Classical music piped in from hidden speakers. A real class act, this cash-only tailor of Vincent Peele's.

The tailor lifts his lanky frame, exhales, says he has something that will work while Clint waits for the bespoke, vanishes. Clint lowers his arms, tries to look like he's comfortable here, but I know better.

"How close to getting that land for Peele?" I ask.

"Acquisition. Assembling smaller parcels and bidding on the largest property. There are competitors."

"Shocker."

"Dude named Scott Charles Booth owns three-quarters of the property. Grandfather was a lumber baron. Big player. Established. Doesn't need the money, and so has to be offered other incentives."

I'm about to ask incentives like what when the tailor glides in, sets a charcoal-grey jacket against Clint's chest. I'm having a hard time making things gel, watching my brother get dolled up for the in-crowd, thinking about Daree and my daughter and somehow that makes my blown-up leg start hurting. The tailor gives Clint his new slacks, tells him to put them on, takes a measurement, says they need a quick hem. Clint sits beside me in his boxers, picks up an *Architectural Digest*, flips through it. "You should visit the old man. Sooner than later."

"Why sooner?"

"Cuz he's expecting you."

I take this in while the tailor returns with Clint's slacks and they discuss shirt and tie colour and pattern combinations. Apparently there are guidelines for these decisions, protocols, a world of masculine knowledge Clint and me were never privy to. If men's fashion were the only way the old man failed us maybe I'd go see him. Clint begins getting dressed. It's a nice suit, glen plaid in muted grey-brown, understated, not too slick.

"Second time I've worn one, not counting that piece of shit yesterday," Clint says, posing in front of a gilded full-length mirror. "First was when mom died."

"I remember that thing," I say, standing. "A rental, right?"

"Sure." The tailor makes some adjustments, fiddles with Clint's collar. Says he wants to try another tie. Clint waves him away. "Felt awkward as hell. Goofy shoulders riding up to my ears."

"And now?"

Clint smiles at his reflection. "Feels fuckin' mackin'."

"Mom should see you." My brother hands the nameless tailor a hefty stack of bills. "She wouldn't even recognize you."

The railroad tracks ran straight through the middle of Chilliwack to a sorting yard behind a bottle depot that reeked of stale beer and a warehouse where guys like us but a couple decades older made concrete culverts. Nights after mom died we used to sneak out, although with the old man down for the count by nine or so what we really did was make sure he wasn't going to drown in his vomit and then yup that's us strolling out the front door, ashamed and laughing it off, lighting smokes before we made it out of the yard.

I was seven or around there, Clint nine.

Late eighties, before the internet and smartphones and social media made staying indoors, holed up in your bedroom, a bearable option. Bunch of us kids on the streets back then. Indians from the reserve, some younger than me, who I hadn't learned to look down on yet. Other broke-ass fuck-ups from the apartments around where we lived. I was beginning to think about the places I saw on TV, Hawaii and New York, London and L.A., even Vancouver, big places that meant something because they were on TV, and I was beginning to see me and my brother and the kids out on the streets weren't shit to anyone, and I was beginning to be okay with that.

Least I understood my place.

And something else was going on in my murky prepubescent brain. From the railroad tracks, low in the valley, on the floodplain of the Fraser River, I could look up to the nice neighbourhoods, Little Mountain, Chilliwack Mountain, Promontory, where the kids had new clothes and backpacks at the start of every school year, where parents drove down the hill to take their kids to soccer games, music recitals, and I was beginning to get that foul taste in the back of my throat, acidic and bitter, and even the first sign of pain in my temples, physical manifestations of rough, unformed, and unnamed emotions that had nowhere to go, and I remember, even back then, thinking—although *thinking* isn't quite right, because this was very pre-thought, instinctual, a hardwired survival signal—that the motherfuckers on that hill were the cause of me being shit, if not directly, then at least in spirit. It was an emotional truth. Nothing logical about it. But we all felt it, and what I didn't know was that we'd all react differently to that shared instinct, and that how we handled it would end up shaping our lives.

So we'd wander around, break into cars, smash things, light shit on fire. Kid whose name I forget got gasoline spilled on his leg and his buddy lit him up. Nothing cruel to it; just curiosity. Once the burns healed he drew little eyes and mouths on his shiny-smooth scar, pretended Freddy Krueger was emerging from beneath his skin, scared the shit out of us. We'd pummel one another, steal candy and chips and pop from the 7-Eleven beside the high school by running in en masse and snatching whatever we wanted.

But mostly we'd hang out at the rail yard. There was a chain-link fence we'd scramble under. Security patrolled sometimes, though they were rare and fat and underpaid and we'd always see their flashlights way before they got near us and besides, the off chance of getting busted only added to the attraction. We'd climb on the parked trains, stunned they were actually silent and still, sit on top of boxcars and smoke cigarettes or pieces of hollow grass, maybe some weed stolen from someone's parents if we were lucky. The air smelled of engine oil, creosote, overheated brake drums, horse manure. I remember thinking about those giant trains, where they came from, but I couldn't imagine much farther than say Hope to the east and Vancouver out west. The world was one big question I was afraid to ask.

Sometimes we'd break into the grain cars and play around in the mountains of grain inside. A kid found out he was allergic to the dust or fertilizer or some shit and his face swelled until he couldn't breathe; we dragged him out the top entry port and carried the poor fucker to the road, flagged down a car, and took off through a field when it stopped. I think he was okay.

We'd steal shopping carts and load them full of rocks and leave them on the tracks to watch the trains plough into them, then go digging through the blackberry, searching for the mangled shopping cart, in awe of its tortured metal, testament to a power that would eventually wreck us too. There was a parking spot where the older kids with cars used to take their girls, a road that dead-ended at the tracks, pavement littered with fast-food wrappers, crushed beer cans, cigarette butts, and spent condoms, and we'd hide in the blackberry and wait until the windows steamed up and throw rocks at the car, those nice, uniform-sized crushed rocks they lay the rail lines on. Some dude would burst out of the car—usually a lowered Mustang or a jacked Ford 150, sucker probably spent almost everything he made on the payments—right pissed, half-naked, tucking his prick into his ginch, screaming, and we'd take off running while he thrashed through the blackberry toward us, getting even more worked up when he realized there was no way he was gonna catch us and maybe sensing that was his whole fucking life right there.

Except one day, we were ten or eleven by then, I didn't run. I stood on the tracks while the long-haired skid teenager raced at me, his pants undone, his Slayer shirt riding up over his flabby white belly. I remember he looked oddly feminine. Soft, even though he was screaming he was going to eat my heart, tear out my eyes, fuck me with a stick, all that. The guy gets to me and I call him something, I can't even remember what, and he slams into me and that was the first punch I ever took that wasn't from family. It sent me hard across the tracks, blinking against the ringing in my ears, and then the skid kicked me in the gut and I shrieked and the fight left him, which is when I learned most folks have a small tolerance for inflicting hurt. People talk big. But you stick a knife in someone's hands, a gun, most of them won't use it, and if they do it'll ruin them.

That's important to a guy like me.

Another thing we'd do is follow the train tracks to where they crossed the TransCanada at an overpass and climb out over the bridge beneath the tracks. Cars would zip by at a hundred or more beneath us and we'd cling to the steel girders, inching along until we were in the middle of the overpass. And then we'd wait. Semis with maybe a foot of clearance would roar beneath us and we'd have to hold on tight to the bridge or the shockwave would pull us out into space and we'd fall into traffic. We'd scream and thrash our heads back and forth when the semi-trucks hit, air frothing around us, wind roaring in our ears, whipping our hair around, prying our fingers from the girders—like being trapped inside a thunderstorm. But even that wasn't the best. Best of all was when one of us felt the entire bridge begin to vibrate. We'd be calling it all night, hoping it did and didn't happen. *A fucking train's coming!* we'd shriek, panicked and psyched.

Most of the time it'd be a false alarm.

But sometimes, if we were lucky, the kid who called it would be right and a confluence of chance events would conspire to put a half-dozen shitbag kids under that fucking railroad track at the precise moment a fully loaded freight train roared through town. We'd wrap our arms and legs around the girders and wait in the dark, breathless, cheeks pressed to cold rolled steel, feeling the train's power materialize in welded metal. There would always be naysayers. *Nah, it's nothing, piss-ass.* But there was a point when the majority of us felt the overpass tremble in advance of the train, and then something switched and the kids who weren't in it for real would scramble through the girders back to land, desperate to escape, and we'd call them every name and then some because my brother and me, the Ward Brothers, we stayed put for the freight train every single time, if for different reasons.

Clint stayed because he cared what people thought. He was already on the up by then, accumulating a posse of delinquents that—in a few short years—would be dealing dime bags and eight-balls, stealing cars and joyriding them into ditches, doing dope runs for established crews to Vancouver or Calgary, Prince George or Kelowna, humping backpacks full of weed over Zero Avenue in the dead of night, curbing rivals outside the youth centre and shithole bars like the Princess, and basically doing whatever he had to do to make bank except get a job making concrete culverts.

I stayed on that overpass because when a freight train hit, for the forty or so seconds it thundered over me I forgot everything about who I was and where I came from and where I was heading. Forgot me and most of my friends were beaten before we knew what the fight was about.

So there we were. Two brothers wrapped around these massive steel girders with semi-trucks roaring below while the overpass began to ripple back and forth from the shockwave of the approaching train, gradually at first, then faster, the entire span rising and falling, only an inch, maybe less, but it felt like the structure was suddenly adrift on a rolling ocean and the train would inevitably blow its whistle as it approached because the kids smart enough to bail were out there throwing rocks at it, pissing the helpless conductor off.

Maybe the train took a half-minute to get to the overpass, and in that time we'd go through it all: fear, regret, self-hatred, excitement, terror, resignation. We'd imagine the face of a loved one grieving over us, even if that loved one's face was vague and unformed because, really, the fact we were out in the dead of night fucking around on a train overpass meant there wasn't anyone specific. We'd scream that it was the raddest thing ever. A kid named Tommy Something would piss himself. Someone else would be crying, wishing he'd run when he had the chance. Me and Clint would lock eyes, daring one another without saying a word—

Now the fucking freight train hits, the diesel engine sinking the overpass under its barbaric weight and the vibration tearing through our chests, making our stomachs churn, and the smash of air forced downward threatening to blast us onto the TransCanada and our fingers slipping, shaken loose by the implacable might of old-school iron and industry, and holy shit now we're screaming, this was a bad idea, oh fuck oh fuck, but there's no escape, all we can do is hold on and pray we're strong enough. The engines pass overhead and we get a respite until the bulk of the train crosses, car after fully loaded car rolling ten feet above us, making the rocking motion even worse, the noise like a mountainside cutting loose, throats raw from shrieking, someone throwing up and the vomit whipping sideways and then, if we're *real* lucky, right then, right when the force of the freight train is about to hurl us onto the TransCanada, a semi-truck passes beneath us.

A semi-truck is not a streamlined vehicle. A semi going over a hundred pushes a wall of air out in front, and this air spills over the top of the cab and curls behind the trailer in a roaring, violent mess. So when that semi passed under us, compressed air smashed up from below while the train bucked and thundered above, rocking the overpass back and forth, and for a second the two forces would come together in some ungodly clusterfuck of physical law and *lift us into the air*. We'd hover there, asses floating a few inches above the girders, arms and legs locked against a power that was now threatening to throw us upward into the train's meat-grinder undercarriage. I'd be sure I was gonna die, maybe already had, bile rising in my throat, spittle spraying from my lips, road dust stinging me blind, and the strangest thing is that for kids like us the dying didn't come until a few years later.

Jasminder Bansal

Tuesday morning. First time in an airplane, flying north, pitching like a pinball. The plane cabin is all eighties umber and exposed rivets. Spend most of the flight with the shade drawn, staring at the bolts securing the door, imagining the employees responsible for tightening them, how miraculous it is, given what fuck-ups we are, that any of this works at all. We smack down in Smithers, a town tucked against the Coast Range in Northern B.C. A local landowner named Les Hutchins picks me and four American investors up at the single-room airport. A coffee machine in the lobby burps black fluid into a plastic cup. I pile on the Splenda, buy an Oh Henry! from a vending machine, and call it breakfast.

We're shown to a rental van. Les drives us into a cutesy faux-alpine downtown, shows off a life-sized chainsaw carving of a woodsman engaging an alpenhorn. Selfies for all. Then we drive into the mountains. The snow has melted into puddles that stretch across the gravel road. Les fishtails the van through them while yelling over his shoulder. We stop beside a partially iced-over river and climb out, turning three-sixties, marvelling at granite walls plunging sheer to the valley bottom, the stone dusted turquoise-white with ice and snow. I notice an urge to talk louder, assert myself in the silence.

We skid and slide to the water's edge. Les settles beside the river, oblivious to the silty mud staining his knees, props his torso like he's doing a push-up, slurps at the fast-flowing water. He's a big guy, thick, with a ruddy complexion and a shock of white hair clustered around his ears. A crow or raven, wish I knew for sure, squawks from the far shore.

I've never sipped water from a mountain river. The cold air, the flight, being hired full-time at Marigold—all combine to make me feel a welcome sense of future possibility. Mud squishes around my boots while the Americans chuckle, check their phones, mutter about the lack of service.

Cup my hand, bring glacier water to my lips. I feel far away from Knight Street particulate . . . but it's still only water. I brush the sand off my palms, feeling let down, unsure what I expected.

A bald eagle arcs from a bleached snag. One of the businessmen, I believe his name is Donald-from-Arizona, tells Les the property will do fine, and two hours later we're back in the shuddering twin-prop and I'm trying not to be sick and the Americans are discussing property rights, how the only way to preserve natural resources like air and water is to privatize them so there's an incentive for conservation and that's when Donald-from-Arizona whispers I always was curious about you squaws, long winters and all. I put a paper bag to my mouth and pretend to vomit. Later, in Marigold's offices, Vincent finalizes the deal, and I realize I haven't thought about Amar all morning.

Marigold's offices overlook False Creek: Yaletown's stately glass towers magnifying a chance ray of light in an otherwise overcast sky; boats in the harbour still neatly winter-moored, sails folded and tucked away; joggers and cyclists threading beneath cherry trees a couple weeks from flowering; the city tuned to spring, relieved another long rain is nearly finished; the changing season evident in faces turned skyward, hopeful.

In the boardroom, helping Vincent sort through paperwork, careful not to let my real intentions slip, noting the companies Marigold is involved with, hoping I find something solid to connect Peele and Bo Xi. Seated at a polished concrete slab that Vincent told me weighs more than two tons. Apparently they had to cut a hole in the exterior wall to crane the thing in. It took a team of a dozen guys a full week. I said wow at the right time. Vincent said yeah but it was worth it, he knows the artisan personally, locally sourced aggregate, non-toxic polish, very sustainable and resource-efficient, nothing else like it in the city.

Shoulders are appropriately slumped. I'm watching Vincent indirectly in that new-employee way, hopeful and nervous. I ask him if the Smithers deal went well? He laughs, says stellar. Says he knew he was right about me, that I make people feel good about them-selves. I study the paperwork like it's all a bit over my head, imagine him being charged for money laundering or worse, but the truth is it's difficult to keep my excitement in check. I'm loving the feeling of accomplishment, something I've missed since Langara. Travelling, meeting people, making small talk, being scheduled in. And living close to the source of the story, watching and recording.

Vincent *ooh*s with childish enthusiasm as he looks over the offers. He's standing beside me, too close, resting his hands on the table, wearing brown corduroy and a tucked-in golf shirt. I'm wearing straight-legged black slacks from the Sally Ann and an incredible pale blue blouse I borrowed from Meeta. Tonight I'll have to go home and sort through my clothes. The thought punc-tures my mood—I haven't checked on my mother since Saturday. Is she doing okay? Should I call Meeta, ask her to make sure? And right behind the worry is Amar—

An assistant hurries in, hands Vincent a note. He reads it, sends a text. I use the time to compose myself.

Vincent plucks his beard, hits a few numbers on a calculator. "Great times, red-hot leads!" Checks his tablet. "Tomorrow you have an appointment with Longcon Investment. Taking them to see a parcel in Lillooet. You psyched?"

I hesitate, remind myself not to let my guard down, or maybe appear to let my guard down? "It's just . . . all this is . . . wow! And I'm new? Might be feeling overwhelmed? I love this table?"

Vincent sets his hand on my shoulder. Heavy. I let him feel me shrink from him. "Normal. No probs. Look at this office. Bustling! Can't get enough of it, for sure. I feed on human energy. Powerful stuff, emotional energy, is what my therapist says. Calorie-dense. Like you, a moment ago, looking upset at me, even angry? Kind of glaring? See how I picked up on that? Is there something you'd like to talk about?"

Bastard. Take a second, force myself to stop fidgeting with my pen, give him my best willing-to-confide look, blurt: "I'm sorry. This Saturday is the anniversary of my brother's death. My counsellor says being angry is . . ."

Peele looks delighted. "Ah, your brother. Not me." Lowers his voice. "You see a therapist too?"

Move slightly closer. "Grief counsellor. Is it the same thing?"

Peele folds his arms across his chest. "No, your problem's simple, mine's highbrow. Comes from having such an obliquely inquisitive intellect. My therapist keeps everything tidy. Like a French maid of the mind."

A nervous laugh while I run my fingers along the edge of the table. Peele watches me with a smirky leer that he might be mistaking for flirtatious. I smell the fabric softener in his clothes, his piney beard. "I guess there are all sorts of ways to deal with trauma?"

"Can't repress, that's for sure. Builds, unhealthy, bursts. Big no-no."

"Right. Maybe redirect?"

"Such as how?"

"Creatively?"

"Gotcha."

I doubt it. "What about you? Your family?"

"Super normal." Pretends to read a document. Whistles. The man is a pro at talking about everything but what matters. I need something personal out of him. A direction, a place to start. I take a chance: "Vincent? I guess I'm looking for ways to improve. A friend mentioned working on my conversation skills? Is that something you think I could work on?"

Without looking up: "Huh? How so?"

"He mentioned I could be . . . more clear when communicating with clients?"

Vincent looks puzzled. "You're making strides, Jasminder. Wardrobe was the big thing." Eyes my blouse, smirks. "Your boss loves the new look."

I tell him thanks, but sometimes I'm afraid I'm not connecting with clients, you know, because of my heritage? And did he experience anything similar?

"No. My heritage is normal." Vincent smacks his lips in distaste. "And are you, um, accusing me of not being local?"

Forcing an embarrassed flush, waving my hands at him, over-the-top conciliatory, hoping he can't see me laughing. "No, no, of course . . . I just thought, I'm sorry . . . but not entirely European?"

"Born in Vancouver. Bit of Italian. Still very European. Ultra-European, in fact. On my mother's—"

"Sure. My bad. So communicating was never a concern."

"Flawless communicator. And besides. I used to teach English as a Second Language. Don't listen to whatever moron told you that. Your English is fine, or I never would've hired you. Although . . ." Vincent leans a skinny hip against the table, frowns. "It could be a positive if you had an accent? Unique selling feature."

Feign surprised interest to cover my real interest. "Oh, ESL? That's cool. Before law? Here in Vancouver—"

Vincent doesn't answer. Spends a minute messing with his phone. "Hey, have you seen this? Scientists predict in thirty years Vancouver will have the same climate as San Diego. So awesome! Will we be able to grow limes?"

"Thirty years? That's—"

"Soon! I love key lime pie. Have you been?"

"California? No."

"Travel, Jasminder. Broadens minds. You should do it. Anyway, desertification? That's what we have coming. Forest fires. Rising oceans. The globe's going hyper-dynamic. Can't sourpuss about it."

"Priest and shipmaster. Top careers for the millennium."

Vincent giggles, gathers the property deals into a stack, slips them into a suede bike-messenger bag. "Although I do worry about the snowboarding. Can't imagine life without fresh pow."

"And if it's that hot in Canada, imagine what it's gonna be like farther south . . ."

Peele puts on a fretful face. "Can people even survive in that kind of heat? Probably barely. If they have the means? I love that, though. Don't you? Sure." Shakes his head, seems to forget about mass extinction. "As you suggested, new challenges present new opportunities. Innovate or die. Competitive environment. Dog eat dog!"

"Except we're not dogs?"

"Well . . . biologically hardwired? But of course it's all about the technology. I embrace change by shopping for the hottest new app. Global warming? Consider the markets all that death will open up. Levee expansions, sunscreens, seaweed farms? Boom times! Global warming is Mother Nature's way of spurring entrepreneurial innovation. And culling the bloated herd. SeaSteading? What a grand adventure! Columbus redux! What about a forest of condo towers floating west from Vancouver Island? We could sell those. Floating cities so expensive there's no way the low-lifes will get in. Structurally exclusive, just like Vancouver."

"Manufactured beachfront."

"Exactly! We chillax on our SeaSteading viewing platform, munch nori, chat about launching a Christmas Eve artillery bombardment toward shore, laugh at the losers fighting it out on land where it's sucky and they eat each other with like no salt. And we volun-tell the women we want on board! But even now we all have to do our part. Of course, I'm an optimist who believes in . . . uh . . . never doubt that a small group of thoughtful, committed citizens can change the world? Especially when they're rich?"

"Oh, for sure. Challenges and . . . um, building community networks to explore new opportunities?"

Vincent glances over his shoulder, lowers his voice. "Of course no free-thinking person can believe a word of it."

"Of . . . ?"

"Ha, yeah. Gotta be critically minded. Global warming? As if. Who benefits? Government needs to get out of the way, let business do the heavy lifting." Peele shakes the messenger bag at me. "Like these deals? Tied up for weeks. Regulations. Bureaucracy. So some oaf can gorge at my trough? The taxes they say I should be paying . . . please! Massive money-transfer scheme. But whatevs. I'm incorporated in the Caribbean. Bring it!" Vincent picks up his tablet, opens a news site. "I try to read a couple headlines every day, to stay informed. I mean, I like being free, and free markets are super free because it says so in the name, so what's wrong with that? Logic much? Freedom's here forever. Or until people like me decide it isn't! *Ooh*, look at this article. *University Scientists Claim Left-Wing Violence Is Caused By Global Warming.* Science! Keep it in your pants, Che! Or how about this one: UN *Official Claims Global Warming Hoax Is All About Eliminating Capitalism!* Wow, Jasminder. That's an actual UN official saying that. Can you believe it? I read something about that yesterday. It's amazing how misinformation spreads. Like the plague? Hey . . . you went to that cheapo journalism college. What was your experience?"

I lean over, read: "*Global Warming Collapses Symbiotic Gut Bacteria, Kills Insects, Humans Next.*"

Vincent waits to see if I have anything to add. I don't. He's wide-eyed, tapping the tablet. Seems he finds this shit rather agitating. "That's exactly it! I affirm gut bacteria, freedom-hating lefties don't. Truth in journalism. Although it was only a diploma at Langara? Not a real degree?"

"A diploma, yes. It's considered a real degr—"

Vincent gives me a sad face. "Ah, and here we are, with you only a sales assistant. Ah, well. Get what you pay for in education, too. Of course I'm a properly educated man. They made me skim-read an Edward Said excerpt. So I get it must be especially difficult. For you in particular? To understand how things work over here? Which is why I'm so proud to have you at Marigold." Peele stuffs his tablet in the messenger bag, pushes his chair under the board-room table. "I can't imagine what it's like, you know . . . uh, to be . . . trapped, yes . . . trapped. Caught. Helpless. Between two cultures. Mine and . . . whatever one is yours? Stuck in the middle?" Peele brightens, looks like he's about to sing the chorus of the Stealers Wheel song, manages to restrain himself. "Anyway. I'm glad we can speak so openly. And thinking about your struggles? It's hard. To think about? Always confused, never feeling you belong, never . . . well, I guess never truly knowing yourself? I mean, how hard is that? And sad? For me to have to think about?"

"Thanks, Vincent. It's a real trial."

Peele bows his head, clasps his hands like he's at a funeral. "I commend you, Jasminder. Super glad we had this talk. You're an incredible person. Almost a hero. From Canada . . . or at least in Canada? Because we let you in? You give me hope. You know, I have friends in the industry. Film? Documentaries? I could call in a favour, ask so-and-so to do a mini-doc on you, something upbeat to show the world how fantastic you're doing in Canada, for everyone to see?" As he's about to leave Vincent hands me an envelope, says, "I guess what I mean is . . . it all worked out in the end? Was rough going like a million years ago but now we're all good? No sense dwelling! I mean, look at that view!"

I take the envelope. Stuffed with cash. How much? And what do I do with it? Count it in front of him? Or pocket it, cool, pretend I'm fine with whatever he deigns to give—

"So . . . this is cash?"

"Payroll, accounting, need to get you updated in the system. Problem?"

"Well, taxes? And . . . legally? I'm pretty sure—"

"In the end? Always works out. Look at you now, killing it in Vancity. Bygones! So now that's over, ancient history, and we're looking back . . . it couldn't have been all bad, or bad at all, could it?"

I tuck the envelope in my purse.

Carl "Blitzo" Reed

Oh, to wake naked, crusty-eyed, lathered in vomit, in the driver's seat of a Tesla Roadster at forty-nine years old. I need an infusion, something lacy that begins with a needle and ends with me falling asleep. Paw beneath the seat. Scrounge the glovebox. Sweating. Leaking urine, let's qualify that with a *perhaps*. Give me the benefit of the doubt, but the truth is I'm as well put-together as the renminbi. What would Mao do?

When I hear the word *culture*—

"Hey, Blitzo? I mean, Mr. Reed?"

"Nobody calls me that, Narc."

One of the painted boys is in the backseat, ass up, hugging himself while Holdout licks his face. Cross-fertilization. Interspecies menagerie. Don't think I haven't considered it. I'm for heterogeneity. Everything at once. You with your petty morals. The walls torn asunder. You with your stick-in-mud repressions. Take a peek, marvel at the boy's stubborn tumescence. Like the *Titanic*: that fucker will never go down. Something about hubris. Vanity.

"Will you take me . . . ," the boy mumbles, painfully endearing, and I'm listening until he says the word *home*.

Hannah. Check the clock on the dash. Two hours late! My teeth chatter. "Speaking to the young person I did not invite into my vehicle: you need to get out."

"Home?"

I tell the feckless miscreant my daughter's waiting at the airport, for me not him.

"Don't you have, like, a limo to send?"

"Too impersonal. Uptight. Wrong message entirely."

"Then like how about you loan me your lim—"

Holdout interrupts with a flurry of snorting. Useful for a change. I ask him when he forgot how to talk. Lovely timing, though, this revert to the mean. I empty the contents of the glovebox, claw at the leather seats, praying I was smart enough to pay a mechanic to build in a stash box, a secret passage, a Silk Road cyber-key. Me and Dread Robby are tight, Green Lead backed the pioneer onion routers early, although that dude's politics are like Ayn Rand and Yosemite Sam mixing fluids. I'm digging under the seat for my gear, babbling, trying to get used to living in constant terror, feeling nameless security agency scan-bots red-flagging me, tagging my identity, geolocating good ol' Blitz, so I take out my cellphone, scrawl texts and Tweets like:

XKeyscore/NSA/lonewolf/riseup/anarchistchef/MotherofSatan/
death/death/jihad/allseeingallknowing/MUSCULAR/revolution/
holywarforever/death/LOLCATASSASSIN/death/stircrazy/
CHAOS/killthepresident/mad/sex/boom!!!/FIVEEYES/death/
werewolfpacklove/revolution/chickenCOUP /turnupthenoise/
allahandjesussittinginatreeK-I-S-S-I-N-G!!!/seededdeep/
DEEPDIVE/secretconspiracytoconsume/RAMPANT/boom!!!/
bloodmakesmehorny/YokotaAirForceBase/hatemakesmereal/
vampiredominant/QUANTUM/deathcult/doyoufeelsecure?/TAO/
overthrowsupranationalundead/eveofdestruction/yourdataisourdata/
SpecialCollectionService/madhattersex/TATP/
ucantstopmehaterzforlyfe/stickyfangs/cybercommando/death/
TEMPORA/alldownhillfromhere/Semtex/unconventionalwarfare/

coup/TimMcVeigh/boom!!!/callingallheros/
weseeuforwhatureallyare/revolt/WEKNOWYOU/revolt/riseup/
revolt!!11AbAG!!1!!!!!1!!

Hit send, wait for the Black Hawks to come thudding in, consider purchasing a fully loaded Belgian Malinois, try not to think about Hannah—

"You find the gear?" Holdout asks. "Cuz you don't look so good."

—seriously fucking with the Tool's automated tracking searches, hurling syntactical wrenches in the cyber-snoop transmission, feeling low-level NSA analysts zeroing in, scanning my usernames, indexing metadata, dusting digital fingerprints, reconstructing network activity, parsing private emails, profiling, searching for that needle in the ceaseless shitstream, hoping they get lucky, bland and blind sticky-fingered moles nosing through my business, well it's all right here, guys and gals, in the open sunny sunshine—

"I think I'm missing *Housewives*," Painted Boy sulks.

—but they won't take me head on, nope, the spooks'll flame me, doctor my image and my rep, cyber-steal my shit, remotely disconnect my internet or my refrigerator, threaten me in other chickenshit cyber-bully ways I'll have to google for like three hours just to realize I should be scared, am being offered the weak-kneed digital equivalent of Tony Flatface tapping on my door with a lead pipe—

"Time is it?" Holdout says. "Hannah might still be at the airport."

I'M AFRAID

PLEASE DON'T HURT ME

I TAKE IT BACK

YOU'RE BIGGER THAN ME

I SHOULDN'T HAVE SAID THAT

Truth is I think I blew it, missed picking my daughter up, creating domestic distress even in my absence. Try to pry open the Tesla's

centre console, resort to biting the dash. The human face is not opti-
mized for gnawing something flat. Nose gets in the way. Eyes water.
I find a seat corner and begin in earnest. Holdout bounces from
front to back, snorting, spitting, licking, his face rotating through
the zodiac signs. The pig's feeling inspired, gets hung up on Libra,
decides to substitute Gandhi.

"Be the change you wish to see in the world."

"Shut up, prig. I'm still evolving. You eat my gear?"

Painted Boy starts belting a tuneless round of "Wonderwall,"
which has either deep-seated emotional significance for the lad or
has, unbeknownst to me, accumulated a sinister retro-cachet. Holdout tells him to shut up, then joins me in chewing apart the seats.
Solidarity among species.

I tell Holdout: "Regardless, I'm not sharing my stash."

Who knew Tesla Roadsters were stuffed with newspapers from
London during the wwii bombing campaign? Yellowed and crum-
bling, they disintegrate in my hands. For a second I feel I've broken
the code. Directed energy weapons? Eidetic thought?

Cast aside. More pressing needs consume.

And then I find it. Not my rig, but the most secret of encrypted
buttons hidden deep in Teslaean viscera. A button disguised as a
keyhole? Ah, you tricky buggers. Tinfoil hat, my ass! I'm shooting
lasers now! Give me something to throw money at! Holdout's shaking his rump in an excited manner, inviting me to deploy. I press the
button. The Tesla's interior shifts, swells, pulsates. Like being trapped
inside a stomach.

More favourably: a womb.

Yes. I'm blinking, tearing up, awed by the bigness, awakened to
life inside the sacred yoni. The divine mother Herself reborn as a
luxury electric sports car. That bitch is splitting lanes! A stretch?
Hardly. Either way I relax, make a semi-conscious effort to go with
the flow. An odd strip of fabric descends tight across my shoulder,
securing me into the seat with an ordnance-like click. I scream,

flow-going forgotten, while a greasy leather tube, a straight-up proboscis, elongates from the dash, forces my mouth open, stretches
my lips back, worms down my throat, flares with universal teleforce.
The leather tube's saltwater-taffy sweet, tastes of Coupland's free-
form future, the next era of techno-organic triumphalism. Suck on
that, QUANTUMSQUIRREL.

The Tesla roars soundlessly to life, continues its transmogrifica-
tion. It's like Easter, only more credible. My mind explodes, or
rebuilds, hard to tell. Bright light, all of it at once, and then, like it or
not, the Tesla's backing Herself down my driveway and we boys are
hittin' the road.

"Coming in hot!" Holdout screams, breeze ruffling his bristly
eyebrows while I moan and flail around the quivering proboscis, trying to remember if this was in the brochure—

✳

Irritated my cyber-animated Tesla decided not to swing by Michael
Zenski's house so I could show Her off, give the sulking micro-
manager the finger, claim another conceptual triumph for Green
Lead, prove I'm the ideas guy once and for all. Greasy proboscis is
lodged in my throat, leaking salty fluid, teasing gag-reflex tolerance
points. Eyes watering. Vibrating from my . . . core? Thinking lube is
the new must-have performance-driving accessory. The Tesla's on
autopilot, all systems go, rocketing down Oak Street, scaring the shit
out of everyone. Seems the car can sense traffic patterns, see the
future in real-time data uploads, perform anticipatory manoeuvres
to avoid collisions, which makes driving less interesting than a
Timbit. Only the proboscis makes it worthwhile. Still, I fret about
the car being more capable than me while waiting for the propulsion
thrusters to flare up. Holdout's fallen behind the times, reverted
to chewing on the upholstery, spitting and slobbering, while the
ochre-painted boy lolls in the backseat, filthy feet pressed against

the ceiling, whining about the data package on his phone; he has to check in, newsfeed, slow connection, this is so not chill.

We slow for a red light, pull up beside a soccer mom and her fuck-eyed toddler spawnling. Mom's got the radio cranked, window cracked. CBC. Something smart, upmarket, a panel discussion about the Libyan civil war. Informed and engaged voices. I slurp some drool, try and remember where Libya is. The Middle East, for sure.

The Tesla taps into the grid, digital superstructure, flashes a glowing green screen in front of my eyes. I watch the spawnling's life play out in social media images. See his birth at St. Paul's Hospital. How the family took him to Tofino when he was three months old because his father's a surfer and his mother wanted him to hear waves crashing against the shore. I see the child cry when he first heard the waves. See his mother dipping tiny toes in the rolling Pacific, how her body curves, holding her infant son over the water, a conflicted gesture, both sheltering and cruel. She wants him to be strong, isn't certain she has the will to make him so. The ocean's a big place, Mom. Sink or swim.

Through the Tesla's interface I glimpse the child's first solid meal, fresh carrot purée. His first birthday, at the Granville Island Kids Market. I see his future memories. Collected and curated. A careful process of image creation. And from these images the Tesla predicts the child's tastes in music and fashion, how he'll make love to his first partner, what he'll dream of becoming, how he'll adapt to failure, how he'll vote, what he'll read, who he'll scorn, who he'll lionize. This is a life lived in a constant, super-luminous glare, completely exposed, without secrets. A life lived on a barren, shadowless plateau, trapped between unremitting lines of earth and sky, lacking contours, hiding spots, foxholes, shelter. The child will not discover himself. He will have nothing that is his alone. He's already been discovered, blown up, played out, put to rest. His needs calculated and accounted for. The Tesla runs the numbers, predicts only two possible outcomes for such a life: absolute deviance or conformity.

There is no middle ground. The boy will become a cannibal or a paragon. Based on available data, the Tesla predicts the odds of the boy becoming a deviant at a scant .0049 per cent. He's born lucky: the child will mature into the happiness allotted for him, the life that is his birthright.

The glowing screen vanishes. Soccer Mom glances over, sees me deep-throating a yonic proboscis while Holdout smears snout-snot across the Tesla's half-open window. Flinches, spritzes the poor pig with hand sanitizer, no doubt thinking about germs, airborne particles, avian flu, mad cow, holy hell.

Holdout shrieks as cucumber-melon sanitizer splashes into his eyes. The pig uses his snout to roll down the window, but before he can shout something crude and disruptive the light goes green and the Tesla instantly shoots forward, no lag between idea and action. The G-forces hurl Holdout into the backseat. Painted Boy panics, smacks at him. From the sound of things—grunting, squealing, wailing—Holdout fights back.

A few seconds later we're approaching the airport's domestic terminal. Traffic slows. The Tesla zangs right and left, cutting everyone off, slamming on the brakes, riding hard up the shoulder. Horns wail, Vancouverites lean out windows shouting mild admonishments. I always knew intelligent machines would be adolescent, passive-aggressive assholes. Only consequence, fear of punishment and retaliation, the social contract, keep us lowly humans in line, and the Tesla lacks all those. Then we're up the final approach ramp and there she is, Hannah, my lovely young daughter waiting for me like she did all through prison, sixteen and already aged in the eyes, smallish, pale-skinned, maybe a bit elven, fae, a bit fantastical, parasomething, her straight black hair sitting flat against her broad skull, bangs cut in a sharp horizontal line—

The Tesla screeches to the curb. Painted Boy flings Holdout out the window, attracting the attention of a security guard and three RCMP. Shit gets real. Holdout, blind and screeching, runs erratic circles in front of the airport's sliding glass doors. Collides with a luggage cart, knocks over an elderly woman. It's not looking good for the pig. A cop gives the go-ahead and the security guard brandishes a set of hoofcuffs, leaps at my pet. Hannah staggers backwards, clutches her backpack to her belly like she's considering bolting. I moan her name through the greasy proboscis, indecipherable, while thinking *please stay don't go I'm sorry*. Holdout worms his way out of the rent-a-cop's grip, runs toward the Tesla, leaps—

Looks like he's gonna make it?

Not a chance.

Smashes headfirst into the passenger door. I try and scream at the idiot Painted Boy to let Holdout and my daughter into the escape pod so we can cyber-Tesla the fuck outta here but manage only a muffled *mmmph! mmmph!* because the goddamned proboscis-thing won't detach from my throat. Language stolen by the machine! Realize I'm living a primordial fear and the panic sets in for real.

Hannah's frozen on the spot, shaking her head slightly, eyes even wider than usual, wavering like she's about to collapse. The twerp Tesla revs Her electric engine, which is evident only by the RPM needle hitting the red. Cops circle, hands on holsters, eyeing the car. I look for the movie cameras and claw at the slimy proboscis, my body quaking. It comes out in painful millimetres, slicked in an opaque milky substance. One of the cops draws his lightsaber. I mean his Taser? My daughter plucks something from her backpack, drops it in the garbage can—

There! That's where I'll find her passwords if the snoops abduct her!

The proboscis pops from my mouth, sniffs the air, retracts into the dash. *Phew!* Finally free to be analog me!

Out the door, man of action, paternal capability, let me sort this nonsense out. Forget to check for traffic. A speeding yellow cab rips the Tesla's door off, spins me against the hood. *Whump! Bang!* Whoa! A cop shouts something memorized. My hands are up. I realize I'm naked and proud but the timing's off so I lean into the car, scramble to wrap myself in the foot carpet, make myself decent, which might take more than a carpet. More authoritarian shouting, easily ignored. I've fallen out of love with the Tesla, buyer's remorse, beginning to wonder why everyone's so fucking psyched with progress if it doesn't actually do us any good. Speaking of which, Painted Boy's snapping cellphone photos like mad, getting all the best angles—

"But I'm a productive citizen," I scream, clutching the carpet around my waist. "Almost a baby boomer!"

Tasers bared. My daughter's shaking her head in fast increments that could seriously blossom into a full-blown seizure or attack of some teenaged sort. Holdout, sensing opportunity in the form of a public full-frontal, sprints around the Tesla, latches onto the foot carpet, rips side to side like a Rottweiler on a baby. I smack the pig's head, tell him he's outgrown his welcome, he's supposed to fit in my satchel. The pudgy bastard must weigh fifty pounds. I tell him it's time to start skipping meals. Hannah gasps, clutches her stomach, unwraps a cold lozenge like she's buttering a porterhouse.

Holdout holds on, unfazed.

One of the cops makes a move, a guy with neck rolls who's really grooving on seeing my potbellied pig try to eat me. I dodge the cop's grip, spin a three-sixty. Holdout whips in a circle, caught in centrifugal force, clocks the cop in the ballsack, flat-ass bowls the Tool to the ground. I scream at Hannah to get in the goddamned car. She says something about a cleanse, makes me feel self-conscious. The cops hesitate, stunned by my unanticipated show of force, and in that instant the three of us leap inside the getaway.

The Tesla looses a not-so-welcoming cyborg-bee buzz.

"Is your car snickering at you?" Holdout asks.

"Watch this, honey!" Smacking the wheel, stretching my jaws wide, summoning the all-knowing proboscis.

Nothing happens.

"Dad my stomach hurts what are you—"

Rooting under Hannah's seat. "Uh, just a sec, hun. How's the flight? Turbulent? Nice weather in Vangroovy, eh? Sorry, pardon me, secret button buried in here somewhere—"

"The *what*, Dad? I'm seriously light-headed. Oh god, I ate too many barbecue peanuts, and the police—"

"Police? Are we in a no-parking? Gosh. Really cracking down—"

Frantic now, hitting every button, rooting under the seats while cops circle the Tesla, growl into shoulder-mounted radios, seal a perimeter. I ask Holdout if he remembers the mind-clearing code, scatter my rig across the front seat.

"Oh god Dad I thought I could deal but I can't deal seriously digestive buildup what are you looking for?"

"The fucking proboscis, Hannah! Wait for it!"

Hannah holds her hands to her throat, like she's physically pulling a breath from her lungs. "Mom was right I knew I shouldn't have—"

Where's the future when I need it? "No big deal hun don't listen to your mother waaay conservative the yonic proboscis early adopter paradigm changer think like a leather dog bone sprinkled with sea salt, smeared in molasses and insert—"

"*Aargh!* Leather? Do not say that word! Dad why are the po—"

"She's right," Holdout says when we lock eyes under my daughter's seat. "I smell bacon."

"Do not say bacon. Hemp seed, Dad!"

"Yummy fried bacon," Holdout moans, rubbing his belly and rolling between Hannah's feet. "Smelling greasy fresh sizzling fried fatty fresh bac—"

"Driver! Exit the vehicle. This is your last—"

"—secret inscription goddamn it Hannah trust me fuck you Holdout it was right here don't move the fucking latch portal button sinkhole legtrap switch icon key it's the coolest thing since—"

"Your Dad drove like this, Hannah," Painted Boy deadpans. "On the road. With me in the car. Wearing zero seatbelt."

Hannah glances in the backseat. Covers her mouth. "Oh god Trent is that you? Trent . . . not photos. Not online. Please?"

"Trent?" I ask, my fingers closing on the hidden button while the cops close in on me. "You two, uh, know each—"

"Yeah, Mr. Reed. Blitzo? Hannah and me went to elementary together."

"My stomach seriously hurts—"

"Elementary school? Small world, hey hun? That's wond—"

"I was like, three grades ahead of Hannah. So yeah. Hello again."

"Three grades? That makes you . . . *phew!* Hello to you too, freshly minted but legally adult young 'un—"

"Bacon! War! Bacon! Blood!"

"Hands up! Now!"

"Fuck you! No—I mean the talking pig! No, I mean . . . give me a second I'm a goddamned engaged parent!"

Cops. Boring. Socially conventional. Not down with my tech. Fucking dinosaurs before we discovered they had feathers, were basically oversized chickens clucking around the Phanerozoic grasslands, no wonder we triumphed over that backward-looking shit—

"Elementary school!" Hannah shrieks. "And you're both naked, Dad? Do you know what that *means?*"

A better me just might. "Trent's an all right kid," I tell my daughter. "If a bit unbalanced? Prone to . . . we need to discuss peer groups—"

"Adults are super hurting," Trent says, twisting in his seat and snapping a selfie with me and Hannah in the background. "Mega hurting."

"Ouch! Dad? The pig bit me! It drew blood!"

"You have blood?" Whoops, wrong thing to say, wrong time, tsk Holdout instead; he bares his teeth, bastard's rolling a fresh diamond grill—

"There!" I yell, hearing the hidden latch click. "Discover all that awaits!"

Settle into the seat, giddy, thinking coronal discharge, ultra-magnetics, thinking about proving them all wrong, making amends, anticipating my cyber-Tesla's Supreme Infiltration Upgrade, the one they don't sell to bitch-asses and yes I got the preferred rate. Instead something cold presses against my neck. A blue-white flash, would be quite pretty minus the urinating-lava feeling. Arms and legs go rigid. Heart balloons. The Tesla rockets forward, my mind stuttering along synaptic roads more blasted than an Iraqi border town until I realize, sweet mothership, I've finally been Tased!

"It wasn't all that!" I scream as the Tesla ploughs into the back end of a Whistler tour bus, ruining long-awaited holidays, and all I can think is: *street cred.*

Jasminder Bansal

A ction, the search. The city peeking from under the covers of an afternoon rain shower, streets cool and wet, clouds opening to the south over the Richmond delta and the sun coming in quiet and mellow. Spiral notebook in hand as I make casual inquiries at a dozen Vancouver language schools. The thrilling sensation of witnessing myself as journalistic sleuth. Trying to get an impression of how I'm coming across from the looks on the faces of the administrative assistants I speak to. A dozen schools, a dozen variations of waiting rooms and reception desks. Office chairs lined against a wall covered in nineties tourism posters. The Grouse Mountain gondola inching its way up a forested hillside. The Capilano Suspension Bridge swaying over a rocky ravine. I've never been to either. A glass or laminated-wood coffee table covered with magazines. Plastic plants in colourful pots. Tightly woven beige carpet. Light through half-open vertical blinds, a microwave beeping in the staff lunchroom, a class repeating verb tenses. I introduce myself at another reception desk, say I'm looking for a teacher here, Vincent Peele, does anyone know how I can get a hold of him? A dozen variations on *no, sorry.*

Then finally: I think so let me check the name sounds familiar. A few minutes later I'm speaking to the school's manager, a man named Alister, midthirties, rumpled shirt and fraying ponytail. He says he used to work with Vincent Peele here in Vancouver before Vincent went overseas.

"Overseas? Where?"

Alister stirs coffee in a mug that says *this might be merlot*, says Shanghai. He and Vincent kept in touch because he thought he might want to join him, or at least request a reference. I ask if he remembers the name of the school. Alister sips his coffee, tells a student waiting at the door that he'll be right out, says, "Yeah, not easy to forget. The school was called Globalized Success College."

Walking back to Marigold, feeling confident I can do this when a jacked-up truck hops the curb a half-block ahead. Parks like an asshole, forces pedestrians to swerve around the bumper and I'm only half noticing, not really paying attention, thinking about the cash I've already earned, plenty to get my brakes fixed, pay the electricity bill. Eric texts, inviting me to dinner at his friend's house tomorrow night, and it's the best I've felt in a long while, almost normal until a man steps from behind the truck and at first it's nothing, he's glaring at me but sure, he's an asshole, he probably walks around glaring at everyone, it's his default expression. Resting Asshole Face. I alter my trajectory on the sidewalk, give him space because I can't be bothered, pretend to window-shop and after a few steps Clint Ward grabs my arm, says see how easy that was, you stupid bitch.

Mark Ward

Me and Ryan work on the Alma house all Tuesday. Fuck all happens. I don't hear from Clint. No one's around; the homeowners are absent, and the house, a character home from the twenties, is filled with furniture but dark, empty. Feels all right, working in the mist and muck. Peaceful. Lots of time to think, if I choose, but mostly I turn my brain off, sink into the rhythms of work and an Oxy fog, blink and four hours have passed with barely a word spoken. Only the crack, thud, scream of tools, metal on wood, metal on metal: hammers, nail-pullers, Skilsaws, jackhammers. An occasional curse. Ryan, thankfully, is the kind of enthusiastic talker with the rare gift of knowing when to shut up.

One thing feels odd, though. Different than other jobs. It feels a bit—as we scramble around the house's foundation, hammering plywood to shore up the trench—like there's no reason for us to be there. And possibly no end, either. Jobs have a finish line. Do the work, go home. But on this house I half expect Clint to come around when we're done, tell us to tear it all out, begin again, and we'll spend the rest of our lives milling around the base of that lost structure, hands against wood and concrete, soft skin to mute object, covered in sweat and mud and sometimes blood, vaguely sensual, vaguely making me want to fuck, but no longer understanding what the object we're labouring on is for. Sometimes I'm filled with dread, and in my mind this dread takes the image of a welded steel tube filled with nails, machine bolts, ammonium nitrate and fuel oil and buried in the earth.

Other times the dread is even more messed up, two words flashing neon red in the bay window:

IMPENDING DOOM

IMPENDING DOOM

IMPENDING DOOM

which is enough to make me retreat to the Ford, fumble for a smoke, pop the cork on an Oxy. Sometimes the dread becomes a sound like a ringing cellphone and my wrecked leg buckles and I'm forced to sit down in the mud and Ryan says hey man you good and I say what are you looking at, keep digging. Other times I imagine lighting the Alma house on fire. The neighbourhood. The city. But of course that doesn't happen.

Me and Ryan suffer smashed thumbs, stubbed toes, aching backs. I nearly cut my foot off with the concrete saw. A half-pallet of bricks falls off the truck, almost crushing Ryan. He slips into the trench and almost impales himself on a spike of rebar. I call him careless, clumsy, tell him to watch out, he's going to get himself killed. We spend the day enveloped in dull pain, the ache of manual labour, and occasionally this pain is marked by the sudden, much sharper pain of trauma. The exchange is timeworn: we sell our bodies for cash.

I spend mental energy, on my smoke breaks, noting my work is similar to war, being *engaged in theatre*, stuffed in a metal coffin called an armoured vehicle, slowly roasting alive because the AC's out, choking on dust, being shot at, maybe shooting back, smoking, waiting, talking about nothing, and maybe it's your day to catch a bullet in the face, have your hand torn off when it gets caught in the chain of an

M242 Bushmaster, have the LAV saw you apart when it's shredded by an IED because the politicians were too busy bickering about the MEXAS add-on armour kit, a costly upgrade.

Labour has always served as peacetime boot camp to war. The body adapts to physical discomfort. This is the kind of thing I think about, driving in the rain across the Knight Street Bridge, over fishing boats floating in the choppy grey-brown Fraser, smelling tire rubber, fresh-cut cedar, and river tide. I think: pain connects us to our physical selves. Provides blunt, undeniable evidence we are of this world.

During lunch break me and Ryan are sitting in the Ford when he says he wants to go to California. I ask why. He says because it looks nice. On TV? I ask. Yeah, he says, looks nice. Sunny. There's an ocean there. We have an ocean, I tell him. Theirs looks nicer, he says, ashing his smoke out the window. Says their ocean's warmer, has waves you can surf, boardwalks, pretty girls. For some reason I get pissed off, tell him not to be a sucker. Tell him he's being sold something. Tell him the grass isn't always greener. Ryan looks upset. I tell him California's a dump, a fucking cesspool, full of money-grubbing thieves. Dickbags? Ryan asks. Yeah, I say, arrogant dickbags everywhere. And polluted as fuck. Don't . . . don't believe everything you see on TV, dumbass, half that shit's filmed here anyway. But the girls look nice, he says. Fuck you, I say, really starting to wish he'd be quiet. The girls are horrible. Shallow. Money-grubbing. Plastic tits that bust and leak. Ryan looks at me, says not all of them. They can't all be like that? I think for a second, say the ones you're talking about are.

Ryan picks at a blood blister on his thumb. It's silent for a long time. I get lost in a not-great thought about never seeing Daree or my daughter again and how much cash can I get to them because I got a feeling shit's gonna go haywire real quick. Then Ryan says, besides, it's cheap to get to California. How you figure? I ask. Because you're driving downhill, Ryan says. I laugh, ask why the fuck he thinks that, and Ryan gets angry, like he's being made a fool of, indignant in the fierce manner of a person talked down to his entire life, and the kid traces a circle in the air with his hands, says duh look at a fucking globe dude driving to California is all downhill, which is when something goes weird in my throat and when I can breathe again I say yeah, you might be right and offer him another smoke.

After lunch we're in the trench, exposing a cracked and leaking foundation when Ryan comments on how most of the houses we work on are empty, says he's never seen anything like it, which reminds me of something I saw online, maybe bullshit but who knows, about entire cities in China built up and never lived in. Condo towers, shopping malls, highways. Brand new and completely empty. Not a soul. Arid wind blowing dust through broken doors. I think about how odd that condensed time is. Even our ruins are contemporary.

Did the ghost-city urban planners design a skid row? A prison? Government buildings with stern-faced bronze statues guarding central courtyards, security cameras, defensive landscape architecture, precautions against the nonexistent population staging a protest? Were all contingencies considered? Disaster plans drawn up, outcomes accounted for? And, more pragmatically, I think about the point at which waste on a city-wide scale becomes a form of viable economic production.

My thoughts are interrupted by the trench slumping in, three hundred pounds of clay hardpan nearly crushing me alive. Leap out of the way, trip, sink to my knees in a foot of icy water, scream. Ryan laughs, tells me to be more careful or I'm gonna get myself killed. Later, back in the truck, I chew my peanut butter and jam, think about the people who died building those ghost cities. Ghost deaths. Counterweights slipping from cranes and bringing the whole mess down. Plummeting from ten storeys up because the bamboo scaffolding went. How absurd their deaths were. Why does it feel like those workers were fed to something massive, sharp-toothed, with a body made of mist, or dragged to the top of a pyramid, hearts cut out and consumed, corpses hurled down stone steps, only no fervent believers waiting to celebrate their deaths, no prayers, ritual robbed of significance? What will they do with those ghost cities, if they even exist, if it's not an elaborate hoax, joke's on me, Marky failed the internets? Tear them down? Build them back up? Rinse and repeat?

That's what's happening in this town. Tear it down and build it up, sell it, do it again, like Clint said the first day I arrived. Don't even need to move in. Remove use value from the equation, cycle speeds up, unrestricted capital flow, rising GDP, a river of cash. *Investment vehicles.* Everything clicking along, gaining speed and momentum, humming, tickety-boo. The only thing in the way is *us*. Consumption is very meatspace. Slow, antiquated. Obsolete. We're shifting to a higher level of abstraction. Creation and destruction in the same instant. Like a Hindu god. A subatomic particle.

Day's done. Pack up the tools. Still no word from Clint, fine by me, that Reed daughter work sounds like nothing but hassle. Drive Ryan to Commercial Station. About to boot him out when I'm like, fuck. Tell him he can crash at Clint's condo if he wants. Ryan doesn't ask about me knowing he sleeps rough or say thanks, just gives me a blank look, like it doesn't matter where he sleeps, like he hasn't slept in the same place for more than a few days in ages.

We get to the condo around six. Tired, filthy. Eat microwave pasta, smoke a joint, play *Call of Duty*. Ryan sits cross-legged on the floor because there's only one chair. The television flashes red and white. Things explode, reform, explode, die, get reborn. I'm feeling edgy, pent up. You have to sleep on the floor out here, there's only one bedroom, I tell Ryan. That's okay, Ryan says, hands twitching on the game control, staring at the screen. Outside there's a city, and beyond the city a forest, maybe something called Canada, but we're in a condominium, concrete walls, no lights on, only the television glowing and popping, and we might as well be in suspended animation or on board a nuclear submarine, asleep in the bomb shop, snuggling an eighteen-foot cruise missile because it's nice and cool, dreaming a coffin dream.

After he kicks my ass at *Call of Duty* Ryan goes to the bathroom, returns to the living room naked. Covering himself with cupped hands. Looks like a child who crawled out of bed and has to go pee. I ask what the fuck he's doing. I took my clothes off, Ryan says, chin raised, looking straight at me, defiant, refusing to be ashamed, refusing the weakness he thinks feeling ashamed would betray. I say yeah, I fucking see that. I took my clothes off, he says again, uncertain. A few seconds tick by, slow, protracted. I tell him yeah, whatever, now go get dressed. I can't pay rent money, Ryan says. I say good, cuz I'm not your fucking landlord. What are you? he asks. I don't know, I tell him. Something from the woods.

Ryan stands there, motionless, covering himself. I'm conscious of the world outside the condo, low overcast, muffled city sounds, strangers. I say: Get your clothes on, I'm getting a Pizza Pop, want one?

Is it because we're not fags? Ryan asks, trying to sound angry. I tell him, you need to hate someone, at least hate the right fucking people. He looks confused, standing in the empty condo, skin grey-blue in the light of the paused video game. Who's that? he asks, frowning, serious, goosebumped. I say that's for you to decide. We're silent for a few breaths. It's not a heavy or a bad silence. Can we play more *Call of Duty*? he asks. I say sure, for a few minutes. Then I turn away, light another joint, tell him I'm getting tired, got a long day tomorrow, then ask how he likes his Pizza Pops. Ryan returns to the bathroom, yells that he likes 'em warm but not super melted. A while later he comes out dressed in dry clothes, settles on the floor, resets the game. We share the joint, he kicks my ass at *Call of Duty*, looks at me, says fuck dude, I thought you were getting Pizza Pops.

∗

Can't sleep. Four a.m., sucking on a jawbreaker, scratching, staring at the ceiling fan, debating paying Mr. Craig Williams another recon visit. Scrap the idea. I know plenty about the target. More than I need. Going back serves no purpose, only adds unnecessary risk. Mr. Williams has a public profile on one of those social media fitness sites. Fit-tracker. Fit-wanker. I know his preferred running route if he's working on low-end endurance instead of intervals designed to build sprinting power. I know his maximum heart rate during various training phases and how he tweaks his diet for each phase. His weight. His favourite playlists. I know what days he meets his business partner and what days he runs alone.

This is a nice time, before engagement, when things feel solid, in control, and I'm in no rush. So all I do is grab my laptop, go online, find Williams's picture again, stare at it, say good morning, good sir.

It's still dark when I roll off my Therm-a-Rest. Drink water from the faucet. Do fifty push-ups. Hundred sit-ups. Three squats before my leg's killing me so bad I have to quit, pisses me off, the goal is five. Add fingertip pull-ups off the door jamb to get rid of being pissed off. Decide not to take an Oxy until after lunch at the earliest. Go to the kitchen, eat a PowerBar and an apple, boil cowboy coffee, pour it into a Thermos. Eat a boiled egg while I make two tuna fish sandwiches. Make a mental note to buy a slow cooker because I'm tired of paying too much money to eat shit food at gas stations. Then I walk around the island between the kitchen and the living room to wake Ryan up.

He's gone.

Search around, not expecting to find him. But he's curled up on the balcony, wrapped in a waterlogged blanket, lying in the narrow strip of dry vinyl beside the sliding glass door. I stick my toe in the small of his back, ask him what the hell he's doing out here and he says he can't sleep inside, it's too hot, he needs a lot of space around him. I say no problem, now get up, time for work.

Jasminder Bansal

Wake in the middle of the night sweating, blinking through an afterimage of masked men wielding machetes and grinning men with gold incisors. Blankets wrapped around my neck, where am I, militiamen carrying machetes and was that Amar standing at the foot of the bed?

Mangy yellow light through paisley curtains. Horrible taste in my mouth, stale gin and cigarette ash. Traffic noise so loud it vibrates the door. The door of where? City Centre Motor Hotel on Main . . . *shit*. The cash from Peele . . . three grand, more than I've ever seen. Then later with Eric on the Granville Strip because I didn't want to be alone after Clint Ward tracked me down, told me to get the fuck out of Marigold. I bailed on Eric halfway through the night. And now I'm alone in a dive hotel, not hungover because I'm still drunk.

A silhouette against the window. A man, heavily built, standing outside? Setting his hand against the glass, like he's trying to *feel* if I'm in here?

No, nothing. No one.

A shitty seascape painting hangs beside the bed. A two-masted schooner bathed in heavenly light as it crests a wave. Stormy seas. We shall persevere?

Lying wide awake, arms folded behind my head, watching head-lights slide across the ceiling, wondering how much would be enough? To make me forget Amar and walk away? Who can say five hundred grand wouldn't be enough? Or five million?

I think it would. Of course it would.

Reach for the bedside light, change my mind, decide to lie still, and the creepy feeling builds that if I move I'll be spotted, but by whom I can't say. The security chain on the door is ridiculously flimsy, a child's toy bracelet. I lie awake, thirsty, uncertain. Should I call Meeta? Eric? Sim? Pick up the hotel phone, wanting to say hi to someone. Say hello, I'm here. Do you have a second? Just to talk? I discovered something that might be big, a connection between Clint Ward and Vincent Peele and someone higher up but now I have no idea what to do. The dial tone buzzes impatient in my ear. Then I have an idea. A silly idea—

"Hi, Amar," I whisper into the phone. "It's me? Jaz?"

Nothing. Of course there's nothing. There has to be nothing. Because if there's something, a sound, a voice . . . no. There's noth-ing at all, which means I'm mostly okay. I flip onto my side, turn my back to the door.

What would Amar say? If he were alive with me now? If we were talking on the phone about what I know?

Clutching the phone to my ear. Dial tone painfully loud. Wanting to set the receiver down, hang up. But needing to hear him, or imag-ine hearing him, his unhurried voice, that smooth, self-assured manner. Amar had it all figured out. Right and wrong. Who he was and who they were. Where he stood and what he stood for. How did he discover his answers so young? Where did they come from? Who told him?

I hang up the phone.

Mark Ward

Fuck Wednesdays.

Carl "Blitzo" Reed

Prison. Jail. The slammer. Doing the bird. Will jail teach you a lesson, Mr. Reed? Will you be reformed? Improved? Nope, sorry, guess you'll have to accept me as I am: weak, flawed, imperfect, prone to embarrassing bouts of this and that. Trouble is this time around they didn't even give me a proper cell. I'm in the medical ward, for Chrissake. Zero street cred. No interesting people to lie to, be threatened by, mule dope for, make love to. Lying on a single bed, not even strapped down. Not considered a threat. Not happy 'bout nothin'. Feeling much too clearly. A small room, painted pastel yellow, with a rather sinister stainless-steel band of sheet metal running from the floor to about four feet. Prison wainscoting.

Designed for what? To contain fluid splatter?

And a single fluorescent light hanging directly overhead. Rusted wires. An obnoxious, fascistic light. Making my eyes water, making me moan and shiver. Illuminating pragmatic industrial fixtures and ugly, government-issue furnishings. Three sturdy aluminum and orange-vinyl chairs lined up against the wall. Chairs made to last. Made to cry in. Made to have long, drawn-out, heart-to-heart conversations in. Made to assist in reaching new levels of understanding, have breakthroughs, repent, be sent home to try again, try very hard, a non-stop trying machine, talking through it, communicating, maintaining positivity and optimism, learning life skills, strategies, coping mechanisms, while unbeknownst to us the orange-vinyl chairs snicker among themselves, knowing we must feel their unsettling sticky-warm seats yet again, fail again, sin again, repent again, the cycle continues, gotta laugh or court insanity, sorry there's no such thing as real change in the human heart, they lied to us, it's a racket, an ethical pyramid scheme, only good people believe change is possible because they've never had to try, we are who we are, nature and nurture, can't fight it only ride it, this is who I am, leave me be and for Chrissake please turn off the light, because:

I'D WAY RATHER DIE

THAN SIT BACK DOWN

IN YOUR FUCKING CHAIR.

Sensation of my body ends at my neck. This is the only upside. I can move my head, examine my body like it's not mine. No recognition of this pale, sunken chest, pudgy abdomen, flaccid cock hanging left, wormy, insignificant, what are you, overhyped, more myth than reality. So my body's waaay down there on the bed. Doing bodily things it was designed to do. Events shrouded in mystery. Guts doing digestive stuff. Blood pumping around, carrying whatever, heart beating. All involuntary, on autopilot, keeping me going for what? This is an appropriate time for an epiphany concerning the illusion of control. An appropriate time for humility. Gratitude.

Something like: *Thank God I'm ali*—no, fuck it, truth is I miss getting high with my potbellied pig, feel incomplete without him, way too drug-free for gratitude.

No windows in the room. Air pumped through a machine. Sliced through giant fan blades. Calculated, accounted-for air. A metal door, painted the same yellow as the walls so it blends in, and a

security camera mounted above it. On instinct I smile for the camera. I've been awake for days. Years. There's a squat, sturdy-looking
table beside the bed. Water in a paper cup. Pills in smaller paper
cups. Nothing worth looking at. They won't give me methadone.
Too expensive for inmates. So there might be some Gravol in there,
a few other mild packets of disappointment. Besides, I refuse to
take their goddamned government-issue poison pills. Pollute my
body with their neurotoxins and bovine hormones. Mush my mind.
Big Pharma's behind it. Forced vaccinations. Chemical castrations.
Secret test subjects. Aligned with the Agencies. All the information is there; you just have to believe it. Check out the quality blogs,
not beholden to Big Media, do your own research, courageous
down-home folks risking it all to reveal the truth about how they
ate a Snickers bar laced with Roundup and whatzit, felt a conver-
sion to Islam coming on, sawed off a cat's paw, drove backwards
three times around L.A. to cure themselves. Who stands to gain?
Big Pharma. Big Insurance. Big Guv. Toxic this and that. Madness.
Mind control.

Hospital pills? Nice try, nope. Big no thank you.

A prison nurse flings the door open, snorts, stumps in, leaves the
door open, a fact I find unsettling. Was she paid to do that? My name
on a jailhouse kill list, Helplessly Shanked, sounds like the name of
a wicked porn flick, leaves me feeling elevated. So I'm grinning at
the prison nurse, daydreaming about a solid prison shanking
where the only thing I can feel is my face. The scowling nurse ignores
me, goes to a stainless-steel table, fiddles with medical stuff, utensils,
tools, probes, esoteric apparatuses swiftly incorporated into my
ongoing shanking daydream—

This is a burly workhorse of a woman. A real take-charge type. In
my daydream I'm compelled to call her OVERSEER. Compelled to
beg, shriek her name while she orchestrates her collared and howling inmate posse across my penitent flesh. OVERSEER is possibly
Germanic but way beyond age twenty-five so no longer beautiful.

Now OVERSEER glances over her well-muscled shoulder, lifts a gleaming set of pliers, snarls.

The security camera zooms in on me strapped to the bed, writhing.

OVERSEER approaches . . .

"Pills?" she asks, her voice appropriately baritone.

"Sorry? I'm uncomfortable with your pharmaceutical approach to healthcare."

OVERSEER brandishes a device made of latex and stainless steel. "You habitually consume substances mixed in bathtubs, Mr. Reed. Did you take your prescription medication?"

"If you ask the right question I'll say yes."

OVERSEER glares at me in a not-sexy way. Not getting a potential illicit-encounter vibe. Not getting a carefully-orchestrated-for-my-benefit-inmate-posse-shanking vibe or even a like basic utilitarian nine-to-five hand-job vibe. OVERSEER does offer a tight, humourless smile that says: Do not fuck around. I deal with your kind all day long.

"Mr. Reed, have you taken your medication?"

"OVERSEER?" I say, raspy, anticipating. "GHB? Ketamine? Crystal meth? Cocaine?"

"No, Mr. Reed. Certainly not."

"Prison orgy?"

No answer. Could be a yes.

OVERSEER checks the PharmaPoison mind-control water in my paper cup. Checks my blood pressure, harrumphs. Empties a plastic bag of something. Does other routine nursing things I don't bother paying attention to. I'm trying real hard to hold on to the shanking daydream but the awful squinty-concentrating look on OVERSEER's face forces it away. One should never have to concentrate during an orgy. Totally ruins it.

"You ruined it," I tell her. "Could've been good."

"Don't piss me off," she whispers, which, all right, makes me freeze up, go silent, bug-eyed, studying her movements, guarded, afraid she's going to slip me something mass-produced, wondering why we've yet to mechanize this process.

"I need for-real drugs," I say. "ASAP."

The nurse encourages me to take my medication. Drink some water. Rest.

I nod, thinking if I could feel my body I could walk right out of here. Get up, walk through the pale yellow door, down the hall, out a well-marked exit. Jail break. The nurse touches my forehead, inspects something, takes me a while to realize she's changing my bandages. I tell her I can't feel my body. She says that's probably for the best, clearly doesn't believe me. She asks if I have any other questions. I consider: Would I like to know what happened? Where I am? What day it is? How long I've been here, and how long I am required to stay? I tell her no, thank you, I rather like not knowing. There's no mystery in the world anymore. Then I say: I will pay you a thousand dollars for real drugs. You already have drugs, she says, not making eye contact. Your pills are on the bedside table. Two thousand, I tell her. Two thousand dollars for not-fucking-around drugs. What kind of drugs? she asks. I already told you, I say. The nurse studies me for a few seconds. Fine, three thousand, I tell her. For a day's worth of proper drugs. Twenty-five thousand dollars a week for as long as I'm locked in here. But only for drugs that turn my brain into a bush party bonfire. The nurse smiles, touches my big toe with her index finger, says no thank you, Mr. Reed. I smile as well, tell her fine, I didn't mean it anyway, entrapment, she's free to go, passed the test, good girl.

Jasminder Bansal

At the Vancouver library, being myself, not wanting to go home. Quiet library sounds, respectfully restrained conversations, books flipping open and closed, carts being wheeled, a child hushed. Sitting at a second-floor desk facing a curving interior promenade, a tobacco shop, pizza joint, and ATM machine staring down the stacks across the courtyard, tense gladiatorial spectacle. Angled glass panes refracting building and sky into one another, folding the hypertrophied Coliseum knock-off into itself.

Pretending to read a hardcover coffee-table book about xeriscapes, endemic grasses, sustainable and water-wise, all the right choices, trying to imagine a life where shit like that matters, like maybe my sister's. Regrouping after last night at the City Centre Motor Hotel. Remembering how it felt at Langara when I was researching a story, a student enjoying one of her favourite places in the city, the whole world in front of her.

Healthful Vancouverites bustle through the promenade swinging shopping bags and leather briefcases. I'm wary of bumping into anyone I used to know, but secretly hoping I catch sight of them from my superior vantage. Interested in observing a former friend or classmate, studying how they move, what they're wearing, are they

with anyone? Are they enjoying successful careers? Trying to guess
the shape and timbre of their lives from a safe distance. What would
I say about my life? I'm in real estate, not a dream job but it pays the
bills, perfectly reasonable decision, nice to see you too . . . *blue oat
grass, prairie dropseed, summer aster.*

After a while I pack up, walk to the washroom, seclude myself
in a stall, phone Eric against my better judgment and because the
shitty truth is there's no one else to call. Voicemail. I hang up, irritated, about to leave when my phone rings and it's Eric sounding
surprised but not entirely happy saying hey Jaz what's up he thought
I'd be out with that great guy Vincent Peele.

"You're in a bar? I can't believe you're drinking after last night."

"Is that an apology? Ghosting usually happens online. You vanished. I called."

I sit on the toilet lid, tell him yeah, I needed to be alone, sorry.

Bar noise drowns out Eric's reply. He repeats his question about
Vincent.

"Seems not that bad? Why?"

"Listen to yourself. Only a few days and you're all-in? Jasminder . . . shit! Heads-up? You could've come worked with me.
Decent company. But not interested? Okay, listen. So you have . . .
a smidge of an inkling what Peele's about? How he does business?"

Interested now, digging for my notebook. "What about how he—"

"Fuck it, that's what." Eric takes a loud swig, yells at the bartender for another. "Know how he got started? Legend! Early
twenties, just graduated. Before law school. Bachelor of science
something. Anyway, Peele gets an idea . . . windmills, I dunno, solar,
renewables? Patent app, lawyers, whole nine yards. Business plan,
airtight. Goes to the gubbermn . . . federal . . . what's it called?
Research Council? Anyway, bullshits!"

"Bullshits?"

"Straight up! Hires a bullshit science guy to say it'll work,
straight-up bullshits the gubbermn guys. Talks his way into a sizable

grant. For some renewable nonsense? So . . . big business potential, congrats, everyone's excited, up-and-comer, green tech. Sure. Vincent Peele . . . fuck."

Eric's voice drops lower. Now I have it on paper and I'm feeling tense, excited, breathing quick, blood pumping like it always does and no, the money's not better than this feeling, not by a long shot—

"We're talking a couple million. For a bullshit patent and a decent pitch. Taxpayers! Woo-hoo! Anyway, Peele plays around a few months, sits on the cash. Then he's like, fuck this. Takes the cash, uses it as seed capital for a big development. Out in . . . wherever? His first real estate play. Speculative! Ten years ago, different times, bigger risk. Taxpayers! Course he's in it with other investors. Get me? No, pretty sure you don't. Hold on—goal!" The bar erupts in cheers. Beer bottles clink. ". . . shitty goal, but we'll take it. So no way, right? You're thinking, no way Peele can get away with it. Sink a bucket of taxpayer money into . . . not even into *anything* to do with solar! Into a condo build! But he did. Love the guy. But watch yourself, Jaz. Anyhow, gubbermn beans come along, say how's the windfarm-thing going? Peele says, oops, sorry, that shit went totally bankrupt. My bad. And ps I'm bankrupt too!"

"He went bankrupt, but the money—"

"He just *took* the fucking money. Paid guys to write receipts for blah this and whatever that. Y'know? R&D doesn't come cheap. So we got our team of fake scientist salaries, and our nonexistent management salaries, and our fake warehouse leases, and our fake materials outlay and now that material's all gone and oops there's a cool couple million gone in eight months, easy."

"But he invested in the development. That would've been traceable."

Eric's ice rattles. "Know what, Jasminder? I wonder what you're about. Since day one. Anyway how's it going? You . . . Marigold Group . . . you and Peele? Eh?"

Oh my fuck. "Eric? What are you asking? Exactly?"

"You and Peele? Y'know?"

"I'm not with Vincent Peele. If that's what you mean."

"You sure?"

Asshole. I let it slide, keep him talking. "I successfully completed my probation period as an entry-level sales associate. I'm now working with Vincent's team. Is this an issue? And yes, I have you to thank for getting me the job in the first place. And no— "

"Uh-huh, c'mon."

"C'mon what?" I give him a few seconds to see if he chickens out. He does. "So . . . Eric? Investing in the development would've left a paper trail?"

"Y'think?"

"Legally—"

"That a concern? Really y'think?"

"Peele invested cash straight into the property."

"Scores! Now let's say, you or me, average Joe or Jane, walk up, couple million bucks, hey, here you go! Mind if I sink this into your spec build? Nah, I don't need a contract. Or a receipt. No legal proof at all. I trust you guys! Whad'd happen?"

"Okay."

"Right. Means there's another system of checks and balances operating. 'Scuse me . . . ugh. Fucking kiwi vodka? Another extensive . . . underground system?"

"And the government—"

"Gonna do what? 'Cept not talk about it because it's so embarrassing? And that's 'ssuming . . . even you know . . . guy on the Research Council, big mortgage, retirement coming, hundred k kickback, no sweat ol' buddy? Or even, hey listen, better do the deal Mr. Gubbermn, because if no deal, burn your house? Yeah. That's Vincent Peele. Case you were wondering."

"Wow."

"Telling you, Peele's an asshole."

"Then why'd you give me a reference?"

Eric pauses. "You asked. Maybe I wish I didn't? Maybe I wish you'd quit? But you don't believe a word. That it?"

"I'm leaving room for embellishment brought on by booze and insec—"

Eric laughs in a way I've never heard: bitter, harsh. "'mbellish? . . . That right? Okay, Jaz. You're way in it, it's cool, we all are. Just thought you'd want to know. And it must be even worse for you. I've seen . . . because I know where you come from . . ."

Someone enters the washroom, slams the door, startles me. "Where I come from?"

"It's cool, really. Your gangster brother, that beater car, I saw, y'know—"

"You saw what?"

"It's . . . I followed you home, other night? Because you're always so . . . cagey about us? Like when we're out together, you're only half there? That's the feeling I got. So I wondered. Is she fucking married, something? Can't blame me."

Close my eyes. I thought I'd outgrow feeling ashamed about being raised broke. A family of four in a one-bedroom apartment in South Van, a brother who wanted out so bad he . . . and am I any different? Like Amar, only less honest with myself? Vincent Peele offering to take me skimboarding and that moment where I wanted him to—

"—so I get how you feel now, finally . . . doing well for yourself? Fucking journalism! Jaz? Can we look back, have a laugh? How young and dumb we were? I mean . . . what were we thinking? Journalism? Get a real job!"

"Yeah, journalism! Ha ha! Can you imagine? Get real!"

"Yeah, shit. What a laugh! Getting called a liar scumbag, trolled twenty-four-seven, can't afford a basement suite in this town? What a waste. So . . . do me a favour? You don't believe me about Peele? Think I'm being . . . fine. This is still a small town. Word gets around.

Check North Van last weekend. See what's up over there. Bet it's not all pretty."

Tell him thanks, dodge a question about dinner tonight, hang up. Head to the library computers because I have a silly but unshakeable suspicion my phone has been hacked. Search recent news stories out of North Vancouver. What a waste, huh, Eric? A violent home invasion pops up immediately. Two intruders, masked. Father assaulted in front of his family. House vandalized. No suspects. Father was a real estate attorney who did consulting work for Marigold—

An image of a howling Clint Ward kicking in a door and behind him another man, built lean, ragged black hair hanging over his eyes, pacing and spitting and scratching, furious, forgotten—

Close the browser window. Take a look over my shoulder. The library hasn't changed at all.

✳

Night. At my desk at Marigold, pretending to work while the janitor makes his rounds. This awful feeling of being stuck on the outside and wanting in but having no idea how to get there; this growing suspicion that if I work for Vincent much longer I'll forget what I set out to do, wake up one morning with absolutely no recollection of Clint Ward, memory erased, adult decision, the money sure helps.

The janitor's cleaning Beckett's office. Most of the lights are out. Beige cubicles with computers and printers, family photos, sticky pads, and I thought by now I'd have uncovered a hidden clue or secret sign. Isn't this when I discover an innate skill like telepathy or lock-picking that sees me through and saves the day? Isn't this when the real hero runs in for the rescue, smiles, says let me take it from here?

The janitor locks Beckett's office, unlocks Peele's. I wait until he's vacuuming, then interrupt, say the vacuum's too loud for me to get any work done, ask him if maybe he could do another floor and come back in an hour or so? He says sure, sorry, and after he leaves I spend twenty minutes rifling through Vincent's desk and photo-copying documents—

Mark Ward

Me and Ryan kill Thursday morning building a concrete-block retaining wall at a house on West 17th. Kid's dragging his heels, slacking, hungover. I'm not feeling too shit-hot either; leg's locked up, forces me to limp around like an ass, submerge myself in a deep blue Oxy sea. During coffee we smoke a joint on the customer's front steps, argue about whether I should let him drive the work truck. Ryan gets lippy, bugs me about slurring my words, picking. I tell him my skin feels thin. Like it can't hold all my blood inside? Kinda like the atmosphere can't hold all of us inside? He laughs, says this is only my first week working and how about we bet a c-note I don't make it two full weeks and I tell him to shut up.

Clint rolls up around eleven, honks. Ryan gives me an excited look. I say stay put 'til I call you, wander over, hop in the Dodge. Ryan gets to work cutting blocks, suddenly going balls-out to impress the big boss. Makes me want to smack some sense into him.

First time I've seen Clint since he got fitted by Peele's tailor. He's wearing his custom suit. Truck stinks of Colts, Cool Ranch Doritos, and Axe body spray. My brother's sweating, pale, eyes rolling in his head, hands twitching, legs bouncing up and down. Totally ripped. Ask him if he's meeting Vincent Peele today? Ask him if he has a tee time lined up?

Clint grimaces, tells me to piss off, looks across the street and into the yard where Ryan's working, seems surprised. "Twll still showing up?"

"Yeah. Wants to see you. You're the boss."

"Huh. That I am." Clint rummages through a backpack sitting between us, pulls out a wad of bills and a Red Bull. Hands me the cash, cracks the Red Bull, downs it. "I miss this shit. Crazy. Last thing I thought I'd say. But getting up, going to a job. Building something, you know, with my own two hands. Standing back and looking at it. Being satisfied. Go home, have a beer, forget it, do it again the next day. Now . . . you know? Business follows me around. Clings. Stinks. No downtime. Can't sleep."

"You do stink." Clint doesn't laugh. "Right now I'm not minding work. It'll get old soon."

"Leg's hurting. See you limping."

We watch Ryan work for a minute or so, then I ask how shit's going with Marigold.

"Peele said the loser he tasked me would bow out easy, this bullshit Indian said there's special bones buried in North Van, fucking straight-up trying to shake us down."

"Didn't bow out easy?"

Clint's hands skitter over the steering wheel, to his knees, to the steering wheel, to the dash, where he fucks with some dials on the GPS.

"I need to say this. Marky? You asked the other day. After you met Peele. You can get lost. You're out."

"That right? What about the money? I still owe—"

"Fuck the money. Chump change. You're out."

"Peele wants me out?"

"Maybe. Yeah."

Stretch my shoulders until my lower back pops. "That the truth? I had a long chat with Peele, remember? I know his kind. Any chance he gets to put a guy like me under the thumb, he takes."

Clint gives me a sideways look I don't like at all. "I don't think he's in it for the money. Not really. I think he's . . . more like you? He's got . . . something else going on. In the head?"

Clint picks his fingernails, reaches in the glove, pulls out the wolf's tooth, tries to tap out a bump but he's shaking so bad he spills half the blow on his lap, says *aargh* fuck me dead and licks his fingers, sticks them in the blow-mess, sucks on his fingers one by one until most of the blow's gone and here I am looking at my brother all sketched out because of fuck knows what horror and something inside me goes *zip-shoo* like a pressure valve releasing and I'm real calm, breathing regular, thinking clear, leg not hurting, colours brighter, landscape crisply defined, hands steady and this is how it was in Afghanistan during my only firefight, no one thought I had it in me until OPFOR rounds started whipping in and the shit-talkers shrivelled up and it was me first out of the LAV, not rushing, mellow, sighting the enemy down slow and careful, smiling, returning fire.

"That's a smart way to think about Vincent Peele, brother. I think you're right about him not caring about the money." Ryan shuts down the concrete saw, glances at the truck. "He's going to come over here," I say, nodding toward Ryan. "You top up his phone?"

"Phone?" Clint mutters. "Gets a pay cheque is all."

Ryan's peeking over the retaining wall, trying to play it cool, but I know he's trying to think of some legit-sounding excuse to come bullshit with the grown-ups. "So. It's you that wants me out? Not Peele?"

"Yeah. I think so."

I light a Colt, hand it to my brother. He takes a drag, winces, tosses it out the window. "Can you get out?"

Clint tugs at his tie, paisley, makes me want to puke. "Not now.

Don't think so? No."

"Why not? Tell Vincent Peele to fuck off. You're the muscle. Make that known. Bring the knuckles. Bring me."

Of course Clint can't do that. But I want to hear him say it. He's silent for a while, breathing too fast, then he sneer-laughs, bitter, self-directed. "You were right. Peele can talk a steaming pile of shit, but he's low-level. Not worried about him. But the people he works for?"

"That guy Tectonic?"

"Nah. Doubt that Chinese dude even exists. Mostly it's us."

"Cleaning money."

Clint jerks upright. "Make more money doing it. Perfect racket! The whole city." Clint sounds proud now, bragging. "I was in small 'til Peele came along. Helped run cash through a few houses. I buy the house, fix it up, get paid top dollar for the reno work, sell the house to a contact for a hundred grand more than it's worth, flow most of it back to him. I walk away with ten grand, find another house."

"Contact has a legit house to flip at an inflated market value," I say, "plus the clean cash from you."

"That's how I met Peele. Name got mentioned. Lawyers are exempt from reporting to Fintrac. You want to do a big deal with dirty cash, you use a lawyer. Snakes take a cut and it's done."

"Nice play. How you get the cash back to the buyer?"

Clint laughs. "Remember smurfing in high school? Sending the crew to make cash deposits under ten grand, all over town, so they weren't flagged and flew under Fintrac's radar? Old-school. Huge hassle. For a while I had a thing going with a precious-metal dealer on Hastings. I'd use cash to buy bullion, gold guy doesn't give a fuck, takes my money, I get a receipt, give the gold and the receipt to my guy, he banks it, rolls it into a legit investment, sells that and runs it through more properties. Tight." Clint presses his fists together, bulks up his chest. "With Peele it's . . . even better. Top-tier banker connect. I get the cash, banker drops it direct into the client's account, doesn't flag it as a cash transaction, takes his cut. Everyone happy."

"'Cept here you are, down at the bottom looking up. Like old times."

Clint bristles. "Took a risk. Money's real in the bank. Or it would be, if I hadn't spun it into Peele's bullshit syndicated mortgage . . . fuck! Used it to borrow more—"

"You want out or what?" Clint picks at the blow stuck to his pants. Says nothing. But I see him, and I know. "Only one thing to do. Exactly as they say. Hope when the Solstice is built and sold they let you walk."

My brother looks me in the eye. Can't remember the last time I saw him scared. We were kids, for sure. He was afraid of the old man until about grade eight. After that, he was only scared of looking scared.

So there it is. Clint's fucked.

"That's it?" he says, hunched over. "Do what they say? You went to school. You know . . . more about these people than me. Lawyers? Fucking bankers? And that's all you got? Keep working, hope they let me through?"

"What d'you want? A big plan? Nah. Too big to jail. Only way out is through them. Even me. I probably couldn't get out now. Look at Peele sending me those texts. So that's it."

"What?"

"I don't like you very much."

"Same."

"How it turned out. Didn't mean it. Not my choice. Different priorities. Philosophies."

"Hear that. So?"

Ryan takes a step toward the truck. I shake my head. Don't come over here, kid. "Not gonna cut you loose to them, brother. Not to Vincent Peele."

Clint gives me a look like he's trying to figure me out, sets a piece of paper in my lap. A scribbled name, Sebastian Price, followed by an address, vehicle description, licence plate. "Peele says it's go time. The Reed daughter. Squeeze job."

"Shit going down in Denmark?"

"Huh? This one's not too bad."

"Cuz he's breaking us in easy."

"Lord Byng Secondary. Old boyfriend." Clint taps his hands on the wheel, watches Ryan, tells me to send the kid over.

"What for?"

"Like he said. I'm the boss."

I tell him yeah, okay, head outside, memorize what's on the paper, crumple it, toss it down a storm drain, wondering if I'm being played by my own brother and maybe that's how I end up, willingly marching to the front lines like I did four years ago, full circle, feeding myself to it—

Jasminder Bansal

Home in bed, phone going nuts, a full hour after blowing off a client meeting. Sheets tacked to the ceiling drifting slightly, responding to invisible currents, filtering the late-afternoon light. Wall collage: pictures of friends from high school I've been meaning to take down since forever; images of Michael Moore looking harmless and unassuming and intentionally silly in his investigative persona and Sid Vicious with his lip cranked over-the-top cool; black-and-white video stills taken from one of my mother's performance pieces where she strapped heavy plaster constructions to volunteers and had them walk around the city while she filmed their restricted movements; Amar and me on the river delta, laughing, holding sticks and covered in sand; headlines from news stories I've filed away for study; me and Meeta at the PNE, fingers stained cotton-candy blue.

The documents I stole from Marigold are spread out on the bed. Read and reread, highlighted, heavily annotated. Lines and arrows connecting superficially discrete pieces of information, client and company names, account numbers, addresses, building permits, dollar amounts, fragments. I've cut out words and phrases and account balances and pasted them together and moved financial figures from one column to the next and changed names so everything makes sense like it has to.

Not enough emotional energy to get dressed, go to the office, settle into my persona, deal with Vincent and the rest of them. Not enough energy to lie. I take out my notebook, full of scribbled leads, try to find the words to open the story. My mother's been immersed in her screens all day. Hasn't spoken a word. Eric texted and reminded me we have dinner plans. Is he the first person I should tell? No. Not him. It has to be someone who wants to believe. I read a series of correspondence between Vincent Peele and a project manager named Russ Fuller. On the surface it seems like a normal everyday discussion about a rezoning application, but when I compare it to the document that shows the projected return on investment from one of Marigold's condominium developments in Steveston, and combine that with a landscape architect's conceptual rendering . . . then it makes sense, what they're really discussing, between the lines. Doesn't it?

Seems like I've been here for days, secluded in my oak-panelled study, chasing the truth, the dream materialized, in need of a real meal, sunlight . . . but I did it? I think I did it? It's all right here?

"Nothing goes up forever," Zachary says, his eyes distorted though red-framed coke-bottle glasses and clove cigarette smoke. "That's an historical fact."

On Zachary's balcony, bundled in a plaid Hudson's Bay blanket, appreciating the glow of the heat lamp overhead, watching a few beleaguered stars peek through a high layer of evening cloud. Made the mistake of answering Eric's call a couple hours ago; he enticed me out with an offer of G&Ts. I stashed the Marigold corruption research beneath my bed and, realizing I felt like celebrating the breakthrough, agreed to drinks. Zachary owns a web design company named, for reasons no one has ever explained, BLAPT! Another friend of Eric's, an investment advisor named Brice, is manning the hibachi, grilling pineapple slices for a March-in-Raincouver taste of the tropics, and the charred-sweet smell mixes with Zachary's clove cigarette and the juniper in my gin. The booze is almost worth a night with Eric and his friends.

"It's different this time," Eric answers, half-snickering at aping such an overused line but clasping his hands like a court judge about to deliver a verdict. He's seated next to me, sharing the same blanket. It's gotten to the point I don't even like looking at the man, never mind his voice. A long sip of my drink while I consider the least hurtful way to write him out of my life.

"There are less than fifty thousand single-family homes in Vancouver proper," Eric continues. "Not enough supply. Never will be, even with the laneways. Interest rates at historical lows—"

Brice flips a pineapple slice. The grill flares up. Flames reflect in Zachary's glasses and for a second I'm convinced it's not a reflection but real fire. The image fades as quickly as it arrived. I haven't suffered a grief vision since I started pursuing the story in earnest.

"It's true," I say, tired of the shoptalk but curious to see where it goes. It's not every day I get to hang out with people like Brice and Zachary, different social strata. I tell Zachary the bar has shifted and it's a very exciting time, surprised by how the lines sound natural after only a week. "Frankly, Zachary, I'm surprised you haven't—"

Zachary pinches his clove cigarette like a joint. "I'm very happy renting. Like they do in Europe? This fixation with single-family homes is *very* North American."

"So you wouldn't buy a home even if they were within range?" Brice asks, pointing the barbecue tongs at Zachary while sirens sound ten storeys below.

Zachary pauses. "I'd need to do the math."

"The math always works, long-term," Eric says. "Zero financial advantage to renting. Not building equity. There's a reason they're called land*lords*. Property—especially in Vancouver—is an incredible wealth generator. I mean, the average—"

"We know the averages, Eric," Zachary says. "And there's more to the equation. But you're either in or you're out, correct?"

"Well," I say. "Everyone needs to make the decision that's right for them. But for me, personally—"

"I'll tell you what's ridiculous," Brice interrupts, draining his Scotch and handing it to Zachary for a refill. Brice is twenty-eight, wavy blond, wearing thrift shop jeans and a five-hundred-dollar T-shirt. "Take someone like me. Born in this town. Went to school here. Make a good living in investment. Like, a top-three-per-cent kind of living? I care about this town. And I'm priced out. How does that make sense? Top three per cent?"

When Zachary's finished pouring Brice's drink I hand him my empty glass, stop myself from pinching Brice's limited edition T-shirt when I say, "Um, at top three per cent I don't believe you're truly priced out—"

Brice sets a charred pineapple slice on a plate, hands it to me while Zachary sections lime for my drink. "Oh, I am. For sure."

An unwelcome whiff of BBQ ribs is grilled into the pineapple. I tell Brice thanks, set the plate on Eric's lap.

"That's the market right now, Brice," Eric says, adopting a diplomatic tone while he sits up to eat the pineapple. "The best is to get in—"

"It's an artificially inflated market," Brice says. "I mean, c'mon guys. We all know what's going on. Look at the class photos of my high school. Look at the ratios, Caucasian to Asian, between say 1990 and now. Look at who's buying these houses. I mean, really? We're all friends here. Tell me I'm wrong?"

"Condos too," Zachary says, blowing clove smoke rings that wobble toward the window and dissolve on contact.

Eric watches me down my gin and tonic, gives me a fretful look. "I estimate only thirty per cent of buyers are foreign. Most want to move here. This foreign buyer thing . . . it's a lot of spin. There's no hard data. It's entirely anecdotal. And frankly, Brice, a lot of the rhetoric degenerates into xeno—"

Brice laughs. "Do they pay taxes? Is their money legitimate? That's what I'm saying. It's not racist. It's math. Why aren't we tracking this stuff? Shit. If you knew how many of my friends, professionals, smart, hard working, had to move to . . . Langley . . . or one of these . . . ugh, suburbs, simply to have a home to raise their family . . ."

I set a lime slice between my teeth to stifle a laugh or angry outburst. Check my phone. Hoping who called? Sim?

"It's true," Zachary says, taking over the grill while Brice is distracted. "People are moving. Especially in the creative industries. Soon Vancouver'll be banking and—no offence, Eric and Jasminder—people involved with property. And the mega-rich. Is that what we want?"

Brice nods. "And there's this incredible tsunami of money, and no one has a clue how it's being earned. I'm not asking to limit foreign investment, people. I'm *in* investment! All I'm saying is a guy like me should be able to afford what he wants. There should be controls—"

"Controls are a good idea, sure," Zachary says, serving himself a pineapple slice and turning off the barbecue while Eric sets his empty plate on the floor and I watch two indistinct figures make love in a condominium across the street. "Shouldn't owning a home be, like, a human right? It's clear we need government regulation."

I finish my drink, set it down, tired of putting my teeth through my tongue. Toss the blanket off my lap, stand, stretch. Pour myself straight gin on ice. The men watch, waiting for me to settle.

"It's the market," Eric says when I stay standing under the heat lamp and he realizes I'm not going to return to my seat. "Supply and demand's calling the shots, guys."

Brice clues in to me avoiding Eric, gives me an interested glance. "I've seen it again and again. Junk bonds. Tech start-ups. Mortgage-backed securities in the U.S. only a few years ago. All the boom and busts. Something has to give, and when it does it won't be pretty. We should act responsibly now to limit the fallout. I mean, even a goddamned plumber makes six figures in this town. And if he flips houses—he makes millions."

"Is that terribly unpalatable?" I say, sounding way more snarky than I intended, but I take a quick sip of gin and decide to roll with it, so what?

Brice raises an eyebrow. "Pardon me?"

"Is it so horrid for a plumber to make six figures? Millions? Because he's a tradesman?"

Brice shoots an accusatory glance at my drink, then at Eric. "I'm sorry, Jasminder, you've misunderstood. It's not horrid. It's inflated. That a man with barely a high-school education—"

"Has the gall to make as much as a white-collar professional?"

Zachary snickers, lights another clove smoke, apparently keen to play the rebel, sit back, let this drama unfold—

"I make significantly more than a plumber, thank you." Brice lifts his glass in self-congratulatory cheers. Only Eric obliges. "It's not a value judgment. It's an economic truism. The market can only support—"

"Oh, shit, Brice, the *market*? That's fucking rich—"

"Jaz—"

"Do not do that, Eric. Please let me finish. Brice? You're a big fan of the market, right?"

"Well, I—"

"Yes or no."

"Sure. Yeah. Of course. I mean . . . what else is there?" Brice looks around, slightly confused, like *who is this chick?* The men shrug and nod.

My hand's on the door handle. I could leave now, or take it down a notch like my mother says, but instead I say, "Great! Because this is the free market at work. Right here. And you, Brice, who gets paid to argue why markets should be free from regulatory interference in China, in Cuba, in South America, arguing all day long, lobbying, suing, pressing for so-called free markets so your big-business clients can move in, now, suddenly . . . when the market doesn't advantage you over others, suddenly . . . you're all for *regulation*? Isn't that the fucking straight-up opposite of everything you stand for?"

Eric tosses the blanket on my unoccupied chair, stands. "Jaz, is it getting late?"

Zachary, through a cloud of exhaled clove: "Okay, I think you're right on the money and all, but it doesn't need to be said—"

I open the barbecue, take a bite of pineapple, wash it down. "Like hell it doesn't. Please let me finish. Because here's the thing, Brice. The market privileges few at the expense of many. Always has, always will. Only . . . you've never experienced this other side. You've been riding this incredible tsunami—to use your awful expression—of advantage your entire life. And now, by some fluky collision of global circumstance, the market doesn't work only to advantage Bricey and his born-in-Vancouver Sauder business buddies. Suddenly there's—*gasp!*—actual competition for resources in this town. Valuable, scarce resources that are in global demand. And now, golly shucks, it's time for government regulation to protect your interests. It's time to whinge and whine and point fingers at all those criminal foreigners."

Eric's trying to wave me down, makes me furious. "Jaz—"

"Eric, yup, I'm a little drunk. Don't like it, too bad. Am I such an embarrassment? Could you get any more boring? Seriously. You're like a fucking walking Ambien."

Zachary laughs, pats Eric on the shoulder, and before Eric can interrupt again I continue. "Bricey! Take home, ha? You feel absolutely entitled to homeownership. It's an integral part of how you envisioned your life. Your colleagues in Seattle have houses. You're in the top who-gives-a-fuck per cent! But the market entitles you to exactly nothing. This is a lesson people all over the world—in far less advantaged circumstances than yours—have been learning for a long time. And you, unlike so many others, are still fortunate enough to have *choice*. You know, all those hard choices people very unlike you have always had to make to own property. Zachary, lovely view, thanks for the pineapple. Eric, goodnight. I'm a big girl. I'll find my own way home. Do not call me."

My key's in the lobby door when a man slides from the shadows behind a pillar and I get a conflicted fear that's all about fighting the urge to scream and not wanting to look foolish should the threat be imagined.

"Hey, easy," the guy says, and I laugh, embarrassed, when I see who it is.

"Anyone ever tell you you're a beefy brown dude, Sim? Sneaking around in the dark? You already have an image problem."

Sim makes an unimpressed sober-person-speaking-to-drunk-person face.

"Sorry. Shitty thing to say. You could've called?"

"I did. Several times. Why's your phone off?"

"Because I want it to be."

Sim looks at my apartment's flaking pinky-green stucco and the weird thing is with him I'm not embarrassed. We came up together. I dig my nails into my palms, remembering how good Vincent Peele's envelope of cash felt. Slump against the door, almost slide onto my ass, ask Sim what the hell he's doing here.

"You all right? Jaz?"

"Ducky. You?"

Sim's wearing designer jeans with a slight sheen to them, a white dress shirt, and a black leather jacket. His bulk fills up the jacket very nicely. I notice the worry lines around his eyes, realize we've both aged. My oldest and only friend Sim Grewal is exactly how I want the night to end. He catches me looking, returns a glance that feels heartworn, makes my pulse quicken in unwelcome ways.

"Let's get outta here," I say. "I still haven't seen your new place? Then I'll be all right. I miss your legs."

Sim almost smiles. "Legs?"

"Sexy legs . . . something wrong?"

"Sexy legs? No. Just . . ."

"I miss all the usual, too."

"Sorry, Jaz. Not what this is."

"Lucky me. Not only not getting laid but making an ass of myself. Seems to be the theme tonight. Thanks for stopping by—"

Sim widens his stance, lets me know he's not leaving. "You got a new job. You didn't tell me."

"This is your business because?"

"C'mon, Jaz. I'm a friend. Remember? My business because I know why you're at Marigold."

Sim's tone makes me want to kick him. "So you're ambushing me to say congrats? Celebrate? Because that's what I'm doing. Less than a week and I'm already working on several significant property deals. There. You're the first person I've told." I hiccup, cover my mouth, apologize. "Maybe I'll even get my brakes fixed. Imagine that! This mouse is moving up. It's about *risk*, isn't it, Grewal? Risk and reward. Amar knew that."

Sim withers at my mention of Amar. "Not here to celebrate."

"You never look happy anymore. Where's that gorgeous Grewal smile? Too much time holed up in the club?" I lurch from the door, do a passable job maintaining my balance as I walk to him. Sim holds his ground. It's a cool, cloudless night. A man filters out of the apartment and walks past, head down, pretending not to notice us. Drape my arms over Sim's shoulders, tug him away from my shitty apartment, my mother up there, miserable, grief-stricken.

Sim takes a step away but I hold on, pushing into this man I loved, remembering the quiet girl I was with him only a few years ago, feeling him here now, wondering why I've changed and he hasn't, that I want him tonight but not in my life—

Sim steps out of my arms, plants a hand on my shoulder, pushes me away. "You have your brother's ambition, Jaz, but not his street sense."

"Has-been," I say, shocked at the fury in my voice. "Don't you mention Amar. You're not in the same league, and never were. What've you done after him? A sort-of pimp. A wannabe with pretensions, couldn't make an honest living, and now that I am—"

"Honest? You fucking serious?"

"I'm not disinfecting brass poles."

"Hate on me. But you have to quit that job. Those are not good people. Phone Peele now. While I'm with you."

The stolen documents are stashed beneath my bed. What if I don't write the story? I heard the sales numbers Beckett and Elodie trotted out in the Flowroom. "What if I don't care who Vincent Peele is? What if all I want is in?"

Sim waits for a semi-truck to crest over the Knight Street hill. "Doesn't matter. You're not hearing me. Quit the job. Fuck's the play, anyway, Jaz? Money on the line for that project . . . you think Peele will risk having you around if Clint outs you?"

I cross my arms, try not to think about Clint's warning. "Peele's a twerp. All talk."

"That right? Here." Sim shows me his phone. A photo of a recent arson on a block of Main slated for redevelopment. "That look like talk?"

I'm stunned, try to rally. Sim waves his hands in appeasement like hey little girl sorry to deliver the bad news but it's time to wake up, like I haven't made my choices knowing the consequences full well. "Are you not hearing me, gangster man? Everyone's into something. Why should I be any different? Because you have a teenaged bullshit fantasy of who I am? Here, let me find my fucking sari . . ." I stop, wait for my voice to strengthen. "I made three grand this week. Maybe that's not much to you. But to me? That's life-changing."

"Jaz, money's not enough."

"Really? This brown bitch makin' real bank. And you hate it?"

Sim retreats down a few stairs, seems about to say something, stays quiet. It's late, but there are plenty of people around. I know what he's thinking. *Drama. What a fucking heat score.* I could call after him. What would I say? What if Sim's involved? These guys are all connected. Sim learned from my brother's death. Invested in the club. Other legal businesses. It was wrong to call him a pimp—

A blacked-out suv speeds by, the rear window rolls down, a man wearing a balaclava raises an ak-47, and I almost shout a warning when the suv accelerates and its muffler roars and I'm left alone, staring into shadows.

Mark Ward

Pacing outside Lord Byng Secondary, staying close to Sebastian Price's car, waiting for the kid to come out from evening basketball practice, shake him down for dirt on Hannah Reed, piece of piss. Kid's family's loaded. I'm guessing he's never been in real pain. Maybe not even afraid. Easiest kind of shakedown there is. Drop my smoke, step on it, keep walking. Voices drift from beside a three-storey brick building that houses the classrooms. A group of guys come out of the gym, wearing basketball jerseys despite the rain, walking quick, jumping and smacking at one another, whole life ahead of 'em.

The jocks reach the street and split up, heading to their cars. Beamers. Mercedes. Lexus. Sculpted cars, streamlined by a heady mix of money and aggression. Cars that speak like weapons. That convey a very specific message. Cars that are more articulate than their drivers. I see my target: gangly, no chin and big nose, sweaty blond hair, carrying an army-green backpack. Walk by him, take a look as he hops in his gunmetal-grey 911.

Alone. That's good news.

Problem is the target's buddies are hanging around bullshitting. Decide to take a risk. Hurry past my target, get in the Ford, tear down the road a few blocks, thinking about where Sebastian's house is and the route he'll take to get there. I could wait outside his driveway. But that's dogshit. I need to cut him off before he gets too close to home, so I crank a right, then a U-turn so I'm facing the street I think he'll take. Out of the truck, hang back from a stop sign, listen to the kids' pimped-out cars as they leave Byng, throbbing bass, squealing tires, performance mufflers. Pull my hoodie up. A car slows at the intersection, not the target's. Bend down, pretend to tie my shoe, nearly miss Sebastian, the fucker, coming in fast behind the first car and rolling through the four-way—

Leap in front of the Porsche, deploy, no time to put my balaclava on. Sebastian slams the brakes, clips my good leg. I take a dive, slam my hand on the hood as I fall. Face first on the road, rain thundering down, the Porsche's lights blinding me, five hundred idling horses rearing to charge. The puke floors it, tries to pull around me. Hit and run. Or maybe Sebastian's not a total moron, senses something's off, carjacking, *stay indoors*, it's a scary world full of people who want what we have, son.

Either way I fucked up.

The car doors will be auto-locked. Sebastian's pretty safe unless he gets out. Which is what I need to have happen. So—not thinking; acting on instinct—I fling a handful of gravel at the Porsche as it screeches past.

Kid's a dumbass. Cocksure. He's a *somebody*. This is his neighbourhood. His sports car. Who am I? No one. A vagrant, a beggar, maybe a junkie out casing houses, and now I'm throwing gravel at his Porsche? The nerve of a nothing like me not knowing my place? This is a big affront to a kid like Sebastian, fucks with his world view, his pride and vanity. He slams on the brakes, hops out, blinking against the rain, chest swelling up like a jungle bird, amped to kick this junkie dirtbag's ass—

"What the fuck was *that*?" the kid shrieks, his voice cracking.

I let Sebastian lift me, let him raise his hand to smash his fist in this junkie loser's face, look him in the eye and knee him straight in the balls, real solid, *whump*, oh you need those? Kid crumples, throws up, just misses me. So now we're roses. Sebastian's a baby-doll in my hands, limp, moaning. Grab the target by the hair, drag him to the Porsche, shove him in headfirst.

Slip my balaclava on, set my watch timer to four minutes, tell the shitbag well hey buddy that's that.

Carl "Blitzo" Reed

My wife's lawyer visits, bringing good drugs and bad news. Name's Leon Burris. Leon's short, bulbous in the middle, squished. Wearing tennis shoes without socks, dorky pleated shorts, a lemony golf shirt that matches the walls of the room, leads me to believe there's a weekend occurring somewhere. Leon is completely unassuming. A slack-jawed shuffler. A man unconsciously avoided for fear his loser-dom can be caught like a cold. Heels brush the floor as the lawyer shuffles to my side, puts his body between me and the security camera, plunks a Ziploc bag filled with white powder in my palm.

"Forever yours," I say, sincerely grateful. "Anything she wants for more of this. You tell Heather that. Tell her she doesn't even have to come to the surprise summer solstice party they're throwing for me. Have we nailed down dates? So I can pencil it in? Because, uh . . . unjustly incarcerated, and possibly for quite a while? Speaking of which, Leon? Is today Saturday?"

Leon doesn't say a word.

Takes a lot of self-control not to place the entire Ziploc over my face. A giant bump reveals icing sugar. I choke and sneeze, dust myself in sickly-sweet powder, too disappointed to scream. Drop the Ziploc on the floor.

Leon doesn't move. Just stands there, looking like a loser, winning. "It's Thursday, not Saturday, and yes, you're in prison again," Leon observes, his voice lispy but lacking inflection, breathing on me on purpose. "You owe me fifty dollars."

"Huh? Did we bet—"

"And . . . you pretend not to remember. Which means you owe me another fifty."

I decide not to let the message boy into my head. "Holdout's digging an escape tunnel. Gonna chew through that lino any second. Don't make me sic him."

"Your super-pig's not here, thankfully." Leon sets a manila envelope on my chest. Taking his sweet time. Taps it and says, "Divorce."

"Capital *D*?"

Leon taps the envelope again.

"You sure?"

"This time she means it."

"What's different?"

Leon rubs his nose, sniffs his fingers. "The teenager, Trent, your lovely young daughter's elementary school friend, has provided ample photographic evidence of your most recent aberrant behaviour. We were very fortunate to acquire those photographs before they were made public. An embarrassing state of affairs for the minister of the environment, as you might imagine. But we have them all. Among other evidence. A carefully curated history of your various studied and storied . . . perversions."

"If you only knew."

"We know plenty."

"Nah. You weren't around for the real Heather Reed. Honourable Minister, my bumpkins! Uh . . . bum kiss? What if I air it out? Another ruling-class drama? I hear the hoi polloi can't get enough. Set it in the seventeenth century, somewhere exotic, boobs and bad language, score a Netflix deal! Cuz you want to talk perversion, I once saw Heather—"

"You won't do that, Carl. Everyone knows you won't."

"I almost could too. Why won't I?"

Leon pretend-smiles. "Because you're weak, or good, which in your situation amounts to the same thing. You care about your soon-to-be-ex-wife and your emotionally fragile daughter. Don't go down that road. The ethical course of action is to let yourself be destroyed, spare your family, take that quiet victory to your grave."

"Had my fill of self-sacrifice when I turned myself in. Besides. Smacks of unenlightened ego."

Leon opens his arms. "Then please, air it out, as you say. Hannah on the stand. Sobbing."

"Heather's tired of the close calls? Fine. Tell her I want to hear her demands delivered in person. Tell her I do not negotiate with the undead."

"The undead are beyond making demands. We've risen to feed."

I close my eyes, wave the lawyer away.

When I open them Michael Zenski's sitting in an orange vinyl chair, looking tired. I tell him his facelift is slumping. Ask when I'll be released. Michael says it depends on how I behave. I tell him that's wonderful, thanks for taking the pressure off so I can focus on staying sober.

Michael sets a cellphone on the bedside table, talks about impending criminal charges and all I hear is: driving under the BAD, possession of BAD, resisting BAD.

I try and appear concerned, ask if he wants to get right in my face, yell BAD PERSON. He calmly assures me I'm not a bad person, I just make bad choices. I say oh my fucking god are you serious? Michael doesn't answer. I tell him substituting a watered-down definition of a word for the word itself doesn't help in any way, only serves to confuse the issue, delays the fact that I must accept and come to terms with the truth that I am a BAD PERSON in order to move on, recover. Michael says no, you're not a bad person, but your behaviour is bad.

I say Chrissake, you did it again, please say what you mean, please respect me that tiny bit, please treat me like an adult who is capable not only of dealing with the actual honest-to-god truth of what I am but also understanding when I'm being bullshitted to death and talked down to using ridiculous condescending euphemisms. Ask him if a person who consistently makes BAD CHOICES is not, by fucking definition, a BAD PERSON.

Michael says no, there's a moral dimension. I say bet your ass there is, and you're on the wrong side of it. Michael says it's about not being judged. I laugh, maybe a bit too shrill, say look around, I'm in PRISON. I've already been JUDGED. Then I say, wait, no, this is fun: I'm not in PRISON; I'm just LOCKED IN A ROOM AGAINST MY WILL. I'm not SICK; I just have DIARRHEA, NAUSEA, A FEVER. I'm not CRAZY; I just BELIEVE THE EARTH IS A FLECK OF ALIEN TOE JAM.

Michael says okay okay, there's a finality to calling someone a bad person, it robs said person of the opportunity for change, suggests that if I am bad in the past I will always be bad, whereas highlighting specific behaviour emphasizes what the person does, their choices, which are changeable, as opposed to what a person is, which maybe isn't? I ask if he's saying BAD PEOPLE CAN'T CHANGE. He says maybe? Then he tells me he's done talking about it, it's not why he's here.

I say: wait, we're finally getting somewhere, is that why it's so hard to say BAD PERSON, because really deep down you believe it's for sure FOREVER? Michael stays quiet. I say because that sucks, Michael, really really sucks, because the truth I want to hear is that I am a BAD PERSON now, and was a BAD PERSON then, but can work to become a VERY GOOD PERSON forever, TRANSFORMATIONAL CHANGE, chemical as opposed to physical, an entirely new substance, chrysopoeia, OURO-FUCKING-BOROS!

Michael asks can you please keep your voice down? I say all right but never mind, I'm not in LOVE with you, I just want to LAY DOWN AND CRY WHEN YOU'RE CLOSE BECAUSE I'M AWED THE IDIOT UNIVERSE OFFERS SUCH JOY.

Michael sets his forehead on his knees, hugs his legs, rocks back and forth, tries not to cry too loud, makes me worry. After a while he straightens, blows his nose, sets a manila envelope on my lap. I tell him I've come to hate the things, what good news was ever delivered in a manila envelope, ask him if he's been successful calorie-restricting Holdout.

He doesn't answer, tells me the envelope contains an offer to buy me out of Green Lead. Says I've become toxic to those who care about me. A living pollutant. I tell him I have an addiction, that the opposite of addiction is not sobriety but community. Michael sighs, says he knows, that's what makes this so hard, but you can only take a friendship for granted for so long before it ceases to be one. I ask him if he brought me quality drugs. He says no. I say: Then are you here just to hassle and depress me?

There's a flat-screen TV mounted on the wall. I ask Michael if it's new, that I didn't notice it before. He says how the hell would he know? I settle in to watch a reality show filmed in some aging movie or rock star's mansion. The washed-up star is doing an interview in front of a wall of memorabilia. Bobblehead dolls. Trophies. Glassware. The star looks like something long buried and recently exhumed. The sound is turned off. I study the star's face, making up dialogue to go along with his puffy Botox lips. I tell Michael this is very odd, I don't remember a television being there last time I woke up. Michael asks if I'm sleeping a lot. I tell him yes.

"You seem fairly together," he says. "I'm offering you a hundred twenty-two million for your position in Green Lead."

"*Pshaw.*" A hand wave.

"If you don't sell Green Lead I'll liquidate my position to be rid of you."

"*Pffft, pssss . . .*"

"Carl, I mean it. Stop watching reality TV. It melts your brain."

"That's best case. Sell your shares to who?"

"The first person interested."

The animated corpse on television grins. His teeth are rotted out. "How do people watch this nonsense?" I mutter, completely riveted. Then: "Fine. I'm the first person interested. *Na-na-na*. I'm offering to buy *you* out. So there."

The TV goes to commercial, something about fear-sweat stinking four times as much as normal unafraid sweat and now we have this groundbreaking antiperspirant specially formulated for such a shocking betrayal, why do our bodies hate us so bad, secretly conspire to kill or at least socially cripple us, won't life be better when we're finally rid of them, giddy disembodied floating brains, cosmic consciousness, but hey wait a sec isn't that kinda like being dead? "Do you hear me, Michael Zenski? I'm offering to buy you—"

"What's your offer?"

I snap my fingers. "A universal big bang of glorious cashola. You happy? That much money."

Michael smiles. "A billion infinity?"

"And then some."

"The end of Green Lead."

"You've always overestimated your import, Zenski. Middling, unimaginative micromanagers come cheap. Where's the remote? Watch TV with me?"

Michael hands me the remote. "You don't have the financial means to buy me out."

"I do so." I change the channel to a reality TV supermodel show. Six half-starved teenaged girls transformed into computer-blurred blobs. I watch for a minute or two, biting my tongue, trying to be a polite communal television-watcher, but then I can't stand it anymore and I'm like, "Whoa, Michael? Does she look real to you? Because, no? What I'm seeing is a creature that used to look like an actual real if slightly depressed and malnourished human being, but they've rounded everything down, removed all unique distinguishing features of humanness, like look at her face? Bejesus! Is that really her face? A flat plane with software-coded objects made to resemble a human's eyes and nose and chin that they've plunked on, like Mrs. Potato Head, but now conforming to some creepy cyborg-imp ratio where the eyes are waaay outsized and the lips are . . . *ahem?* Michael? Are you seeing this?"

"Carl, sell Green Lead to me. You're frightfully close to broke."

"It doesn't even look like the same person! Am I the only one seeing this? Have they discovered a new genus?"

"I'm sorry, I thought we could have this conversation, but apparently now's not—"

"The real question is, why aren't we on television? If I were on television I wouldn't need drugs. I'd get high basking in my own computer-generated perfection."

"That's the problem. Real life would never feel perfect enough. That's already the problem. Or one of them."

"Michael? What is 'real life'?"

"Stop it."

"Serious. Look at that one! They erased her nose? Is that sexy these days? Might take some getting used to. I'm game to try. Noses *are* weird, when you think about it. Is it bone or cartilage or an unsettling interstitial nether? Anyway, because it seems 'real life' assumes its opposite—"

"Carl, enough. I only came to offer you—"

"—'unreal life,' and I don't believe it's that binary anymore, right? That oppressively categorical?"

Michael laces his fingers behind his head, stares at the television. "It might be more like a field? Like a fluid scale or spectrum, with these CGI models being heavily weighted toward the unreal side of things? Or more charitably: the fantastical. Which isn't necessarily *bad*—"

"See? Gotcha! *Mmm?* You're not that pissed off. You can't resist engaging me. You find my mind impossibly sexy. Always have. Are you getting . . . because I am—"

"Seriously, Carl, you don't have the means."

"Oh, I do so. Wanna see?"

"The money. Christ."

"I said I do so have the money. Never forget the Nugget. Whoa! Look at that one! Michael? What's she supposed to be? A sexy amorphous supermodel nun? Never mind, the concept *is* kind of hot. I'd kneel on the altar and let her flog the sin out of me. But I can't believe they pay these CGI guys for this, you? Whatever happened to makeup artists? That was a real skill. Like, actually working with and accentuating the myriad differences of the human form instead of obliterating it with some prewritten software code. Huh-huh, yep, let's drop the feature icon 'Oversized Eurasian Eyes' onto the facial platform 'Sexy-Lipped Black Person,' see how that looks, wow, that's real bleeding-edge super radical you must be so proud of your life's work YOU SICK FUCKS! HEY CGI GUYS: YOU SUCK AND I'M NOT BUYING! Call me a crank if you want, but *jeesh.*"

"Crank. Please don't yell at the television, though."

"Too lowbrow?"

"Trash. Plus, I have a headache." Michael turns his chair to face the TV. "Pretty soon the CGI thing will fade. We almost invested, remember? Said no thank you, regressive, male gaze. It was the right call. Soon it'll be risqué to show someone's real face."

"Ha, yeah, like in Victorian times if a woman I dunno had a rip in her stocking and everyone went all crazy abhorred, what's the horrible world coming to, DEVIL WORSHIP? Michael? Is that your real face?"

"You keep shouting, the nurse is going to sedate you."

"OVERSEER? Hopefully. But . . . since incarcerated I've been fretting about Satan? Like wondering if I've been reincarnated as

Satan on earth . . . but maybe not conventionally-male muscly Satan, but scrawny pubescent Satan? Anyway, the fear seems cyclical? Like rotates from vampires to cyborgs to Satan to religious extremists to spy-spooks? And I think what's happening is these fears are melting into a single ceaseless lava-terror roiling in my head? And . . . um, influencing me in not-so-great ways? Because maybe me being reincarnated as juvenile likes-to-party-wet-dream Satan is a response, you know, to living in constant fear? And instead of the fear quieting me, it's doing the opposite, and making me want to yell louder and party more? Like some kind of survival mechanism? Which OVERSEER says is proof I lack life readiness skills, that there are biiig multinational forces ready to squash or squelch me if I don't gratefully guzzle her PharmaPoison?"

Michael giggles, makes me giggle too.

"Squelch me? Michael? Are you giggling at the word *squelch*? To both suppress and noisily suck! See how that links to Agency spies and vampires? Whoa! But wouldn't it be cool if the CGI guys didn't sprinkle the supermodel's facial features on at all? For a change? What if they left the girl's face totally blank, no eyes or nose or mouth, how tech-amazing would that be, just complaisant non-opinionated smooth skin to rub—"

Michael picks up the manila envelope Heather's lawyer delivered, peeks inside. "Not after the divorce, you won't have the money, by the way."

"Never happen. I'm loved. Look at the TV! *Eeesh!* Who knew our latent ideal of beauty is basically like these indistinguishable walking flesh sacks with feathered hair? Technology's great: it allows us to fully manifest our self-loathing."

"Self-erasure."

I watch Michael watching the television, realize it might be the last I see of him. "Yup. Which is way cool, if you have some kind of bizarro eschatological fetish—"

Michael smiles. "Drench me with that silky eschat—"

"Fucking soak me in it, baby. Smear me—"

"Beat me with your throbbing eschatology. Whip me like a smart-ass schoolboy."

"'My gawd, he breathed breathlessly, wincing in anticipation, I've never seen an eschatology quite like that before ...'"

We laugh at the TV. After a while I say, "Michael? I miss you. I'm glad you're here."

"Heather's pushing through with the North Van bid," Michael says. "I talked to Vincent Peele. He's a slick bastard, but I think he's getting nervous. Carl? This affects you directly. I'm afraid Bo Xi is going to sniff us out, bail on the deal, and stay hidden. Did you contact Caltrop?"

"I guess I'm having doubts. Must be the sobriety talking. But Bo Xi won't bail."

Michael straightens. "How can you be so sure?"

"How much could he wash through the Solstice?"

"Looks like ..."

The reality TV show sucks me back in. Twigs and leaves are threaded through a Gia-supermodel's hair. Gold-dusted cheeks. Eyes burned out. Gia, my love, is that you? Did you trip, fall face first onto a red-hot stove? Oh, that's the new beautiful?

"Carl? Focus. Bo Xi? I said a couple hundred—"

"Okay, naggy nagster, I hear you. Millions. Even to a man like Bo Xi, that's not pocket change. He falls asleep thinking about it. If he can sleep at all. He wakes up, *boom!* First thing in his head. I mean really, it's probably driving him insane—"

"He's already insane."

"Yeah. Two decades funding militias to roam around with machetes and protect his diamond mines? Now look at him. He's over sixty. Shit's waning. And the money's right there ... so close ... right there ... and he can't have it. Holy heck! Makes my hemorrhoid flare just thinking about it. What do you think he does to keep his mind off the money that's his and not his?"

Michael stretches, looks for the door. "Last thing I want to think about."

"Rest assured he does something. And he wants this North Van property more than he wants to live. Michael? I've never told anyone this before. Sometimes I feel him."

"Who?"

"Bo Xi. Like we're . . . connected? Not like telepathics but more . . . I'm like a walking mood ring? My physical self divines the man's moods from across the Pacific? I feel his horror alive in my bones, like when he's unhappy with his Peking duck my left knee-cap tingles? After what he did to us back in Bute and all these years craving a revenge killing, it's like an invisible psychic bridge, an alien or extra-sensory tissue has grown to connect us, maybe a new organ we're yet to discover, hyper-evolution, anyway, yeah, I feel him sense him intuit him whatever and it fucking creeps me out, and that's how I know he's coming, for sure, the money's driving him batty, I feel his madness as a craving for drugs and senseless sexual encounters, it manifests as migraines, dry scalp, bad breath, broken social taboos . . . sorry I've never told you this, it's cool but scary, psychosomatic link, damn it feels good to finally get this off my chest, forgive me, I'm not entirely to blame though, see, it's also because of him? That guy? Over there? His fault too? Not only me?"

Michael laughs, asks if that's really supposed to be Gia.

"Michael? I'm saying I believe Bo Xi sent OVERSEER to sexually intimidate me. Perhaps chemically neuter me. Are you listening? Should we turn this show off? Talk? I feel a break-through coming on."

Another model, maybe a bag lady, dressed in rags torn to reveal smoothed-down breasts and thighs, leaning over a shopping cart filled with empties.

"I understand what makes these shows so attractive," Michael whispers. "I'm feeding on their hopes and dreams, humiliations and failures."

"Uh, should we keep watching this? I'm getting creeped out. Are you making a slurping sound? You want me gone, why don't you stage an intervention? Violate my personal liberty for my own darned good? Because you've grown to despise me?"

Michael waves me away. "I'm sorry, Carl, but I honestly hope Heather finally goes through with it. Might be the wake-up call you need."

I turn off the television.

"Wake-up call? You sententious twerp. I'm on the front lines of a war. A casualty. Lying bleeding out in the muck. Psychosomatically connected to an international criminal psychopath. And you, Mr. Zenski, are bolting for the goddamned chopper."

"Good god, cut the shit. You had a drug-induced psychotic breakdown. That's all. Nearly drove over an RCMP officer—"

"Doesn't sound like me. Mostly pacifist, until it's no longer convenient. Don't believe in—"

"Can you *please* cut the shit—"

"So that's their story? Won't hold up, you'll see. I was assaulted. Tasered in broad daylight. Like that Pole—"

"Christ, Carl. Hannah was at the airport. Your ... what? Sixteen-year-old daughter? So please cut the shit!"

I sit up. "That's the problem, Michael. It's only shit if you're looking in from the outside. They wore you down. You're all out of fight."

"*You* wore me down."

"Fine. Doesn't matter. You got old. Happens. Heart not beating with the same fiery passion. Spending too much time in the past. The what ifs. You can't sleep, lie awake wondering what it was all about. You're white, male, rich, mostly hetero. So you don't live the effects in your day-to-day. Everything happens over there, way over yonder, to some poor sonofabitch somewhere else. You're not a moron, not ignorant either wilfully or otherwise, so you're aware there's suffering, a whole lot of it, linked directly to you, to us, to this culture we've created. But the suffering seems so far away. And who knows? You've grown up not trusting the media. Maybe half that shit's not even real. Maybe it's not all that bad. For *them*. And, you worry—because you've been reading all the recent limp-dicked bullshit—isn't it kind of presumptuous, even neo-colonial, to fret over how they're doing? You know—the poor starving war-torn exploited people? Isn't that proof of your entrenched agency? And so on? Isn't it a sign of your privilege, your position in the dominant culture, that you have the luxury of having this conversation with yourself? Oh, you're implicated. Sure as shit. But so is everyone. So, who cares? Isn't it better to hang back, not interfere, while they find their own way? Despite the fact that the moment you let up the fight some predatory piece of shit moves in to capitalize? Because it's not them. It's you and me! It starts here! But you know what? When it's all said and done? What have we changed? Not much. Maybe nothing. What's the point? Am I wrong? As if there could be a conceptualized, coherent end point. Come on! You know there's no finish line. This fight is *forever*. And that thought's exhausting. Whoa! No end to this! Capital's not human. Doesn't live and breathe, except through its human pets. And it's everywhere at once! How can you fight something like that? You're getting up there. Did what you could. Time to put your feet up. But here's the thing: I am *not* ready. Am I addicted to drugs? Shit yes. Did I overestimate my ability to deal? Yes. Am I harming myself, everyone around me? Yes. Do I hate myself for that? Yes. But don't come in here, with your condescending, holier-than-thou, centrist bullshit, and look down your nose like I'm a lost cause. Like I'm subhuman. Don't denigrate me, make me into your poster boy for failure and defeat. I made the call, a long time ago, in a prison like this one, to get right fucking high. And I'll make the same call again and again. Just like I'll keep calling the bastards out, again and again, even as it kills me." I settle into bed, winded, exhausted. "Now. Turn the TV back on. The world has some splainin' to do."

"You were something, Mr. Carl Reed," Michael whispers. "I would've followed you to the ends of the earth."

"You already did. We took a piss and kept on fucking."

"Now we're lost."

"Who's lost? *I'm* not lost. I'm in prison. Again."

Michael leans into his chair, rubs his eyes. "A kid named Sebastian Price from Lord Byng got a solid shakedown."

"So?"

"So the man doing the shaking was after Hannah."

hannah whre r u??!! answr plz!!

hannah its dad whr r u??!!

hannah im srry its yr dad yes im in jail agan im srry plz contact me now its urgnt

hannah im frekking out pls contact me

going 2 call cops for real like now

going 2 call cops in 3 mins if u dont get bck

dont want 2 call cops but will vry soon

just say u r ok

just called mom but no answr

call yer mom if not me ok?? but me 2 ok??!!

not angry jst wnt to talk but if u dnt want 2 tlk jst text me & say it and itll be ok I luv u MORE than u know truly LUV

answr yer phone dont u want 2 float down amazon with me see distinct unspoiled cultures see how it all endz 2 begin? See varanasi dead people floating? What do u dream? Plz answr!!

not happy not cool least u cn do is text me sy yer ok??!!

yer mom cntacted cops *not me* dad is *not* a rat fink snitch cop cntacter u can trust me plz call

ok cops r mega looking for u. best call me or mom!!

sory 4 my long absence power trip nurse OVERSEER took phone

while eating soup lights out soon PLZ cntct me!!!! :(:(before nine or
they take phone again :(:(

ok iget yr pissed you hav evry right 2 b but PLZ say u r ok??

totlly selfish. totlly not cool pssv aggressv BS …I LUV U tho.

nurse OVERSEER early taking phone total fascist will b back tmorro
at 9 AM PLZ TEXT ME OVRNGHT!! WILL GO 2 RHAB
SWEETY!! WILL GO 2 HELL 4 U!!! WILL TRY REALLY HRD
THS TIME!!!

Jasminder Bansal

So pissed off at Sim I don't even bother going into my apartment.
Driving across the Knight Street Bridge, punching it, stereo
cranked so I can't hear my brakes screeching even when I'm not on
them, terrified I've put the people I care about in danger.

Late-night fog restless along the Fraser, spilling over the bank,
reaching inland through strips of black-barked cottonwood jack-
hammered between pavement and flood dikes, drifting through shipping yards and recycling stations and gravel pits with piles of sand
and rusted-out sorters, teasing through industrial mechanic's shops
and wholesale distributors and I'm driving east on the River Road,
cutting across the yellow. Quick downshift and where could I go to
begin again? And more importantly, would the memory of my
brother fade?

My Honda rattling and whining, hitting corners too fast to
brake and the river only twenty metres left, how long for the
water to filter through vents and implode windows? Hearing
nothing but bubbles and odd metallic pings as the engine rapidly
cools, the current flipping my car until I can't tell which way is up.
I speed past an RV lot, *Adventure* and *Adrenaline* and *Discovery*,
seasonal pad rentals, satellite dishes and frozen entrees, barrel cacti,

and are those headlights up ahead through the fog? Oncoming traffic?

The cottonwoods open up and I see the river flowing swift, a doubling of dark into dark, a path winding through a forest, and there, in the middle of the river, blurred by fog, is a centuries-old schooner run aground and foundering, heeling hard to starboard, mainmast shattered, sails shredded. Headlights approaching fast around the corner and the ship decayed, rotten, ghostly. My car tracking through gravel on the left shoulder and the headlights getting brighter. The steering wheel pulling hard toward the river. I'm on the wrong side of the road and the thought hits that I hold their lives in my hands and Sim's waiting for my word. The steering wheel shaking so violently it tears my skin. The smell of tidal mud in my nose. The ruined schooner listing in fog and darkness. No beginning again, no undoing. People, strangers in the car ahead, driving home, unknowing but trusting. I hold Clint Ward's life in my hands or he holds mine or it's both. The oncoming headlights feel inches away. I crank the wheel. A car horn recedes. We almost never do it; we're better than we believe. I have to believe that.

The image is paused in a state of dissolution, grainy, nearly indecipherable, halfway to nothing, a rough copy of an even rougher original, a Sony Portapak cassette transcribed to digital and made valuable by the years accumulated since its creation. The scene is outside, in an East Vancouver alley. Spray-painted dumpsters against a brick foundation. A man and a woman, both dressed in flowing black robes, strap an odd construction to a third man's back. The man is naked to the waist. The object is an accumulation of cubes, small and large stacked and stuck together to form a single mass. I can't tell from the video, but my mother told me she made the sculpture from a white bedsheet wrapped around a chicken-wire armature and layered with plaster. Party streamers and what look like pom-poms hang off the construction, swaying as the man moves. The object doesn't appear heavy, but it's large, maybe five feet long and around the same width, sprouting from the man's back, bending him forward, supplicant. The robed assistants, moving methodically, hold lighters to something glued to the cubic construction. The viewpoint widens, reveals a crowd of a few dozen gathered in the alley.

A bright flash, a shower of sparks. The performer flinches as glowing white embers cascade around him. The assistants step aside. A woman says something in a language I don't understand and the performer begins dancing, slowly at first, sparks streaming from the cubic sculpture and skittering across the pavement, following his path, tracing a transient pattern in the air. Light shimmers through grey-black haze. No music, no cheering, only hissing sparklers and the man's feet brushing concrete, and those quiet sounds create an even more palpable, almost material silence. The performer's eyes are closed and his lips are moving in what could be prayer and there's something joyful in his expression, and now the hot sparks falling from the plaster cubes run over his bare shoulders, shower down, burn skin, and watching the video I smell the man's scorched flesh, see him grit his teeth, the dance now beautiful and hurt-filled.

The performer quickens his steps, bends at the waist, leaps from side to side, skin slick with sweat. His face relaxes. I'm sitting upright on the edge of my bed, watching the first artwork my mother created in this country, not trying to understand what the dance means, what context it belongs to, not thinking or questioning but only being, lost in physicality, the beauty and incomprehensibility of flesh in motion, *alive*, and the intimation of a violent end that pervades the dancer's every step. The burning sparklers fade. The dancer collapses to his knees, cries out. The attendants remove the sculpture from the wounded performer's back, and in the smoke drifting through the alley I see the unmistakable image of my brother.

My mother named the piece *sedition*.

I play the video while skimming through Peele's documents, adding a few notes, dreaming of a takedown. My mother comes in, asks what all the mess is. Before I can answer she sees me playing her video, asks me to turn it off. I do, and she sits on the edge of the bed beside me, says she heard voices outside, saw Sim and me arguing, asks where I went so late.

Looking at the blank screen: "For a drive."

"You still taking those river drives? What about your brakes?"

"Looks like they held up. It was pretty out."

My mom lifts a bank statement. "What's all this?"

"My work." *My life.*

What I read into my mother's silence is that she knows I've decided to keep things from her and she won't try to drag them out of me. Sometimes I wish she would. "It's not only my work at Marigold? I mean it is, but it's . . ."

She puts her hand on my knee. "What?"

I know who murdered Amar. When did the truth become a distance between me and those I love? There's no way to explain to my mother why I'm at Marigold without telling her the whole story. I stuff the bank statement in a file folder. Lying makes more sense than truth ever will. "They're just financial documents for my clients. I think I'm going to do okay there."

Mark Ward

Daylight filters through floor-to-ceiling windows, a toneless morning light, soothing, welcoming, saying you're okay, Mark, everything's cool, it's gonna be all right . . .

And that's how it is while I'm standing naked smoking and making scrambled eggs until I look down and written in the cast-iron pan in the snotty half-cooked egg mess are the words END OF DAYS and what the fuck who wrote that in the runny half-cooked eggs did I write that and for a second I'm horrified but then it strikes me as fucking hilarious, silly as hell, END OF DAYS what kind of stupid doomer shit used to justify all sorts of hateful atrocities END OF DAYS all flaccid and silly made of watery scrambled eggs not big and powerful but what happens too bad for me is my leg gives out and I smash into the cast-iron pan and drag it off the stove and the snotty egg mess splatters all over my thighs and belly END OF DAYS and I'm still laughing as I grab the dishtowel and wipe the sticky egg mess off, fuck sakes, yuck.

About to hop in the shower when my brother yells from out in the hall, bangs on the door, rapid and demanding, the day going from weird to worse. Pick up my smoke, consider not answering. My post-post-apocalyptic mood is shit, convinces me to chase two Oxys with a double vodka and sour milk. Clint and me are going to go our separate ways, make real the internal rift that happened years ago.

Take my time looking through the peephole, stalling to irritate him. My brother looks monstrous, so tweaked out and warped by the fisheye lens I barely recognize him. Clint sees my shadow in the peephole, screams something about it being his fucking condo, bangs on the door hard enough to rattle it against my forehead. I pop the security chain. He barrels in, talking super quick, sentences compressed, like he has a vital secret to share and only a few seconds to do it. Wearing a rumpled flat-grey suit, tie off, collar undone, jacket unbuttoned. Have to admit, he's growing into the suits. Skulks from the kitchen counter to the sliding glass doors and over to the bedroom, smashes a fist into his palm, grunts, spits.

I ask how he's doing.

Clint tries to speak, stutters, kicks the chair in front of the TV, shouts holy shit Marky it's on!

"Want some food? Breakfast?"

Clint blinks, dumbfounded. "Huh? *Breakfast?*"

Pick the cast-iron off the floor, toss my smoke in the sink. "Yeah. Morning? Making eggs."

"Morning?" Teeth-grinding sounds from across the room. "Don't fuck with me, Marky. You . . ." Clint winces, staggers against the wall like I shot him, covers his eyes. "Are you . . . fucking naked!"

I lift the cast-iron. "My pad."

"Ugh! Prick out? Put some . . . fuck!"

Dig in my duffel bag, put on a pair of boxers. "All I said was hey, want some—"

Clint lunges, faster than I hoped, and he's in my face yelling fuck you Marky bullshit breakfast I know when I'm being screwed with I said it's your time to shine! Stuffs some cocaine up his nose, laughs, slices his hands through the air like a video game karate dude, does a few jumping jacks, breaks into a wheezing cough, asks for a smoke.

Hand him the pack. "Whatever then. I'm having a boiled egg."

Put the dirty cast-iron in the sink. Pour water in a pot and set it on the stove. Dig a thumbnail into an orange.

Clint watches me peel the orange, then, triggered by some hidden affront, tries to sweep-kick me in the head, falls against the fridge, howls, drops into a lame-ass martial arts fighting stance, says, "Peele crazy dawg dude looks clean but the guy can party, paaartaaay." My brother does a few clumsy dance moves, laughs, then a half-second later looks angry enough to rip my guts out. "Tried calling you asshole you didn't pick up you should've seen this yacht! Big shot owns it, picked us up in Coal Harbour, hot tubs, fucking themed rooms and—get this! A scavenger hunt to get the secret codes to get into the themed rooms to get the girls! This is us now man, thug life. Yacht owner, fuck's his name, runs a mega internet-gambling deal. Shoulda seen him, whole posse follows him around like that show *Entourage* but only not his buddies he's got lawyers hackers accountants designers top-notch security and of course bitches bankers investment advisors fawning over him, coolest shit ever, his architect for this oceanfront pad he's building on some private beach pissed him off and we almost tossed the egghead overboard. Come a long way!"

Check to see if my water's boiling. "What room you pick?"

Clint sticks his finger in the corner of his eye, blinks, swats at something I can't see. "Fucking hell that orange stinks."

"Was there an outer-space room? Mars? Cuz that'd be cool—"

"Ugh, that orange-stink is killing me. Saying you better answer when I call." Clint's face lights up. "Where's that puke? Twll? He around?"

Drop an egg into boiling water, put an orange segment between my teeth, strip the tough pulpy membrane off, spit it in the sink, eat the juicy orange capsules while my brother makes a disgusted face and what I'm thinking is no way, not the kid, not a word. "Ryan? Nah."

Clint checks his phone. "Fucker's not answering. Hey, last time you saw him?"

Wash my hands, not psyched about turning my back to my brother. "Dunno. Day is it?"

"Dayzit? Uh . . ."

". . . uh . . . fucking . . . uh . . . um . . ." Bust out laughing.

Clint roars, lunges across the kitchen island, snags my arm. Blood leaks from my brother's cracked lips; his pupils are black pinpricks floating in yellow-grey swamp. I'm guessing right now Clint doesn't even know who or what I am, only that he wants me ripped in half. But he's also weak and hungover so I pivot, slip away, rub my arm all pretend-upset. "Fucking hell, bro. Joking? Chill."

Clint smacks the marble countertop, seems not quite happy with the effect, does it again. "Simple question. Answer me! My condo, all I get is you—"

"Saw him yesterday at work. Same as you. You called him to the truck, remember? Here. Piece of orange?"

"Course I remember! I mean since . . . last night? He come here?" Stalks to the window, cracks a blind, winces. "Lightweight. Shoulda seen him on the yacht, out of his head, might'a fell off?"

"'Kay. Piece of orange?" Waving half the orange at my brother.

"Piece of—fuck sakes! You see him, liar dope fiend, you tell me. Got it?"

Crack the softboiled egg, say sure, I got it.

Clint gives me a look that makes me hear burning metal hissing and popping. "What I'm saying is you were right about when I went all pussified and you said hey, brother, you gotta go all the way in to get out. With Peele? That was warrior-style. Needed to hear it. Easy to daydream about the simple life. But that's gone. We're way in now."

"We?"

"Course. You and me. Like old times? Gross, Marky, first the orange and now that fucking *egg*, I mean, get some real food!" Clint tries to light a smoke, but the lighter outsmarts him. I snatch it, light a smoke, take a drag, hand the smoke to him, pocket his lighter.

"Marky, dude, lighter?"

I eat a few raspberry gummies, ask how far we're in.

"All the way. Lighter!"

"Why?"

"Lighter!"

Drop the lighter in his hand, watch him almost lose it again, begin to feel the Oxys kick, wondering if I should offer Clint some vodka, maybe we spend Friday hanging out on the balcony getting shitfaced—

"We're going to kill that bitch, is why."

"The Reed daughter—"

"No, no, no, Marky. Stay on point! Not her, we *need* that one, the Reed girl's not for killing. That Bansal sister I told you about. Tired of her. Told her to fuck off the other day. Don't think she's gonna listen."

"You told Peele about you and Amar—"

"Hell no. Do I look like an idiot? Peele'd make me kill her, then kill me and you. She's up to some bullshit, is all. Why else she at Marigold?"

Pour Clint a glass of water. He looks at it like it's sewer sludge. I shrug, drink it down. I'm standing behind the kitchen counter, watching my brother pace through the condo. The light softens his features, the edges of his body, makes him appear immaterial. I think I'm saying goodbye. I hope he is too.

Clint reaches in his pocket, sets something on the counter.

"Fuck's that?"

"You know exactly what. Your all-time favourite."

Don't even have to look. Settled on this beauty when I was ten years old and me and Clint were hanging around the Chilliwack mall scoping blades in the army surplus store. It's a seven-inch, matte-black KA-BAR United States Marine Corp combat knife, carbon-steel clip point.

"Take it," Clint says. "Got it for you. Want to see you holding it."

I make no move to touch the blade. If I'd left the balcony door open I could probably take a run and push my brother over the railing. But it'd be a risk. Clint's built lower than me. A hard man to unseat. Now he's digging in his coat pocket again. Pulls out a camera, says, "Okay happy days here it is. Nice work with the basketball kid. He led us to the Reed daughter's boyfriend. Hannah? Horny Hannah!" Clint laughs, shakes the camera in my face. "This shit gets out . . . yeah, that politician's mom's gonna wish she stayed in the kitchen . . . but oh man Marky you gotta see this . . . sixteen and a freeeak . . ."

Call Ryan after Clint fucks off, leave a message telling him there's no work today but he can meet me in front of the condo in half an hour if he wants cash for the days he worked. Course he's there when I go down, leaning against the wall, messing with his phone, hoodie tight around his face, wearing sunglasses despite the cloud. I hand him an envelope, ask what he's doing this weekend and I guess he forgets he's trying to keep his face hidden because he looks up and I see he's rolling a mean black eye. I'm about to say hey what's up but he brushes me aside, says he doesn't need a ride any-where, vanishes down the street and I'd like to be the guy that presses the issue, runs after the kid, offers to help, kindness, all that. But I'm not.

Instead I spend the rest of Friday morning doing a horseshit errand for Vincent Peele: muling two suitcases to the HSBC office building downtown on Georgia. Clint knows I hate ferrying crap around, but Peele called after my brother left and said it had to be done. He also said I did good work with Sebastian Price and that soon—possibly as early as tonight—it'd be time for me to deliver druggie old-man Reed a fuck you. I told him fine, though the whole thing's shit. I googled Carl Reed and he seems like a dickbag, but the daughter? Dunno. Sixteen. Doesn't sit right. Best case is Reed uses his head, convinces his politician wife to fold the province's bid for the North Van property. Worst case isn't worth a thought.

Traffic's backed up along Georgia, commuters heading to their holes, and by the time I park the truck I'm nearly an hour late and feeling wound up, wrecking ball. The day's gone dark. Some sort of protest or festival going on at the art gallery. Hippies dancing and chanting. Hop out, grab the suitcases, minding my own business, wishing I'd put on a clean pair of jeans, wishing my skin didn't feel so flimsy, feeling stage lights beam down, too hot, and the audience out there laughing but not in a nice way. Couples stroll by, yuppies dressed for success, hand in hand, meeting each other for brunch, and seeing them makes me think of Daree, which makes me think of Sarah, which makes me bite my cheek to stay on point for work, which puts me in a shit mood all around.

A tensed-up knot forms in my neck, creates a stinging pain around the left side of my face. I decide to call Daree once I'm finished delivering Peele's suitcases. When a bomb explodes beneath your feet, you lose time. A minute, maybe five. Like blacking out from booze. And when your brain finally returns to normal temporal flow you're somewhere and someone else. Changed forever. Maybe blown apart, maybe dead or wishing you were. Makes sense. But the trouble is: that's what's been happening to me since I landed in Vancity. Small increments of life gone missing. A couple seconds here and there, that I skip past, and there's a jarring effect, like stepping off a moving sidewalk at an airport, and I get this goddamned pain behind my eyes, and the headache, and the sense that I'm living outside my real life and there's nothing I can do to change it.

A group of ESL students totter past the Ford—Japanese, Korean, a couple Latinos from well-off families. Friends holding arms, sending texts as they walk side by side, giggling at their phones and nearly walking into telephone poles. A few are carrying shopping bags, and for a moment I think about Bangkok, sprawling shopping malls and skyscrapers built right beside sheet-metal shanties, men pedalling rickshaws through overflowing streets, the energy so different than this monstrous city, unpolished, infectious, potent, like something vibrant burst from the dirt, straining for sunlight, struggling, a place where it's still okay to make mistakes. Here we don't permit mistakes. They've been written out. Market-tested, refined. A young city, we never had the opportunity to form a richly sedimented history, the layers of culture and difference that collide to create something vital. Vancouver skipped the past. Went straight from sucking her thumb to being embalmed.

Now she's being dragged through the streets, on display, bled out, stuffed with preservatives, sanitizers, disinfectants both modern and ancient while the townspeople poke at her dried flesh, marvel at how lifelike she is, gaze into her sparkling glass eyes, chanting, *see, ain't she pretty? Stunning! Lovely!* And you either nod and say yes she's the prettiest thing around or you slink off, outcast, afraid of what you don't understand, wondering why no one's bothered by the stink of natron and myrrh, cedar oil and liquefied insides. And as the corpse moulders, the devout rise ever more vehement in her defence, their lives invested and committed, fawning over her, shrieking *look how pretty she is! how gorgeous!* while her limbs rot off and her belly splits open; she's hussied up real nice if you cover your nose and don't look too close; the devout closing rank, with slitted eyes and mouths stretched for a feast. The chorus drowns out opposing sound. That's what's happening to me. There's only one song in this town, and I'm not singing.

Which means I'm out.

It starts to piss rain. Toss Peele's suitcases in the cab, put on a hoodie, crawl inside, feeling suspicious and vigilant about nothing specific. I'm a mess. Muddy work boots, stinking filthy jeans, rosy-red blood smears around my scabs. Lay down with my knees curled to my chest and my hands tucked in my hoodie pocket, shivering, freezing out of all relation to the temperature. Will I get back to Bangkok, deliver the money I'm saving for Daree in person, say

goodbye in person? And with the thought comes guilt, because I
have a mission, a defined target, and I'm already daydreaming about
pissing off, and if I slink away and Craig Williams lives free and easy
I'm nothing, I mean really nothing at all with no purpose at all, and
right then there's this huge need to you know hear someone, say
something to someone, a few words, something honest and real, and
I'm dialling my phone and Daree's saying hello Maak is that you?

First thing I do to sort myself is dig a couple Oxys out of my
work bag. I'm slumped across Peele's suitcases, watching headlights
on Georgia sparkle and smear through dirty light, trying to think of
something soothing to say, then *zip!* an instant one-eighty in terms
of mood and I'm feeling contrite, needy for this mother of my child,
mother is all, sorry, that's all I feel—

"Sarah?"

"Sleeping."

"Better?"

"Still not good."

"Me either." A silence so long and not awesome I finally cave.
"Say something."

Nothing. Silence.

"Fuck sakes Daree I phoned—"

"Not for many days. We argue . . ."

Fiddle with the locked suitcase, try and remember how long it's
been since I called her. Can't be that long? Day or two? "We argued
yeah so what everyone argues get over it that's what people do.
Argue and fuck."

"We only argue. You called last Saturday. Six days. You could—"

A headache starts up, focused on the side of my face that got
smashed by the LAV, feels like getting stabbed with a screwdriver,
time does that ugly *skip-skip* thing and Daree's talking but I can't
hear and the Oxys aren't doing shit and I'm cradling a suitcase full
of that motherfucker's filthy money—

". . . going to go . . ."

"Go? *You?* No. I'm hanging up . . . hey! Fucking met someone? That's why you won't come to Vancity?"

Daree works at an internet cafe on Khao San, in Bangkok's backpacker tourist slum; it's where we met. She doesn't answer. Bangkok sirens across an ocean or Vancouver sirens right here?

"Is it more money you want? I'm good for it, my daughter—"

"Not money. We want you—"

"—but I have money—"

"—back with us. Me and Sarah."

Breakthrough pain. Super-severe new pain that confronts terminal cancer patients as they move implacably toward death. An unwell body becomes accustomed to a certain level of pain and a concomitant amount of painkiller, then the body goes FUCK YOU and the patient catapults to another level of suffering and another plateau, and this happens again and again and can also describe a life—

"But I have money!" I shake a suitcase, tempted but too afraid to open it, all this cash so close and I can't have it and it can't help.

"You're not coming. You sound scared. Are you—"

So I hang up.

Dead-ended. About to crawl out of the truck when my cell beeps and there's a photo from Vincent Peele showing Daree's rundown pollution-stained apartment in Bangkok, then another of Peele carving a snowboard in steep rocky terrain with the message *yo me crushing Horseshoe double black Whistler* and a final image of Daree exiting her apartment with Sarah wrapped in a tie-dyed shoulder-sling I bought her in Krabi.

My phone rings. First thing Peele says is, "Ernest Hemingway?"

"You fucking hurt—"

"Oh, nothing to fret about. Chillax. More uptight than a

Torontonian. You have la moolah? Unmolested and safely in la possession?"

Tell him yeah.

"So then. No worries, mate! Trace a phone call, contact an associate overseas—you like that Whistler photo of me trouncing the gnar? You ride?"

"No."

"Been thinking about you. Flattered? This history of yours, university and war, the warrior-intellectual. Drawing historical precedent, came up with our man Hemingway. He dabbled in war?"

Take a sec to watch a cloud engulf an office tower, get my shit together. "High school. No university. Self-educated. Wasn't a big deal back then, and besides, it helps if you're brilliant. There are better examples."

Shit. Fucker baited me.

"Ah . . . still. A potentially volatile combination?"

Across the street, at the art gallery, multicoloured protest banners are draped from fir trees and marble entry columns. The rain pounds in on an angle, making it hard to see, and through the headlights on Georgia Street the rain looks like static on a screen.

"Peele, fuck you on about? I got work, remember?"

"Bit of a romantic, that dog Hemmers," Peele continues. "But my suspicion is he's not your model. There's an interesting relationship, historically, between university-educated intellectuals manipulating what could be called the working class."

"Well, like you, I'm no intellectual."

"A rare impulse these days, isn't it? Class war?"

"War is only war, Peele. I've been swinging hammers for a long time. Never seen one glow with blessed revolutionary light."

"No stormin' la Bastille? The dream dies hard. Wait. Flowroom! Me refereeing the Ward Brothers cage match—"

Peele hangs up. I say fuck off to the dialtone, stuff the phone in my pocket, think about how best to murder him. Knock him out, tie him up, take him into the woods, sink him into concrete up to his knees, cut him, leave him for the cute forest creatures? Yeah, maybe that.

Climb out of the Ford, grab the suitcases, lock the doors, plunk a few quarters in the meter, glare at the protestors. Booths, covered in ratty blue tarps, are set up in a rough semicircle around a waterless mosaic fountain facing Georgia. A drum starts up, sharp, arrhythmic, inspires scattered cheering. I'm rolling the suitcases behind me as I limp toward the bank, wheels clunking when they hit an expansion joint in the sidewalk. Are the real people on the street looking at me? Do I stand out, filthy, unwashed, afraid? Can they sense I don't have an inside?

At the front doors of the HSBC building, thinking of the working stiffs and cheap suits coming through these doors every day, diligently paying their outrageous mortgages and car loans, fretting about usurious credit card rates and the GDP and RRSPs and their kid's tuition and taxes and gas prices and the stock market, passive versus active investment strategies, asset allocation and risk management, dividend tax sheltering, getting royally nickel-and-dimed if not outright stolen from and shuffling back for more, mostly honest and hard-working people, straight rubes and suckers, perpetually stooped, never in the know, making money for guys like Vincent Peele and his bosses, trying to develop a relationship with their banker in the blind hope he won't fuck them, while I—bagman, thug, criminal, low-life, deviant—stroll through the front doors carrying suitcases stuffed with stinking blood money, money from ruthless international drug syndicates, from companies who purchase industrial waste and dump it in the ocean, from factories in Indonesia and Sri Lanka where employees are slaves in everything but name, money from pornography rings, from chemical-weapons dealers, from mining companies in Africa who send children down shafts like canaries, money from Western-backed despotic regimes and murderous dictators and jihadi terrorist cells, money from narco-warlords and corrupt officials of every description and nation, and the whole thing—not the bank or the city but the whole heartless, avaricious shebang—strikes me as ritually absurd, a violent, nihilistic farce, and before I know it I'm laughing so hard I can't breathe, and my laughter rises to mingle with traffic noise and protest chants. Trying to choke the laughter down because people walking by are glancing in my direction and even though I don't give a rat's ass what they think this is still work, and I was raised to take my work seriously, even when it's senseless, even when it is a farce.

Take a few minutes to get my head straight.

The protest chants and singalongs grow louder, more strident.

And the energy in that crowd, chanting in the rain just to be unheard, standing up for what they're told to believe in; how cunning they were to misdirect us way back when, convince us peaceful resistance could effect structural change. The new idiot orthodoxy. Maybe Peele's right. Give me two, three of those protestors, real committed, a bit unstable—

A banner strung up outside the gallery reads *Affordable Housing Is a Human Right.* Another I can only half see is about a single-room occupancy hotel on East Hastings. Same old story. We could've had this shit figured by now, if we really wanted to. But we don't. Hippie reruns about my age wearing baggy hemp pants and shirts that hang to their knees have their hands linked together as they spin around the dried-up fountain, chanting and singing while others whirl fire poi, the red-orange orbs cleaving circular tracers through the air and *ooh* isn't that pretty and oooh how cool is that and oooh I feel so alive and free!

Stagger through the bank's front entrance, duck under a massive swinging pendulum sculpture cleaving the marble foyer, spot the side door Peele told me about. Punch the entry code, tug the handle. Nothing. Door won't budge. Outside, the protest erupts in cheers. Cars honk in easy support. Try the code again, chest tightening, a cellphone signal . . . tear at the fucking door, shake it, thrash against it. A guard lowers his chin to his radio. Yeah I look like a fucking thief, a madman, nervous as hell because I have Peele's filthy money and it belongs in this fancy bank with its gilded offices and ocean views. Both hands on the door, tearing and screaming while the protestors dance and sing. The security guard's got a buddy with him, and right when I'm about to go straight out of my mind I see Peele's play.

Motherfucker's having a laugh at Marky.

Sprint outside, heart going *wuuump* way too slow despite how jacked I am. Stumble into Georgia Street. A delivery van hits the brakes. Side mirror misses my nose by an inch. Rush of blasting air, big HA HA at Marky, cars slamming brakes all around and I'm in the middle of the four-lane street ripping Peele's suitcases open to get at the filthy money . . . and they're stuffed with nothing but back issues of *TransWorld Snowboarding*, *Fast Company*, *Canadian Art*, the *New Yorker*, *BIKE*, *Dwell*, *Wired*, *Artforum*, *Surfer*, *Fortune* and I'm screaming punching laughing kicking in the middle of the street with cars swerving and horns blaring and a shattering crashing noise follows the first rear-ender and I feel Peele laughing at me, the city laughing at me while I smash my fists onto car hoods and drivers stare straight ahead both hands squeezing the wheel thinking *oh god what is this I so don't need this where are the police get off the street you loser reject skid derelict why don't you just leave why don't you just die oh my god I think I want to kill you.* The violence seeping from the commuters washes over me, forces the air from my lungs, and all I can do is pace and pull at my hair and toss the magazines at speeding cars. They smash and scatter and torn pages whirl overhead and the whole shitshow makes the hippy reruns clap and squeal, real happy, far out, peace.

Jasminder Bansal

Brunch at Hawksworth. Mirrors and mahogany and a sculpted plaster ceiling, backlit, its curves matching the calla lilies placed on every table. I enter breathless, feeling undeserving, afraid I'll be spotted, asked to leave. Vincent introduces me to the minister of the environment, Heather Reed, and her husband, Carl. Ms. Reed is a small-boned woman whose dismissive nose highlights the honed diamond pendant around her neck. She's seated when I arrive and immediately gestures me beside her, then whispers please tell me you're capable of discussing something other than business, unlike that boor Vincent. She says this loud enough for Vincent to hear while offering him her hand. Vincent fake-kisses Ms. Reed's hand, says business is booming thanks for asking, introduces me as his most talented recent hire, a compliment that makes my cheeks warm. *What's the play, Jaz?* That's what Sim asked. I wish I knew. Not feeling terribly hungry, I order black coffee and a hamachi tartare, resolved to see this thing through after telling Sim to back off.

Ms. Reed orders a cocktail called an Income Tax, something made with gin and other people's money. Everyone laughs but Mr. Reed, who stares out the window and picks his fingernails. Mr. Reed could use some sleep, a healthy meal. He's gaunt, wearing what look like baggy pyjama bottoms and a faded denim jacket, with a nose less hawkish than hooked. There's something of the washed-up prophet about him, a sadness that separates him from the rest of the table, and I get the feeling Mr. Reed is a man who made the mistake of outliving his convictions.

Ms. Reed asks how I like working with Vincent. I smile, tell her it's totally next level. Chuckles all around, which seems to ease the tension. I sip my coffee. Ms. Reed downs her cocktail, asks the waiter what he recommends for ten thirty on a Friday. Vincent interrupts the waiter, says it's pouring rain, let's drink Scotch, and Ms. Reed laughs and says you know me too well, young man, you're a bad influence.

Vincent winks. "Bad in a good way?"

"Bad in every way."

"I see. Carl? Jasminder? Scotch?"

I tell him no thank you. Mr. Reed doesn't answer.

Cars slow for a red on Georgia Street. Vincent prattles about the LEED-certified beach house he's building on Salt Spring Island until the waiter returns with drinks.

Vincent toasts an early and beautiful spring in Vancity, then explains, in his usual casual fashion, that the delightful Minister Heather and Marigold Group are locked in fierce competition for a very fine piece of development property being assembled in North Vancouver. My plate arrives. No one else has ordered food. Vincent asks Heather if the province has secured municipal support for her pricey taxpayer-funded venture. Ms. Reed raises her glass to Vincent, says of course we have, you smarmy bastard. Then she turns to me and asks if Mr. Peele's unfortunate reputation is warranted.

Vincent pretends not to listen, runs a finger along the rim of his Scotch glass.

Everyone at the table studies me, including Mr. Reed—who blinks his bloodshot eyes like he's having trouble keeping up with events in real time. I slide my fork through my tartare, try and marshal an accommodating smile. "I'm very excited to be at Marigold. I haven't heard anything."

"Damien Hirst sprinkled real diamond dust on that painting," Mr. Reed interrupts, rising off his seat to point at a painting hanging over the bar, his voice blustery and hollow. "That ridiculous one right there. The heart? See it?"

Ms. Reed whispers a *tsk*, which I interpret as a suggestion to please humour her husband. Vincent's staring at Carl Reed in a way that makes my mouth go dry, a look that reminds me of Amar's expression when he desired something very badly, a new Cadillac or power boat. Sim's words are in the front of my mind, *these are not good people*, but I force them away, turn my attention to the painting, a silkscreen of a giant red heart stretching across the canvas. The cartoon heart sparkles in chandelier light while bartenders busy themselves polishing martini glasses.

"Of course, the man's a brute," Mr. Reed continues. "Low-class London boy content to suck on moneyed teats, felt compelled to state there's diamond dust in the painting in the goddamned title. *Big Love with Diamond Dust.* Eh? Success is the subject. *Blech.* Puffery. And I bet this pretentious, vampire-invested kill room paid a fortune for that insipid piece of shit. Send our art into the system. Send our songs. Send our youth. A closed loop—"

"Carl—" Ms. Reed says.

"Send us all! Artists, poets, moms and pops, schoolteachers, welders, backwoods survivalists. Everybody in. Let's hold hands. Guilty and proud! That's what that painting says. *No use trying!* Bravo, Damien!" Mr. Reed claps, drawing ruffled stares from everyone within a twenty-foot radius.

Vincent tries to pat Carl on the shoulder. Carl flinches, leans so far off the edge of his seat I'm afraid he'll topple. "Carl my man! Long time no see. Thanks for joining us."

"Did I have a choice?"

"Prison again? I heard . . . another embarrassing police brouhaha?"

Ms. Reed stiffens. Hunches over her Scotch like a veteran barfly.

"Yes, I was in prison," Carl answers. "Which is where you should be."

Ms. Reed's head snaps up. "Carl, enough. The development? I told you—"

"Ha! I'm happy you and I go way back, Carl. Otherwise that would be not a super-appropriate thing to say?" Vincent grips Carl's forearm, shakes it so hard Carl's hand flops back and forth. "Carl's the creative force behind Green Lead Investment, Jasminder. And what a force he was. Forward thinker. Finger on the pulse. Isn't that right, Carl? When you're at your best? Which is certainly not now?"

Mr. Reed digs his fork into the table.

"Venture capital?" I manage. "That must be interesting? The . . . people?"

Carl harrumphs.

Vincent swirls his Scotch, says he likes how cheerful and generous the cartoon heart painting is, leans close to me, says those are dead butterflies stuck to the canvas, very neat, even admirable, that level of sincerity, imagine being so comfortable with your own vulnerability, being comfortable with sappy sentimentality, it's totally speaking to him, do I want to try slacklining?

"Slacklining?" Ms. Reed says, frowning in confusion, then, likely realizing she sounds dated, laughs and says, "Is that when those crazy people balance on those ropes—"

"Webbing," Vincent corrects, smoothing his beard. "Tat."

"—across canyons?"

"That's it, Honourable Minister," Vincent says, almost rolling his eyes. "Balance. Vertigo. Flow state. This is something real West Coasters understand intuitively. Take that free-form focus and apply it to a high-stakes business environment. Technology, real estate, finance. I'm stepping over the void right now, folks. See me? I've been slacklining since before you could buy those pre-made kits from MEC. Bowline, water knot, figure eight. Lost Arrow Spire?

Yosemite? Super-famous slackline? Did it. Smoked a bowl, fully Left Coast, turned around and did it again! Hey, Heather? Marigold will succeed in acquiring the North Vancouver property. At any cost. Understand? You're going to lose, might as well fold. Saggy government will always lose to honed industry. Way of the world—waiter! Government be gone! A Paleo smoothie chaser, surprise me, something with complex sugars, big ride this evening."

Ms. Reed fiddles with her hair bun, ignores Vincent. "Slacklining? I bet this girl would be good at that kind of nonsense. Her life does seem to be one helluva balancing act."

I'm about to speak when Mr. Reed mutters, "The fatalistic, adolescent twerp probably sprinkled diamond dust into his semen to stick the butterflies to the canv—"

"Carl!"

A single word spoken by Ms. Reed and Carl freezes midsentence, shrugs, says maybe Hirst didn't use his semen, if he did he would've told us about it in the title. Then he mumbles about needing fresh air. Mr. Reed's elbows are on the table, dug in, his narrow chin resting on scrawny fingers. The sleeve of his jean jacket slips down and I see a line of partially healed bruises that look a lot like—

"Carl. Dear? We've moved on from the painter and his assorted fluids." Ms. Reed nods at her husband's sleeve. Carl starts, tugs his sleeve up, glowers out the window like a sulky schoolboy.

"Yeah, Carl. I mean, sourpuss much? Cheer up old chap!" Vincent throws his arms behind his head, stretches, yawns, works his fingers over his forearms, apologizes for being sore because of his brutal training regime. "Wonderful arty interpretation, Carl, although I disagree completely. About the painting? Still, a very interesting perspective, if beholden to a cranky top-down ideology that isn't doing you any favours. I'm a bit of a collector myself. A hobbyist! Big warehouse full of my remarkable art collection in Richmond. One in Orange County as well. I own several of Mr. Hirst's pieces.

We should go take a look sometime. I'm interested in destroying your thoughts. Junkie?"

The final word whispered, so quick I'm not even sure I heard it.

Carl Reed remains perfectly still. "Excuse me?"

"Oh, ha! *Hearing* your thoughts! What did you think I said?"

"I thought I heard—"

"Heather? Should I be concerned? How's Carl doing? Legally medicated?"

Ms. Reed waves her empty Scotch glass at the waiter. "He's fine."

"Fine? Carl? Are you su—"

"She said I'm fucking fine, you—"

"Wonderful! Because Michael's been in touch. He's refreshingly reliable and sane. We're excited to have Green Lead on board with the Solstice—"

"It's a heart," I stammer. "I like it. What could be wrong—"

Vincent waves a hand in my direction. "Okay, Jasminder, thank you. See? Always welcoming constructive opinions. Open communication is the foundation, isn't that right? Multiculturalism? Tolerance?"

"What the hell are you on about?" Mr. Reed says, mouth twisted in disgust.

Vincent turns to him. "Acceptance, Carl? Try to stay current. As a proud Canadian, I can tolerate a multitude of voices. For a few minutes. Jasminder? I hired you. What's your experience? Please share."

"Well . . . for me . . . tolerance is about—"

"Listening! Exactly. That is *so* what it's about. You're a fantastic interpersonalist, Jasminder, despite . . . Heather? See the talent you're up against? Here we are, the tech-savvy next-gen neo-Futurists pushing you obsolete old white-tops into your graves!" Vincent strokes his beard like a Russian czar overseeing an execution. "So. As we were saying, Jasminder, Heather and I are at odds over this stunning piece of property."

"It's a friendly rivalry," Ms. Reed says, smirking at Vincent. "But things do get . . . rather heated?"

Carl groans, covers his face. Ms. Reed fiddles with her diamond pendant. Vincent pretends to dust off his suit.

"Friendly because Marigold contributes generously to your campaigns. *Zing!* I very much appreciate a competitive spirit, especially in a woman. Makes my inevitable alpha domination more exciting. There are no losers. Except you. I've spoken to Scott Charles Booth's assistant, Heather. He says the man has zero intention of seeing his property lie fallow while the province galvanizes the behemoth of bureaucracy. Tell you what? When we reach escape velocity, break free of totalitarian government altogether, I'll let you manage my chicken coop. Waiter, my beverage? A smoothie, yes. Should I write it down for you? And another Scotch for the lovely-if-not-totally-honourable Minister Heather Reed. Food, anyone except Jasminder? No? Not much of an appetite, Carl? Go figure. A shame, really. Amazing food. Michelin and so on. Waiter, I'd like the iron steak sandwich, blue. Very bloody. Like . . . bloody meat in my teeth. Protein? Rebuilds tissue damaged by elite-level exercise. Simple, true-to-ingredients food here at awesome Hawksworth. Locally sourced, duh."

"I've eaten at fucking Hawksworth," Carl spits.

"Delighted, Carl. Charmed. And the other interesting tidbit about this North Van property, Jasminder—if you'll permit a tumble into vicarious gossip—is that Mr. Reed himself, our aging peacenik Carl here, has agreed to back Marigold's bid for the property to the tune of . . . what was it, Carl?"

Mr. Reed waves his hand, nearly knocks over a crystal vase filled with origami orchids. "Piss off, Vincent. Ask Michael. He's the numbers man."

"Piss . . . oh! Michael's numbers, *hmm?* And what are you? The dreamer-visionary? Pardon us small-minded skeptics. Us bean counters and contract writers. You know? We who make the world go round? Like your hard-working, pants-wearing spouse? In any case. We're excited to have Green Lead on board. Aren't we, Jasminder?

Say yes. Ethical-investment visionaries! Twenty-something million. Isn't that amazing? Opposed property bids within the same family? Whoops! Wouldn't want to be in your shoes, Carl. Dragon lady! I've felt her . . . uh, not-always-friendly fire! In any case. Must make for interesting late-night conversation."

Silence.

Ms. Reed scowls at her husband.

Carl straightens. "Green Lead has its own strategic priorities. Independent of the province. Or my wife."

Vincent glares at Carl long enough to make the older man look away. "Is that so? Maybe. But . . . strange bedfellows. Heather! What's your take on your husband's involvement with Marigold?"

"Carl's a big boy."

"Oh, yes! See? That's the problem, isn't it? Because really—and with all due respect, Carl—Heather? Your husband is a lifelong degenerate and layabout—"

"You snake sonofabi—"

"—and I find it difficult to believe that a man like Carl is operating independently of you, which means—"

Ms. Reed reaches across the table, grabs Vincent's hands and holds them. Vincent gasps, tries to fight her grip, realizes she won't release him, pretends to be okay with her holding him, licks his lips, tries to speak, stammers something indecipherable. It's the first time I've seen Vincent at a loss for words, and suddenly it's like Mr. Reed and me aren't even at the table and the feeling is *very* uncomfortable—

"Young man. Is something troubling you?"

Vincent glares at Ms. Reed's hands on top of his. "Troubling? Human contact? Well . . ."

"Are you worried my husband and I are in cahoots—"

"Ha, in *cahoots*—"

"—scheming, plotting to sabotage the Solstice development—"

"And everyone says I'm the paranoid one!" Carl yells.

"Carl, shut up!"

Ms. Reed strokes Vincent's hand. He looks about to be sick. "Well? Are you?"

"Don't be ridiculous. We're simply—"

Carl whispers: "It was you. You depraved sonofabitch. Those scumbags in North Van! And the Price boy . . . and Han—" Carl cuts himself off, goes quiet.

Ms. Reed glances at her husband. Vincent takes the opportunity to tear his hands from hers, shouts at the waiter for a moist towelette.

"What was him, Carl? Tell me."

"Yes, Carl my man, what was me? Exactly? Mind all right? Feeling okay? Paranoid delusions? Not quite sure who and where you are? Or is and were?"

Carl flinches but stays quiet. I look into my coffee cup, make mental notes. Ms. Reed glances outside and for a moment her hard businesswoman-politician demeanour vanishes and she looks a lot like a mother, worried—

A commotion on Georgia Street brings several diners to the window. Car horns, a horrible crunching sound, screaming. Was a pedestrian hit and then I'm standing at the window beside Heather Reed and she's whispering that poor man that poor poor man see Vincent this is why we need green spaces, mentally rejuvenating and there's a guy in the middle of Georgia stumbling through traffic, shrieking, wild-eyed as he hurls magazines at passing cars. My breath catches as a Mercedes suv nearly runs him down and for a second I can't tell if this is happening or only a grief vision created by my unwell mind until Vincent puts a hand on my hip, says, "See, Jasminder? What a shame. For us to have to see that? Even in beautiful Vancouver? And with all the money we've thrown at those rejects. Why are they still here? Oh, look! My steak sandwich—"

We turn from the window and what does it mean, what does it say about me, that I'm able to live with that man's suffering, keep going like nothing happened and when did I learn to do it so easily and before I'm settled in my seat the image of the unstable man on

Georgia fades and here I am now, confronting my own problems—

Vincent folds his napkin as the waiter sets a plate on the table. "Waiter—thank you. And thank you too, Mr. and Ms. Reed, for putting my ills at ease. I feel better! Heather, enough chitty-chat. I'd like to make the province an attractive offer. Our team— through Jasminder here, amazing work, yay team, very global—has recently acquired a rather sizable property outside Lillooet. Could hold a thousand pretend back-to-the-landers like your husband. Waiter! Come here. Look at that sandwich. Is that cooked blue? I sincerely hope so. I asked for a blue steak sandwich. It appears slightly grey-brown? Anyway, it's fine. I'll take the high road. I'll eat anything. Leave it alone. Heather, this property I'm offering in exchange borders Upper Lillooet Park. Drop the North Vancouver bid and we'll offer you the Lillooet property in total. Expand the boundary of the park, big political win. It's a beautiful parcel, right, Jasminder?"

"Gorgeous," I say, too quick. "Absolutely stunning."

"World-class?" Carl hisses.

Vincent clears his throat, asks if Carl would like a nibble of his meat sandwich.

"Eating dead flesh causes living rigor mortis. Plus, laced with—"

Ms. Reed rattles her Scotch, says she's surprised Peele is caving so early. Says she thought he had bigger balls. Vincent says he believes his balls are normal sized, says he's feeling an emerging spirit of co-operation between crazy-free enterprise and repressive government.

Carl groans, rubs his face.

Ms. Reed checks her watch. "Shit. Running late. Nice to see you, Vincent. Let's do it again when I'm in town. Oh, and by the by . . . the North Vancouver property is already in my over-the-hill hands. Haven't you heard? Scott Charles Booth has expressed a firm desire to gift the land to the Canadian people. The man has finally taken an interest in his legacy. The green space will be named in his honour, of course."

Vincent sets his sandwich down, dabs blood from his lips, asks if Heather possesses Mr. Booth's alleged agreement in writing. Being drawn up as we speak, she answers. Carl leans over and smacks Vincent on the shoulder, says she skunked you this time, I told you my Heather Hellcat's a goddamned sharp-toothed feline.

"You're right, Carl. About what you said earlier? It was me."

Something in Vincent's voice makes me reach for my purse, eye the door.

Carl grips the edge of the table, chokes. "What have you done, you—"

"Carl!" Ms. Reed snaps. "What's going on? What the hell is he—"

Vincent plunges his fingers into his beard. "Hannah must be . . . how old, Heather? Sixteen?" Lifts his steak sandwich. "Yum! Look at this delectable . . . tender flesh . . ."

"Get the fuck out," Ms. Reed says, the muscles in her face bunching up.

"Sulphur!" Carl says, sniffing the air. "Anyone smell that? Sulphury putrescence? Goddammit! Peele chose this uptight kill room, I *knew* it—"

Ms. Reed waves her hands frantically. "Carl . . . easy now . . . no!"

"Sulphury-rot-stink Heather baby this is ageless malevolent evil sorry I've been expecting this all along It-Peele baited us into a cursed demonic feeding trust me Heather you're way outta your league I googled this shit let me deal with—"

"No!"

Carl dips a hand inside his jean jacket. Vincent turns in time to catch a face-full of white powder Carl's plucked from a tiny purple satchel. Vincent leaps up, pawing at his eyes. Slams into the table. Glasses shatter across the floor. The entire restaurant's staring at us, men are making their way over with angry or helpful expressions and Carl's brandishing the satchel, cackling and muttering a very unusual fluid-sounding language. Vincent flings his arm over his face as he staggers for the door and I'm left gaping, speechless.

Ms. Reed shoos the crowd away. Takes a sip of Scotch. "Shit, Carl. *Again?*"

"Got rid of It, didn't I? Not easy, sorcering on the fly. Banishing that kind of pervasive nastiness. Did you see It not having a reflection in the window? You're welcome."

"Bastard. So much for me bluffing him into a deal."

"Won't hurt It too bad. Garlic powder. Bit of burning. No permanent damage. Heather? When will you listen? I *told* you this joint was a bloodsucking—"

Ms. Reed cackles. Leans across the table, tousles her husband's hair. "Fuck me, Carl. That was madness! Look at these stiffs. Fully freaked! I think we're gonna get kicked out!" Downs the last of her Scotch. "Hey . . . Blitz? I got a room. Let's do it in a heptagram—"

"So, it was nice meeting . . . ," I manage, throwing myself into the tornado of waiters and fellow diners swirling around us.

"Not quite yet, Jasminder," Ms. Reed says. "Stick around. Girls only! But you—husband. You can leave. Upstairs. Ask the front desk for a key." Carl makes to go and Ms. Reed grabs his arm, pulls him close, hisses: "Vincent threatened our daughter? Crossed the line! Get that crazy motherfucker Caltrop booted up. Tout suite!"

Mr. Reed shakes his head. "Y'know, Heather, *jeesh*. That's what I've been saying all along."

Heather waits until her husband leaves, tells me to sit down. Orders two more Scotches. Watches me drink mine more quickly than I mean to. Asks if I'd like anything else. Puzzled, mind reeling, conflating images of a crazy guy on the street and a garlic powder assault, I tell her no, thank you. She smiles and asks how's the digging going?

"The . . . what?"

An impatient huff. "Digging? The dirt? C'mon, Jasminder. What do you have for me? On that sewer rat Vincent Peele? And the big bad Bo Xi?"

An ally, a confidant, someone on my side? "The phone call? Was you?"

Ms. Reed presses a fingernail to her lower lip.

Mark Ward

Flee Georgia Street before the pigs roll in, find what's left of my mind hiding in an alley dumpster, manage to track down my condo, stuff two Oxys in a Twinkie Ryan left in the fridge and wolf the thing down, collapse on the living room floor with my mouth slimed in petroleum whipped cream.

Phone wakes me up a few hours later. Ryan. Sounds wheezy. Says he's sorry dude but he fucked up. Stretch, try and lift my head off the floor, fail, ask where he is. Says he doesn't know. Sounds like he's been crying, which is fuck. I ask: Someone's house or condo? A hotel? Says he thinks it's a hotel. Then a thump as the kid's head hits something and I'm shouting at him. No answer. Tug my pants on, try to get in my shoes, scream at Ryan to stay with me, answer me, crushing my phone while sweat drips down my brow. The stupid fucker. A part of me's worried sick and another part, small but still there, is thinking fuck sakes, I hardly know the kid, why'd he get me wrapped in his bullshit.

Very quick, but so quiet I can barely hear, Ryan says the Astoria. I ask him what room and the phone goes dead. Run downstairs to the truck, tear ass. The Astoria Hotel's not far. Blow through a few reds, crank the truck over the curb in front of a four-storey building with a brick facade and a neon sign out front, letters lit up white, framed by a burnt-orange border and hovering stars. The liquor store at street level is open but like a lot of shitty hotels in this neighbourhood the lobby doors are locked. Hit the buzzer. Nothing. Pound on the door, scream for the clerk to open up. My yelling scares the shit out of a dude sleeping under a tarp in the doorway. He jumps up, tries to run, falls in a tangle of tarp and soaked blankets. I'm kicking on the goddamned door, thick reinforced steel, trying to smash it down when a voice from inside says hey what the hell you think you're doing? I scream a friend's in your dive fucking dying and the voice, a man's, rough, guttural, says he's calling the cops and asks me what room and I yell open the goddamned door, I don't know what room.

A silence so long I start screaming again and someone in the hotel opens an upstairs window and shrieks at me to shut up, tosses a coffee mug onto the street, nearly hits the homeless guy, who's staggering across the sidewalk with the ripped tarp half-wrapped around him, muttering insane-sounding shit about insects, and then it's like someone flipped the fucking madhouse switch because in two seconds assholes are screaming at me from windows all around. More shit gets thrown onto Hastings. The dude in the tarp takes a run at me for no reason other than I guess he feels galvanized by the madhouse screaming, fuck knows? I dodge him easy while a shadowy shape hovers behind the hotel door. I yell for the asshole clerk to open up, and he does, a couple inches, leaves the security chain attached.

The clerk's big, his hair stringy out the sides of his head. He asks what my friend looks like and I have to resist the urge to shriek in his face because all I can think about is Ryan up there with his heart popping.

"He's young. This short. Wavy dark hair. Maybe had a backpack or a busted toolbox—"

The clerk asks if my friend had a guy with him.

"He didn't say. Yeah, a dude, fucking cares?"

The door swings open. The clerk rubs sleep from his eyes. Push past him, make for the stairs and he says you need a room key and I turn around, yell then get me the fucking key and the guy, fuck this guy, he lopes real mellow to a wooden alcove built into the wall, moving like a slug. Takes his time rummaging through a cardboard box while I pace and curse, hands me a single key with a twist-tie threaded through it and the room number written on a bottle cap, says he called the cops and should he call the ambulance and I tell him hell yeah, fuck you think, he's only a kid.

I'm about to run upstairs when I glance out the window, see someone in a T-shirt and boxers crawling into the passenger seat of my truck, realize it's Ryan. The bastard must've snuck down the fire escape. Throw the key at the useless clerk, run outside, and as we pull from the curb the cops arrive behind us and Ryan, eyes closed, head hanging, says fuck dude I left my toolbox in there.

Jasminder Bansal

L ater that afternoon I meet Heather Reed in front of the main elevators at 666 Burrard Street: Park Place Tower. Is there unseemliness in the air, or only strange vibes left over from Mr. Reed's garlic powder assault? I wave to the minister from across the foyer, thread through pink granite pillars trimmed in copper. Ms. Reed's on her phone, orbited by two assistants. She's sipping from a stainless-steel travel mug in between blasting instructions to whoever's on the other end of the line. The elevator dings closed. Ms. Reed snatches my elbow and holds tight, like I'm a prize she's afraid of losing. The elevator's packed, makes me feel claustrophobic. The unmistakable juniper scent of gin fills the elevator, wafting on Ms. Reed's breath.

"... you tell that wannabe Robertson if he wants his bike lanes ... election year ... I was green before it was hip ... got him by the short and curlies ..."

Half the people in the elevator lean closer, the other half pull away.

"No, I said the goddamned ... livable city! Uh, sustainable ... excuse me ..." Ms. Reed covers her phone, shakes my shoulder in too-friendly greeting. The diamond pendant's gone. Her dress is wrinkled. She doesn't seem to notice half her hair has slipped from her bun, is hanging in a lopsided nest behind her shoulder. "Jasminder?

Thanks for coming, but here's the thing: I'm late for a meeting somewhere in this hellhole. For a design project. You tag along, we'll talk?"
Before I can answer she returns to her phone. The elevator doors slide
open. The crowd jostles out and one of Ms. Reed's assistants—a
distraught-looking waif with tortoise-shell glasses and a floral-print
blouse—shouts for someone to please hold the door while she lunges
for the button. Too late. The doors glide closed.

"Oh no," the assistant whimpers.

Ms. Reed whirls on her. "Christ, Syrah! Do *not* tell me that was
our floor . . . no, Minister. Not talking to you. Syrah! Duh! Anyway,
Clyde? Straight-across deal, no haggling. Bike lanes in exchange for . . .
holy shit I'm so sick of hearing about the UBC line! Aren't we the
Green City? I'm pretty sure we say we are. So let's put a subway out
there alr—oh. Yes I've been to your home on Alma. Gorgeous thou-
sand-year-old koi. Underground vibrations from the UBC line would
disrupt sensitive fishy brains . . . and oh the premier's cousin has a
house on . . . and is that right . . . okay . . . I mean what the fuck are
they thinking, underground transit to the university? Three hundred
million a kilometre. That can buy a lot of condoms and kombucha!"
Ms. Reed snaps her fingers at Syrah, who holds up a tablet for her
boss to read from. "Clyde! Telling an elf like Robertson what he wants
to hear is the easy part. Infrastructure, waste, tragic. That's right.
Repeat after me. Sustainable, mindful, green. See? Talking points.
Zero commitment. I lead, you follow . . . Jasminder, I so cannot wait
to crush that yappy ankle-biter Vincent Peele."

The elevator doors open, revealing an empty corridor.

"Syrah! Is this finally our floor? If we miss it again I'll force-feed
you a suckling pig . . . no no of course not you, Minister, I did not
call you a fucking sexist pi—yes, I understand. You're very sensitive
to name-calling after the . . . alleged incident?" Ms. Reed points at
the phone, sticks her finger down her throat, gags. Syrah and
another assistant, a guy about my age wearing pressed khakis and a
navy Big Brothers Charity Run T-shirt, snicker at Ms. Reed's

antics. Ms. Reed taps the elevator wall, asks if it's freaking freezing in here.

"Slightly under-heated," I say, clutching the stolen Marigold documents to my chest. "Ms. Reed? Heather? If you have a momen—"

She's back on the phone. "Clyde? Speaking of pigs, my husband believes his is . . . never mind. You still call him Blitzo? He's out of prison, thanks. Yes, I'm still into nettle switches, but no, we shouldn't plan a get-together at your Hornby Island sweat lodge. I'm miffed at you, remember? North Vancouver was my deal from the start. And now, Clyde, here you are, trying to take credit? Do not poach me. You're only Community, Sport, and Cultural Development. I'm the entire environment! Can't have any of what you are without an environment." Ms. Reed's voice rises to a shout. "So what if you and Scott Charles Booth are frat buddies? You care; I don't. Did you rub Tiger Balm into his jockstrap? Did he pretend not to like it? Syrah! Is this is our floor? Yes? Yes! Out out out! Everyone outta-tha-way!"

Pile into the corridor, fish-tank-coloured walls, rose carpet in blotchy herringbone. Smells of burned coffee, Calvin Klein cologne, microwaved miso soup. The hallway's deserted and dead quiet. I shiver, wonder at the haunted-horror vibe pervading the office tower. Syrah doesn't quite make it out of the elevator in time, gets knocked sideways by the swooping doors. Ms. Reed cackles, shoots her assistant an I'm-astonished-you're-smart-enough-to-breathe look. I white-knuckle the stolen files while Ms. Reed tugs me down the hall.

Syrah races in front, punches at her tablet.

"Ha, those two!" Ms. Reed says to me.

"Most of the files—"

"Clyde, be quiet a second." Ms. Reed hands her phone to the assistant trailing behind her, yells at Syrah to hurry up and find wherever they're going. "Jasminder? My husband and Vincent Peele? Peas in a pod. Dicks and death."

I hold up a file for her to see. "This looks like a bank state—"

"Both of them nattering about the big stupid system! Carl wants it torn down because it's a capitalist-imperialist front. Peele wants it torn down because it limps his liberty-laissez-faire Shopify boner. Both trying to out-shout each other and guess why?"

Ms. Reed hits her drink, pauses while Syrah reads a door number out loud, whispers oh god no, furiously punches at her tablet, scurries down the hall. Ms. Reed slaps the assistant in the Big Brothers T-shirt on the butt, tells him to hustle. "Anyway, Jasminder, the bastards want it all torn down because we're finally here. Centuries of old boys sitting around patting hairy backs saying *ooh* congrats for us we created democracy free speech the market all that Enlightenment fairness and equality. Crock of shit! Because now we've fought our way in . . . and look how pissed off and pouty they get! Boohoo, gentlemen. We're here to stay! Jasminder, you have some nerve, digging into Vincent Peele and Marigold. Excellent initiative."

"Thanks. It seems like the right thing to do."

Ms. Reed frowns. "There's also that, if you prefer."

Chasing after Syrah, trying to listen to Ms. Reed while mentally rehearsing my spiel.

"Mason!" Ms. Reed barks. "Hand me my phone!"

"Ms. Reed I really need you to look at—"

"—no, no, Clyde! What do you mean, Peele intends to sue my husband because of the Hawksworth fracas? It wasn't an actual assault. Only spilled garlic powder. More like an April Fool's prank. You know how boys are. You're one of them! Peele's a faker. A transparent attempt to undermine our bid. He cries every time I . . . just a sec."

Syrah stops in front of another office door. Knocks. No answer.

Ms. Reed hurls the door open. Arctic air blasts into the hall.

Syrah bites her lip, stifles a sob.

"Syrah? Wrong room again! And there's no one here? Does that seem strange? Is this building condemned? Where the hell is everybody? Clyde, Jasminder . . . hold on. Holy hail Mary mother of . . .

long night, eh, Syrah? Think I can't tell? I've seen solar eclipses smaller than your pupils, girlfriend. Give Mason the tablet; he might figure out how to turn it on. Where's Mason? My adoring supplicant? Clyde, relax. I'll be there soon to take charge, if I ever make it out of this living nightmare of an office building. Lost in purgatory!"

Mason pipes up: "Are you a repentant soul?"

Ms. Reed freezes. "What?"

"Because if not it can't be purgatory; it's just normal hell. I'm guessing eighth or ninth cir—"

"You a closet thumper? Makes sense." Shaking her travel mug: "Regardless, things are gonna get a lot less fun when the go-juice runs out. Clyde, trust me, Booth will come through. I'm with my secret weapon right now." Ms. Reed pinches my arm. "Jasminder! Hurry up, documents . . . whaddayagot for a sister?"

Syrah and Mason glare at me with a mix of relief, exhaustion, and envy. "This is sensitive material? Maybe it's best if we speak in private."

Ms. Reed slams the door closed. "No such thing. Twenty-firstcentury politics, lesson number one: there are no secrets. Blast it out there, let the masses wallow and fling. Make shit up if you gotta. Controversy, name recognition, branding. Only weaklings snivel and deny. Mason! Write an outrageous sexually inappropriate story about me right now. Then post it. I'm feeling media thin."

Mason nibbles on a pencil. "That you once seduced—"

"*Seduced?* Are you shitting me? I never seduce. I tackle and take! You are suuuch a thumpster. Fill in the blanks on: me, cigar boat, ball gag, Bieber. Got it?"

Mason taps the update into his phone. "Sure do!"

Ms. Reed inspects her arms. "*Ahhh* . . . there it is. Shares! Retweets! Pokes! Love it! Seriously addicted. Social media's like a Zelda potion, regenerating me in real time. Carl doesn't know what he's missing. Now. Jasminder? *Brrr!* You want a job? I'm about to fire an assistant. First one to get me to this meeting wins."

I am energized by challenges in my business.

Mason sneers in my direction, snatches the tablet from Syrah. She leans against the wall, wavers. Ms. Reed puts her phone to her ear and marches down the hall. "Clyde! Jesus H! So what if Vincent says I lied about Booth already signing? *I'm* saying I did or did not lie and neither and both. Mason! C'mere . . . this meeting we're on the way to, about what?"

Mason positions himself a step or two behind his boss. "Park-Pods?"

"Park . . . what in a manger's fuck? Hey Jasminder! You have exactly ten seconds—"

I snap to attention. "I found a provable link between Bo Xi and Vincent. I know where they met, but what I need is someone with the . . . resources . . . to access financials on several numbered companies."

Ms. Reed stops so fast I nearly stumble into her. "You need my resources? Are you pitching me?"

I try and hand her the documents. She doesn't touch them. "No. Of course not? But I thought since it was you who clued me in to—"

"The fact that we share a passion for marble cake!" Ms. Reed yells, covering her phone and sticking it in my face. "You're kinda lousy at this high-level corporate sabotage racket. Smarten up. Who knows who Clyde's working for?"

Synchronized who-is-this-moron headshakes from Syrah and Mason. I swear I see a gaunt, tortured soul frozen into the floor beneath my feet, but I take another look and it's only my mind mis-reading patterns in the herringbone carpet.

Ms. Reed keeps her phone covered. "You're a shot in the dark, Jasminder. Background research into Peele's team, found out about you getting hired, murdered brother, truncated journalism diploma. I figured why not? But that's not to say I'm willing to risk implicating myself. Or risk anything at all, for that matter."

Another dead lead. "I see."

"Here we are!" Mason yells, waving at a door identical to every other. "See, Ms. Reed, I found it before Syrah!"

"Did he just shake his rump?" Syrah whispers.

Ms. Reed wags her finger in Syrah's face. "Rump-shaking is permitted if and when I say."

A lecherous voice from Ms. Reed's phone: "Oh you girls want to see rump—"

Ms. Reed shudders, tosses the phone at Syrah, tells her to hang up, asks Mason to remind her what a ParkPod is before she signs off on it.

"The ParkPod's like a—"

"Time's up! Elevator pitch! Think I have all day? Lazing around, stained sweatpants, boogers, reading fucking novels?"

Mason joke-punches his boss on the shoulder, says no, even funnier, writing them. Then he flings the door open, gasps.

Ms. Reed shoves him against the wall, huffs in. The room is furnished but deserted. "For lease? Mason! What the Henry Frick? Another wrong door? Give me twenty!"

Mason drops into push-up position. Ms. Reed sinks a heel into the small of his back. Syrah sneaks around, kicks Mason's hands out from under him, giggles when he flattens, snatches the tablet, tells Ms. Reed the ParkPod is like an outdoor La-Z-Boy recliner enclosed in vines and greenery, the proposal is to build them throughout the city, private rejuvenation spaces, like those sleeping pods in Asian airports but more Vancouvery.

Ms. Reed looks at the ceiling. "That's what I'm wandering around a freezing hellhole to talk about buying? An outhouse with weeds?"

Mason sits up, says no, not Oppenheimer Park, way more upscale, brushed aluminum like the bus stops.

Ms. Reed snatches the documents from my hands. Skim-reads the first one, says nope, nice try, hands it to Mason, he shakes his head, says big fail, hands it to Syrah, she smirks, says I'm way out of my depth, hands it back to me. Second and third files get similar treatment. Ms. Reed mumbles a name after glancing at the fourth. Mason stuffs it in a slim briefcase. Ms. Reed goes through every file, says hell yeah Jasminder the long shot comes through you might have something. Talk to my team, see where this goes, I'll be in touch.

Mark Ward

Vincent Peele calls, sics me on the Reed father. I tell him I'm on it and hang up. A while later Ryan and me have the talk. In Clint's condominium, playing *Call of Duty*, not facing each other. It's dark out. Wind whips rain against the windows. Ryan looks like a limb that got pulled from the ocean. Pasty, shrunken, pale. Hasn't eaten a thing since the Astoria. Ask him how much he uses and he says not much. Ask him what and he says meth mostly. Things that make him go bang. I ask him if he's ever been high on the job and he says, "Want a piss test?"

"Have you? On my jobs?"

"Only weed. Gonna fire me?"

My soldier shoots his in the face. "I don't know."

"Cuz it's not really up to you."

Not super psyched on the kid's smartass tone. "That right? Who's it up to?"

"Clint."

I'm glad we're not facing one another. I don't want him to see my expression. "Think so? My brother owns Redline, but these are my sites. I hire and fire."

"You can boot me. Clint has other jobs. He'll put me on one of those."

I'm wondering: why the rock-solid sense of job security? "Why would Clint go out of his way, against my word, to keep you on? When I tell him you're a total fiend? Had to call me to rescue you— which, by the way, a thank-you wouldn't be out of line."

"Thanks. Was amped is all. Shouldn't've called. Especially since you're ruining my Friday night doing this shit."

"What shit?"

Ryan doesn't look at me. "Power-tripping bullshit. Like you don't get high. I see you with those pills. High all day. High right now."

"Had my leg half blown off."

"Yeah, well."

Something got ripped out of me, too.

The game ends. Ryan hits reset. We're both reborn. I decide I'm done playing. The rain makes a pattering sound on the windows that gets louder when a gust of wind swoops in. I think about the wind whipping through cedar and hemlock trees out in the woods, picture the condo windows exploding inward, glass piercing skin, take a long swig of beer, decide I'm gonna cut the kid loose. He resents me for helping him out, hates I saw him weak and fucked up. Fine.

Across the street, in neighbouring cubbyholes, normal people are cooking dinner, watching TV, chatting on their phones, relaxing after a long work week and the lines of the cityscape are gridded, severe and sterile, goal modelled, reminds me of a computer chip.

"How long you been doing it? Not drugs. The other thing?"

Ryan manoeuvres his soldier up a flight of stairs, kicks in a door, hurls a flash grenade. Death cries from the OPFOR targets hiding in the room. Ryan's soldier leaps from a second-storey balcony, lands, ducks and rolls, slips his combat blade into an OPFOR soldier's spine.

"Are there places you go? Spots? I dunno . . . corners?"

Ryan slides a glance in my direction. "Fuck off."

"Nope."

Ryan's soldier bludgeons an OPFOR to death with a chunk of concrete, which means he gets to take the dead soldier's AK-47. "Fucking *finally* I got a real gun. Look out, bitch, elite special forces killer DEATHDREAM on the hunt!"

"Ryan?"

"Really? Can't we just play the game? I fucked up I'm a shithead I'm sorry you're way better than me, there." Ryan's solid with the AK, sinks four rounds in my soldier's chest. We start over. I light a joint, hand it to him. He smokes it for a while, hands it back, says, "There's usually a somebody. Like I know somebody and he knows somebody and there's a party, usually, not a big party but a few people."

I hit the joint to make the twisting in my stomach go away. "You don't have to do it. You make okay money."

"DEATHDREAM," Ryan yells. "On the warpath."

Stuttering pain-pressure builds behind my eyes. *There's a somebody.* Limp to the sink, take a sip from the faucet, slide on my ass because my fucked-up leg starts quivering. It's guilt, is what it is. The pain in my leg should be gone by now. That's what the military docs say. They tell me the pain *is* gone. It's in my head. *Ghost pain.* Pain that's not real but still hurts, and I'm like: Split hairs much? Because that's a pretty fucking iffy ontological distinction. Doesn't even allow me the satisfaction of suffering legit pain. The military shrink, fuck him too, says it's manifested guilt. Which I'm beginning to think is maybe not total bullshit. Because I should've known we were driving over that IED, should've sensed it somehow, sensed the hidden OPFOR fingering a cellphone detonator, yelled STOP to the VC, STOP THE LAV. I don't know how I should've known . . . but why didn't I? Because the fact is I don't have feelers. I took a drag of my smoke even though it's against the rules to smoke in the LAV, you can do it if you have a cool VC, and next I was crawling from a cage of red-hot metal and burning tires and black diesel smoke, too shocked to scream, spitting blood and sand and a brown guy, fuck, an Afghan local ran into the smoke and flame, held his *kufi* over his mouth and nose and pulled me away from the burning LAV. He ran in and rescued me even though the OPFOR likes to detonate secondary charges to kill first responders, people trying to help. That local Afghan guy, some stranger, not a saint or perfect because no one is, just some guy, a son or brother or husband or father, a fucking *person*, he pulled me out of the flames even though I was leaking shit through my pants and I stank like shit and blood and oil and money and war and whiteness. What I did to the guy trying to rescue me is I almost shot him dead, had my hand on my Browning 9, almost shot that fucking Afghan right there in the dirt with my shit-filled pants and black-smoke sky and the LIGHTROAR, *we summoned it like gods*. I almost shot that Afghan because I thought he was dragging me to a pit in the ground to cut my head off, make me famous just by dying, and the Afghan man saw me reach for the Browning and ran away *betrayed*. I'll never see him again, say *sorry*, say *thank you*. The LAV gunner and the vc didn't come out at all so why didn't I sense the bomb, a fucking buried pressure cooker filled with nails strapped to decades-old unexploded ordnance, UXO, maybe *our* ordnance, what a laugh, UXO OXY, all our fancy warplanes, all our buzzing drones and those two guys, good enough guys, fuck what were their names, melted skin, flesh to metal, kids piled against factory doors, please tell me their names, meat and soft bits is all we are, meat and nothing else, *ghost deaths*, fed to something, *can't hit reset* and why can't I remember their names, please my brother *hold me* I love you and please my brother you didn't do that, not to this boy, this *child*—

"Twll means hole," I whisper. "It doesn't mean bro."

"Dude you playing or what?" Ryan yells over the exploding video game noise. "Your soldier's standing in the open like a jerkoff. Find some cover. I could've killed you ten times, easy. Clint was right. You're a whack-job, but you're not even cool. You're a total pussy."

"That right?" I drag myself out of the kitchen, pick up the game controller, move my soldier behind a stack of cinderblocks, swallow. "When was this? What Clint said? When you guys were—"

"Fucking partying, yeah. Last night. Glad you weren't there. Clint said he can't believe you went to war. Said with soldiers like you no wonder we keep losing."

"Clint's my brother. He's allowed to talk shit."

I let the threat hang.

"But he's right. Look at you. High all the time and not even for fun. He owns Redline. You don't own shit. Not even a truck."

I remind myself the kid's venting. "I guess I don't own much. But look. I asked you. If it's not for money, why do it?"

"Money never hurts."

"Of course it does."

"So you gonna fire me?"

I sigh. "No. But I tell you this. Phone me strung out? I'm not your mommy. You had a tough go. But know what? You're making choices, friend. Bad ones. Choices with consequences. They're yours to face."

I keep my voice lean, but it feels shit, saying I won't help the kid. He's fifteen. My life growing up wasn't roses, but it was nothing compared to what this kid's been through. But there it is. I toss the game controller on the floor, tell him there's a pizza in the freezer. Ryan ignores me.

Grab my Therm-a-Rest and sleeping bag and head out the door, pausing in the hallway to listen, see what's up. I've been keeping an eye on these condos. The mail, parking spaces, lights. Walk down the hall, wondering which one to use. I push through a fire door, take the stairs up one flight into another identical hall, which leaves me with a not-cool sensation like I've doubled, become my own doppelgänger and now I'm sneaking up on myself, about to stab myself in the back. But that doesn't happen, and instead I find unit three thirty.

Stand with my ear pressed to the door for a few minutes, working on slowing my breathing. Nothing. No one home. Door's locked. Crank the handle, slam my hip where the deadbolt penetrates the frame. A splintering sound as the cheap frame rips apart and then I'm inside, examining the damage, making sure it's not too obvious.

The condo's dark except for rectangular patterns of light shining through the windows and stretching across the living room. An unearthly silence made even heavier by the rain lashing the windows. Smells of carpet glue, drywall dust, fresh paint. I do a quick search. No furnishings. No food in the fridge. Hasn't seen a human soul in a long time. Maybe never even lived in. Eat, fuck, die. Never that. No money in living.

Drop the sleeping bag and Therm-a-Rest on the floor. Head back into the hall. Close the door quietly. Three potentially empty condos on this floor alone. Fifteen floors. Lots of empty units.

Time skips and stutters, drops me into the alley behind Clint's condo, soaked, walking close to walls, slinking, scowling. I find who I'm searching for a block away, huddled in the bushes in a concrete planter box outside the MacMillan Bloedel building on Georgia. The building's deep-set, gridded windows tower overhead, a brutalist fantasy in concrete and glass, the architectural equivalent of a billy club in the face. The homeless guy's soaked, covered in layers of flattened cardboard and scavenged plastic bags, his eyes glassy and uncomprehending, so filthy he looks caked in soot, reeking of sweat and sickness, maybe even infection. It takes me a half-hour to talk him from his sort-of shelter. He's not wearing shoes. His feet are swollen and covered in sores. He says shit like who are you and please don't hurt me and I shush him, tell him he's safe, that I'd never hurt him, not someone like him, hand him a lit cigarette, talk to him in a quiet, measured voice, like I'm calming an animal caught in a leg trap.

During this business I'm not thinking do-gooder thoughts about how kind or generous I am or about what an amazing thing I'm doing. Truth is the guy disgusts me. He stinks, he's filthy and piss-stained, wretched, cast aside and beaten down. He cowers as I sit on the edge of the concrete planter box in the darkness and pouring rain talking to him about fuck all, and when he reaches out to touch my shoulder I shy away, say what the fuck don't touch me.

Truth is I want nothing to do with him.

Which is why I'm out here, fighting that ugliness in me, confronting it, sucker-punching that nastiness, struggling against the disgust this guy makes me feel for no other reason than I'm human, ugliness is in us, we have to fight it.

My thinking on tonight's mission, its meaning and intent, is crude. I prefer it that way. Professionalism reeks of death. Necrosis. The fully formed, already known, and already spent. In the twenty-first century everyone is forever being right about everything. Give me the freedom to be passionate and wrong, to mistake a Hallmark card for high art. Give me the amateur, the hobbyist, the dental hygienist who spends her weekends taking photographs of red-barked arbutus, the welder who secretly writes prose poetry, the administrative assistant who sculpts soapstone. Give me creation in all its banal, perpetually worthless glory. Give me bad ideas, incomprehensible logic, misplaced aims, theories shot full of holes. Give me failure, make me suffer its joy.

It takes another hour to coax the vagrant into the empty condo.

He looks around the room, blinking, probably feeling lost, suspicious, afraid, not sure what happens next. Truth is neither am I. We're in uncharted territory. I tell him it's cool, he should try and get cleaned up, not make a nuisance of himself, how long he makes it here before the cops boot him will depend on him. He drags a blackened fingernail across the pristine countertop with an expression like he's been beamed into a starship. He might only get a single warm night. Maybe he'll get a week, a month. Who knows? The point is he'll get something. He walks into the bathroom. I head for the door, not expecting thanks, thinking the guy's likely too stunned to speak, but as I slip into the hall I hear him running a bath. That night I bring three more in from the rain and when I return to the condo Ryan's gone, not sleeping on the balcony but really gone and I sit alone and naked outside, glaring into darkened condominium circuits while the rain stings down.

Jasminder Bansal

On the night he died, Amar texted, said he wanted to show me something, said I should dress nice. He'd been out of our apartment for several years. Mom refused to see him, or said she did, but I found out later from Sim that she was still taking Amar's money to pay our bills. I refused to judge her for it; Meeta had other opinions and made sure they were known.

Amar parked his silver Cadillac suv outside our apartment. I hurried to him, stepping around puddles, feeling anxious and slightly ridiculous, which was always how I felt around my brother. I wore a long overcoat to hide my floral print dress; I didn't like the fabric, how it clung to my skin.

It was early evening. The clouds were stalled over the ocean in a broiling line, cavalry awaiting command. Amar reached to hold my hands, his customary greeting for family and close friends. He was always the physical one, quick to bear-hug and tousle and rough-house. I spent my childhood swatting Amar away, or laughing and squirming out from under a tackle. But that night I was glad to have him hold my hands and lead me to the car. Glad just to see him. It had been months.

Amar had begun to feel like a stranger. *He's changed*, family friends would say, if they said anything. *This is not our Amar.* And the news-papers? I'd stopped reading them. Stopped watching the news. Which was difficult, considering I was saving up to apply to Langara and knew I wanted to study journalism. A gang war, everyone called it. A terrible breed of gangster. Bold. Vicious. Another daylight shooting in a leafy Vancouver neighbourhood only blocks from an elementary school. Cut to an image of a cherry-lined street cordoned in yellow tape. Cut to an image of the Downtown Eastside. Cut to an image of an RCMP officer standing beside a table heavy with cocaine and automatic weapons. Cut to an image of my brother rolling gold and a custom suit, or a tattooed Vietnamese rival wearing aviators. The problem was right there, if unspoken: the immigrant gangsters had gone public, started overstepping themselves. At that time the province was the largest producer of black market marijuana on the continent. Everyone knew there was a vast amount of dirty money involved, and that the dope was being traded across the bor-der for hard drugs and automatics. Which was fine as long as the enterprise involved white growers in the interior and white bikers stabbing each other in strip clubs. But throw a brown kid in the mix?

Now we have a problem.

You want to be seen, little sister? Amar used to say. *You have to bring down an airplane. Shoot a man in a mall parking lot. Then they pay attention.*

He was right. My brother got noticed. Amar couldn't walk down Robson without being called out—either by a fan or a rival. I don't think he realized he'd adopted a role laid out for him in advance. Maybe it doesn't matter. Gangster. Criminal. Terrorist. Different paths leading to the same place. Maybe Amar really was that per-son. *Murderer.* Maybe I still refuse to see him. Maybe I refuse to see him in me.

✳

Amar discovered fame can feel like a shield. A nothing brown kid finally commanding the spotlight. The more attention he received the bolder he became. But it was a lie. Fame only made him easier to murder. Made his life into reality TV ritual, his death a prime-time exorcism, a superficial cleansing of the corrupt body politic.

"No one steps now," Amar said as he eased the Cadillac to the curb. "I'm known."

Everyone in line at the club turned to watch us. I held my hands clenched on my lap so my brother wouldn't see them shaking. Amar was wearing a glossy, cream-coloured suit. Gold chains and rings gleamed against his skin. It was his trademark look, cobbled together from movies and music videos. Half pimp, half investment banker, all high roller.

"Amar," I said. "I don't want to go inside."

Amar paused, slung his arm over the steering wheel, glared at the crowd outside the Euphorium, said he was worried about me being holed up in that apartment. "Start calling your shots, Jaz, instead of letting motherfuckers call them for you." A white guy wearing a black T-shirt with a rhinestone skull emblazoned across the front tapped on the passenger window. Amar lifted two fingers from the steering wheel and waited until the guy wandered off. "See that? Fuck that guy. Year ago he wouldn't have nothing to do with me. Now I'm in demand. Most people let the tide carry them. You want to be like everyone else? School, debt? What do you want?"

I remember thinking of Sim.

I tried to say something to sum up everything I was feeling in a way that wouldn't destroy the last of what little relationship we had. I thought about telling him, right then, about me and Sim. But maybe Amar knew. Even then, on the last night of his life.

An unfriendly fist thumped against the Cadillac's hood. Amar's expression changed instantly. "You want to be a good Western Paki girl?" he said, sneering. "Go to school because everyone says you should, get married, wear a sari, spend your days hunched over a karahi, make nice with the whites? A fucking mouse. Spend your life wondering what you could've been? Haven't you heard a thing Mom's said?" Amar smoothed his hair, laughed at the people waiting in line. "I haven't waited to get into this dump in three years." Then his voice went cold. "The hate I can handle. Being ignored I can't stand."

I could have said anything in that moment. *Take me home.* Could have insisted. *I don't want to be here.*

Instead I stayed quiet.

Amar gave that look he'd been giving me since we were kids, half frustration and half disappointment, like I was the one who wasn't living up to potential, not him. Then he slipped out of the Caddy, unhurried. I watched him from inside the parked vehicle. It was quiet, the air slightly stuffy and smelling of Calvin Klein cologne and Armor All. I watched Amar's lips move. His gestures and body language. They were different now. *He* was different. Blustery. Aggressive. He leaned into people. Laughed in their faces, his gold rings sparkling as his hands waved through the air. *You're tellin' stories.* That was his line when reporters accused him of being connected to a recent shooting or a drug deal gone bad. *You're tellin' stories.* A popular YouTube video showed my brother rolling up in his Cadillac, leaning his head out, glaring at the camera through his gold-framed sunglasses and delivering the line. Then a laugh so carefree and infectious people didn't seem to mind it wasn't genuine.

I sat in the Cadillac and watched Amar walk around to open my door. Can you be wrong about a person for so long? Kind, generous, peaceful. Had he charmed us as well? No. Not Amar Bansal. Not my brother. His enemies were telling lies. *Tellin' stories.* But that night, as Amar opened the Caddy door, I began shivering, and less than ninety minutes later the truth of my brother, whatever it was, wouldn't matter at all. Amar played his part right to the end.

Clint Ward.

I know what Amar would say.

He'd give me a hard look, say the little mouse is still playing nice, ask if I want a fucking roti.

*

The anniversary is tomorrow. I'm scheduled to fly a group of investors to Osoyoos. An exclusive retirement development, golf course, recreation complex. Medical support staff. High brick walls and a guard posted at a wrought-iron gate. Instead, after meeting Heather Reed, I phone Vincent from a coffee shop on Commercial Drive, tell him I've come down with something. He asks what's wrong and I say I'm not sure and he says he'll send Elodie to Osoyoos, although the deal really could've used my international flair. I thank him and say I'm still okay to work, I just can't fly. I'll be by the office tomorrow and he says great we can play foosball, he has some ideas about the Solstice project he'd like to wing around the Flowroom, get my feedback on.

I ask him how the North Vancouver property bid is going.

He says Scott Charles Booth is playing hard to get and has yet to sign anything, but Marigold has a solid in with one of Booth's most trusted advisors so it's looking like a go.

We hang up. I'm expecting Heather Reed to call at any moment and say she'll help with the story. Waiting to see the deal ripped from under Vincent Peele and Clint Ward. Because of me. An ugly knot forms in my stomach. Is exposing them enough? Lawyers, a trial, and . . . what then?

I invest in myself and my business every single day.

I will not bear silent witness while others decide my fate.

I grab my phone, search for a list of companies Bo Xi is currently on the board of. There are four in North America, but only one with an office in Vancouver. Pillar Investment. A venture capital firm. Thirty seconds later I have an email address for the manager at Pillar Investment, a woman named Joyce Arnell.

I settle into my chair. Try and see what I'm missing. Sim's out there, waiting for my word. Clint Ward gone. Vincent Peele gone. Bo Xi will still need that North Vancouver property. It could be me that gets it for him. *It's a big play*, Amar would've said. *The only kind worth the time.*

My mind wanders to the pitch.

Mark Ward

Carl Reed looks more like an unemployed math teacher than a man sitting on a quarter billion. Lanky, maybe six three, all of a hundred and fifty pounds. Sandy blond hair flecked with grey and thinning on top, revealing a dry and freckled scalp. Eyes hidden in shadows no detox will ever brighten. Jittery. Wearing a dumpy hippy outfit, rough baggy cloth shirt, looks like hemp, and those wide-legged capris like the poi spinners at the art gallery. Leather moccasins. All he needs is a tie-dye bandanna. I dislike him immediately. A fuckin' armchair subversive, nattering about working-class oppression from his ocean-view estate. Only blister dude's had is from hot-knifing. Takes me a half-second to know him for a tweaker.

Reed's sitting on a bench overlooking Lost Lagoon in Stanley Park, smooching and cuddling a hideous hairless dog. The rain exhausted itself last night. A patch of blue sky reflects in the murky water, along with leafless oak and low-rise West End apartments built in the sixties. I stealth beside Reed, decide to fuck with him a bit, settle in so we're touching elbows. He doesn't look at me, slides to the far end of the bench. Clint was right. This is going to be piss-easy.

A snorting sound and suddenly I'm glad there's some space between us. Reed's holding a potbellied pig, not a dog. He lifts the nasty thing in my direction. Fat rolls jiggle on its legs and neck. The pig squeals, licks its glistening snout, snorts.

"You don't like him?"

"Barely know him."

Hooves thrash and shake. Reed sets the pig between us. Toss my arm over the bench, check my phone, see if Ryan got back to me, decide there are worse places to spend a Saturday morning. "Pig in the middle?"

"He's the only non-swine on this bench. Name's Holdout. My only true and loyal friend."

"Tragic."

"One more than you, good sir."

"H?" I ask, returning the jab.

"Only to sleep. Sometimes speedballs. Sometimes whatever."

"You're getting up there. Stims help you hang with the kids."

"I'm forty-nine."

"You look sixty-five. That's being generous. Time to kick back, old man."

"Thanks. Next time I want unasked-for advice I'll hurry to the reprobate attempting to blackmail me."

I light a smoke, pick up a handful of pebbles, huck them in the water. A flock of ducks hurries over, webbed feet paddling furiously, the bigger ones nipping at the smaller as they race for the grub. They dive, emerge crunching rocks. We are ever hopeful. "You high right now?"

Reed says nothing.

"Matters because you need to follow what I have to say. And follow it to the fucking letter."

The pig rubs its filthy ass against the backrest, glares at me, animal-dumb. I exhale a cloud of cigarette smoke in its face.

Carl, frantic, waves the smoke away. "Whoa! Really? This is a living being. Do you know what they put in those? Big Tobacco. Fibreglass. Stearic acid. Ammonia. Hydrogen cyanide. Ring any bells? Nazi gas chambers."

I fake outrage. "No way. Is that like confirmed?"

"From the American Med—"

I start laughing. Even the pig snuffles, which okay is fucking weird. Carl lifts the pig to eye level, whispers be cool don't let him in, makes my skin crawl. Sets the pig down, says, "Holdout likes you."

"A pig? First for everything. Sober?"

Carl sighs. "Clean a couple days. Since I got out of jail. I'm terribly coherent. Able to hold a conversation. Able to know I'm being divorced. My business partner, former best friend, and lover is abandoning me. My daughter's missing."

"That'd be an interesting story. If I gave a shit."

"You been doing this a while? Because it doesn't suit you. Maybe you're with Fintrac. Undercover on Vincent Peele and his crew. Of course you don't know Peele bought off your bosses in Ottawa. Or maybe you do, and that's why you're here, hassling a man in the vulnerable early stages of recovery."

"Your instincts are lousy. The simplest explanation is—"

"Useful until it isn't." Reed smiles in a way that says I ain't shit. "I know you're not a Fintrac Tool. But you're not entirely of this world, Mr. Mark Ward. Pretending to be someone else, pretending to be an idea of someone else. There's something atavistic about you. The Fraser Valley hick caught up in his older brother's big-city bullshit. You smashed your head on that corporate criminal ceiling yet? It's not made of glass, not for lowborn grunts like you. More like concrete. And when you hit it you fall right to the bottom, into the liquid manure you came from."

I think I do an all-right job hiding my surprise, but apparently not, because Reed says, "Vincent Peele found a lucrative eddy in a torrent of sewage. But the rain comes, he'll be washed away. Like the rest of you. Me? If I have anything, it's staying power. That's been proven."

"Fuck you on about?"

Reed nuzzles the pig. "Consider your sources."

I pull out the camera. Hold it inches from Reed's face. "Your politician wife's gonna drop the North Van property. She can spin whatever bullshit she wants, long as she doesn't mention Marigold Group. Also. Green Lead is going to double its investment in Solstice Homes. Then this ugly goes away."

Reed's silent so long I give him a sideways glance to make sure he didn't fall asleep. Then he whispers, "You watch it?"

"No."

"Could be anything."

"Anything named Hannah Reed, yeah."

"Drugs. Sex. Both. What kind of a man are you? To resist watching that video?" Reed reaches in his pocket, pulls out a bag of gummy bears, feeds a handful to the pig, pisses me off because I feel like asking for some. "You brutalized Sebastian Price?"

"With gusto."

"And the Bryant family in North Vancouver?"

"My homecoming present." Check the time, say I'm due somewhere. Say I need an answer.

"Everything's rotten," Reed says. "Rotten all the way through. Some kind of disease. Woke up one morning and couldn't shake the feeling I'm as guilty as everyone. No more believing I'm above it. Realized the rot is in everything. Realized it *is* everything. The kids talk about being online like it's an inherently liberating experience. *Pffft.* The internet's a shopping mall floating on an ocean of excrement. Instant access to questionable information doesn't make you liberated. It makes you tired. Awash in trivia. The repressive regimes and canonical fascists sought control above all else. Information. Sex. Ideas. All required an iron fist. Imagine the energy they expended maintaining control. The resources? We've moved beyond that. There is no singular oppressive force. No material enemy. We're decentralized, coded in light. The new century demands a new us. You know I could have you killed right now, at this very moment? Think about that. In the middle of the breath you're drawing . . . perhaps I'll ask the pig if you should live. Holdout? Should Mark Ward the former soldier live or die? *Hmm?* Or should we let him prove his worth?"

The pig wipes snot on my leg. I smack at it, send it scurrying onto Reed's lap, examine Reed, try and figure out if he's bluffing. Wish what he was saying didn't make so much sense, wish there was a way out that didn't involve . . .

"Killing me isn't worth the risk," I tell him. "Besides, won't do you any good. We have copies. You'd have to kill—"

"Quite a few."

"So. You agree? The politician wife calls it quits on the property. You toss some more money in Peele's direction. Easy. This video, it'll destroy your daughter. You're right about the internet. This'll go viral, trust me. It'll live forever and Hannah will never live it down. It'll destroy your family."

"That ship sailed."

"Okay. I might be fuck all. But the people I work for? You know this is a shot over the bow. Wifey keeps pressing the bid, we fire a real shot. Maybe the next video it's not your daughter doing something. It's something being done to her. You'll never recover. Even with all your money."

"All. My. Money." Reed repeats, slowly, his eyes unfocused as he nibbles the arms off a blue gummy bear. "You really do hate it? Remarkable. You honestly hate it. Last of a dying breed. Must be lonesome. And maddening. Remind me of an old friend."

Reed slides closer and I'm feeling not so shit-awesome, not so sure this work's gonna be so straight-up—

"Speaking of friends," Reed continues, "have you seen yours recently? The kid? What's his name? Ryan?"

I fight to keep myself from unsheathing the KA-BAR.

"You keeping a close eye on that Ryan boy? He's around the same age as my daughter."

I dig my teeth into my lower lip. "Nothing to do with this."

Reed shakes his head. "See? Your inexperience is showing. These things you're involved in, dark matter, they have gravitational fields. They pull objects, people, toward them. Sometimes a person's floating way out there, clear of harm's way . . . and they get sucked in. That idea we're all connected? Nice idea? Like we're all in this together? Sense of solidarity?" Reed smiles. Sickly but confident in a way that makes me scan the tree line across the pond. "They never said what we're connected *to*."

Me strangling the skinny bastard. Right here, in broad daylight. Wrapping my fingers around his neck, crushing his windpipe, and next thing I know I'm reaching for the KA-BAR—

A roaring boom, so loud it feels like my brains are being blown out my ears and the wooden bench explodes beside my left shoulder. Splinters stab my cheek. A heavy-calibre round, most likely a Cheyenne Tactical, precision range up to two fucking kilometres.

OPFOR, a ragged bit of metal moving fast and I slam into the target, press behind him, edge the KA-BAR to his throat. Scan the apartments ringing Lost Lagoon, thousands of spots for a comfy nest and the joke's on me, Marky's a bonafide asshole, meeting a target in the open, exposed—

"Tell your boy to stand down." My voice going *warba-warba* in my ears and Reed's not even trembling, the junkie set me up, in fact the bastard seems real cool considering the blade's cutting his neck, blood leaking onto his ugly-ass hemp shirt and I have to look away, killing's so easy, so easy, him or me or maybe us both. The potbellied pig screeches and tears off into the woods. That seems to get to Reed because he sounds sad when he says, deadpan, "Holdout won't stop growing. It's his tragic flaw."

"Where the fuck is he? Reed! Tell your man—"

"I never could see him. He used to go out and hide and we'd get high, walk through the woods looking for him. I stepped on his arm once. What am I connected to, Mark? That's what you should be asking. How powerful is *my* gravitational field?"

"Tell your man—"

"To stop shooting? Not kill you? It appears he's already made that decision."

Reed's right. The shooter didn't miss. He set the round exactly where he wanted.

"Another question, for fun? How long do you think my 'man' will let you hold that knife to my throat?"

Five seconds tick by. Pissing sweat, ears ringing, trembling, not from fear but from being such an asshole, underestimating a target so badly, not paying attention—

I sheath the blade, inch away from Reed, lift the KA-BAR so the shooter sees it, set it on the ground, kick it onto the lawn. The ducks waddle over and peck at it.

Reed dusts off his shirt, sets a finger to the nick on his throat, stares at the crimson stain, says his friend wants to meet me.

"So tell him to come on out."

"You keep assuming I tell him what to do. That he's under some sort of control. Let me assure you, that is *not* the case."

Tongue feels like a fucking brick and I tell myself now isn't the time to be pawing for a goddamned pill bottle. The slug punched a fist-sized hole through three inches of solid wood. I try and muster a smile for the shooter's benefit, show him I'm not squirming on the mat just yet. "Looks like your boy mistook me for big game."

"He's not known for understatement."

"Like I mistook you. You're not the man. You're the messenger."

"You want to reduce a thirty-year friendship to some sort of bullshit power dynamic, you go ahead. *Jeesh.* What a sad life you lead. I'm becoming less enamoured of you, Mark. Let's say there *is* a signal. Let's say you're alive because I've decided to give you the benefit of the doubt. For the time being."

The pig waddles out of the woods, burps. Reed pats his knees, calls it, laughs when the thing leaps into his lap, snorts and happy-giggly snuffles all round.

"I'm not the only one with a copy of this video," I say, feeling shit.

Reed twirls the pig's tail, doesn't bother answering. After a while he says, "I made my money on a prison card game. True story."

"Don't want to hear it."

Which is when things go haywire, because something changes in Carl Reed. Not one thing, but everything? His posture. The look on his face . . . that blank-eyed junkie stare replaced by a supreme or supernatural confidence, a power, and the hippie burnout—swear to fuck—he seems taller, larger, his hands not only narrow but *huge*, bony fingers stretching a foot long and this has gotta be the drugs or lack thereof, drugs and adrenaline from the sniper shot, death having a grand time toying with my mind because Reed doesn't seem like a washed-up rich prick poseur anymore and his eyes are bright and turquoise blue, glowing, blinding, forcing me to shield my face from those empty all-seeing orbs and while this *thing* sitting on the bench stares at me my heart goes *pingpingping* on its way to the *pop* and I know with sick certainty that Reed's doing it, an ageless power, sorcerer, shaman, deity, and his voice, if it even *is* a voice because I'm like fairly fucking certain the alien-thing's lips don't move but his voice booms like a Cheyenne bullet through my head, and what I hear is:

"SON, THIS IS WHEN YOU SHUT THE FUCK UP AND LISTEN."

Then air being drawn into my lungs and my heart rate slows and the hallucination's gone, drug-mania, delusion, because it's only the pathetic has-been Carl Reed sitting on a park bench, nuzzling his potbellied pig.

"You hear me, Mark?"

"That was . . . uh . . . pretty wild?"

Clamp my teeth together, fumble for a smoke, offer Reed one, try and get in front of this mess. He looks at the smoke in disgust. Spread my arms on the bench, dig my fingers into the bullet hole, imagine a second Cheyenne ripping through my chest, punching my sternum out my spine. Not a bad way to go. There's way worse.

"A prison card game," Reed says. "You with me now? Or do you need to check your feed? Find the perfect emoji? Didn't understand until it was too late that the world was pissing in my face. This was in the late eighties. Berlin Wall torn down. All these former East Berliners going west. An exodus. Wait! I never killed anyone—let's make that clear from the get-go. Believe what you want, everyone else does. Anyhow, one of these folks, former Eastern commie type, a wizened old man, shows up in Kent prison. You should've seen him. Ancient fellow with nearly see-through skin and watery eyes the colour of driftwood. Had a habit of dragging his fingernails over his skin. Not scratching, just dragging them along. Had scales on his skin. Tiny scales you could only see in perfect bright light, which there never is in prison. I am not insane. You might be, but not me. I've wished it, though. So we all saw the old Berliner and his tiny scales and when he dragged his fingernails across them they'd flake off, leave a shimmering trail in his wake. Anyway, he set us on edge.

"We had our theories about him, for sure. Paid a guard to pull his file. Nothing in there. Not even a name. Just something that looked like a serial number stamped on a yellowing index card. Can't remember what the number was. Doesn't matter. Point is, no one knew why this guy was in prison. Complete mystery. All we knew is he had scales. Prison, best not to stand out. Scales on your skin? Even tiny, kind of pretty silvery-blue ones? You stand out. This was a man who chilled any room he walked into. A man whose presence ruined appetites. Never spoke, which was maybe his only redeeming quality. We called him the Monk. He had that air about him. Something of the dark sacrament? Remember when the media was all into devil worship? Nineteen-eighties? Kids getting abducted and sacrificed easy as chomping a Cheezie? The Satanic cult next door, cutting out virginal hearts? Heavy metal records played backwards? Pagans in a huff because no one can tell the difference between Pan and the devil, for Chrissake. I'm big into religious cults, you?"

"Not so much. I like Cheezies, though. We done?"

Reed rubs the pig's belly. "Thing is, I wish I had your will. Trade all my money for a will like yours. Shame you're a waste. Won't amount to anything. You aimed too low. Maybe a product of your time. You want to leave?"

I try and say yeah. People are waiting. But something in Carl Reed's voice doesn't let me. More than what he's saying, it's how. It's tough, interrupting a man during his last words. That's how it feels, listening to Reed. So instead I tell him hey, fuck it, we're here, there's a high-calibre rifle aimed at my chest, you the boss.

"The Monk didn't last long. You're so distasteful you ruin a convict's appetite . . . I think he lasted eleven days? That's a sacred number, understand? He was my cellmate. One night, I'm on the top bunk, I feel the bed rocking back and forth. At first I thought . . . but it wasn't that. And a wet grinding sound. *Snn-chnnk. Snn-chnnk.* You can hear a knife contacting bone when you stab someone, especially if it happens, say, thirty-eight times. The insides of a mammal, humans included, have a particular smell. A ripeness. Maybe you know this?"

"Yeah."

"You do?"

"Used to road hunt for deer."

"Oh, gross. That doesn't count. Anyway, that was it for the Monk. No one said anything to me, and I laid in the top bunk all night, not moving, wide awake, staring at the ceiling, smelling the Monk's insides as they cooled, waiting for the guards to find him and take him away. Next morning, that's exactly what happened. Tool came in, carted the Monk off. Searched the cell. Interrogated me, which really meant I sat in a room for six hours drinking coffee because Michael made sure I was taken care of. While later they sent me back to my cell. They'd hosed it down. I'll never forget the stink of that disinfectant, an institutional fake-floral bleach that didn't quite mask the smell of the Monk's punctured insides. The two smells collided, created a reek that was unbearably offensive. I started coughing, choking. Kinda like you just then? When I revealed my true self?

"Anyway, the guard laughed, said you're better off than the other guy, took a whiff, said no maybe not, locked the cell door. So there's this vile stink driving me nuts. This was when there were still sinks in prison cells. Stainless steel. You could wash your face, brush your teeth. So I have this lavender-bleach-blood-burst-intestine reek driving me mad, and to get rid of it I smear mint toothpaste under my nostrils. Yeah . . . toothpaste smeared all over my face and a big gooey wad of it caked in my mustache. That's funny, huh? Then you've never smelled what I smelled. Anyway, I pick up the tooth-paste tube and give it another squeeze and there's something inside, about as big as my pinkie, that the Monk hid in there before they spilled him open.

"I take it out, scrub the toothpaste off, hold it up. Fuck is this? Meanwhile I'm still choking on the horrible death-smell. Wash my discovery in the sink, realize it's made of extremely shiny metal. Looks like a spaceship coupler of some kind, a high-tech fitting. And I'm holding it and . . . the death smell vanishes. *Poof!* Normal, breathable air. Whoa! Funny to say I didn't think too much of it then. Main thing is I had this polished piece of metal and I thought it might be worth something. Maybe sharpened to make a shank I could trade for drugs? I pocketed it, paid the guards to find me another cell, and the first chance I got I traded the metal thingy for not-excellent drugs. Didn't think a lick of it. But then, month or so later, a few of us were playing cards out in the yard. Not a proper adult card game, but with hockey cards, like kids. Lining cards along the wall and flinging other cards to try and knock the ones we wanted down? I was lousy at it. Whipping cards all over the place. But a card got lined up against the wall that I really wanted. A Mario Lemieux, eighty-six, the one of him sitting on the bench watching the game, which I liked because of his expression, confident and intense, calm and joyful—even a touch mischievous—all at the same time, while he watches a game he's about to absolutely dominate, how young he is, clean-shaven, handsome, with that enviable look of a young man who is completely in sync, understand? A man who is completely at one with his surroundings, united in mind, body, world in the way maybe only professional sport can give us now. Maybe we were all like that once. Hunter-gatherers? Living seamless in the world. Who knows? I doubt it. I think we lived in terror, and still do. But imagine how it felt for Lemieux on the Penguins bench in eighty-six. How hard he worked for it. His life whittled to a fine point, sacrificing breadth of experience for depth, all action directed toward a single goal, day after day as a child, a teenager, driven, and now he's finally there, he made it, he's *there*. Imagine that sense of fulfillment. Of belonging and purpose. And all this is coloured, of course, by the fact that the man's body, what made him, was programmed to betray him in his moment of triumph. That Lemieux card—I think it's the best hockey card of all time, just for the look on the kid's face, and this from a man who loathes hockey. What can I say? The Lemieux card struck me. That's all. I was struck by how disparate two human lives can be. I had never, never even once ever, felt anything like the emotion I saw on that young hockey player's face. Lemieux might as well have been another species, he was so different from me. And of course I thought he was sexy as hell, very nice to look at, so there was that level as well."

I pat the pig on the head. "You won the card."

"Fuckin' A, I did. Fluke shot. Zipped the Lemieux down fair and square. And the owner of the card reneged. Some batshit biker with face tattoos. Said he wouldn't give me the Lemieux card, but he'd give me *this*. And he pulled out the metallic object from the Monk." Reed shakes his head, like he still can't believe it. "It happened like that off and on for the next twelve years. I'd get rid of the thing and it always came back. Eventually, as my mind went, I came to believe the object had totemic power. When it was in my possession I schemed ways to be rid of it. And when I didn't have it I lusted after it, searched for it, plotted to get it back." Reed laughs. "It helped pass the time. Gave me something to do. Ritual, habit, whatever. Maybe kept me from killing myself."

"What is it?"

"Ask Troutman—I mean, Michael. I found it stitched into the tongue of my hiking boots when I was released. The boots I wore when I walked into the cop shop, confessed to two killings I didn't do. Michael saw me pull it out of the stitching. He took it, gave it to some hush-hush tech researchers out of Berkeley. They scratched and poked at it, told us it could be worth something. We sold it to Tesla. It's in their cars. A crucial piece of electro-tech. Tesla has some godawful marketing-babble name for it. I call it the Nugget. The Monk and his shiny object became the beginning of Green Lead. So fucking strange, when I look back. Nothing happens for a reason. Everything happens for a reason. Michael keeps telling me what the Nugget does. I keep forgetting. Can't make it stick. It infuriates him."

"What do you think it is?"

"I think it made me believe in magic. Forces beyond our scope and scale of knowledge. Vastness. A universe with intent. A design we never see in total but might be able to tap into now and then. It made me believe everything is invested with spiritual power. Made me feel small and large at the same time, worthless and valuable. Reconciled opposites, sustained contradictions. A shiny piece of metal stuffed in a toothpaste tube kept me alive. For what, I have no idea. There's a reckoning on the horizon. For our species?"

We sit in silence, watch ducks swim and dive in the green-scum lagoon, days devoted to food security, procreation. Traffic noise filters through the cedars. I'm about to leave when Reed grabs my forearm. The pig hops off Reed's lap, circles at my feet, roots in the cigarette butts, sunflower-seed shells, gum wrappers.

"You need to find that boy," Reed says, his voice halting. "Ryan? Find him and get him away. Send him to another planet. Another solar system. He's going to get sucked in."

I can't help myself. I ask who he's in danger from.

"From you, Mark. From the dark matter you're becoming."

Reed releases my arm, tucks the potbellied pig into a sunflower-coloured satchel, asks if we're done. I say fuck if I know, I was waiting for you, is your boy gonna pop and drop? Reed says follow me and find out. I stay seated on the bench, watch him shuffle away, head bent low, bony shoulders jutting. The creepy mentally slipping feeling lingers; I half expect him to fucking levitate outta here. He's almost out of earshot when I yell hey what about the video and Reed waves a hand vaguely in my direction, doesn't turn around, doesn't say a word and I'm left with an alien voice lodged in my mind, a diesel-burning taste in my mouth and a leg that's full-on killing me. Reed walks across a rolling lawn toward a parking lot, bumps his head getting into a white limousine. When he's gone I phone Ryan. Try and leave a message. His inbox is full.

I AM DRIVEN

BY PASSION

AND

PURPOSE

Carl "Blitzo" Reed

A few hours after meeting Mr. Marvellous Mark Ward I charter a floatplane up to Knight Inlet. Clouds mass against the North Shore Mountains, and the city, still wet, gleams like a glacial stone. The Pacific stretches west to Vancouver Island, the forested land-mass pale and blue, draped in fog and low cloud, the ends of the earth inscribed on vellum, and to the south Mount Baker's ominous American bulk rising above rust-brown cornfields in the Fraser Valley. The plane vibrates, its engine drone settling into my teeth. The pilot's a friendly freckled kid with a knack for minding his business. I resist the urge to tell him to keep flying, not outward but upward, until the plane's propellers slip through air grown too thin to support our mass. But I say nothing, stare out the window, realize there's a relationship between skyward fixation and drug addiction, wondering why I've stayed sober since they let me out of the slammer, thinking maybe I should be all here for *this*, whatever it might be. From the air Vancouver appears impossibly fragile. The mountains, rugged crest beginning in the Arctic and ending, with a few hops and skips, in Tierra del Fuego, could shrug and knock her headlong into the ocean. Eventually the city will drown, in water or something less appealing I'm no longer certain.

The pilot brings us down gently, like he's settling skin-to-skin, on the remote eastern shore of Knight Inlet; guides the plane toward a half-moon beach beside an abandoned BC Hydro powerhouse. I hop off a rocking pontoon, splash into hip-deep water, numb with cold, bare feet on slippery kelp and asshole barnacles, feeling like there's never enough time. The pilot tosses me a neon-yellow waterproof duffel bag, asks if I'm sure I'm all right, confirms the rendezvous. I stagger ashore. The airplane buzzes off, leaves me with the lapping sound of water against continent, a caress dreamlike and implacable that hovers at the edge of sinister, and with the sound comes the feeling I've slipped far away from any recognized bearing.

I strip, feeling strangely exposed, naked in the wilds, unarmed and defenceless. Find a change of clothes in the duffel bag. Caltrop emerges from the woods like a rumour, well within killing distance before I'm aware of him. He's over sixty but built compact, a body that will remain efficient until his last breath, no slow, nagging decline for this man, hair so grey it's white, skin furrowed deep around his eyes. The face of an old-time sailor, a farmer stubborning grain from a Manitoban field, the face of a man who spends his waking hours guiltless beneath an open sky. He's clean-shaven, dressed in jeans, hiking boots, a blue T-shirt, a Gore-Tex jacket tied around his waist. He makes me tight-lipped with envy, something I've long hoped to grow out of.

Now, as in most things, I've become resigned.

The abandoned power station looms behind him, wires fallen from towers and snarled around the concrete foundation, windows broken out, a chain-link fence crushed beneath windblown hemlock. It's easy, given my current timbre, to glimpse a skull, memento mori, lurking in the shape of that forgotten building. I make the effort to remind myself the world does not exist solely to reflect the moods of humanity, toe the duffel bag, tell my friend there's a quarter million lurking inside. The same amount he's received for

decades. Every year I deliver the cash and expect my man-at-arms
to mention inflation, declining purchasing power, expect him to
shake me down, prove who's really in charge, show that despite
my money I remain the weaker man, but he never does, which
leaves me feeling crass and even more unworthy.

Clouds drift up inland fjords. "It's magnificent out here. I hate
it."

Caltrop inhales, studies me much too directly.

"You were in town. That was somethin'. Kid nearly peed himself.
We could've met at—"

"Less distraction in the bush," Caltrop says. "Easier to think."

"Waaay too easy."

"You afraid, Carl?"

"And freezing. Nature? Totally over it."

"Forgot what it's all about."

"I've sure been trying. You weren't at the lagoon today just for me."

"It was never for you."

"You've been watching the Ward kid for how long?"

Caltrop opens the duffel bag, looks at the cash like it's a worthless pile of laundry, zips the bag closed. "Since the night he flew in.
Was keeping an eye on the older brother. Followed him to YVR, then
to a house in North Vancouver. The lawyer Michael sent to sniff
around Marigold? Didn't deserve what he got. Neither did his wife
and son. Working for you sure costs plenty, hey Carl? I watched the
Ward brothers come out of the house in high spirits."

"And yet you didn't stop them."

Caltrop's lips twist. "Stop them? How? Kill them? You think it's
easy only because you've never done it."

"And now?"

Caltrop stares at me like I'm a big rock he has to move. "Now I'm
glad I didn't shoot first. The Ward brother, the younger one—"

"He's what we've been looking for. Reminds me of you, at your
best."

"If only we could all be remembered at our best." Caltrop kneels, runs a hand through beach pebbles. There are a few spots on his skin, but otherwise his hand looks young, unaffected by swelling, wrinkles. "Sorry about Heather."

I sit on the duffel bag, nest my hands between my legs to warm them. "Me as well. Looks like it's a done deal. Been a long time coming. So that's a life. Open and shut. I was lucky. Not everyone falls in love even once. Not everyone is permitted happiness, even once, even for a moment. It happened to me twice. I'm trying to feel grateful. Hannah won't answer my calls."

"I've removed her from the line of fire."

Relief and regret and resentment all at once. I slump further into myself, don't bother asking how Caltrop found my daughter, how he took care of her when I couldn't. "You have an idea of the kind of man you want to be. The kind of husband and father. Then your kid grows up and you realize how far off the mark you've been."

"Kids are an opportunity to think about someone besides yourself. You never took that opportunity."

"You were smart not to have any."

Caltrop hurls a flat stone into the waves. We watch it skip, sink. "It wasn't a conscious decision. How it worked out."

"Ladies not keen to shack up with a man who lives in an abandoned powerhouse?"

"Hannah will pull through. She has her mother."

I sit cross-legged, feel the ocean beckon. "I used to lie in her bed. When I got released? I used to lie in Hannah's bed when she was at school. She must've been seven or eight. It sounds pervy and gross but it wasn't. I missed her so bad in prison. We were strangers. I used to lie face down in her pillow and craft the word LOVE in my mind, over and over, LOVELOVELOVE, hoping she'd go to sleep at night and *feel* the message, my love for her, as if I could invest the pillow with some kind of emotional resonance, some frequency or aura she could tune to in her dream world, LOVE, and I would lie there knowing it wasn't enough, not even close, but maybe she would feel it and forgive me. And this is tough to admit, even to you . . . lying in my daughter's bed felt safe, sheltered . . . it healed me . . . with her Strawberry Shortcake pillowcase and the blinds closed and the world way far away outside . . . it made me feel young, guiltless."

"Which you're not."

"No. What about the video of Hannah? I keep asking myself. Do I want them to die? Peele and the rest? Even Bo Xi? Is that what I want?"

Caltrop yanks me to my feet. "Mark Ward will give me the video. I'm arranging a sit-down. The rest is already finished."

I listen to the waves, hating how they persist in washing ashore, one after the other, relentlessly keeping time. Drowning has to be one of the worst ways to die. Holding your breath until you can't anymore, seconds ticking past, then a helpless gasp and the water searing in, then another and another, plenty of time to remember, to think and feel. And right then it's decided, never could commit, how it happens says so much, but now I know and Caltrop gives me a searching look like he senses something's wrong and I want to hold my breath until water turns to flame, see-through skin, tiny silver scales—

"Protect my daughter? I never could."

"Bullshit. You never wanted to badly enough."

I take a step closer. Part of me believes simply being close to this man, absorbing his energy, has the power to strengthen. "The North Shore deal is progressing. Marigold Group has their ducks in a row. You were right. This gig might lure Bo Xi into the open."

Caltrop shrugs. Talk like that is above my pay grade, even though I'm the one doing the paying. "Tell me I've been useful," I say, trying to keep it together. "Tell me I've made a difference."

"Because it's all about you? Go ahead and tell yourself that, Carl. Sink into the pit between what you could've been and what you are."

Before the flight out here I dropped Holdout off in the financial district, told him grow piggy grow. He seemed to fit in okay. "Fifteen years of my life for this. For what?"

"Longer than that. They let you out of prison. You built another for yourself. Came to covet the chains. That wasn't my doing."

"Tell me things are changing. That it was worth the fight."

"You still think in terms of years, maybe decades when you're inspired. We're talking centuries. Thousands of years. But there's little romance in that perspective, and zero glory. You trudged off to prison because you wanted to be a hero. Wanted to be recognized, even among our anonymous faction. You've always been selfish. Motivated by ego, not principle. Even now, when you stick that last needle in your arm it won't be due to despair. You'll do it to prove that the people you care about failed you."

"Am I that petty?"

"You tell me. Better yet, show me."

An airplane appears from behind a disk-shaped cloud, leaches a heavy contrail, makes me hope the sky's being spiked with toxins that can remake my mind. "How do I know it's not bullshit? What you're doing with the cash? Maybe you have it buried in your backyard."

Caltrop tosses the duffel bag over his shoulder. "Maybe I burn it. Bake it into my brownies. You offered, I accepted. I will say the money has permitted some ideas to come into being, prevented others from doing so."

"You intend to deploy Mark Ward to assassinate Bo Xi? Feed a troubled young man to the lions? He's not innocent, but he's not that guilty. Not yet. And you say I've fallen."

"Mark will be given a choice."

"Bo Xi isn't an idiot. He'll sense you coming."

"Bo Xi is a man. He won't sense, but he might *uncover*. Do not compromise us."

"Are you going to kill me?"

"No need."

"I was wrong. Ward's not like you. He's simpler. Purer."

"Even the most incendiary powder requires a spark."

Wind whips the ocean. A floatplane flies low and level across the inlet. It's a long way back to civilization.

Jasminder Bansal

At Marigold, on the phone with a client, praying Heather Reed comes through. A man wearing a dark grey suit slips into Vincent's office. There's nothing immediately remarkable about him, particularly since I only get a quick glimpse before the door closes. But something in his build, how he carries himself, those subtle clues of body type we pick up on without being conscious of—all these inconsequential nothings add up to a feeling like I know who he is. The air becomes stifling. I walk into the waiting area. Vincent's assistant Harvey looks up from behind the admin desk, asks if I'm okay and I say sure, why, and he says because you're pale, you look unwell.

"Who is that?" I ask quietly, nodding toward Vincent's office.

Harvey glances at Vincent's door, clearly conflicted. "A client. Why?"

"Not a client. Maybe a construction guy? A project manager?"

"Why?"

I'm about to ask more but Harvey gives me a look that says don't bother, that's all you're getting. I say thanks and return to my office, resolved to put the visitor out of my mind. But sitting at my desk, staring into my tea as if it has divinatory power, I realize I need to see the man's face. Head back out, give Harvey a wan smile, settle into an armchair in the reception area, plop my Mac on my lap and pretend to work. After a few minutes Harvey puts his jacket on, says don't work too hard on a Saturday, especially if you don't feel well, leaves.

I open and close webpages at random, listening to the muffled conversation filtering through Vincent's door. I can't hear what's being said clearly, but it's a heated exchange. Then the door bursts open. Vincent storms out. His eyes are puffy and red from Mr. Reed's garlic powder assault at Hawksworth. Before he sees me he yells over his shoulder, "—I said we put our soldier to task!"

I'm seated to the side of Vincent's office, about fifteen feet away, hidden behind an easel that has a promotional poster for one of Marigold's residential developments tacked onto it. Vincent slams his hand on Harvey's desk, mutters something about his under-performing assistant putting in an appearance but not doing any real work, makes a phone call. I sink deeper into my chair, feeling like I should announce my presence before I hear anything compromising, wishing I'd followed everyone's advice and resigned from Marigold, thinking about how often Amar chided me for not minding my own business.

Vincent hasn't seen me yet.

Maybe I could sneak into my office, pretend to—

Someone answers Vincent's call, and Vincent, in a voice completely lacking inflection, says, "Hey homes. What are you up to? Cradling a shotgun? Tapping the trigger with your big toe? Pulling a Cobain? Thought that was a hoax? Heard it was. Yeah. He's on Playa Mazunte, writing sasquatch porn for Amazon. Making a killing. The glum loser abandoned us. Ha-ha! Yeah. I'd abandon us too. No shame in being honest. In fact, I like that about you, Mark. Okay. New mission. You're gonna love it. Time-sensitive. That means hurry? Remember the Reed family?"

The heavily built guy marches out of Vincent's office. His hands and neck are covered in tattoos. Peele whirls to face him, sees me and hangs up the phone, no goodbye, nothing.

Clint Ward.

My laptop clatters to the floor.

Clint's eyes are dull and dark, his face expressionless, and rather than acknowledge me he stares over my shoulder, shrugs his suit jacket on. Clint and Vincent don't look at one another. Clint walks out, composed and casual but very intent on leaving. I'm nearly choking, trying to pick up my laptop and fumbling it, afraid to see what Vincent's doing, afraid he'll see through my persona while dry ice drifts on the dance floor obscuring half-human half-animal dancers and a handgun rises behind my brother's head.

Vincent hurries over, beaming like he's the happiest man alive, says he didn't know anyone was here, rubs his eyes, says man that Carl Reed is a worthless human being. Asks why I'm working, Saturday, nose to the grindstone, trying to impress the boss? And why am I in the reception room instead of my office, where I should be?

I manage to pick up the laptop, stammer something silly about my room being stuffy. Vincent says is that so? Walks over, sticks his head in my room, inhales, says it seems fine to him but smells a little off and maybe he'll phone to have it freshened.

I wipe dust off my keyboard, pretend to examine the screen, hope I sound casual when I ask, "Vincent? Who was that man?"

Vincent bends, squeezes his calf muscle. "Who? No one."

"I know what I saw."

Vincent straightens the promotional poster, plays it cool. "Is that so? You know all about my office?" Waves a hand in a possessive arc. "Where I conduct my business? For this company? Where you are currently employed?"

Vincent's between me and the door. This isn't the right time, I tell myself. Let it go. Wait for Heather's help. And right when I decide it's settled, that I'll make the safe choice and stay quiet, I hear myself say, "I . . . I know who that man is. And why he's here."

Vincent looks puzzled. "Okay? You know whoever you know? No probs. And now you want to know why whoever you think that was

was in my office? Well I'm sorry, protected client privilege, no problem at all Jasminder, still learning the ropes. Of course I'll forget you even asked."

Close my laptop, set it on the coffee table. "His name is Clint Ward."

Saying it out loud . . . my voice surprises me, sounds composed, true to who I am or want to be.

Vincent blinks, chooses another approach. "Small world! You know Clint? Wonderful, awesome, yes. How do you know him?"

And how Peele's studying me, like he's seeing me for the first time, furious, lips pulled back to expose his teeth and it's the hungriest, most cruelly needful look I've ever witnessed—all this combines to make me climb awkwardly over the side of the chair to put some distance between us.

"Clint Ward killed my brother, Amar. I saw him."

Witness.

Peele can't get a word out. Looks very small when he's not spewing bullshit. Shocked at not knowing. Wondering if I'm lying and hating he can't tell. Thought he had me pinned, gripped, and held down. "I don't understand? Are you saying . . ."

"Clint murdered Amar. Three years ago."

"I don't think . . ." But he doesn't finish.

Peele had no idea who I was. Clint never told him, probably doesn't know I saw him murder Amar. I was inside . . . and nobody knew. I was succeeding. This past week I've been living it . . . a truth displaced and doubled but still mine . . . and now Peele knows about my connection to Clint Ward and of course there's no way he'll keep me on at Marigold. But I still have the stolen files. And Heather Reed.

Peele swallows. "I had no idea . . . about him? Jasminder?"

I say yeah, slide past him, unflinching, walking away free and clear, thinking I've won and how sweet it'll feel to break the corruption story. I'm nearly at the door when Peele says oh by the way he almost forgot he met Heather Reed yesterday. After I saw her at Park Place Tower? And was that what I was doing this morning? Stealing more private documents for the competition?

Room feels tilted at an angle, like I'm about to slide off, and I lean against the reception desk to keep myself standing. Not succeeding at all. Heather Reed played me. Sent an anonymous tip that kept me on the story. Maybe it was all bullshit, the link to Bo Xi made up so Heather would have the leverage she needed—

Peele's laughter sounds far away. "You trusted Heather Hellcat? Super-bad call! She phoned me like five minutes after you gave her my files. Said Vincent, I have something you might be interested in? Said hey honeybun, let's renegotiate sticking points? Said how 'bout I return these stolen files, you design a green space into the Solstice development? Everyone wins! Except Jasminder?"

Only a few steps from the door but too weak to stand without support from the reception desk. That lying, careerist asshole. Peele's walking toward me. Grinning. I can't look at him directly but I see him out of the corner of my eye and I have my phone in my hand, searching for Sim's number, afraid for my safety but that's not even the worst part because without those files I have nothing.

Vincent takes my phone, sets it on the desk. "Aw, look at poor you. Cased the knuckle, pretzeled your rim on the last gap. Fully rag-dolled, eating shit!" Vincent smacks the files onto the reception desk. "So . . . anyway? Not sure where you were going with all that? A career-making exposé? Lies, rumours, a few numbers in a column. Biiig stretch! Langara journalism? Bargain basement!"

Voice dull, resigned: "You're laundering money through Marigold's developments."

Vincent flutters his hands, fakes being horrified at my accusation. "Airing dirty laundry? Says Jasminder who? All above board. No proof. And even better . . . nobody cares! So what is it with you? Hater? Jealous? Incredible times, huge upside. You're missing out!"

Is he right? Is it only jealousy? Do I want to drag him down so I can take his place? Do I even believe my own story? The splintered feeling of wanting something more than anything and at the same time not believing in it at all, of being wilfully self-duplicitous as a means of survival, of hating yourself for wanting what you know is wrong—

Vincent strolls around the reception desk, sits in Harvey's chair, puts a fist to his chin, gives me a fake-friendly look like we're chatting about weekend plans. "Curious about your angle, though. Did Heather steal your thunder? You were gonna squeeze some cash out of me? Extortion! Grrl power! Awesome! You're way cooler than you pretend to be. Do you want to go bouldering?"

Pick up my phone, walk to the door, grip the frame. "Go take a flying fuck—"

"Oh, yay! You took a shot, went wide. Happens. Few months at Langara and here she is, Miss Hunter Thompson, living the story—"

"I prefer Michael Moore."

Peele holds up his phone, shows me a photo of a recent gangland killing in South Surrey. Says he knows nothing about it, super unfortunate, a few bad apples won't spoil this incredible city.

"Those files aren't everything."

Peele pockets the phone. "I doubt that. Otherwise you would've gone to some control-freaky lefty media outlet. Ah, Jasminder. I finally get you! Muckracking sjw journalist girl on the up!" Peele fidgets with a 2010 Olympic snow globe on the reception desk. "Here's the thing. Those Valley hicks, the Ward Brothers, yuck. Total low-lifes. I mean . . . Clint seriously disgusts me, he's worse than garbage. And to think people like him are allowed to vote. And Mark . . . *cuckoo!* So what I'm saying is: I can forgive. You made a mistake. Driven by misplaced ambition, all that. See how magnanimous I am? Clint fucked you; he apparently fucked me by not being an upfront guy. I'll have Harvey deposit your final cheque, no diss track . . ."

He's lying, of course. But right now all I need is away from him. "You're right. I made a mistake."

Peele shakes the snow globe, studies it. "Absolutely. Nothing to see here. Big criminal conspiracy blah? Secret power-elite exposed? Nope. A few loopholes, opportunities exploited. Business as usual. Bizzy-ness? Heh. Like Wall Street in 2008: I'll be gone, you'll be gone! Numero uno! As in: looking out for? Where's the big story in that? Seems like everyday stuff, normal people trying to make a living. Sorry for the letdown. No one's running things. That's what's so sweet! Dude on the button's an imbecile, and more power to him! Power-elite scheming, marshalling resources, world domination, look at us helpless little people caught in their horrible schemes?" Peele sets the snow globe down, texts something. "Not how it works. Nice to have someone to blame though, isn't it? Because there's just you and me, protecting numero uno. Day after day. And that gets us to where we are."

My phone vibrates.

"Jasminder? Take a peek at that photo. Bad apples."

Refuse to look at the photo or give him the satisfaction of seeing how afraid I am. Cock my index finger at him instead. "*Kapow! Kaboom!*"

Peele clutches his heart, tips his chair until his feet lift from the floor, flails around, laughs. I walk out without another word, drive to the gym, get on a spin bike for the first time in months, set the gears to their lowest, put on my workout playlist, do Tabata intervals until I collapse, dizzy, disoriented, nauseous, and even then when I get home I can't sleep and when I close my eyes I see blue-black lesions flowering on the sides of buildings, Carl Reed's emptied-out eyes, a shadowy half-man hunting through old-growth forest growing inside an ice-cold office tower, a handgun at point-blank range through strobe lights and fog, six six six . . . and I hear Heather Reed's corrupt laughter and *my brother you were right*, you make your own way in the world or someone makes it for you—

Mark Ward

No one's safe. We're aware of this, knowledge buried in animal minds, precognitive fear-scream of cave dwellers. And because no one's safe we go to great lengths to pretend otherwise. Build fences, lock doors, carry firearms. But a guy like me wants a target dead, at night, in his home, there's almost nothing to be done about it.

Here I am, calculating the distance from the target's front door to his bedroom and from the back door to the alley. Noting the neighbours. Any insomniacs? Late-night smokers? Making a mental count of the number of stairs. Noting the flooring. Carpet? Hardwood? Thinking about friction and footwear. Here I am in a condo stairwell, timing myself as I run up the steps. Adding a ten per cent tolerance to account for darkness, the unexpected. Here I am, visualizing myself moving through the target's home in the dead of night, seeking possible interruptions, planning escape routes and startled Plan Bs.

Surprise is speed. Which means speed is everything. Stealth is for television. Killers tiptoeing around, picking locks, slinking down halls with the cops close on their tails. Nope. There are no police. Best forget them. What do a high-school shooting, a sidewalk assassination, a roadside bombing have in common? *It happened so fast.* A mind surprised is unable to process events with anything close to enough speed to make a difference. There's always an exploitable lag between shock and action. An untrained citizen needs five seconds, at least, to realize the pops they heard weren't fireworks or a car backfiring and the man in the mask carrying an automatic machine gun isn't pulling a tasteless prank.

A person sleeping, three thirty in the morning, woken suddenly? Takes a full minute to realize they're awake. It takes me ten seconds to reach a bedroom after I kick in the front door. Enough time to murder a target three or four times before he's fully awake.

That's the only goal. Kill him while he's asleep.

Him awake means I've failed. Means I'm at risk.

Add another half-minute, at least, for the target to crawl out of bed, secure a weapon, find an effective defensive stance. There. I've murdered him eight times.

But let's say a target wants to make my mission even *easier*.

Maybe he's lived a sheltered life, coddled by privilege and graced with power and blessed with wealth. Let's say he's a man in his prime, fit and strong, at the peak of his career. He is, in his mind, invulnerable. That's why it seems reasonable to run alone through an isolated, densely wooded area, working up a solid sweat, heart pumping, his playlist blaring in his ears. A difference between women and men. Women still live close to fear. Few would go out of their way to make it this easy.

I'm talking about my bro Mr. Craig Williams, who just topped a steep hill rising from the ocean and gained the peninsula of land called the West Side. Williams is in the woods now, grinning, feeling mighty fine, enjoying the brisk ocean air and sunlight settling on salmonberry leaves and fern fronds. Lovely day for a run. He's been running in this forest for twenty years. The man knows every turn in the trail, every puddle.

But he doesn't know me.

Step from behind a fir, SAP raised. Weighted leather cracks on skin, echoes through the forest, makes me believe all of this is real. The target's on the ground before he knows he's hit.

Speed. Shock. Terror.

Don't bother putting my balaclava on until the target's down. Williams looked right at me in the instant I hit him. Won't remember a thing. Takes ten seconds to drag him into the woods. He's moaning, blood leaking from exploded lips. Starts to struggle, make an effort, keep fighting, don't give in, be a winner—

Two more and the target quiets.

A man like Williams has spent his entire life lording over others. But now, three blows from the SAP, on his belly in the muck and moss, now I'm taking him back to the fucking swamp. Everything that props this man up—family, money, custom, gender, race, rule of law, every advantage that gives men like Craig Williams free rein in the world, makes them tyrant kings—none of that counts for shit down here in the swamp.

Check my watch. A countdown timer set at four minutes.

We're already twenty seconds in.

Sink my knee in the small of Williams's back. Not thinking much. Not worried about much. Moved outside my mind, beyond buried roadside bombs of emotion, sinkholes of memory, the compulsion of time, the stream of language, symbols, and delusions that aggregate into the cesspool we call consciousness. Beyond doubts and second guesses and moral circle jerks. Way far from good and evil. Only a thing in motion. Meat. Living a single isolated moment. The terrain of prophets and warriors, a gale-force wind stinging sand into my eyes, tasting the enemy's blood. This is peace.

Lean close to the target's ear. Slip the KA-BAR from its sheath, metal on leather, a sound like a last breath, makes me want to whistle a tune. Williams hears the blade freed, dry-heaves, grosses me out even though he's doing it unconsciously, body reacting to terror, fight or flight, and I have to spend some time mellowing him or Williams won't truly be with me for what comes next.

So I smooth-talk him until we're ninety seconds in. Returning a terrified man to the world takes patience.

Williams gasps, spits. I keep on him, whispering sweet nothings until he says, "You fucking thief. My money—"

"Not money, Williams. You're all I want. You're what I have."

". . . why?"

I let the KA-BAR speak. Run it over the back of the target's neck, not hard enough to cut him but softly. Williams flinches, grinds his head into the leaves while a breeze rises off the Pacific and we're in a sweet-smelling forest with dewy dappled light and gorgeous super-verdant moss and cheerful birds chirping a hymn to another glorious day in Vancouver and man Peele's right this town sure is pretty—

"You know why, Williams. You feel it."

Silence, then weird choking sounds.

"Williams. Listen. I'm holding a seven-inch combat blade to your neck. Next is I cut you. You know why. Answer me."

"Not money?"

"No."

Williams squirms, bucks, tries to toss me off, whispers, "Bang Phli? My God. Here? *Bang Phli.*"

The name has power over him.

"How many?"

"Not my doing," Williams says, struggling to look over his shoulder. "Cost overruns. Material outlays. Doesn't matter. Not my fault. We subbed the fucking factory—"

A smooth stroke, forehead to chin. Slam his head into the leaves and dirt to silence him. "It matters now, Williams. It matters a whole lot."

The ground's damp, the air sharp and cool. Smells of earth, rotting leaves, changing seasons.

Two minutes in.

Williams babbles some pain-filled nonsense, pulls it together to moan, "How it works. You're in this . . . look at you!"

"I am in this. That's why I'm here. Dog eat dog. Every man for himself. Only the strong survive. This is your ethic. This is where it takes us. Two in the swamp. Thing is, you never thought it'd be you. Losing beneath a piece-of-shit trash like me."

Sobbing now, horrified at his world being yanked from under him, maybe wondering what he really is.

"Williams? Have you prayed for them?"

"No."

"Dreamed of them?"

No answer. I lift my head. We're still alone. The sun emerges from behind a cloud, warms my face, reminds me of holding my daughter. "But you've thought of them. Or maybe . . . you only thought of yourself through them. Will *you* be punished? Will *you* go to hell? Will it ruin *your* life?"

"Better them than me."

"It's you now. Understand? You fucking made me."

I look to the sky.

Jasminder Bansal

Watching the front doors of Marigold from across the street, fidgeting behind an umbrella, nervous as hell but trying to play it cool, furious at Heather Reed and Peele and Sim and Eric and even Amar and this whole fucking town, trying to be an anonymous woman in the crowd, trying to get Peele's hungry expression out of my head, and after a couple hours of this hell Peele and Elodie walk out, laughing and brushing hands. They barely turn a corner and I'm crossing the street, letting myself into the locked office building.

I turn the lights on and enter the deserted waiting room with nothing defined except a will to truth. I scramble through the front desk, searching for correspondence with any mention of Bo Xi or Pillar Investment. Nothing. Try Vincent's office. Locked. But Elodie's isn't.

Hold my breath, slip inside. Her desk is bare. Pens and papers are scattered across the floor, seems unlike the neat-freak Elodie. And lying beside her desk is Vincent's bike messenger bag. I tear it open, stifle a triumphant yell when I see his silver laptop and before I've thought about consequences I'm tapping away, trying to figure out the password.

Not happening. Turns out I'm lousy at computer espionage, no cyber-spy skills revealed in the knick of time—

The elevator chimes in the hall.

I hurry into the waiting room, say hello to Beckett. He asks why I'm not in Osoyoos and I tell him I'm feeling unwell. He flinches, says I do look awful. Maybe even feverish? I laugh, say you better stay away, could be contagious, and he frowns, says that's not funny Jasminder I have a crazy-busy week ahead. I tell him he's killing it, that I can't wait to hear his numbers, that getting him sick is my diabolical plan to try and even the score, and when he nods and retreats to his office I race outside.

I make it three blocks before it hits me. What a tremendously stupid thing I've done. A car horn makes me aware I'm standing in the middle of a crosswalk at a busy intersection. I run to the sidewalk, check if I'm being followed. What if I return Peele's laptop? That's what I'll do. Tell everyone I was confused, ill, grabbed the wrong laptop by mistake. The laptop's tucked under my arm while I shove through the crowds on Broadway, worrying that people know I'm a thief. I can't keep the laptop. That's clear. Clint Ward's a killer. They'll hunt me down. The only way to make sure that doesn't happen is to break the password and give any information to the newspapers and police. It's the only way to protect myself.

I decide to go straight to the cops. There'll be an investigation. Isn't that how it works? So instead of getting on the SkyTrain I walk downhill toward the Cambie Bridge. The police station's nestled at the foot of the hill, in the eastern shadow of the bridge, a stodgy brick building with tinted glass windows that remind me of a highway cop's sunglasses. Walk inside, shoulders back, chin up, trying to appear like I'm in the right but feeling security cameras recording my image. Ask the man behind the desk for the Gang Unit Task Force, a special investigation unit I'm all too familiar with. He directs me to a chair at the edge of a brightly lit hall. Sounds of photocopiers, radio dispatchers, office chatter. I wait, clutching the laptop to my chest, trying very hard not to bolt because where would I go?

A woman arrives, introduces herself as Officer Sandra Dawson. She's in her early thirties, short hair, bit of an overbite, and the problem is I can't tell if I can trust her. But she smiles in a way that says she's happy to see me, leads me into an interview room, closes the door. Speckled linoleum, beige walls, and grey furnishings, and something about how unremarkable the room is freaks me out, not a single distinguishing feature, and as I sit at the table and try to smile for Officer Dawson I see identical rooms spreading across the city, across the country and continent, a maze or nest of anonymous self-propagating interrogation rooms. Have I made another mistake? Is this going to help? Old World paranoia hits, some vestige handed down from my mother. Basically: Officer Dawson isn't going to let me leave without paying a bribe, and I consider how best to excuse myself.

Officer Dawson offers coffee or tea. I decline both, say thank you, try to be polite, rational, remind myself I'm doing the right thing but appearances matter, I need to be clear, composed, tell her exactly what happened. Officer Dawson asks me what I need to talk about. I tell her about Clint Ward and Vincent Peele and that I'm certain Marigold Group is laundering money through real estate deals.

I put the laptop on the table. Officer Dawson doesn't say a word. I'm fighting the urge to yell. This is the right thing to do. All the evidence is in the laptop. To convict these men. An international money-laundering syndicate. Officer Dawson looks capable. She'll realize what a treasure of evidence I've delivered.

"Will I have to testify?"

Air whispers through the ventilation system. Officer Dawson folds her hands on the table, says okay Miss Bansal please listen very carefully. Return the laptop to Mr. Peele's office immediately.

I shake my head. I'm not communicating clearly. She doesn't

understand how serious this is. "Is it because I worked for them? At Marigold? Is that some sort of conflict? Because I didn't know."

"Return the laptop to its legal owner, Jasminder. Before it's reported missing."

"I can't do that. Please? I . . . did this? They'll—"

Officer Dawson firms her lips, says the laptop is stolen property, even if it does contain evidence of criminal activity it's completely inadmissible, asks if I have anything else I'd like to discuss.

When I don't answer she gives me a nod and walks out. Vincent Peele's laptop is sitting on the table, mocking me, laughing at a fucked-up failure chasing her ridiculous dreams—

I get everything I want by helping others get everything they want.

"You understand why, Amar," I whisper. "You would've called Vincent Peele a nothing middleman. You would've called him an opportunity."

Cops in uniforms march through the hall, laughing and joking, day-to-day nine-to-five and here I am, not part of anything, inside and out.

Mark Ward

Three minutes and thirty seconds in.

On a winding gravel path, cool in forest shadows. Leg's gone stiff. Otherwise feeling not bad. Not celebrating yet. Not riding some psycho-invincible high. Maybe feeling a bit too vincible? Trying to stay focused despite the pain, manage the details, make sure I didn't commit a grievous tactical error. Thinking about Carl Reed warning me about Ryan. Replaying the target's shock when he realized I wasn't after his money. That was the only way Williams saw himself being harmed. Robbery, blackmail, kidnapping for ransom. Not plain ol' aggravated assault. Physical suffering's for us poor folk. Not men like him. I guess, though, sometimes life goes off the rails, even for a hard-working, upstanding guy like Craig Williams, and shit, that doesn't bode too well for an asshole like me, does it?

Leafless alder and birch branches fan across the trail, brush my chest and cheeks, leave me soaked. Bloody clothes, combat knife, and balaclava in a backpack. Now dressed in running gear. Another neighbourhood guy out for a jog. I'm not far from Williams, but I'm not worried. I gagged him, tied him to a tree. It'll take a while for him to be discovered. There's an odd aftertaste in my mouth, bitter and burnt, and my ears are humming, just a bit, evidence of the endorphins racing through my blood. Other than that I'm calm. No shakes.

Smooth, even breathing, nice for a change, hope it lasts but know it won't.

I break out of the woods and onto the sidewalk. This is a well-established neighbourhood, Blanca at 16th, renovated early-century stucco bungalows with peaked roofs, and boxy two-storey Vancouver Specials from the seventies. A couple newish Darth Vader houses with black aluminum trim and patches of faux black brick. Cypress trees, birch and elm in the yards. A tidy neighbour-hood. Quiet now, no traffic. A dog barks a few blocks down as I cross Blanca, make my way up 15th, a slight incline, leg starting to stab at me, street lined with cherry trees yet to bloom, cement lions perched on fence posts, my leg getting bad, mind going oxyoxyoxy, sweating, knowing I'm pale, not looking great, get in early, nice place to raise a family, plenty of upside.

Thinking more about Ryan than Williams. Asking where I'd go if I were the kid. Gotta be partying again. Likes his job too much to quit. So he'll show up soon enough. Hopes Clint will wait until he's eighteen, make him crew boss, set for life.

Turn right onto Tolmie and see a wiry motherfucker leaning against my Ford like he's waiting for me. Which he is, because it's the crazy dude in the Datsun that was following me in North Van on my first night in town. He lifts his jacket to show me the Glock tucked in his belt, then gestures me into the driver's seat in a no-bullshit way that lets me know he's military. I follow the command, no use arguing with a take-no-prisoners soldier ghost.

We climb in and the ghost says he just got back from Tunisia, a crucial time in that country, lots of work to be done, good energy.

I start the truck.

"Mind if I tell you where you're going?" he says.

"Mind fucking off?"

"Name's Caltrop. I'm here because of you, Mark. Your work."

Caltrop catches my look, seems surprised, like he's cluing into something and giving himself shit for not considering it earlier. "I'm real, Mark. I'm alive and really here. Any way I can prove that to you?"

"Not at this late stage, nope."

I drive off slow. Caltrop says head down to 16th, then east. "The murdering pig. How's he doing?"

"Who?"

Caltrop laughs. "Hippie takes his son outside, points to the sky, says son, the Man's got satellites up there can count the hair on your balls. The kid thinks for a minute, looks at his father, says, what hair, Dad?"

I stay quiet. We wind though the West Side for several minutes. They'll find Williams soon. I'm wondering who the hell this guy is and what he knows and how to get rid of him and out of the blue Caltrop says you get to know someone well enough, study them, it's like seeing into their future. "I know Carl Reed that well."

My hands tighten on the wheel. "Carl who? Sounds like a dickwad."

"Blitzo," Caltrop says, sneering. "He earned the moniker long after we parted ways. I see you're uncomfortable, Mark, and I want you to know I'm not here at Carl's request. That were the case, it'd already be done. I've had plenty of opportunity. Had another one earlier today, out at the lagoon?"

I try and speak, manage a choking cough.

"Relax a little, Mark. You've had one heck of a week. Another left at the second light. Think about the blood-soaked evidence in your backpack before you ram us into a pole."

"They'd take us both. Something tells me that'd hurt you as bad as me."

"They wouldn't take me." Caltrop seems to be regretting his decision to have me drive. "Steady, soldier. Ease off the gas. Leg's setting you on fire? Sorry about that. Painkillers in your backpack?"

"Stay out of my shit." Blinking, world in the periphery losing focus, trying to concentrate on the yellow line.

"I'm not patronizing. Trying to help."

Caltrop digs in my backpack, finds the pill bottle, taps one out.

I jerk the truck into my lane. "Two. And you want the video of Hannah Reed, fucking take it. It's in there. I didn't even watch it. It's Vincent Peele you want. That muff-faced hipster fuck."

Caltrop finds the camera, pockets it, says mighty fine of me, hands me two Oxys. "There. Moving right along. Get in the left lane. Attaboy. Now. I've known Carl Reed for over three decades. Met him when he was eighteen. Keep in mind people are quick to judge. We meet someone, that single meeting becomes the entirety of a person. It's ridiculous but it's how we work. There's no reckoning for how a life changes over time, its ebbs and flows. Which is to say, you meet a man like Carl Reed as he is now, it's easy to dismiss him. And right now, he's all the things you think he is. At a life low. Been sliding downhill for a long while. Doubt he'll make it through. But it's important you know that when I met him, early on, Carl Reed was the radiant, supercharged future of our organization. He was that rarest of creations: a dreamer who translates his dreams to the people around him, convinces them the dreams are theirs. That's an incredible gift, Mark. A very powerful and potentially dangerous gift. You understand how normal folk will fall in line behind that kind of charisma. People are itching to be led. Another left at the second light. You can order a man to kill, command him to commit any horror. And he will. But eventually it'll destroy him. Means you have to keep replacing your soldiers. This is fine if you work on the scale of nations. But when you work on the scale we do it's simply not sustainable. Someone like Carl Reed, a man who spins dreams, he's invaluable. He gives me too much credit. I'm meat-and-potatoes. Carl is what makes something like us work. *Made*, I suppose. And when he went—we all went."

We drive east along the Fraser River until we hit the sagging belly of New Westminster, the sun languid through high cloud, mountains visible down a broad swath of low-running river, lacking depth in the evening light. Mist shrouds waterlogged alder rooted in the tidal mud between cinderblock warehouses and motorcycle chop shops, shipping facilities and plumbing supply stores. The air smells of vehicle exhaust, an ocean mingling with sluggish river water, the Mighty Fraser now placated by the valley bottom, sucked into our agriculture, poisoned with manure and nitrogen fertilizer, threaded though countless dead-end channels along the delta, beavers and blackberry scrub and the roar of international jetliners lance-like and wilful, and as I drive the stranger named Caltrop to an unknown destination I watch a tugboat captain wearing bright orange caulk boots and a yellow rain slicker hop across a log boom, the logs rolling and bobbing beneath his feet, his movements practised and serene, a single misstep shy of death, a startled cry—easily mistaken for a gull's shriek—before the logs close over his head. The sight strikes me as hopelessly anachronistic, black and white. We still do that here? I thought it was all about flipping real estate?

Caltrop directs me to a row of warehouses built close to the water. The parking lot ends at a rotting wooden fence being taken over by blackberry brambles. Stacked car parts rust in a welding shop loading bay, leaking streaks of red-orange across the pavement, a mangled front bumper, a car door with a shattered window, an old axle, tufts of fur, bits of bone and broken teeth. Beside the welding shop is a small manufacturing company named FireSpot, its logo a circle with flames hovering above a forest. Caltrop tells me to park in front of the unit closest to the river, tells me to bring my backpack inside. The sign above the door is faded and peeling, says *Ace Office Repair*.

Caltrop flicks the lights on. The warehouse is divided in half by a plywood wall about twelve feet high. The front is crammed full of office relics—hulking photocopiers and giant fax machines, printers and office telephones from the eighties—everything covered in dust, archaeological testimony to nothing at all. Wire cutters, needle-nosed pliers, and less obvious tools hang above a workbench piled high with ripped-open office equipment.

"No one pays to get this shit fixed anymore," I say.

Caltrop says yeah, that's the point, no one comes by, then leads me through a side door that opens facing the river. I follow him down a muddy path, across a sketchy platform of roped-together pallets to an eighteen-foot gillnetter. A peeling red stripe wraps around the boat's name: *The Yegg.* We scramble on board, me limping and awkward, Caltrop sure-footed. The deck's slick with dew. A net is spooled onto a reel at aft. The river's silent and broad and deceptively slow at the surface, but there are currents that can drag a man deep, spit him out ten kilometres downstream. The grinding habitual groan of commuter traffic crossing the Pattullo Bridge settles onto us from above. A blue heron, severe and reedy, scrutinizes us from the opposite shore. I duck into a gloomy cabin crammed with torn maps, yellowed paperbacks, navigation equipment, ratty army-surplus blankets, dirty plates, and stained coffee mugs. It smells of dead fish and rotting clothes, of hard work and uncertain outcomes.

Caltrop tells me to wait, lifts a bench seat cushion to reveal a storage cabinet, hauls out a cylindrical object about the size of a guitar case wrapped in a wool blanket. I tell him I need to leave. He nods, says sure, leave, I won't stop you. I give it serious consideration, think about Ryan out there alone, decide to let my curiosity get the better of me. Caltrop slips the blanket off, raps his knuckles on a black plastic cylinder, says this is a monovault munitions burial tube with a gamma-seal lid. The tube's sticky with river mud.

"Waterproof polymer," Caltrop says quietly. "Completely corrosion resistant."

"I know what it is."

"Far as I'm concerned, what happened in the woods isn't a question of right or wrong," Caltrop says, wiping mud from the munitions case. "It's a question of necessity. Like a single life, necessity ebbs and flows. Anyone ever tell you you're needed, Mark?" Caltrop pauses for me to answer. When I don't he says, "On the tactical front, you and I differ. But on long-term, strategic aims—"

"You're mistaking me for someone else. I came to hear fish stories."

"The Hague prosecutes state war criminals for crimes against humanity. But there's not a court in the land that can touch the men we hunt. Shadow kings. Living above the law and accumulating beyond reason. Until now. Until you."

"You still fish with this boat? Must be pretty cool, out on the river."

"Alien comes down to earth and asks what this place is all about. We say, well, that guy has a yacht moored inside his yacht. And half that continent's starving."

"Ever caught a sturgeon? Heard they put up a helluva fight."

"How do you think of yourself?"

I glance through a grimy window. Out there real people are living their lives and a guilty man lies cut open. "I am the thing itself. Without idea or image, theory or ideology. Just an object in motion. Existing before the conscious mind. That's how I'm beginning to think of myself. One day I hope to stop thinking entirely. Thought removes us from our true selves."

Caltrop pops the exterior lid off the munitions tube, reveals another tube protecting the innermost chamber. He lifts a steel toggle and twists, undoing a latch. The seal loosens with a hiss. "I'm curious about your selection process. Your criteria."

"I'm not wanting for choice."

"Exactly. How do you narrow it down?"

"Gut feeling. A bit of research. That might be changing."

"It's early yet. You're experimenting."

"I hope it's still early."

Caltrop reaches inside the munitions tube, carefully retrieves a firearm wrapped in an airtight, resealable storage bag that looks like an oversized Ziploc. Revealing this weapon feels sacred, the gillnetter rocking almost imperceptibly, river water whispering against the boat hull, the storage bag crinkling in Caltrop's hands, and in that moment Caltrop reminds me of a priest at altar, lifting a silver aspergillum in blessing. Murder is always an act of faith.

Caltrop sets the rifle on the bench, asks if I recognize it.

"A C14 Timberwolf Medium Range Sniper Weapon System. Manufactured by the Canadian company PGW Defence Technologies Inc. A civilian precision sport rifle modified for military use. Chambered for the Lapua Magnum .338. Effective anti-personnel to twelve hundred metres. A real sweet weapon, sir."

"How 'bout you pick her up? There. How she feel?"

"Honest."

Caltrop retrieves a box of cartridges from the burial tube. "Men and women working alone. Isolated. Atomized. This is the future for a long time to come. Organizations attract too much attention. Consider what the word *gang* does to a jury, or the word *cell*. Dehumanizes everyone involved. Removes all credibility. Drug gang. Terrorist cell. A prosecutor says those words in a courtroom and they can convict an egg salad sandwich. The culture is terrified of people uniting. Lone wolves are easier to discredit. The narrative is more flexible. Loners can be vilified, ridiculed. Made to appear insane."

"Being alone is insane."

"You don't have to be alone. If you accept what I have to say."

Caltrop tells me about a man named Bo Xi. About how Vincent Peele met Bo Xi when he ran an ESL school in Shanghai. About the sources of money flowing from Bo Xi though Marigold Group to Vincent Peele, then on to my brother and me. I hear about soldiers in Central Africa paid to guard illegal diamond mines staffed by villager-slaves, many of them children. A strategic civil war planned to further Bo Xi's interests in the region. Long sleeve short sleeve. Oil and coal operations in Mongolia that displaced entire villages. Private military contractors rappelling out of Black Hawks to assassinate Tibetan political leaders. Caltrop tells me a lot of things, and I listen real close, and the Timberwolf feels like the first promise I was meant to keep.

Carl "Blitzo" Reed

Starring in my own performance piece. Last hurrah. Don't wait up. Rough cotton breechcloth's riding something fierce, making me snippy. Balancing in a partially inflated red rubber dinghy on the shore of the Fraser River. Misty blue-white light, spectral. Two crows harassing an eagle. Foot perched on the dinghy's gunnel, fists on hips, head held high, imperious colonial coxswain shrieking orders at my slack-ass crew. Anyone who says they knew me is a liar, a wraith feeding on the life force of the living. Biter, groupie, hater.

Keep your leaky aura to your goddamned self.

Hock a loogie, watch it float downstream, try and think of something highfalutin' to say, conscious of posterity, embellished accomplishments, rising into the canon by being shot out of one, rising from the grave, fucking vampires again, eerie hauntings, peasant myths, psychic feedings, malign awakenings, inner circles, why is the future already full of ghosts, post-humans carrying the cosmic colonial torch, territorializing solar systems because it worked out so well last time? Buy me a sunny fiefdom, fire up the generator, duct-tape a vr headset to my face, rename myself NEXT. Hoping it always goes up? Hasn't quite been my experience. Bit afraid now, shivering in the cold coming off the river, pathetic carbon-based creature, balls shrunk inside my belly, testes seeking warmth, involuntary response, life in a nutshell.

Ugly undercurrents and eddies of sadness.

Star waves from behind the camera, zooms in, pinpoints false starts and forgotten ideas. If I could do it all again? Nah, let the artilects have it. Can I get a happy ending over here? Or maybe just an ending? But for now Blitzo's got the last laugh, dude's been around, sending this toxic rational-national mess upriver, back where it came from, straight to the source.

Cleaning house? But nobody invited me in—

The under-inflated dinghy swirls and rolls, nearly pitches me into the drink. A bit premature? Forget Sir Simon Fraser's waaay-too-square buttoned-down overcoat in the old painting; I'm costumed in raw-boned-on-the-road voyageur Captain Fraser vintage attire: torn and shit-stained breeches, crusty leather leggings, itchy flannel shirt, knee-length Melton-cloth Hudson Bay capote closed with a sexy lavender sash I'm using to wipe the blood from my eyes. All topped with a wide-brimmed felt hat stolen off the weirdly undecaying corpse of a former crew member. Nobility, adventure, exploration! A half-eaten sockeye thrashes in the bottom of the dinghy, sheds silver scales, leaves me conflating vague memories of the Monk, Nazis, Tesla, and Simon Fraser into a lurking river cryptid that's pining to transform fins into legs, ooze on shore, don a hazmat suit, infect the population with a positive attitude and productive work ethic. Take a final celebratory hit off a roach, remember I'm like ninety-nine per cent water anyway, fondle my sash, decide to improvise, point to the river, shout: "Upon the mercy of this Stygian tide!"

Scattered applause from the audience.

The guy seriously said that during his voyage. Or wrote that he did.

Anchored the dinghy to Holdout, could be a bad call. My piggy-muffin scrambles up the muddy bank, digs his hooves in, fights against the current, thrashes through alder and blackberry, cusses me out because he's pissed I dragged him from the financial district, says I could've taken pills, slumped into the hot tub like a normal rich loser, done us all a favour, says I always have to make everything about me.

"You're looking especially porky," I tell him. "Big as a fuckin' grizzly, in fact."

The pig leers at me, pats his monstrously swollen belly, waves a futures contract, says he was down on Howe Street feasting on the pork belly market, says he was afraid the wee piglets were gonna grow up and compete with him, says he feels like a rock python that swallowed a pregnant goat; he won't have to eat for years or at least a few minutes—

Gonna miss that gosh-darned pig. The problem with suicide is death becomes another errand. Letters unwritten. Goodbyes unspoken. Wills unsigned. I've spent the past eighteen months trying to decide how to address Michael in my final words. Dearest Michael? Michael my love? Michael my one and truly? Finally smeared on some lipstick and sealed the blank page with a kiss. Michael's not with us this evening, I was afraid he'd interrupt or intervene, talk some sense like a carping, overly cerebral ninny. He can join my channel. I'm broadcasting my spirit wanderings on YouTube. I feel a force tugging at me from beneath the deepening current, sinking sinking sleeper, some kind of psychic magnet or paranormal awakening that makes me hanker to channel Sylvia Plath? Holdout belches, the gust splinters saplings, kicks up waves, nearly knocks off my hat, drives me farther from shore and Holdout wants to know if he can have my High Vitality Points Tesla, says he wants to cruise Kits Beach in August, claims he looks better in it than me—

"Initiate launch sequence!"

Holdout squeals, says I'm finally writing secrets in the web, slips free of the rope anchoring the dinghy, hops onto a director's chair, dons his favourite pair of shades, the ones framed in critically endangered black-rhino bone while the current snatches and waves spill over the dinghy, soak through my maybe sustainable and culturally authentic Gastown tourist trap moccasins. No time for second thoughts: grab the oar (really a pawnshop Stratocaster in hot pink), adjust my hat, yell bon voyage, psyched for a heroic journey played bass-ackwards, monumental undertaking of undiscovery, empire in rewind, decline, leave the vast unknown alone. Sink the Stratocaster into the current, try to stay standing while attempting to paddle the deflating dinghy backwards and upstream. Listen for a groovy soundtrack, feeling like hunter and hunted. Are the rapids murmuring *Lhta koh*?

Star's hands are clasped in front of her breasts like a love-lost Disney chick. She sings she lives only to see me reborn, optimistic, eternally young, doesn't get that all I want is my life, simply ceased.

Dinghy's taking on some seriously frigid water. Past the point of no return. Stuff a pot brownie in my mouth, mumble: paddle, paddle, ever ho! Just made that up, seems to fit. Ever ho! Trying to paddle the dinghy backwards but gripped by roiling current, plunging and pitching, whipped downstream, digging the oar-guitar in, whooping and hollering, singing *For freedom, homes and loved ones dear/ Firmly stood and nobly died* . . . trying to be rid of the lines but they're forever inside me, undying and undead.

Holdout's bellowing tyrannical decrees, being indelicate, sowing discord among the sophisticates, threatening to swim out and eat me, saying I broke or never lived up to my promise. Lost in a familiar land. Are those icy claws emerging from beneath the surface? Or the patriot cryptid's exo-teeth? The dinghy heaves right, I overcorrect left and dig it: airborne, stretched sideways over the rushing water, gripping the busted pink Stratocaster, felt hat flying, trying to swallow the last bite of brownie, seagulls, mist, cottonwood trees and then I'm immersed, released, the water pulling me down, Fraser drowning in the Fraser, autoerotic? Gotta be really into yourself. What cannot be cured must be endured. The vaudeville hook snags my neck. Lights dim. I can't tell where I end and the world begins, and Michael is this perfection? Someone says you're everywhere, Carl, everywhere at once, and there is plenty of time, much too long, to remember.

Mark Ward

Spend a while holed up in the condo, feeling shit about not going to look for Ryan, doing my damnedest to pretend the soldier named Caltrop is a disjointed drug-fiction and there's not a TIMBERWOLF rifle sitting on the kitchen counter. My brother calls and leaves a message, his third, says I better fucking answer. I ignore him, eat a few sour candies, fail to do my exercises, brush my teeth twice.

Decide I need to be outside. Get dressed, walk toward Stanley Park. It's not a bad evening, people out, umbrellas folded, a shiny post-winter vibe. I buy a smokey, load it with Dijon and sauerkraut, eat and watch other people do the same, weekend shoppers, urbanites, and folks come in from the 'burbs, trying to feel the connect that can come with communal eating, but there's only calories, condiments, and ground-up animals, and what I want is to introduce myself to a stranger, say *hi I'm Mark Ward* and the stranger will be like *hey dude* and we'll shake hands, conversation will come easy and the next thing is we're lifelong besties. But what happens is I struggle to swallow the last bite of smokey, walk to the seawall, stare at the Pacific.

It's an ocean, all right. Water, waves. Yellow sulphur piled fifty feet high in the shipyards across the inlet. Is everyone giving me veiled looks and a wide berth? Can they tell what I'm thinking? And even worse is knowing I'm feeling edgy and hyper-vigilant but unable to do anything about it, and the goddamn ocean gets in my head, asks why can't I name a single living poet. Why can't I name a single living scientist. Why don't I know a single word in any Indigenous language.

Why are the famous people I can name all rich? And why are the famous people I can name who aren't rich nearly all killers? Murder is the poor man's monologue. Why must we offer blood for voice?

When will I understand how the atmosphere works?

Flick my smoke in the water, stuff my hands in my hoodie. The Pacific doesn't offer answers. It means shit to me. So I keep walking.

Pause at the overpass where Georgia Street enters Stanley Park, lean against a gnarled cedar, smell it, try to think of something uplifting about nature, its healing power, the grandness of the Canadian landscape, the redemptive sublime, something normal and well rehearsed. Vancouverites zip by on rollerblades, skateboards. People enjoying a break from the rain, smiling. I tear off a strip of cedar bark, think it'd be cool to know how to weave it into a basket. Put the bark between my teeth and taste it, fibrous, chewy, slightly sour, maybe I should've been a homesteader? Land up in New Denver, Sechelt, Comox, a vegetable garden, chicken wire, maybe some sheep if they make sense. I think about shearing wool. I think about falling in love with a sweaty, unshaven Québécoise princess with matted dreadlocks and an STD to tiptoe around, the two of us embarking on a conscious life journey, our children barefoot in the dirt, feral, unvaccinated. Building a cabin, piecing it together over a decade as the money comes in, living with no running water, pink insulation bulging against a plastic vapour barrier, a pot-bellied woodstove glowing toasty hot with burning hardwood, warning the kids about getting burned, life's difficult lessons.

I think about these things the way a city dweller thinks of them, the way a Westerner travelling in Nepal walks by a stone hut, sees children staring vacantly at a field and suddenly life seems impossibly beatific. The atmosphere is so thin, eventually it will slip away. Coal Harbour condominiums surround me, steel and white concrete, sculptural, delicate fins rising from the earth's spine. I think about the thousands of empty condos in this city, the few I filled with vagrants, the comic hopelessness of that gesture. I try and summon hatred for the condominiums but they are too beautiful, resource-efficient, high-density, designed for a future evolutionary leap. We have not caught up to them. Capital is post-gender, post-race, post-culture. It is the most liberating force ever conceived. I have fired a c14. I will fire it again. We used to laugh at my mother because she was afraid of squirrels. I don't understand what the internet is, how it works and came to be. Living in a new condominium seems a terrible affront, a sacrilege. Without the atmosphere all life will be torn into space. We'll be buried in the heavens. Our bodies will never rot. We'll never be alone. Our condominiums should be hermetically sealed until we are absolved of skin. We, who remain plagued by dreams of dirt.

Not even locked. Open the door and there she is, a crazy bitch sitting at her kitchen table in a dumpy South Van apartment, cool as a cucumber, like she's waiting for me. Close the door quiet. She doesn't move. Back turned so I can't see her face. Slide the security chain across the door. Still doesn't move. SAP's tucked in my belt and the KA-BAR's hidden in a sheath so I'm all good. Small bit of night work.

Apartment's a tiny cage. Nowhere to go.

But I can't see the target's hands. Which is fuck.

"You didn't run?" Watching her while I scan the room. Faded fruit-basket wallpaper. A carpet rust-stained from someone else's furniture.

Dead houseplants in cracked pots. A bed in the living room with sheets tacked around it. Can barely see the floor for all the mess; clothes and blankets and papers scattered everywhere and I get a not-cool feeling of familiarity, of sharing something with—"I need to see your hands."

Jasminder Bansal folds her hands beside what I'm guessing is Peele's stolen laptop. Not shaking, pleading, running. Not afraid? Batshit insane? Not good—

"My mother's in the bedroom. Asleep. She doesn't sleep enough. Please leave her be."

She should sound more afraid. *Trap*. Move to the bedroom door, listen. Crack the door open, see the shape of an old woman covered in blankets on a foam mattress on the floor, stacked boxes piled around her like the family's in the middle of moving, a disassembled bed leaning against the wall, framed photos piled in a corner, the old lady so still she could be dead and truth is the place is starting to fuck me up a tad, like: sadness? Like: loneliness? Which is some bullshit I'm not interested in dealing with in the middle of a straightforward job. And Jasminder's tone, how she's talking to me, calm, unafraid, that's lousy too, maybe a superiority thing? Fine. Works for me.

Way better than nattering too much.

Walk into the living room. "Nothing to do with your mother. You fucked up. Went to the cops. Peele wants to talk. We're gonna walk outside, get in my truck. You explain why you acted so stupid. Use words like that. *I acted stupid. Panicked.* Peele's a dickbag but he can't risk exposure. Gets his laptop, nothing's going to—"

"He's a better liar than you. He's going to kill me."

And, that's a fucking fact. Clint gave me the address. Sent his dog on the hunt. No way I thought she'd actually be here. Giving up, I guess. Seen it in Afghanistan. Terrorizing show of force. OPFOR wets pants, throws down weapons. Smart move. Best possible outcome, least loss of life—

I'm behind her. Walking slow, the SAP in my right hand. Clint said make sure no one sees you with her. Only one reason to say that. A couple steps away now. The city's outside. People doing their thing. My head feels like a screwdriver's stabbed into my ear. I do this work and then I wait, like Caltrop said, for Bo Xi. The man they call Tectonic. Me and that sick motherfucker settling into the swamp. Getting comfy in the muck and madness. Jasminder doesn't rate. Sad but true.

Raising the SAP—

Eyes focused on the back of her head. Softness. Straight black hair. Pretty shoulders and neck, not too skinny. Clint and Peele, they're gonna do lousy things. The soft spot where spine sneaks under skull. Important to hit with a precise amount of force. Learned anything in life it's that. Still breathing regular. Still in control, but the pain behind my eyes, battery acid taste, *hold me brother*, only get one shot, piled against the door burning we feel them in our wicking outerwear, piled against the door burning we feel them in our ski holiday hot tubs—

"I was going to call Sim," Jasminder says. "He could be here right now, waiting. But I couldn't. I guess I don't want it badly enough."

I glance over her head. She's watching me in the reflection in the window. Watching me creep on her. Not freaking out. So . . . fuck sakes. Her face is calm. She's been crying. Smeared mascara. But now her face is calm. Resolved.

"You're Clint's younger brother," Jasminder says, meeting my eyes in the reflection. "Mark Ward."

Feel stuck to the floor. Events gather momentum. Take on a will of their own. But the opposite is also true. Sometimes things rip apart. The natural state of the universe is disorder. Meaning's a fucking fluke. And the SAP's not smashing down. Summon my will. Remind myself I'm the bad guy. Make myself make sense.

"I'm Clint Ward's brother." Repeating Jasminder's words without knowing why. But it feels right, like a confession.

"You can't stop now," she says, looking at the SAP. "This is what you do."

Closes her eyes. Death wish. That's what this is. Suicide by me. *Wants* me to do it. Get her out of this mess. Maybe I'll do it for her, save her from what comes next. So easy now. Power. Will. Logic. Structure. Sense. Send a command from my mind to the muscles in my shoulder, downward motion, it'll all be over soon—

"Not here," I mumble, weak, blue-black light flashing in my eyes, vision narrowing, not sure why but wanting so bad to sit down, plead, say I GIVE, PLEASE, I GIVE, lay my head on the table—

Jasminder Bansal

"Where?" I feel him behind me. Hear him wheezing, his teeth smacking together, and a dry choking sound when he swallows. "Take me where?"

"Peele has somewhere."

"To do what?"

"Trust me, fuck, you don't want—"

"Don't be a pussy, Mark. Isn't that what your brother would say? Man up. I have a right to know." I open my eyes. Look into the reflection. The apartment fades until only Mark is in focus. A leather club trembles in his hand. He's sweating, glancing over his shoulder. Terrified. "I saw you yesterday. On Georgia Street."

Mark blinks. "This isn't what I am. Weakness doesn't interest me."

"You're wrong about who's weak. Peele should've sent your brother. I see you."

Mark Ward

What's she mean, she sees me, she sees me, what's she see, fucking with me, what am I, what does she see—

"Put the stupid thing down, Mark. No one's watching."

A semi-truck roars up Knight Street. Shakes the floor beneath my feet.

"How you sleep with that racket?"

Jasminder says nothing, but I see how tired she is, worn out and worked over and I guess she's been through it, not some uppity bitch like Clint said, just a girl who's been through it—no, is *going* through it, right now, with me. And the thing is I like her, not as in I want to dick her but you know . . . maybe as a living person? A human being? A person maybe not too much like me but maybe not too much different?

And she's right. The SAP looks stupid. Doing nothing except being limp, useless, silly, hanging in my hand. And then it's not.

It's tucked in my belt.

Jasminder Bansal

He brushes his sweat-slick hair out of his eyes and tries to laugh, nervous and awkward, like he's not sure where he is or what he's doing, but the laughter becomes an awful grinding cough and he scratches his forearm, grimaces, closes his eyes and presses his index finger to his temple and the muscles in his torso and neck tense and bulge and it looks like he's trying to push his finger through his skull, like he's trying to physically push an idea or image or memory out of his head. A few seconds tick by and he starts trembling from the exertion of stabbing his finger into his temple and then he spits, stuffs his hands in his hoodie, looks at me like he has no idea who I am. I'm about to call Sim when Mark's phone rings and when he answers it everything about him changes and he sounds like a father or brother fighting to be calm and reassuring when he says slow down slow down tell me where he has you—

Mark Ward

Rich men die easy. Tile nice and warm on the soles of my feet. Travertine, slate, some shit. Dude sprung for the radiant heating upgrade. Bathroom like a fancy spa where you pay 'em to rub dirt in your face, say relax, *om*. All-around sweet crib. Coal Harbour fuckpad only a couple blocks from Clint's. Bathroom feels like inside a rocket ship, teeth humming, liftoff. I drop the toilet lid, cause of death, and the crash makes me want a cigarette.

Left side of my face numb as hell. Leaning against the vanity, swallowing, trying to clear the nasty taste in my mouth, trying to stay standing. A dusty taste, like Kandahar road grit. In my eyes. Still feel it even now. Gets in everything. Clogs up kit. Wears out machinery. Grinds everything down.

Looking at the creep in the bathtub, scenting him, this big beautiful bathroom, all light and polish, not thinking about Ryan out there, or Jasminder, or my brother, ossuary, a big secret, something like that, waiting for a hard-earned insight to carry me through.

Legs hanging out of the claw-foot tub. Half in half out. Looks ridonculous. Who is this guy? Naked legs splayed funny. Chubby toes smeared red. And that weird black and red face paint he has on, those weird four-inch curving black-painted fingernails filed sharp.

Wearing Mardi Gras beads, a plastic lei, and nothing else but those sharpened fingernails. What is this guy? Might still matter. Maybe not to me, but to Ryan and Jasminder.

The handcuff key is on the vanity.

That's what I need. Why I'm here.

Not only for that sick fuck.

Move so I can see into the bedroom. Ryan's slumped against the headboard of a posh circular bed, shivering, naked. Faint tank-top tan lines from last summer around his shoulders and neck. Left arm cranked above his head. Wrist chained to a chrome bar. A bundle of nasty-looking bites along his ribs, on the soft skin beneath his arm, across his pecs and beating heart. Pale blue veins. Soaked silk sheets knotted around his waist and for a while I stand quietly in the threshold, blinking, smelling blood and worse, trying to put it together, not so eager to say anything, break the silence—

"He wasn't going to eat me," Ryan says, like he's angry at me but I dunno.

Run a hand over my bastard leg, feel the rippled partially healed-over flesh, think about digging out an Oxy, realize I need to stay on point, Ryan stammering, saying that awful shit over and over—*he wasn't going to eat me*—despite all available evidence, the little shit, chanting it, snot-streaked, and me trying to block out the sound of him, not hear it, last thing I need, but he's getting louder, hitting his stride, rocking on the bed, tugging against the handcuffs, *he wasn't going to eat me*, in Kandahar there are starving dogs that prey on street kids, in Vancouver there are well-fed men who do the same, pretty travertine tile, rocket ship, a dead man dripping down a bathroom drain—

"My brother," I say, loud into Ryan's screaming.

"Clint didn't mean it." Ryan pulls the sheet over his chest, wraps it under his chin. "He didn't know . . ."

Which is bullshit, and we all know it. Clint exactly knew. Ryan's sticking up for my brother even after . . . I think about saying it, decide not to. What good arguing? Check my watch. Eleven minutes inside the condominium. Way too long.

Jasminder's standing beside the floor-to-ceiling windows. Maybe she's looking at Vancouver? The sparkling nightscape. Dreams, poetry, nature, all that. Maybe her eyes are closed. I can't tell. She didn't try and stop me. I wonder what that means, what's changed for her, don't know her well enough to say. She followed me up here even though I told her to stay put in the Ford and she saw Ryan and she didn't try and stop me so that means—

"You know that sick fuck through Vincent Peele," I say to Jasminder, and it isn't a question. "You recognized him. A business partner."

Says nothing for a long while, then, "I'm wasting my life looking through windows." Presses her fingertips to the glass and the gesture reminds me she's pretty, might have a good heart, maybe she gets to live, maybe Ryan does too, and that's best case—

I'm still stuck between rooms. Living and dead and I'm in between. Waffling. Wobbling. Thirteen minutes in now, which sucks. First-responder territory. Cops and so on. Someone heard the screams and called it in, cavalry's coming real quick for the guy in the penthouse. I look at Jasminder's back, her shoulders and neck, smooth and soft, and the thought crosses my mind. To hurl them both off the balcony? Jasminder first, because she'd fight, then Ryan because he wouldn't. Them dead would sort a lot out. Get me right with my brother and Vincent Peele. Maybe get me back to my family if I went that route. But instead I hurry across the room, uncuff the kid, ask him what I should've done instead.

Ryan shudders. "You let him. Like me. Look at this place. He's got money . . . so you let him . . ."

"I guess so. Look at this place."

Truth is my mind's already on other things. Escape. Jasminder. My brother. The next target. But I'm tired. Pain shoots up my leg.

Another pain, deeper and wider, spreads through my neck and fore-head while ugly not-there blood-cell objects float around the room.

Ryan, more together now, wraps the high-thread-count sheets around his body so only his face is visible, says it wasn't only Clint who set it up.

"Who else?" Jasminder asks, beating me to it.

"Mark? Who the fuck is she?"

"My brother and who else knew that sicko in the bathroom?" I ask. "It's all right to tell."

I wait for Ryan to say it, but I have a pretty good idea.

"Like you said to her. Vincent. Vincent knew . . . the guy in the bathroom."

Ryan gives me a look like we're all dead, and it's all my fault, and he might be right on both counts.

"Vincent Peele," Jasminder says, like it's coming together for her. "Clint Ward. That makes sense. Those two."

"Who's she?" Ryan asks me, all wide-eyed and panicked. "Mark? Why's she here?"

"You're going to kill them, Mark," Jasminder says, and I feel her looking at me and the blood-cell spheres floating through the room turn black, get pulled toward Jasminder, and for some reason what she says makes me taste burning motor oil and blackened blood and I dig in my hoodie pocket for a gummy or sour candy to get rid of the taste but I'm all out.

"Mark?" Ryan asks again, finally looking straight at me. "You hear that? What she said? About Clint? Your *brother*. She can't talk like that, dude, what she's saying—"

"Get him up," Jasminder says, and now they're both staring at me like they want something, like I have answers.

"I like Clint's truck," Ryan mumbles. "Can see over traffic."

Sim Grewal's the ace in the hole. So it might work? Maybe all three of us live? Or at least the two of them? If Jasminder will help—

"This could be good for you," I tell Jasminder. "Vincent Peele outta the picture. Bright future. You can have everything, you play it right. You're inside, set up for the North Van property—"

"I'm inside," she says, thinking on something, maybe scheming, maybe realizing she's more like her dead gangster brother than she thought—

"Oh yeah," I say, watching blood stream across the bathroom tile, soak into a cream-coloured rug. "We're all the way up this mother-fucker."

Ryan starts up an awful keening wail, reminds me of kids scream-ing behind a factory door so I tell him to stop, shut the fuck up, but the keening gets worse, high-pitched, irritating as hell, so I grab his chin, pinch the soft spot beneath his jaw until he goes quiet. "I have an out for you, Ryan. Someone who can keep you safe."

I release Ryan's chin. "You're an asshole, Mark. And a loser. At least Clint's not a loser—"

"You're going with Mark's guy," Jasminder tells him, smart, because she knows Ryan will rat us to Clint if we turn him loose.

I ask Jasminder: "Who is he? Mr. Mardi Gras in the bathtub?"

"Scott Charles Booth's financial advisor."

"Booth? Owns the North Vancouver property Peele wants? Important upstanding guy. In the bathtub."

"Yes."

"Course. So Peele and my brother gave the kid to Mr. Mardi Gras. Sweeten the deal. Grease the wheels."

"Gave him. Yes."

"A perk."

Ryan's quiet, listening.

"You never know until you're inside," Jasminder says, heading for the door. "I never thought he was that smart." Bitter now, regretful. "Everyone said I was the smart one in the family. But it wasn't true. Only Amar really saw me."

Fuck it. Maybe she's crying. I dunno. I can't see her face. Maybe she doesn't have it in her after all.

"Get the video," Ryan says, barely a whisper, but both Jasminder and me freeze. Maybe the first thing the kid's said that we really hear.

"What?"

Ryan looks at me like I'm an idiot. "They always video. Wasn't only . . . him? Was another guy too. Real old."

"Might be Booth," Jasminder says, and there it is, the ambition in her voice, what she really wants, what she lied to herself about not wanting, and good for her, must be nice, knowing where you stand. Jasminder helps me, Vincent Peele's going to be done and gone real soon. That means Jasminder's in if she gets Bo Xi the property. Deal's still on. Slight misstep. Nothing we can't handle. Kid chained to the bed. Kid all bit up. Slight indiscretion. Advisor bludgeoned with a toilet lid. Slight gaffe, old fella. Let's stay on point, huge upside—

Jasminder Bansal

The three of us in Mark's Ford. Soaked work clothes in a tangled pile at my feet. The camera from the penthouse tucked in my handbag. Blood stink in my nose. A bright future ahead of me, opportunity, success? Vincent Peele out, me in?

I ask Mark for a cigarette. He hands me one without looking over. Ryan waits a few seconds, hands me a lighter. Ryan's sitting in the middle seat, looking straight ahead. Mark's on the phone with Peele, feeding him bullshit about having me and Ryan and the stolen laptop and offering to trade everything straight across if Peele lets him out free and clear. Peele's voice carries in the cab, tinny, muffled. I tune him out. Mark's wearing filthy too-baggy Dickies pants and a faded plaid shirt under a black hoodie that smells of sweat, smoke, and gasoline. He looks like hell: scabbed, twitchy, chain-smoking, popping pills, voice fast and then slow, loud and soft, erratic, unpredictable, and he better keep his side of the deal, see it through for Ryan's sake.

Mark hangs up. Says he needs me to take Ryan . . . to this guy named Caltrop. Says otherwise it's all set with Peele, asks if I'm good.

"Why were you working for Peele?"

Mark pulls the truck into an alley. Parks. Kills the headlights. "Me? Fuck. Sorta happened. You?"

Ryan's listening when I say, "Money. I wish it was something more."

"More?"

"You know? Bigger? More meaningful?"

Mark eases out of the truck, winces. "Maybe money's all there is."

"I guess we'll see if you mean that."

Mark flips his hood over his head. Ryan doesn't look at him.

After Mark's gone I get in the driver's seat. Phone Sim. He doesn't sound happy to hear from me.

Mark Ward

Phone Daree while I walk. Takes her a while to answer. Says hi are you feeling better and I say yeah I'm feeling not bad, you? We go on like that for a few minutes. I light a smoke. Daree puts Sarah on. My baby daughter burbles and burps and giggles and I seize up, inhale cigarette smoke the wrong way and end up choking, saying I didn't mean it over and over and I'm sorry I'm not better for you guys and Daree's saying no no and this is it, this is why I shouldn't have called, it always happens like this, fucking drama, and then Daree she kind of I dunno bucks up, takes a steadying breath and sounds more calm, like reassuring me and she says it'll be okay it'll be okay we'll make it work and I'm like *make it fucking work?* because she has no clue about my brother and Vincent Peele and Jasminder and Ryan or any of this, only a week since I landed in this shithole, all happened so fast, speed, shock, terror, and I know Daree's hurting and yet here she is trying to raise me up and then it hits me: what I need is there with her and Sarah and it's not gonna happen.

Daree says hey check your phone, I sent you something. I open the text and at first I'm like what the fuck because my phone's wet and I can't make sense of the image. Shelter under an awning, wipe my phone, see a picture of a concrete wall painted cheery-teal and I realize I'm looking at a wall inside Daree's apartment in Bangkok, thousands of kilometres away, and she's strung white Christmas lights across the wall, turned them on so they're glowing pretty and bright, strung the lights up so they spell a name, Mark Patrick Ward, my name all lit up and glowing, she did this, she did this for me, and she says, "Do you like it it's your name in lights we're here," and I'm like fucking holy fuck, I could go to them, drive to the airport, this doesn't have to be it, look at that life with them it's not happiness now but it could be if we work at it, the three of us, *family*, and my name's lit up and glowing like I'm something special even though I'm not and *hold me brother* and Daree's saying it's okay it's okay and it's not okay, she doesn't know and no one does because I never let anyone in.

An hour gives me time to take care of some loose ends. I get ripping high on medical weed grown by bikers and sold by liars, go to an internet cafe on Robson. Filled with teenagers playing video games. Everyone plugged in. Is it true dudes starve themselves to death playing video games? Cuz, fuck sakes? I get online, transfer my money to an account Daree has access to. Not as much as I'd hoped. Thought I'd have more time to work, save, plan for a lifelike future. But there's six grand, and if she's smart and moves out of Bangkok she'll be able to buy her own place or maybe a street cart selling pad thai to tourons, who knows. Maybe she won't take the money. She's odd like that. Doesn't like shit handed to her. Maybe it'll sit in cyberspace, suspended, undying.

Next thing I do is pop a couple Oxys, smoke another blunt, wander to 7-Eleven. Loving the whooshing pneumatic door and cool AC air hitting my face. That same-everywhere 7-Eleven smell reminds me of being a kid. I think about asking the guy behind the counter how they get that smell so perfectly the same in every store. But he'd probably think I was having a laugh. Get his hackles up. So I skip it, hang out in the magazine aisle, killing time checking out fashion and sports mags, travel, art, music, admiring all the fun things I could've been and done if I were someone else. People filter in and out. The door chimes, love that sound. The counter guy rotates blistered corn dogs, sips a neon-green Slurpee. I decide I've got a big night ahead of me, should eat something, fuel up. Use a set of tiny plastic tongs to drop penny candy into a plastic bag, grab some 7-Eleven nachos with lukewarm meat sauce and cheesy slop. Last supper, seems about right, not complaining.

I eat my nachos huddled under the 7-Eleven awning, feeling not much, watching the rain and traffic. Think about phoning Dave Ward, the old man, realize I don't know his number or if he's healthy enough to speak on the phone. Think about phoning Daree, saying sorry. And that's as far as it goes.

Meet Vincent Peele and his posse in the library courtyard, should be an abandoned building, a gravel pit in the Mojave Desert, but here we are. Peele's wearing hiking boots, bib-style snowboard pants, a tight-fitting black Merino wool base layer. I tell him he looks baller, ask where he got the snowboard pants. No answer. Clint's pacing beside his boss, pasty and tweaked. Wearing black kicks, expensive for sure, and a white dress shirt not tucked in. I ask him what happened to the fancy suit. Another no answer, just an exhaled cloud of smoke. Wipe the rain out of my eyes, spit, try to clear the nacho film from my mouth, ask why everyone looks so sour.

Also a dude I've never met. Beast of a motherfuck. Must be six four, two-fifty. White guy, shaved head, all flex and scowl. For sure ex-military. I decide I'm feeling frisky, what's the point if you're not having fun, but the truth is there's this panic building in my gut that comes spewing out of my mouth. So I'm speaking in quick bursts when I ask who's the new guy, Peele? Here for study group? Cuz he don't seem so bookish.

"Duke," Peele says, patting the guy's arm like he's showing off a prize stallion.

"Dick?"

Clint takes a step toward me.

"Duke."

"Oh, Duck? Weird name, Peele. Duck? The new guy has a weird name."

Clint says hey Marky relax, chill out bro.

"West Coast?"

"That's it," Peele says. "Chillaxed. Duke's gonna pat you down. Play along."

So Duke does. I say holy hell you're a big bastard, aren't you? Kill your momma coming out? Or born out your daddy's poop hole? Like a Boschian demon? Duke says nothing. I'm guessing a lot goes over his head. He's wearing Kevlar body armour. Flak jacket. Fine. I don't have Kevlar body armour. I have a soaked hoodie.

Clint leads us to Peele's blacked-out Lexus suv.

"Sweet ride," I tell Peele. "Those are sick rims, Peele. Chrome wires? Pick those out yourself? Or a personal shopper do it?"

Duke squeezes in the driver's seat. Peele walks around front to get in. Clint takes the opportunity to whisper in my ear: "You fucked up brother but it's not a done deal, hear me? You come through, Twll and that bitch . . . it's not a done deal."

I don't answer because I'm afraid of losing my shit and blabbing about what I set up, so I decide to distract myself by hassling the big guy. Slide in behind Duke. Lick my pinky finger, stick it in his ear. Duke roars, reaches around, tries to punch me but the angle's all wrong and he ends up flapping his arm uselessly, which pisses him off even more. I'm laughing, saying I dunno about this Duck guy, Peele. Seems like a loose cannon. Do I hear him quacking? And does anyone want some Hot Lips?

Duke's breathing hard through his nose, killing me over and over in the rear-view. I don't know if Clint believes what he told me, but if he does he's an idiot. Duke's already been paid half up front. Settled into the right frame of mind. I scent it on him, the night work.

I'm guessing Clint's on the way out, too, for bringing me in, compromising the whole operation. So that's the edifying story of the Ward Brothers.

We all do up our seatbelts, seems real funny. I swallow way too many pills as we pull from the curb. Peele twists in his seat, asks where we're going, it better not be far, he's missing an evening half-pipe sesh on Mount Seymour.

"Super kick-ass, Vincent. Hey, uh . . . does it stink like death in here?" Clint gives me a shove. "Or is it my 7-Eleven nacho breath?"

"Speaking of death, what about what *you* did, Mark?" Peele says. "To Mr. Booth's advisor Mr. Knowles?"

"Knowles, eh? You mean Mr. Mardi Gras rapist? With the sharpened fingernails and painted face? You might be right. Maybe I'm still smelling him."

"Tell me something?"

"No," I say, glaring at Clint, trying not to let Peele's pitch-man voice inside my head—

Peele folds his arms over the seat. "Why don't you want what everyone wants? A nice house? A nice car like mine? Life's much more comfortable when you want what everyone else does. You slip into the world and disappear. Now look at you. A deviant. Not part of productive society, so of course you want to sabotage it."

"Oh, I'm thinking about turning it around? Buying a condo? Jasminder had some of those positive-thinking mantras taped to her wall. One of them hit home. *I leave a small dent in the universe with my work.* I mean, what more can you ask for? How's life? Ah, not bad, I'm leaving a small dent! After tonight I think I'll buy a Cuisinart blender. Lemon-pepper kale smoothies are super inspiring. I'm basically tired of chewing."

"Mark, shut it," Clint says.

"See?" Peele says. "That's the thankless attitude I don't understand. Fuck's wrong with smoothies?"

"I like smoothies," Duke says. "Chocolate protein powder—"

"Duke, that's wicked awesome. What about you, Clint?"

"Smoothies? They a'right."

"See, Mark? You're a malcontent. The world could be a shining utopia and you'd still be miserable. Chemical imbalance in your brain. The rest is window dressing." Peele checks his phone. Shows us a picture of a naked chick riding a mountain bike in Whistler. "See her? Living the dream. I feel sorry for you. In this great town. In an amazing time. In this great country. In an amazing—"

"Great country? Canada? Canada is a blood lie of theft and murder."

"Uh, fuck . . . whatever, asshole!" Duke sputters.

"Yeah, Mark. Canada! So much better than! It floors me how ungrateful you are. Less than a hundred years ago, only royalty and the super-rich could travel. Now anyone can travel whenever they want. And that's only the easiest example. Life's better than ever."

"Not for most. You'd know that if you went somewhere besides Vegas and Cancun."

"I've been to Maui, too." Peele laughs.

"It works for you. At the expense of everyone else."

"*C'est la vie.* We're finished kowtowing to wretched human beings like you. I mean, we're all completely different, and I affirm that diversity, but I'm also free not to have to deal with it. You went to war, I didn't. You like. . . cigarettes? And I like cardio fitness! As if the two of us could possibly share any human commonality. As if there's even such a thing! Universalism, metanarratives, no. Super oppressive. We're all individual and unique and free! All with our own opinions and values and stories that we can like nod blankly at but never truly feel or understand because you're inside you and I'm inside me. I need community, get online, find whatever forum feels the most like me in that moment. Mountain bike bros! Melon trellis aficionados! Living life like a mini-nation out to defend and enrich itself. The nation of me! Home team! And way over there, the loser nation of you. Don't cross into my territory! How exciting is that? Totally freaking exciting! As if I want to believe in something bigger than myself. I'm the biggest thing there is, because I'm me! So I embrace hyper-progressive fragmentation. That's next-level liberty. Nations implode because they're top-down and twentieth century, the rich and resourceful form phyle based on lifestyle preference. Super dynamic! And even better, I get to surround myself with people who think exactly like I do. No more Bridgers upsetting me with their obnoxious trucks. It's like a Facebook feed, but forever. You don't believe, you leave. Simple as that."

"Peele? Did you go to private school?"

"Of course. Why?"

I tune the lawyer out, tell Duke to drive to Tinseltown, the underground parking lot beneath the movie theatres. Duke looks at Peele and asks where's that? Peele gives Duke specific directions in his slowest speaking-to-an-idiot voice. I pick a wad of chewed Hot Lip from my molar, decide I'm feeling all right. The rain's let up. The condominiums are still standing. What could be better?

Duke manoeuvres us through Eastside junkies and whatnot, turns toward the theatre. It's gonna happen down there. In the underground parking lot. Not a bad place. Ryan's safe. I do this, the kid's as safe as anyone.

Vincent glances at me and there it is, the hatred, the kill lust, man this prick is good at living underground, way better than me. I'm all on the surface, heart on my sleeve, never was good at pretending to be something I'm not, but this Vincent Peele guy, what did he say? The Ward Brothers cage match? Yeah. So when the time comes he's gonna order Clint to do it—

"Like a boss," I whisper.

Duke steers the SUV down a ramp. Stops at a gate, rolls down the window and gets a half-hour parking ticket. I tell him we won't need a half-hour. Duke keeps it together, manages to ignore me. The gate rattles up. Duke eases us underground, keeps an eye on the metal tube suspended from the ceiling that marks maximum vehicle height. Pretty cool head, this Duke. Professional security detail after his military stint. Personal chauffeur-slash-bodyguard. Good money in protecting rich people. So he's the wildcard. I watch Duke's eyes in the rear-view. Quick with concentration. Brow furrowed. His gut's telling him an underground parking lot is a bad idea, but it's his first job with Peele and he doesn't want to seem like a coward.

So he's keeping quiet. For now.

Peele gnaws on his thumb. Saturday night movies are about to start. People walk by, couples holding hands, teenagers in tight clusters peering at their phones, looking expectant. For what I can't imagine. Some kind of message, a revelation, I dunno. Maybe what movie to see?

"Where?" Peele asks, fingers tapping the dash.

"Stall one hundred eighty-two."

"The place's packed," Duke growls. "No way a specific parking spot's gonna be open. Mr. Peele? I am requesting you transfer control of the operation to me."

"Transfer control!" I yell, making Peele flinch. "Transfer—"

Clint smacks me in the ribs, knocks the wind out. I pick my nose, make to wipe it on him. He swats me away, folds his arms, sulks.

"Control is all yours, Duke. Mark? Shut up! Do what you promised. Where's the kid?" Peele's voice rises an octave. "I need the kid. And the bitch! Where's Jasminder?"

"Yeah, where's the package, asshole?" That's Duke. "Do not play games. This is my op now, Mr. Peele. To be clear: this is where I assume command. Mark! Where are the fucking—"

Mind slipping, something's off, resist the urge to yell STOP THE LAV. "Hey, Duck. You military? Me too! Does that mean we're like cock brothers of death? LULZ! But this Duck guy, Peele, I dunno, can't trust him—"

"Marky you asshole stay cool—"

"—have some faith, gentlemen, *jeez*." Acting all defensive, like they're wronging me, hurting my feelings, but I look over and Clint's wearing scorched CADPAT fatigues and I gotta fight real hard to say, "Park in one eighty-two, Dick. Left. No, your other left. This is a sweet ride, Peele. I never owned a new car."

A construction sign and a few orange cones are blocking the stall. Best thing I've seen all night. Means I asked for a high-stakes favour and it came through.

"Got it. Let me hop out and—"

"You stay right there," Duke shouts. "Clint. *You* do it. Get out and move that shit."

Moviegoers and shoppers part for the SUV. No one looks out of place. Not even us. The parking lot's lit bright. Security cameras everywhere. Hard to bury a pressure cooker in here. Unless it's in your head. Clint jumps out, clears the signs, and climbs back in. Duke's on the ball; he backs the SUV in so he'll have good visibility into the parking lot. Sometimes you get lucky. I got lucky with Duke the ex-soldier turned criminal mercenary.

Duke throws it in park but doesn't kill the engine, reaches under his seat, grabs an MP7, compact submachine gun, manoeuvrable, designed for urban warfare, beauty piece of work, not easy to come by in the Frozen North. Duke sets the weapon on his lap.

"Uh, guys," I say, eyes going cartoon-buggy at seeing the machine gun. "Peele? Clint? I'm unarmed, right? Duck searched me? I mean, Dick? So what's—"

"This is you, Mark." Duke interrupts. "Where are they?"

"You have to signal."

Peele chokes, throws his hands over his face.

Duke grabs the MP7, rotates, points it at my chest, and seeing it there, death, I dunno, it makes me relax, feels right somehow, THIS IS MINE AND MINE ONLY—

"Signal?" Duke says. "Fuck that. Why?"

"Shit, c'mon, Dupe. Thinky-thinky! So Ryan is released."

"*Released?*" Peele shrieks. "By who? You said you have him!"

"What? How can I have him? I'm here."

"Clint, you better—"

"Peele, fuck. I got it." Clint pulls his Glock, aims at my guts. Holding the thing sideways, all TV gangster. I could snatch it from him in a heartbeat. But I won't. "Marky? Family. Don't fuck me. Why aren't you alone?"

"I am alone. Except I'm with you."

Peele snickers.

"Look. I needed someone to watch Ryan. Give the signal and they'll let him go."

Duke shakes his head. "No, no. No signal. Might as well paint a fucking target on my face. Look, where's the kid, asshole? You and Clint fetch the kid, bring him to me—"

"*Aargh!*" Peele yells. "*And* the girl! Where's Jasminder . . . Clint? I fucking told you . . . I said—"

"Marky'll do as I tell him. I said I got him."

"You got me, brother? This is gonna be boss."

Duke grabs the gearshift. "Fuck this. Mr. Peele? I'm officially un-assing."

"What?"

I laugh in Duke's ear, don't mean it to sound so screechy and manic but it does because there's an Afghan man walking across the underground parking lot holding a *kufi* over his nose and mouth. "*Braaap!* Clint! Let's go dirt biking. Like when we were kids? Smooth is fast! *Braaap!*" Arms out, pretending to hold my motorbike handlebars, shaking like I'm riding through rough terrain.

"Hey asshole—shut up! My operation now, Mr. Peele. Look at that shitbag. Op depends on him? Already lied. Wants us to signal? Fuck no. Danger close—"

Mad laughter rolling through the Lexus, feels great to get it out. "GOFO! Peele, I'm saying your boy Dump has a stunning Grasp of the Fucking Obvious. Hey, Dick, return to base, where'd you serve, you're a fucking embar—"

"—too many moving parts," Duke continues, ignoring me. "We stay calm, fully un-ass, no peanuts—"

"*Peanuts?*" Peele screeches.

"Dupe is saying he won't take a bullet for you, Peele. Like backing out? This guy, Dope, I dunno, chickenshit—"

"Shut up Mark!" Clint yells, pressing the Glock to my ribs.

Peele paws at his beard. "Duke? You want to *leave?* I fucking need—*aargh!* Clint, your junkie brother says another word, shoot him in the belly. You! Duck! We're staying right here. That is a . . . command? An order? Uh . . . fucking got me?"

"You already transferred comm—"

"—fucking untransferring it!"

Peele's right in Duke's face. And I mean, inches. Duke has a loaded machine gun on his lap. He's sitting military straight, trying to stay cool, not murder the asshole boss who's spraying him with spittle.

Tap Duke on the shoulder. "Signal, Big Dick."

Clint doesn't shoot and the Afghan man is gone, so good times.

Peele whirls, tries to snatch the Glock from Clint. Clint jerks the gun to the side. Peele misses, shrieks, scratches at my face. I bat him away. Duke's not saying a word, focused on the busy parking lot. After a few seconds of funny flailing hissy-fit Peele stops, breathes in some self-control, and for a full minute, maybe two, it's dead quiet in the pimpin' Lexus SUV.

"Dump, this is fun, not a bad Saturday night, but you still have to signal. Ryan's in here somewhere. What movie's playing? Shit. Can't remember the last movie I saw."

"Who has him?" Clint asks, the Glock shaking in his hand. My brother, no wobbling, warrior discipline. "Who the fuck's got Twll?"

I look at my brother. And I lie.

"It's Jasminder. Is that perfect, fellas, or what? I told her she had to do this thing to get square and cool with like me and you, and the dumb bitch bought it! She's super afraid of you, Peele. She has Ryan stuffed in the trunk. I even showed him to her all tied up. She was sad, but like whatever. Said she wants out. I couldn't leave him alone in there, y'know . . . by himself? 'Case someone heard him banging around? So we signal Jasminder, she signals back, and we go snatch them both. Piece of piss!"

I give my brother a half-smile. There's a family in that smile. A childhood spent throwing rocks at freight trains as they whipped through the valley. *I love you brother.* Clint knows I'm lying. He always did. But he says, "That's a boss plan, bro."

"No," Duke says, unwavering. "It's shit."

Peele rips at his beard. "Tell me the fucking signal!"

Duke shifts the SUV into gear, keeps his foot on the brake.

Not stupid, this Duke. Big, but not totally stupid.

"Duck? Flash your headlights three times."

Duke's going to make sure I die. One way or the other. But for now he tells Peele we should haul ass. Spends a minute explaining all the reasons he's not gonna signal, and when he's finished Peele reaches over and flashes the headlights.

LIGHTROAR

Duke knocks Peele away, snatches the MP7. Nothing happens for a good five seconds, long enough to have me worrying I got fucked. I want to say something to my brother, last words, but the truth is I've stopped breathing—

People walk by. What should I call them?

Civilians? Bystanders? Collaterals?

A nice night at the movies. Maybe a first date, an anniversary, an outdoor wedding procession, and the BLOOD RAIN—

The first round takes off the left half of Vincent Peele's head, all that ugliness just *thunk-spetch* into liquid marring a calfskin interior, strikes me as the prettiest thing ever, real nice image to die to—

There's no sound, or the sound arrives later. Another round hits Peele's headrest, takes a weird bounce, punches into Clint's thigh. Something wet and warm slaps my cheek. A river of blood or money or both, sink or swim, we made their women scream. Heat burns down my throat and the locked doors won't open and the vc or Vincent's dead—

Mist against my skin. Lick my lips, taste the enemy—

The shots start up for serious, rapid-fire, some a quick *pop-pop* and others lower, *duth-duth-duth* like a bass line, and the suv sways side to side from rounds impacting metal and Clint shoves out the door. He didn't fire at me. After all this. My brother didn't shoot me—

Duke smashes back and forth as bullets pound into his flak jacket. He has the MP7 raised above the dash despite getting shot to shit. The MP7 shoots forked lighting. Duke is secretly a vengeful god. Bullets shatter the windshield, punch holes in the roof. Something sledgehammers my shoulder, leaves fire in its wake. Peele ends up hunched against the dash. Clint's crouched behind the door, ducking, shooting, doing a convincing job of being a gangster. Civilians scream, run, fall down, flail, scream, die. No one gets reborn. No one hits reset. Someone is surely doing something poignant and heart-wrenching. The tinted glass in the truck beside Clint explodes. Acrid reek of gunpowder and earthy reek of blood and *my brother, I wish I held you*—

Duke's bulk and body armour act like a shield, blocking bullets from hitting me. I'm trying to fold myself into the footwell, hiding, not really meaning to, instinct, will to live, huddled behind Duke, spitting blood and vomit, not walking boldly into the fray, not doing much of anything, cowering, pissing myself, a pressure cooker packed with potassium chlorate, nails, sharpened rebar. Wired to three artillery shells and this time let's finish the job—

Clint flings himself halfway inside the Lexus. Point-blank shots from right beside us. Someone's crying. Me? I'm sobbing, pleading. We're not plastic inside. We don't dissolve into the ground when we die. Clint opens his mouth, looses smoke and burning sand. Tries to lift the Glock. To shoot me? A guy's standing behind my brother, a civilian coming to help, I almost shot him after he pulled me from the LAV, saved me, *please forgive me,* my mind skipping, past and present then and now and this is one of Sim Grewal's gangsters lifting an AK-47 at my brother's spine. Someone's praying. Is it me? Is this me? I'M ONLY ME. My ears bust open. Duke's foot slips off the brake—

The Lexus rolls into the parking lot, crunches through shattered glass and everything goes quiet—

I'm where I said I'd be. Behind the driver. Did Jasminder tell Sim? Kandahar road dust filters into my lungs. Only this isn't then. This isn't anything. This is what happens when. This is on television, gangland, condominium, I'm getting mine, game changer, we're different here. Black smoke fills the Lexus LAV and I'm sitting in a fancy leather armchair in a corner office, gazing through floor-to-ceiling windows at the city skyline, concrete condominiums and the blue-black Pacific, feeling the yaw and roll of deep-sea waves, the city torn from the continental landmass, adrift, admiring the sunlit ocean, the city unmoored—

Jasminder Bansal

O utside Pacific Centre mall, looking into the entry atrium. The scene stained aqua by lightly tinted glass, an underwater world. Pastel tables perched on steel posts. Towering tropical ferns. Employees in threadbare uniforms and peaked hats fiddling with their phones behind fast-food counters.

I am driven by passion and purpose.

Ryan's standing beside me. We're together and apart.

Mr. Xi's assistant at Pillar Investment arrives five minutes early for our meeting. Joyce Arnell. I recognize her from her employee photo online. Redhead. Midforties. Grey slacks, pale blue blouse. Could be a midlevel human resources exec. Volunteers at her daughter's high school. Enjoys spinning pottery. Has a wheel in her garage. Doesn't use it as much as she'd like. Work keeps her busy. All those secrets. I wonder if she finds it draining.

"Is that her?" Ryan asks.

Joyce doesn't find it draining at all. Her secrets invigorate her. She chooses a table, checks her watch, glances outside, directly at me. I don't think she sees me? Coolness wraps around my throat. Only a few people milling around. I'm grateful for their presence. Shoppers. Witnesses. They wouldn't do it here. Would they? But on the way to my car, or later, at home? Anytime, really. I guess they could do it here, in public. Why not? The newspapers said my brother's crew executed a rival in a South Vancouver parking lot on a Tuesday afternoon. A *targeted killing*. Eighty-three cartridges littering the asphalt.

If this woman says the word—

What if I go inside? Sit down with Joyce. Give her the camera with Scott Charles Booth and . . . Ryan. You can have everything, Mark said. Is everything enough?

Maybe Joyce shows me a photograph to prove who she works for. Who I'll be working for.

I watch Joyce sip her tea. She's outwardly lovely.

Maybe she shows me a Middle Eastern street scene, a mangled vehicle, a crater in the ground, a wrecked and smoking storefront, a bloodstained sidewalk, or a razed village in Central Africa—

My business is growing at exactly the right pace.

I turn from the window. Take out the camera, remove the memory card, crush it with my heel, kick it down a storm drain. When I look up Ryan's halfway down the block, veering around a rain puddle, not quite running but close to it. I'm supposed to take him to the guy Mark knows. I almost call his name, stop myself. He vanishes around a corner, leaving me to doubt he was here. I'm alone outside and the first thing that pops into my head is *some time.* Between what and what? Between Amar and . . . I put my earbuds in. D.O.A. segues to Drake. The red-headed woman is looking through the glass. Her name could be Joyce Arnell. Isn't that who she is or is supposed to be? Does she feel me watching her? Alone on the street, wondering what I've accomplished, if anything, what's changed, if anything. The dream-goal long gone. Ryan? Mark? Did I see them clearly? I walk down Robson remembering Amar, hoping it was worth it, trying to imagine an ending.